FORAYS AND REBUTTALS

FORAYS
and
REBUTTALS

BERNARD AUGUSTINE DeVOTO

Essay Index Reprint Series

BOOKS FOR LIBRARIES PRESS
FREEPORT, NEW YORK

STANDARD BOOK NUMBER:

8369-1604-2

LIBRARY OF CONGRESS CATALOG CARD NUMBER:

78-111826

PRINTED IN THE UNITED STATES OF AMERICA

TO

Lee Foster Hartman

for ten years my editor but nevertheless my friend:
unrivaled among editors in that he nearly always
buys an article when he has commissioned
it, and unique among them in that his
explanation is plausible when he
turns one down.

Preface

~~~~~~

The reasons for publishing this collection of magazine articles are, if not convincing, at least simple. My publishers want the specifically journalistic part of my activity represented in book form. I want the two Mark Twain papers in print, pending a revision of *Mark Twain's America* which must wait on time and opportunity. And there has been some public demand for the collection: no other book of mine has actually been asked for, this one has been, and wisdom bids me satisfy the demand while it can still be perceived.

I confess that the search through my files surprised me. I did not realize that I had published so many essays — not more than a third of them are reprinted here. I had thought of myself as writing novels which few people read and fewer buy, light fiction for popular magazines, and social history of almost professional obscurity. I had thought of my contributions to the "quality group" as occasional interruptions of more serious or more frivolous occupations, always instigated by some editor, usually Lee Hartman, who knew my inability to say no and managed to make his request when I could not possibly afford the time to comply with it. But I find that for more than ten years I have been contributing to the quality group with considerable regularity, that I was practically a staff-writer for *Harper's* even before I took over the Easy Chair, and, surprisingly, that my contributions fall into closely related and fairly unified groups.

All but one of those groups are represented here. That one consists of purely historical articles on the western frontier. They are by-products of a study I have been making for many years, and since I must sooner or later write the book which my publishers and I announce every spring, it has seemed best to withhold them. The articles in this collection which touch on the frontier do so incidentally to some other purpose.

With the exception of "The Centennial of Mormonism," the articles are reprinted as they were written. I have restored the original titles, where the intuitions of an editor required something more resounding, and the original texts where some requirement unknown to me shortened them. Perhaps a dozen times I have changed a sentence to make a vague context clear. I have let the opinions stand as they were. They are not always my opinions now, but I am not writing a book, I am reprinting one, and there would be no point in reprinting such articles as these if one did not reprint them intact. Fidelity to the original point of view has, however, produced one embarrassment sufficiently acute to justify my explaining it here.

I became an "authority on education" merely by publishing in *Harper's* a series of articles which expressed my dissatisfaction with a Middle-Western university where I had taught English for five years. It was the era of expansion, business tie-up and large-scale advertising in the American colleges. The university in question was engaged in a "drive," throughout my term on its faculty. It was building a stadium, a football team, a business school, a sucker-list, and a sphere of influence — or of come-ons; it was engaged in a noisome ballyhoo and a planned degradation of intellectual standards, which were designed to secure it a remunerative place in American education but which it preferred to rationalize as a process of adaptation to the modern world. It did not beautify the American scene, and it annoyed me. I stand on the facts: I should not care to stand on all the conclusions I drew from them.

Ten years ago I was for reforming the colleges. Like all reformers, I outrageously over-simplified the problem. Today I know a good deal more about education than I did then. I know that most proposed reforms are undesirable, and that practically all of them are impossible of achievement and must produce conditions worse than the diseases they undertake to cure. The universities are part of the social equilibrium and cannot be modified from without. Besides, that very equilibrium and the process of history have taken care of most of the obscenities I was objecting to ten years ago. The era of expansion is closed, the Sears-Roebuck age in American education is ended for all time, and its worst abuses have died with it. A simple determinism, the fact that there will never again be money enough to educate the uneducable or to make the universities accessory services to the luncheon clubs, eradicates most of the absurdities to which my *Harper's* articles objected. What I was arguing for was, in effect, greater freedom, more opportunities and better teaching for the best students, as distinguished from the average students and the worst. That cause was fought valiantly but against long odds through the post-war years; the economic pressure applied by the depression has made it a winning cause.

I reprint some of those articles on education because I must accept responsibility for them, because they have some historical interest, and because the whole incident has an illustrative value. I knew very little about education but

I became an "authority" by merely claiming to be one. I was quoted in the most ponderous journals of the trade, I was invited to sit on or consult with some of the most resplendent committees and councils that the vested interest maintains, and membership in several professional societies was conferred on me. Several of the articles became standard works at once, and one of them became a classic: "The Co-Eds: God Bless Them" is still, ten years after its appearance, required reading for all freshmen in at least two hundred colleges. It seems to me in some part untrue, in greater part obvious and irrelevant, and in no part profound, but it appears to be a fixture in the theory of education. Perhaps you will bear that in mind when the next revolt against the colleges breaks out in the quality group. Theorists of education are at best obvious, usually irrelevant, and at worst altogether cockeyed. Progress in education does take place, regularly if slowly, but it comes as the result of more forces than the theorist ever takes into account, hardboiled and empirical teachers are responsible for it, and its revolutionary or "experimental" (in the eyes of science, what an adjective!) evangelists have invariably exploited developments already under way and have invariably interfered with them. I have included "Another Consociate Family" merely to record my present position. I know more about education than I knew when I published, for instance, "College and the Superior Man" (which I am not reprinting) — and I have less fault to find with the colleges.

I have considerably enlarged "The Centennial of Mormonism" and entirely rewritten it. It was originally written as a historical summary, and as such it has attained a gratifying authority in the standard bibliographies. I take this opportunity of expanding it and making it more available to students.

I think I am entitled to point out that "The Well-Informed" was written before "Mark Twain's America" and before Mr. Frederick L. Allen made it obsolete.

The book reviews are included at the request of Mr. Alfred McIntyre.

For permission to reprint material I am indebted to *Harper's Magazine* and *The American Mercury*. I cannot very well thank *The Harvard Graduates' Magazine*, which is now extinct and of which, besides, I was the editor when the essays reprinted from it first appeared. Similarly, it seems idle to thank *The Saturday Review* since I should myself be granting the permissions. I do not know why my contributions to the *Atlantic, The Review of Reviews, The Forum* and other magazines have not proved available for this book. Probably I am by nature a *Harper's* writer and such excursions were a mistake.

I am indebted beyond all hope of proper acknowledgment to the critical judgment, patience, accuracy and good humor of Rosamond Chapman.

BERNARD DEVOTO

Lincoln, Massachusetts
June 1, 1936

Contents

FORAYS AND REBUTTALS

The Life of Jonathan Dyer

A PARAGRAPH IN THE HISTORY OF THE WEST

I

ELDERS Jacob Gates and Martin Slack brought to Hertfordshire tidings of the wrath to come. Curates, deans, even bishops were disturbed by the number of converts the American missionaries made. They were Dissenters of a new and particularly objectionable kind, but their appeal was strong. Sermons were preached against the "Mormonites"; riots began to occur at their meetings; here and there an elder was drummed out of town or set upon with eggs or thrown into a horse pond. Employers were consulted, and some of them took action. Mr. Young Crawley, the coachmaker of Hertford, discovered that an eighteen-year-old apprentice in his shop was explaining the new creed to his fellow workmen. Mr. Crawley acted in the name of an Englishman's religion, and Jonathan Dyer found himself without a job.

We are concerned with Jonathan Dyer not because he was persecuted for his faith but because that faith merged him with the strongest current in the New World from which the missionaries came. Baptized a member of the Church of Jesus Christ of Latter-Day Saints on the twenty-seventh of May, 1852, and discharged by Mr. Crawley almost at once, he did not at once yield to that current. He got work in a linseed-oil mill, where his skill with machinery brought him advancement, and he began to advance also in the hierarchy of his Church. Jonathan became a deacon, a teacher, and finally a fully ordained priest in the Order of Aaron. He converted his mother and two of his brothers but, as a proselyter in the villages of High Cross and Collier's End, found the opposition of the established church too vigorous for him. At Roydon, however, the Paxman family listened to him and were convinced. A daughter of the house was fair: during two years Jonathan found it desirable to visit Rhoda and instruct her in the Mormonite faith. Both twenty-two years old, they were married at Roydon on the twenty-sixth of April, 1856. They resolved to live their religion: to leave England and, joining the current, move westward to Zion.

Jonathan Dyer's emigration is not explained beyond that sentence. He was a mechanic; he had no trouble finding work; he was not interested in the cheap land that tempted millions to America. He was an industrious, methodical, unimaginative young man—no restlessness for the road's end and the far slope of the hill ever troubled him. But for Elders Slack and Gates he would have stayed in Hertford, joined a workingman's library, and ventured no farther from home than a holiday ride on the railroad would have taken him. The voice of the Lord called him eight thousand miles. Of America he knew only what the elders told him and cared to know no more. In a place called Jackson County, Missouri, the Garden of Eden had been planted. The place was man's lost paradise and would be restored to him in the Last Days, tokens of whose swift coming were on every wind. Meanwhile the Saints were gathered in Deseret, "the land of the honey bee," their present Zion, somewhere in a vastness known as the Rocky Mountains. This too was a paradise, a land like Canaan, fertile and beautiful and walled away from the Gentiles. God's will was that the Saints should build up the Kingdom there and await the Last Days.

Passage to America cost from three pounds six shillings to four pounds, exclusive of food. Jonathan's savings were perhaps two pounds. He borrowed two sovereigns from his wife's parents and the rest from the Church. The priesthood would lend money for emigration, the notes to be paid from the borrower's earnings in Zion. Jonathan and his wife and his brother Richard were to sail in the *Horizon*, Captain Reid, in May, 1856, but the ship was full when they reached Liverpool, and they had to await the forming of another company. On June first, with one hundred and forty-three other Saints and lay emigrants to the number of three hundred and fifty, mostly Irish, they sailed in the packet *Wellfleet*, Captain Westcott. Storms sickened most of the Saints; their provisions spoiled; there were quarrels with the ungodly about the cooking arrangements. The superstitious Irish resented the Mormonite hymns. The Irish too were lousy and within a week had infected the whole company. On the tenth of July, one day short of six weeks after she was towed down the Mersey, the *Wellfleet* anchored off Quarantine at Boston. At once a Negro sailor gave the pilgrims a symbol of the new civilization by stabbing the second mate.

The Church thriftily kept on the eastern seaboard all immigrants for whom work could be found until they had

saved enough to pay their way westward. The boom times
of the early Fifties slackened toward the prostration of the
next year, but the country proved able to absorb the Dyers.
Richard found work at Lexington, and the linseed-oil mill
of Field, Fowler and Company, at Charlestown, took Jonathan in and made him foreman. The summer of 1857
brought distress to the Saints and to the nation. President
Buchanan, a "mobocrat" and an enemy of God, rejected
the counsel of Brigham Young, appointed a new Governor
of Utah Territory, and ordered an army west to escort his
appointee. By the end of July the troops were marching,
and soon afterward Colonel Albert Sidney Johnston took
command of them. The priesthood forbade women to cross
the plains but welcomed men for the defense of Zion. Richard Dyer left his wife to the care of Jonathan and departed,
writing back that it took him six weeks to cross Iowa,
through sloughs sometimes so bad that they pulled the
soles off his boots. God moved swiftly to punish a nation
of mobocrats. On August twenty-fourth, the Ohio Life Insurance and Trust Company announced its insolvency. Its
failure carried with it the financial structure of the United
States. Banks failed everywhere, even in New England: it
was believed that no bank was solvent. The stock ex-
changes followed the banks. By autumn unemployed men
were rioting in the cities, farmers were abandoning their
land, trade was prostrate, exchange was impossible. Windows were broken in Charlestown and mobs surrounded the
closed mills or surged sporadically in the direction of bake-
shops. Field, Fowler and Company shut down. Jonathan
peddled crockery. The mill opened again, shut down, re-
opened. But Jonathan was able to pay off his loans, to assist the emigration of another brother, and to lend the Boston branch of his Church fifty dollars.

Wages were very low in 1858, and the mill closed once more. Jonathan moved to South Boston, where he worked as a glass packer. The mill was running again by 1859, and Jonathan's first son was born. Jonathan now invented better valves and pistons for the mill's machinery. His employers promoted him and, the next year, sent him to Brooklyn to build and manage a new mill. The Brooklyn branch of the Church received him as a man of substance.

Jonathan's first daughter was born in March, 1861, on the day before Abraham Lincoln became President of a nation careening toward certain destruction. Jonathan beheld passion, violence, and panic, and he knew that prophecy was on the march. The nation which had spilled the prophet's blood must now meet its doom. On Christmas Day, twenty-nine years before, the blessed Joseph had foretold the rebellion of South Carolina, which Jonathan had now witnessed, and had said "the Southern States shall be divided from the Northern States" — which had come to pass. The world spun toward the Last Days. England too, Joseph had said, must join this apocalypse, and all Europe would follow till "war shall be poured out on all nations." Then famine and plague and earthquakes "and the fierce and vivid lightnings also," and at last the terrible Day of the Lord.

Bishop Penrose had sung to the Church "Thy deliverance is nigh, thy oppressors shall die, And the Gentiles shall bow 'neath thy rod." Jonathan's residence in Brooklyn, his journal says, had been the happiest year in his life, but it was time to enter on the Kingdom. He sold all that he had and by the first of July reached Florence, Nebraska, where the ox trains formed. With Brother Hudson he bought a wagon and two yoke of oxen. Ten weeks of bitter marching through the desert, up the nation's sternest trail, brought them to Great Salt Lake City. Jonathan lived with Richard during the winter, working as a teamster when he could, although "no money to be earned." (Life was not so hard for everyone in Salt Lake, that winter. "The Lady of Lyons" made a great success before crowded houses. Everybody was reading Mr. Collins's *Woman in White*. Tickets to the Territorial Ball sold for ten dollars, and the Governor presided at a dinner whose menu lists four soups, nine roasts, nine boiled meats, six stews, nine vegetables, and fourteen desserts.)

In the spring of 1862 the Church rented Dyer forty-odd acres in the valley of Easton, thirty miles north of Salt Lake City, where the Weber River breaks through the Wasatch. He had no voice in the selection of this land, but he wanted none — it was Zion and that was what counted. So a migration of eight thousand miles ended amid sagebrush on a southern slope above the Weber. The place possessed "a Dugout or a little room dug out of the bank. Quite a contrast this is to my style of former living in Boston and Brooklyn, where I lived in a large house, carpeted rooms, etc., and it has tried my faith very much." The words are the only complaint that Jonathan Dyer ever expressed.

He had entered on the Kingdom. And . . . Jonathan Dyer, of Hertford, had begun the most typical, most fundamental of American experiences: life on the frontier.

II

It is to be observed that Jonathan was a mechanic. He had grown up in a town, he knew the qualities of woods and the tools that worked them, he was adroit with machinery and had invented valves and pumps, but he had never lived on a farm and was as unfitted as possible to exist by agriculture. Commentators too often forget that the frontier held many like him. We are familiar with the thesis — now favored because people who explain things feel that it has some bearing on these difficult times — that the free land of the frontier was a kind of economic safety valve or stabilizer. When previous depressions came, this theory says, the man who was thrown out of work when the factories closed was not desperate, since he could always go west and, starting over, be sure of a living. Just how he raised money for the emigration and just how city dwellers of mechanical training could expect to make their way in an alien trade remains unexplained. The theory also omits to explain why, if the frontier was a sponge that absorbed social unrest, so much of the social unrest in America originated on the frontier.

Well, social unrest did not affect Jonathan Dyer. Utah was not insulated from the nation, and many waves of resentment and discontent traveled across it during his lifetime, which covered the great revolution in our national life. They touched Jonathan not at all. Revolutions are always struggles between special groups; only propaganda tries to make them seem the will of the people in action. The people remain mostly unharried by them, neither willing nor acting, and in the end pay tribute to the old group, victorious, or to the new one which has cast it out. Even agrarian revolt has little to do with the agrarians in the mass. American history exhibits the farmers in revolt from the beginning up to now, and the farmers mostly have worked their land voiceless and unstirred, a mere name invoked by speculators who are their self-consecrated champions. They have paid taxes, gone bankrupt for the profit

of adventurers, and served as the stuff of financial and political exploitation. From Rome to the valley of Easton
there has been no change.

Jonathan's dugout was in a hillside in the valley of the
Weber, a valley which in two hamlets besides Easton held
some two dozen families. The squalor of those first years is
now difficult to appreciate. Life was possible only through
the complete communism of the poor. After a year he had
a house, a one-room cabin of pine logs brought down from
the canyons of the Wasatch, since only soft poplars and
cottonwoods grew in the valley. Its puncheon floor, built-in
bunks, and rain-tight roof meant an advance over the dank
clay of the dugout. Lean-tos were added in time, but a
good many years were to pass before Jonathan could build
a farmhouse. The cabin meanwhile filled with children: his
generation all told was one son and seven daughters, of
whom one died in childhood. It is the children who most
readily reveal to us the conditions of the frontier.

Sarah, the girl who was born in Brooklyn, was nine when
she first wore shoes; the earliest pair were kept for display
at Sabbath school or on the clapboard sidewalks of Ogden,
eight miles away; they were not put on till one got out of
the wagon, and they were passed on to the descending series of sisters. Her clothes during that time, she remembered, consisted of apronlike garments cut from remnants
which Rhoda had brought West with her, from the gunny-
sacking that also made containers for potatoes, and once
from a bolt of calico. She had no underwear, as a rule, but
in the winter Rhoda would manage to fashion for her, out
of God knows what, garments which failed to beautify her
but helped against the canyon gales. She anticipated the
stockingless children and adolescents of the 1930's — in that
early time there were no sheep in Easton and no pennies

to buy knitting wool in Ogden. No shoes in winter, eight miles from a town? Well, children have gone to school, gathered eggs and firewood, and played their games with their feet bound in sacking or rabbitskins. Of those games Sarah remembered most pleasantly coasting down the winter hills in a grain scoop. Once, disastrously, they caught a skunk in a "figger-4" which had been set for rabbits. There was the river, the widening fields, the cottonwood groves — springs, ditches, haystacks — spelling bees, quiltings, Sabbath schools. After a while rattlesnakes grew uncommon.

How did Jonathan bring them up at all? At the end of 1863 he writes, "I raised this year a good crop of corn, some wheat, and some oats." The sentence carries no overtone of the labor so strange to a mechanic. Jonathan would have had trouble forcing this harvest from the earth anywhere, even in Illinois bottomland, where the soil is forty feet deep and is watered by generous summer rains. But at Easton there were no rains and the thin soil was poisoned by alkali. The sagebrush was the index. Where sage grew, there other stuffs would grow also, after heartbreaking labor had cleared it away. Jonathan hacked at that hellish growth. Spines and slivers that no gloves can turn fill one's hands, the stench under the desert sun is dreadful, and the roots, which have probed deep and wide for moisture, must be chopped and grubbed and dragged out inch by inch. Then, before anything will sprout in the drugged earth, water must be brought. Through a dozen years of Jonathan's journal we observe the settlers of Easton combining to bring water to their fields. On the bench lands above their valleys, where gulches and canyons come down from the Wasatch, they made canals, which they led along the hills. From the canals smaller ditches flowed down to each man's fields, and from these ditches he must dig veins and capillaries for himself. Where the water ran, cultivation was possible; where it didn't, the sagebrush of the desert showed unbroken. Such coöperation forbade quarrels; one would as soon quarrel about the bloodstream. A man was allotted certain hours of water. When they came, at midnight or dawn or noon, he raised the gates into his own ditches and with spade and shovel and an engineering sense coaxed the water to his planting

During those first years there would be, besides the corn and wheat and oats of Jonathan's note, potatoes and a few other garden vegetables — carrots no doubt, for this was Utah, perhaps cabbages and surely squash. Brother Kendall, two miles down the valley, had been a farmer's man in England and could help Jonathan with the mysteries of cultivation. Brother Kendall or someone else had a cow to spare and chickens. There was thus milk for the children, and Rhoda churned cream for butter, learned to make cheese, gathered eggs and set hens, acquired the myriad skills of the frontier farm wife who as yet has had no qualified celebrant in literature. There had been settlers at Easton since 1849, but they had not yet been able to harness the Weber to a mill. There was a small affair run by horse power (Jonathan improved the gears) and its crude stones ground the meal for the corn mush which Sarah remembered as the staple of her childhood. The oats, of course, were dedicated to the horses, the wheat to the chickens. Beef was out of the question — cows were too valuable to be slaughtered — but after a while there were hogs, which Jonathan killed and quartered. He had no crop, he could have none till all his land was cleared. Sometimes he would go into the high canyons for several days and fill his wagon with wood. This could be sold in Ogden for the only cash that came to him; but everyone cut wood, and so it could not be sold for very much.

Still these years showed some progress. He began to buy his land from the Church on generous but sternly enforced terms. He cleared it. He gridded it with ditches. He put down larger crops, began to sell part of them, bought horses and some cows. He lamented the failure of the Church to organize Easton — sometimes a month went by without a service and there was neither juvenile instruction nor priesthood meeting. In view of the Mormon care to organize even the smallest and remotest settlements, this failure is strange. But they made out.

The break came in 1868. The crops were about three inches out of the ground when grasshoppers settled on them, as they had done before the historic miracle which Mahonri Young was to relate in bronze and granite. Three-quarters of the green shoots were destroyed at once and ruin seemed inevitable. But at once surveyors followed the grasshoppers to Easton, and suddenly most of the settlers there, Jonathan among them, were working for the Union Pacific Railroad, hauling timber for ties and construction or, as the year closed, rock and rubble for the grade. For the first time there was money in the valley; Jonathan could now drive to Ogden on Saturday night and bring back milled flour, a few groceries, farm implements, cloth, buttons, a mirror. Sarah's first shoes date from this time. She remembered also a strange pleasure surpassing anything she had imagined, rock candy.

By midwinter the rails came through Weber Canyon and the violent town called Hell on Wheels erected itself at Easton. Jonathan says that there were "many bad men" in this company, who drank and gambled and whored to the disgust of the Saints, and says no more about them except that they burned his fences for firewood. The fences had already been pierced, for the roadbed ran straight across his land, and he worked among the bad men as a teamster and did not scruple to sell them produce. Sometimes he mounted guard with an enormous horse pistol to drive the boisterous Irish away. Hell on Wheels passed rapidly on, to Corinne, to Promontory Point, but it had raised the valley out of squalor. Also it had destroyed Easton by building a station two miles farther down the valley than the nucleus of houses that constituted "the settlement." The station was just a mile east of Jonathan's house. Its signboard wore a queer misspelled name which still remains: Uinta.

Sarah's first candles came now — tallow had been too precious for such use — and later there was the magnificent new "rock oil," much better than the rag floating in melted home-cured lard which she had known. This marvel came westward on the "U. P.," which also brought coal from Rock Springs, though Jonathan would not burn it for some years yet. Stoves came too, and many marvelous new things. All the children had shoes by 1870, and Rhoda could make excellent clothes for them. But the railroad's power was best shown by the impetus it gave religion. Jonathan had long since organized a Sabbath school. Now he could get books for it. The valley's new prosperity enabled him to raise, by dances and "entertainments," a fund which, sent to Chicago, bought "between 130 and 140, which proved a blessing for the children."

Now that all the children had shoes, Jonathan was clearly doing well. To this time belongs a story which he remembered when he was nearly eighty. The Bishop of Uinta (the Church "ward" was now organized) came to Brother

Dyer and suggested that since the Lord had rewarded his efforts, it was clearly his duty to take another wife and raise up more seed for Israel. In the only rebellion against his teachers he ever experienced, Jonathan got out the horse pistol and ordered the Bishop off his land, and thereafter there was no mention of polygamy. . . . A grandson has seen the horse pistol but does not believe the story. These folk at Uinta were the humble of Mormonry, and the humble had little to do with polygamy. There seems never to have been a plural marriage in the valley. The story merely means an old man's memory that he had not believed in polygamy. He was one of many Saints who did not. But, be very sure, if the Bishop, a lineal descendant of Aaron, had commanded Jonathan to take another wife, then another wife would have come to share Rhoda's labors and add children to Jonathan's glory.

III

What can be said about Jonathan Dyer? He was a first-class private in the march of America — a unit in the process that made and remade the nation. Yet history can make singularly little of him. You could not write the history of Utah or of the Mormon Church without mentioning, for instance, the "New Movement" which, from the point of view of historical forces, must have shaken this commonwealth to its base. Its occurrence could be guessed from nothing whatever in Jonathan's life and from only a single line in his journal which says that it began in 1869. You could not write either of those histories without detailing the violent disturbance of the public peace which was called the "Morrisite war" — the appearance of a false prophet in Israel and his suppression by Brigham Young. The prophet

Morris and his followers pitched their camp across the nar-
row Weber from Jonathan's lower field and there, a few
rods from him, they were at last attacked by the army of
the Lord. After three days of rifle and artillery practice the
false prophet and some of his flock were killed and their
camp was scattered. It may be that bullets kicked up dust
in the field that Jonathan was plowing, it may be that he
climbed a cottonwood to gaze at the riot, but the event was
worth in his journal only one sentence and an aphorism
about the stubbornness of evil. Of the rest of history during
his lifetime, nothing whatever appears. Mormon and Gentile battled for supremacy, polygamists were hunted down,
at last the whole Church was proscribed and its property
was confiscated. And all this was less than a shadow to
Jonathan, who notes the fall of rain, which counts in a
desert, and the annual increase of his crop.

History, it may be, is not of the humble. Some millions
of Jonathans were creating America. Over all the empty
land such minute nuclei as his stood out. They grew by
aggregation, while men made farms of what had been just
wasteland, and then the land wasn't empty any more. The
unit, the nucleus, the individual kept up his not spectacular
warfare against anarchy, for self-preservation. What had he
to do with the currents of national life? They weren't, for
him, currents at all. They were waves perhaps, which
flowed an unrecognized energy through or around him
and on to his neighbor, lifting both and letting both fall
back, their position in space unchanged, water still to be
brought to the fields. Occupied with his own struggle for
survival, incapable of feeling himself a part of a nation,
Jonathan had a further unawareness in his faith. It was,
the Mormon faith, a superb instrument for the reclamation of the desert, for the creation of the West. It rewarded

the faithful for industry and offered rewards for further effort. It identified with heavenly grace the very qualities that were most needed in a new country: unquestioning labor, frugality, coöperation, obedience. So long as the faithful worked to redeem the earth so long were they building up Israel and strengthening God's kingdom.

So, though Jonathan was a religious emigrant, there was not even much religion as philosophers know it in his life. The Sabbath school which he established became the best in Weber County; it was commended in Quarterly and even Annual Conference, and was permitted to march in Pioneer Day parades. Jonathan was sometimes called upon to advise other educators of the young. He was made a high priest. Sometimes he met dignitaries of the church and listened to counsel. He was never promoted above his sergeancy, for in Mormonism as elsewhere the humble do not become leaders. He accepted the hagiology of his Church and its dogmas and its expectations, but they were merely a background. He did not think about them often or very deeply. He was advancing Israel, making sure his glory, but — and this was what counted — his fields came under the plow and he was setting out fruit trees. If religion was just smoke on the horizon, politics was even less. The grandson who has been mentioned remembers asking Jonathan whether he was going to vote for a son-in-law who had been nominated for some office now forgotten. Jonathan was not, he said. The son-in-law had been nominated by the Democrats, and the Bishop of Uinta had told Jonathan that it was best for the Republicans to be in power. Didn't the leading men in church and party know what was best? You will not write political history by consulting the ideas of the humble.

These were just smoke. It was real when Rhoda and all

the children — five of them at that time — fell sick with smallpox. We have forgotten the terror of that plague. Neighbors whipped their horses to the gallop, passing by, averted their faces and held their breath against infection, burned smudges, wore amulets of vile smelling stuff. No one dared to come to Jonathan's help or even to bring a doctor from Ogden. Somehow he nursed his family through till Rhoda was on her feet and then he too collapsed. The well got contaminated one summer and they all had typhoid fever; there was help this time and they all survived. One year Rhoda's breast "gathered" and she had to drag herself about the grinding labor of a farm wife; she failed slowly, nothing could be done for her, but that also passed and she could go on. One summer, chopping wood, Jonathan cut a gash in his leg. For the rest of the year he could not work; Rhoda and the children shortened their sleep, carried on the irrigation, and brought in the crop. The menace of such accidents was constant. One Sunday noon Jonathan came back from Sabbath school and found that a mule had kicked his son, young Jonathan, in the head and "broke his skull." Jonathan went to Ogden, and by ten o'clock that night had brought Dr. Woodward back. For five hours, by the light of a Rochester lamp in the kitchen, the doctor operated on the boy. The doctor came twice more to dress the wound. Jonathan paid him: "cash, $20; pig, $4; corn and corn meal, $2.70; wood, $6" and, a month later, some more wood. The boy had recovered four months later. And so on . . . "November 21st [1872]. This morning about 4 o'clock my wife confined and gave birth to a daughter; also I took a load of wood to Mrs. Savage."

All that was real and so was the earth. The desert yielded. There was never to be ease or luxury at Uinta — what would a farmer do with either? Education was impossible for the children. The little school at the "settlement" was like its equivalents throughout rural America, and when Sarah wanted to learn more she had to go to Ogden, where she paid her board by housework and walked three miles each way to Professor Moench's academy. The children had to strike out for themselves as soon as possible, Jonathan as a telegrapher down state, and Sarah as a waitress in a railroad lunchroom at Green River. But, if not ease, comfort came to Uinta and security and the rude plenty of the farm. The daughter whose birth is noticed came to a frame house painted green. There was an ell later. The dooryard had a small lawn — astonishing in the desert — and mulberry and walnut trees and Rhoda's flower garden. The ditch that paralleled the railroad tracks in front of it flowed beside Lombardy poplars of Jonathan's planting. There were wells and springs of mountain water. Half a dozen cows and as many horses grazed in the west pasture; a few sheep were about, and annually Jonathan cured hams and bacon from his hogs. These hung beside home-butchered beef and mutton and the children tended sizable flocks of chickens, turkeys, ducks, and guinea fowl. Sheds multiplied, filling with cultivators, harrows, plows, and similar implements which the unseen America beyond the Wasatch was creating. There were hay sheds, chicken houses, a "warehouse" (for Jonathan was English and his wagons were "carts"), an embryonic machine shop, a cider press. The thrashers harvested Jonathan's wheat; it was stored in a granary with his corn and oats and barley. Rhoda made cheese and butter; she "put up" vegetables from the garden and her jams and jellies are nostalgically remembered. She baked every day. There were eggs all winter long.

Is it clear that all this sprang from desert land, that Jonathan created it out of nothing at all? That is the point. Sometimes noticed, it is seldom realized in discussions of the frontier. Some people are pleased by the frontier's pageantry, and the literary are frantically ashamed of what they feel must have been its ugliness; but somehow the plain fact of creation gets overlooked. . . . In 1862 a hillside in Utah, sloping down to cottonwoods along the Weber River, had been no more than sagebrush. The sage, *Artemisia tridentata,* is glamorous in folklore, where it is called Heartsease, and it seems beautiful under distance to tourists of the tamed West, but it is the type-symbol of desolation. There was here — nothing whatever. A stinking drouth, coyotes and rattlesnakes and owls, the movement of violet and silver and olive-dun sage in white light — a dead land. But now there was a painted frame house under shade trees, fields leached of alkali, the blue flowers of alfalfa, flowing water, grain, gardens, orchards.

Especially orchards. Under the sagebrush roots the earth held the ashes of a volcanic age. When Jonathan brought water to it chemistry was set free. Something in that volcanic ash gave a superb flavor to fruit. All the Utah fruits are glorious, but especially the strawberries and apricots and apples, and most especially the peaches. One who has not tasted, fresh from the tree, a peach grown on the eastern slope of the long valley that holds the Great Salt Lake may not speak of peaches. All these fruits, together with cherries and plums and pears, came in time to Jonathan's hillside. How should this Hertford mechanic learn to divine the hidden necessities of trees? The thing is impossible but it happened. He was a farmer by virtue of blind strength and the mistakes of years, but he was a fruit-grower by divination. He walked among his orchards and could read their needs. So that as the years passed Jonathan Dyer's or-

chards became the greater part of his farm, and they were
known.

This in what had been a dead land. Water flowed in his
ditches, stock grazed his pastures, instead of desolation there
were fields and orchards. The children came in at nightfall
to a house built from his lumber. They ate bread made of
his wheat, cheese from his milk, preserved fruit from his
orchards. There had been nothing at all, and here were
peaches, and he had come eight thousand miles. That is the
point of the frontier.

IV

Uinta was eight miles over the hills from Ogden — four
hours when the road was in its April state the time Jonathan drove in for Dr. Woodward, seventy-five minutes in
a buggy behind old Prince when the grandson's memory of
it opens (about 1903), and eleven minutes in 1933. Those
figures speak also of the frontier. The 1903 memory pre-
serves quiet and isolation — summer afternoons beside the
beautifully sited canal in the shade of the poplars, a dusty
road vacant of travel, sometimes a wagon climbing the immense hill which was named for Peg-Leg Labaume, sometimes rails humming before a U. P. train emerged from
Weber Canyon, no other movement except that of clouds
and wind, no other sound but cicadas and the whine of
Jonathan's mower in the alfalfa — the crest of Jonathan's
comfort and success. The fields were clean, the orchards
combed and trim, the sheds plumb. Nondescript cows had
given place to Jerseys; the hogs were now Poland Chinas.
A greengage tree rose in the dooryard; it was followed by
Japanese plums and other foreign fruits whose growth endlessly interested Jonathan. On Thanksgiving and Christmas, when the children and grandchildren gathered, Rhoda

would spend the day cooking great dinners, and every item of them had grown under her eyes. Home-butchered roast beef with Yorkshire pudding is remembered, suckling pigs with Jonathan's apples in their mouths, turkeys, butter and cheese from Rhoda's milkroom, endless breads and biscuits and cakes from flour traded in grist a mile away. Winters were snug; spring plowing turned earth that was ignorant of alkali. This was Deseret, the land of the honey bee.

Yet even in 1903 its doom had been pronounced. A large wagon — Jonathan called it a van — from the Kasius Grocery in Ogden began to make weekly visits to Uinta. Jonathan and Rhoda were sixty-nine; soon it seemed foolish to butcher their own meat, churn their own butter, set rennet for their own cheese. For the rest of his life Jonathan was more an orchardist, less a farmer. Then another corporation asked for an easement over the farm, and steel towers rose carrying transmission lines from power plants deep in the Wasatch. Jonathan and Rhoda were alone. The four hours to Ogden had been difficult but not difficult enough, for none of the seven children had stayed on the land. None had remained in the Mormon church. None, even, had married a native of Utah. Three of them had moved out of the state. The twenty grandchildren were to be dispersed from San Diego to Boston, and though they were to take up trades as wide apart as boiler-making and novel-writing, not one of them was a farmer. They were products of the frontier — which had fallen.

The plenty of 1903 lingered on. But Jonathan and Rhoda grew old. A farm requires vigor and, though Jonathan's remained phenomenal, Rhoda's failed, and it was not always possible to find a granddaughter in her teens who would live with them and help. At last Jonathan began to show the strange mania that sometimes comes upon fruit-growers. He would suddenly notice something wrong about one of his fruit trees and decide that it must make way for a new, young shoot. He would get out his axe. The glorious orchards began to fall. So, a little dazed, un-comprehending, Jonathan made in 1917 the journey which during fifty-five years he had scorned to make — he and the rejoicing Rhoda moved the eight miles to Ogden to live with a daughter. The farm was sold. The buyer kept things as they were, but four years later some ass who had money to spare bought the place, leveled the orchards, let the fields perish, and began to raise silver foxes. He was a Goth plowing the land with salt.

Rhoda died in 1919. Jonathan lived four years more in a growing bewilderment. Sometimes he would disappear from the daughter's house. A grandson would know where to look for him, for the old man would start out unerringly for Uinta but would grow confused and wait wretchedly for a known face. When found he would explain that he was desperately needed at the farm. He had not seen it again when he died, and of the children and grandchildren only the novelist, a romantic, has traveled those eight miles.

What can be said in judgment of Jonathan Dyer's life? In terms of money, his estate, after the expense of six years away from the farm, was about six thousand dollars. He had come from Hertford and labored for fifty-five years to bequeath seven hundred and fifty dollars to each of his children. Or, in different terms, he had raised seven chil-dren who, with their children, had merged with the frontier into the Republic. Not much else can be said: an item in the history of America had fulfilled itself. You must multi-ply Jonathan Dyer by several million, looking westward from the Missouri River to the Rocky Mountains, across a space which your oldest maps will call "The Great American Desert."

After that multiplication you see Jonathan Dyer as something else, and a carelessly parenthetical sentence in a letter from Ogden lights up with sudden meaning. "They are farming your grandfather's land again." So the fox farm has collapsed, with so much other obscenity that belonged to the boom years. There will be crops again on that hillside which slopes downward to the Weber. Alfalfa flowers will be blue in the north field once more and the canal will divert shimmering water to the kitchen garden. Perhaps other orchards will rise in the places where Jonathan's were uprooted; the volcanic ash will once more work its chemistry.

The earth was poisoned, and Jonathan made it sweet. It was a dead land, and he gave it life. Permanently. Forever. Following the God of the Mormons, he came from Hertford to the Great American Desert and made it fertile. That is achievement.

FROM *Harper's*, APRIL 1935

Fossil Remnants of the Frontier

~~~~~~~~~~~~~~~~~~~~~~~~~~~~~~~~~~~~~~

I

SHE was going, she said, to summon Bat Masterson.
We had been tormenting her with the ingenious deviltries
of childhood and, one small blonde girl against a half-dozen
boys, she now proposed to stop it. The invocation brought
us to an uneasy pause. Thirty-odd years later, I remember
the rustle of cottonwoods while triumph glinted in her
eyes and a light buggy came up the road. It drew abreast,
and manliness restrained us from bolting but was not capable of a jeer. Two booted men in flannel shirts and wide
tan Stetsons sat in that buggy, and a shotgun stuck out
from under the seat. They were probably no more than a
couple of neighbors bound up "the canyon road" for quail,
but a dreadful name lent them awe. They passed. The
blonde child said, "That's Bat Masterson and I know him,"
then stuck out her tongue and disdainfully walked away.
The killer-sheriff was not within a thousand miles at the

moment, probably, but in Ogden, Utah, at about 1904, his
name was a sufficient dissuader of boys.

One of my mother's stories dealt with a friend of hers
who married and went to some Wyoming town. There,
after some years, her husband was murdered, "on the very
steps of the courthouse." The misdemeanor may not have
had social sanction but there was no thought of arresting
the misdemeanant. The widow was acquainted with the
usages: before the corpse was carried away she dipped a
token in the thickening blood. She would save it until her
son grew up; then, my mother said, she would give it to
him and bid him "wash the stain from your mother's hand-
kerchief." The tale sounds a theme from the border ballads
of all ages but it is quite true. To a boy growing up in that
culture it had solemnity but nothing of the inappropriate.

The last loose confederacies of rustlers and train robbers
were not much later than my birth. In interior Utah and
Wyoming there was still some gunfire and such galloping
below the skyline as the movies were soon to reproduce,
but it was done by individuals, not gangs, by remnants of
an outmoded lodge, in a tradition already formalized and obsolete. It was as far as the moon from Ogden. We were
Butch Cassidy or Tom Horn. We held up the U. P. at
Tipton; we rode down fanning our guns at Laramie; at
Winnemucca or Castlegate we robbed banks and turned
in our saddles to deal with citizens reckless enough to
level rifles at us; we rode back to Robbers' Roost or Hole
in the Wall for the orgies that convention demanded. But
there was no feeling that such romance was related to our
time and place: we were as ritualistic as the boys I see to-
day in Cambridge, Massachusetts, firing machine guns from

automobiles at government agents who had had the effrontery to pursue John Dillinger.

Utah has little history of Indian trouble. This is due in part to Brigham Young's enlightened policy – he believed, soundly, that it was cheaper to feed Indians than to kill them off – but in greater part to the fact that the Indians of Utah were a degenerate race. The bellicose Utes belonged to the eastward, the Bannocks ranged far to the north, the Apaches seldom came up as far as the Grand Canyon, and the Navajos, who reached our border in greater numbers, were not warlike. The resident tribes were mostly Gosh-Utes and Diggers, technological unemployed, victims of the competitive Indian society which had forced them to the badlands, where such culture as they possessed decayed, sometimes below the use of fire. Thus it was that in the stories of the elders the red slayer was commonly just a beggar and a thief. They had been sufficiently sophisticated to trade on the reputation of their race, so that, finding a woman alone in a farmhouse, they might sometimes frighten her into largesse. But they could not often do even that; my grandmother, startled by the apparition of a blanketed and painted buck singing Injun in her dooryard, simply picked up the weapon known to her generation as a horse pistol. At sight of it the brave forsook the dooryard and the warpath in one stride. The air was full of Indian stories, located elsewhere, of course. Neighbors had ridden to Sand Creek or had campaigned with Custer or Connor or Crook; had fought off Oglalla attacks on wagon trains or stage stations; had galloped to distant settlements and found the naked, scalped, and raped bodies of women, and children curiously dismembered and hung up. Distance was on all those tales, however, and the closest we boys came to them was in the distinction of one playmate. An uncle of his had been captured by Apaches, who cut off his eyelids and the soles of his feet and then tied him to a stake in an ant-bed and left him to the desert sun.

But we inherited the frontier's sentiments about Indians. The ones we saw, to be sure, were just grunting, dour, and mostly drunken grotesques, without terror, whom it was desirable not to approach too closely lest your mother be obliged to wash your hair with kerosene. But the Indian as an image of thought was a savage whose extermination was dictated by the necessities of civilization. The attitude survived long enough to immunize me against one sentimentality of my literary generation. As a historian, I have been able to understand the Indian's side of extermination and to master his strategy, but as a literary critic, I have been withheld from mysticism about the Amerind. I have not found him a beauty lover, the creator of a deeply spiritual religion, or an accomplished metaphysician who plumbed eternal secrets which his brutish conqueror could never understand. Sibylline women and rapt men from megalopolis have been unable to persuade me that his neolithic culture was anything but a neolithic culture. Remembering the scalp-dance, I have found the Amerind on the whole less likely to civilize the American continent than the Nordic; on Amerind art and religion, I hold, the frontier had a sounder criticism than Greenwich Village.

In such ways, remembered violence tinged life in Ogden during that pause between frontier society and industrialism in which I grew up. I cannot say how it affected our libido and personæ. Outwardly, combined with the tradition of the migratory hunter, it did no more than give us a familiarity with firearms earlier than boys were getting it to the eastward. I owned several sub-caliber rifles before

I was twelve. By fifteen I was a good offhand shot and had owned not only twenty-twos but a really formidable arsenal as well. By inheritance, appropriation, and the trafficking of boyhood I had acquired at various times a high-powered rifle, a shotgun, an automatic pistol, and at least three revolvers. My friends were similarly armed, and the gulches above Ogden endlessly echoed with our gun-fire. Firearms were our cult, as automobiles and radios became the cult of our successors. We were competent. I knew no boy who did not regularly strap a revolver on his belt, balance a rifle on his shoulder, and disappear with his gang into the hills; but I knew only one boy who was injured in all that time. Early as we came to them, we used our guns with skill. It was a formalized skill without survival value, so that we consciously practised it as an art, but it was a frontier inheritance.

The quality of all this scarlet was its irrelevance. And that is precisely my point: the West's scarlet, the frontier's violence, was episodic and irrelevant. Our elders and their elders had been lifelong addicts of civilization and community building. The cow-boys arriving at Trail's End, who liquored up and shot one another, were an inconvenience, like the breaking of a water main, and had nothing to do with the life of Dodge City. The schoolmarm took the children out to look for mayflowers through that intermittent barrage. Bat Masterson, on the prowl for a kill, stepped out of the way of matrons of the Eastern Star carrying crullers and chicken patties to a church supper. Just across the Weber River (a very small stream) from my grandfather's south field, the Morrisite war produced three days of rifle and artillery fire. Civil revolt and its suppression get one line in his journal, being subordinated to the record of his plowing. A cattle war, a battle of miners, the

rape of a bank or a stagecoach was just what it is to-day, a
violent interruption of a peaceful process, and was met in
the same way, with the same dispatch. Only, the frontier,
being a large country and insufficiently policed, had few
community safeguards for life and property. That fact put
such safeguards up to the individual: if his safety and his
property were threatened he had to defend them himself.
"The law west of the Pecos" was what one wore on one's
hip or carried on one's shoulder. When someone stole your
horse or dynamited your ditches you could not send east
of the Pecos for a cop. The frontiersman sighed, dropped
his plow, went for his arsenal, attended to the horsethief,
and then came back, got his crop in, and became a private
citizen. He gladly made a peace officer his vicar as soon as
one was available, and if he sometimes showed a preference
for one who had got his training among the outlawed,
megalopolis shows the same preference to-day. Organization achieved, he promptly forgot his earlier phase. It is
not in the West that a tradition of personal responsibility
and violence persists. I have seen more pocket pistols at a
single party in Georgia than in any ten years' travel in the
entire West.

II

Ogden had seen a deeper violence than casual outlawry.
From its first settlement on, Utah was constantly rocked
by the deadliest of all warfare, economic and religious. The
Church of Jesus Christ of Latter-Day Saints was a semi-
coöperative society governed by an oligarchy who claimed
divine sanction and exercised absolute power. It had
reached Utah after a series of expulsions which proved that
the American social system could not adjust itself to it.
Once in the mountains, the Church did its best to establish

its system in defiance of experience. Fifty years of economic war between Mormons and Gentiles, intensified and made picturesque by the religious idiom of its expression, ensued before the compromises which finally permitted the adjustment. In the course of that campaign the National Government once sent an expeditionary force against the Church, and at another time, in flagrant violation of the Constitution, confiscated the Church's property, dissolved its corporations, proscribed some hundreds of its leaders, and attached a test-oath to the franchise. On its part, the Church expropriated the property of many Gentiles, with and without process of law, maintained a Gay-pay-oo for the immemorial purposes of dictatorships, and ruled by terrorism such of its own members as it had to and such Gentiles as it could. If the principles of the warfare were economic and if its strategy was political, the actual front-line tactics necessitated a long series of murders and one massacre in the grand manner.

Yet this gaudy era too was over in that transition period during which I grew up. Ogden, as the railroad center of the State, had an actual majority of Gentiles and so had achieved a working compromise, a forced equilibrium, long before the rest of Mormonry. The violence of neighbors at one anothers' throats, calling upon God, morality, and the national sovereignty for vindication, had subsided, and very little strife found its way to children. Mormon and Gentile, we grew up together with little awareness that our fathers fought in hostile armies. The child of a Catholic father and a Mormon mother, I myself was evidence of the adjustment. One of my earliest memories is of a little girl's prophecy that the Wasatch mountains would be shaken down upon the plain in the imminent Last Days, and that I, as a Gentile, would be destroyed whereas she, as a Saint, would be saved for glory. Her prediction showed the smug self-righteousness as the Lord's chosen that characterizes all Mormons. Children had, even at four or five, a vivid feeling of membership in a unity, a secret and exotic way of life which entitled them to privileges denied the rest of us. They had also an array of duties, organizations, and badges that set them off, but, being children, frequently found them a bore and could be as skeptical of "primary" as we of St. Joseph's parish were of communion class. But this exclusiveness was less marked in Ogden than in other Utah towns, and far less marked than in the farming country where Mormonry was unalloyed.

The Irish priests of my own communion never preached against the heretics. Protestant ministers were less amiable, but it was only an occasional Gantry in the evangelical sects who bellowed excerpts from the filthy and preposterous anti-Mormon literature of the earlier age. We even mingled in Sunday School without shock. A Mormon meeting house was the place of worship nearest my home, and I was sometimes sent there for instruction until I was about seven, when Rome idly exercised its claim. (Somewhat to my relief. No Puritan divine in the Bay Colony ever equaled the long-windedness of any Mormon bishop.) As we grew toward high-school age the lines tightened a little—surprisingly, by the formation of castes. The rudimentary aristocracy of Ogden tended to be Gentile, and a good many people began to feel superior on the simple ground that they had been baptized or married not for eternity but only for this world. As we grew still older, as the efficient Mormon system began to select its missionaries among the boys and point the girls toward marriage in the faith, the cleavage grew distinct. But even then it was unimportant and often humorous. I remember a debate when my high-school class selected a baccalaureate speaker. The Mormon contingent, a minority, proposed one of the Twelve Apostles. An opponent solemnly put Jesus Christ in nomination, and Catholic, Presbyterian, and Baptist united to vote down the Saints.

Polygamy, the sole symbol of Mormonism in the outside world, meant almost nothing to us. The truth of history, which historians have not yet understood, is that to the Mormons themselves it was only a religious symbol, lacked the coercion of economic logic, and was slowly and insensibly found to be a mistake. More briefly still, Mormon polygamy was a caste privilege. "The hierarchy" is the Mormon term for the governing class, the hagiocracy or plutocracy as distinguished from the body of the Church. In general only the hierarchy was permitted to practise polygamy; only the hierarchy could afford to practise it. Thus there were never enough polygamists to establish the tone of any community; there were fewer of them in Ogden than in other towns, and the institution had been driven underground by the persecutions of the 'Nineties. Some of our playmates were known to be polygamous children and the number was increased as we grew up and learned the open secrets of the town. So far as I can remember, that fact meant absolutely nothing to us except as it gave them a certain distinction. By the time we were adolescents some of them, especially the girls, felt, I believe, a kind of embarrassment or social inferiority which the training of the Church did not always transform to fervent superiority. It was, however, frequently compensated by the fact of plutocracy: a polygamist's child was likely to be a well-to-do child. Adolescence also informed us about the furtive practice of polygamy. We saw conspicuously monogamous Mormons paying regular parochial visits to conspicuously unmarried women. But there was no persecution to make such secrecy romantic and, unhappily, they were dreadfully ordinary people. We were just ribald about them. They were easily associated with the folklore that clustered about Brigham Young.

The way in which Mormonism did influence our daily life was to spice it with miracle. In few societies are angels as common as policemen and heaven rather more familiar than a city park: I have had a lifelong tenderness for the world's delusions because I grew up amid prophecy and the glories of the Lord. The whole aim of Brigham Young's policy, after one disastrous experiment, and that of his successors was to abandon the supernatural. The leaders tried to repress the impulses of their people, but the Church had been founded during the Apocalypse by a prophet of God and had always been recruited from the naturally ecstatic. Miracle might be officially denounced but it was a fundamental condition of daily life. Hired girls in my mother's kitchen looked into heaven. God spoke to ditch-diggers and garbage-collectors. On any day, at any corner, any Saint might meet an angel on his way. Patriarchs, prophets, and even deities nightly visited each block in Ogden when the Saints slept. The conversation of all Mormons was predominantly theological, and exegesis might at any moment change to prophecy — and when I say prophecy I mean not only the hosannas of the chosen but literal, detailed soothsaying by qualified seers under immediate inspiration of God.

Miraculous healing, of course, was commonest. The Lord sustained his people in all ailments from cancer to the common cold, from snakebite to St. Vitus' dance. The Mormon elders had their sacred oils and liturgical pantomime, like all priests, but it was extempore miracles by individual

Mormons that impressed us. In time of epidemic these were intensified to the classic symptoms of mass hysteria till terror and ecstasy walked the Ogden streets. But other miracles were more picturesque. The widow's cruse had an exact parallel in a miraculous flour sack owned by a widow in my block. All but empty in the fall, it fed her family through a hard winter and when spring came was fuller than it had been in October. The Three Nephites are the Mormon variation of the Wandering Jew, three survivors of the earlier Church doomed to wander the earth till the Last Days. Rumor of their presence sometimes spread through the back lots; there were omens and marvelous sequels of their passing, and I knew several Saints who had seen them. Piety was rewarded by a legacy which paid the mortgage, by the miraculous provision of clothes or horse-flesh or quails or manna. Sin received equally direct action: an accident that removed a "bad Mormon" was the judg-ment of an angry God, and drouth, plagues of grasshoppers and disastrous forest fires meant that the Saints were not living their religion — usually by skimping their tithes. The destruction of one village by cloudburst and of another by a snowslide was incontrovertible evidence of communal sin.

Deliverance from the plots of the Gentiles was common. The missionaries went forth without purse or scrip through-out the world and they were not always loved. But God's providence went with them. Sandy P——, for instance, had been persecuted by the Austrians. One night a mysterious stranger, bearded and dressed in shining white, woke him from sleep and told him that Satan had prompted the vil-lagers to take his life. Sandy rose and fled, the pursuit swiftly gathering behind him. It grew nearer as he labored through the night, and at last he came to a river too wide and rapid for him to cross. With the Mormon readiness for martyrdom, Sandy commended himself to the Lord. But a deep sleep came upon him. When he waked he was on the far side of the river and the frustrated lynchers were cursing him from the other bank.

That miraculous slumber and that white-clad stranger were constantly with us in Mormonry. Portentous words thundered out of silence. The skies above Twelfth Street opened and Olaf Olafson, teamster or swineherd, saw unfolded the future course of his life. In the deep night Granny Gudmanson heard a sonorous, semi-Biblical apostrophe telling her how to improve a granddaughter's morals, how to treat an ailing cow, or how to build an extension on the chicken house. Celestial messengers overtook wayfarers and told them to turn back or armed them against danger on the route. Angels snatched one back from a train fated to be wrecked or came at night to bid one withdraw money from a shaky bank. And anything might be an omen or a portent. Dreams and visions made all the neighbors rapt. A configuration of the clouds, an egg with two yolks, a blight on the radish bed, even a nightmare had been inspired above and could either be interpreted at home or taken to some neighborhood seer for explanation. The Sandy P—— I have mentioned was greatly gifted in divination. He kept his large family in a continual tension of miracle — and of terror; for do not suppose that communications from God are always conducive to a peaceful life. At about the age of five one of his grandchildren was repeatedly visited in dreams by another one who was dead. Through Sandy's interpretation the dead child's message was seen to be a warning that a third child was soon to die; and before long they took that third child to an asylum for the insane, which showed that Sandy hadn't missed it far. Sandy's youngest daughter was a classmate of mine at high

school, and it was once my privilege to console her when a
Mormon swain took some other maiden to a dance. She
wept on my shoulder, most enjoyably to us both, but that
night an angel visited her in a dream, and she laid the apparition before her prophet-father. Sandy interpreted and
Sally sought me out. The Lord, Sandy decided, had pronounced her swain unworthy and had then given her a
warning. "The Lord says," Sally told me, "that I must not
let a Gentile kiss me any more."

Childhood on the Mormon frontier seems to me a rich
heritage. It prepared me for the economic and governmental miracles of these days. It gave me a good many yard-
sticks for the behavior of the race. It dissuaded me from
asking much rationality in human affairs, and it made my
faculty of surprise abnormally inactive. It gave me laboratory experience in dictatorship. . . . And there was also
my Mormon grandfather's revelation. The Bishop of Uinta
once came to Grandfather's house and told him that the
Lord had revealed an intention to bestow his daughter on
the bishop as a plural wife. Grandfather was a devout man,
a man who had lived his religion, followed the priesthood,
and built up the kingdom. So now his piety was rewarded,
in miracle. The skies were opened to him and he said, "I
prophesy that if you don't get out of here, Brother L., and
if you ever mention the revelation to anyone, I will shoot
hell out of you."

III

The greatest influence on childhood of the vanished frontier was the freedom we enjoyed. It was an all-inclusive
freedom that touched every aspect of our lives. Perhaps I
can best suggest it by the relations of the sexes in adolescence, and of this the most vivid symbol I have is a memory

from my last year at high school. About noon one day a girl and I were coming back toward Ogden over the foot-hills when we reached a barbed-wire fence. Helen stopped and modestly bade me look the other way lest I glimpse her calf when she climbed the fence. It was a request ab-solutely in accord with the Ogden folkways — and yet she and I had been alone in the mountains since one o'clock that morning, had climbed a peak and cooked our breakfast on the top. This, in 1914. It was the privilege of young people, in groups or in couples, to wander in the mountains unchap-eroned and unsuspected of misbehavior — and, let me say, rightly unsuspected. At a time when elsewhere in America stringent restrictions were put on all such intercourse out-side the home, we were quite free to go where we liked at any hours that pleased us. The form which the convention took is amusing: if we went into the mountains to cook supper we must be back before dawn, and if we wanted to cook breakfast we must be careful not to start till after mid-night — otherwise we should spend the night together, which was unthinkable.

The mountains were a force in our freedom. By the time we were eight we went on day-long explorations of the foothills, miles from home, unsupervised by older people. Two or three years later we were beginning to climb the peaks, and by the time we were fourteen we were camping out for days at a time, with or without tents, in canyons a hundred miles up the range. I remember, at fifteen, spend-ing a Christmas vacation in a deserted log cabin deep among the peaks and, with several companions, practising the not inconsiderable skill that such a stay implies. The frontier had left this impress on us, and when the Boy Scout move-ment reached Utah just as we grew too old for it, we were contemptuous of its sterilized and evangelized woodscraft.

Toward the supervised outdoor-life of the Boy Scouts and of the summer-camp movement which followed we felt a frontiersman's disdain for the counterfeit. At fourteen we were able to take care of ourselves in the wilderness. We wanted no lectures on the hazards of cliffs, poison ivy, and rattlesnakes, and no exhortations about the beauties and purities of nature. As for nature, we were realists — and that, I think, is one of the deepest values we experienced.

But be sure we also paid a tax. This was a time, let me repeat, between two ages. The frontier organization had collapsed and the organization of the industrial order had not taken its place. In this very matter of outdoor skills we suffered. We were practising a frontier craft but practising it as an art — survival value had gone from it and so nothing vital depended on it. For instance, I have deeply regretted my ignorance of the native botany and natural history. A generation earlier I should have learned the seasons, qualities, and uses of all native plants and woods, the habits of birds and animals, the use of traps, and the crafts of taxidermy and tanning quite as naturally as I did learn camping and mountain climbing and marksmanship. A few years later I should have learned them from the paid instructors supplied by a community grown suddenly solicitous about its young. I would rather have had the first training than the second certainly, but the second rather than none at all.

Frontier society disciplined children within its necessities; the industrial order taught them from a new sentiment of humanitarian responsibility. Our order granted them the frontier freedom and then, omitting discipline, disregarded them. In some ways it was not a bad system. Psychology approves its impersonality, and it taught children a practical Darwinism — they learned, earlier than children elsewhere, immediate implications of the struggle for existence.

But it was a handicap in many ways, since the terms of that struggle were changing and we were not equipped for the new phase. Also, it had its immediate pangs. A regret that has lasted to my thirty-eighth year springs from my inability to become a really good swimmer. I never saw the crawl stroke till boys just older than I began coming home from college — the first generation of college men in Ogden. Now the crawl stroke is probably not universal in Utah even to-day (no river there has more than a thirty-yard stretch deep enough for swimming and there are only a half dozen lakes in the whole State), but at least the new order teaches it. There was no one to teach me, and that fact has, I think, its significance. A boy who was not born with a knack for boys' skills was simply out of luck. To-day playgrounds and schools swarm with specialists who teach the awkward the approved technics of all games, sports, crafts, skills, and arts. In the Ogden of my time one had them or one never got them. No doubt the preferential treatment of to-day has been carried too far; but one would like to ask analysts and social pathologists how much maladjustment, inadequacy, and frustration they have traced to the wounds inflicted by its lack. Whole areas of experience, whole classes of social adjustment, may well have been thrown out of balance. Certainly it showed in the experience of my generation when we ventured away from Ogden. We had the rituals of our own society, but when we got away from it we had an ineptness that proper supervision of children would have prevented. The elders had brought us into the tribal house, but they had not fitted us to deal with the outlanders.

But one will have to go still deeper into the mind to appraise the basic fact of that frontier remnant. We learned as children, I say, implications of the struggle of existence.

Frontier children always learned them, but the industrial order, at even its most squalid levels, delays that instruction and, above those levels, delays it perhaps too long. Among frontiersmen and those who succeeded to their heritage, such a realization has conditioned the entire climate and physiology of thought. The significance of that fundamental has been insufficiently realized and so has been grotesquely distorted by students of American society. Make of it what you will, to the despair of the hopeful or the apprehension of the merely liberal, one whole division of the Americans was conditioned by it. To that people the struggle of existence is not something that can be repealed by Act of Congress or demolished by rainmakers, philosophers, or the community meeting in prayer.

IV

There remains one frontier-fossil which I touch on with reluctance because, though one of the ideas which students of American life have been most voluble about, it cannot be clearly phrased or adequately defined here. It relates to that cliché of editorial writers — individualism, and its implications in the action of the frontier on the national history.

If as a critic of historical writing I have challenged the simplicities of certain historians about the American frontier, it is because I know of my own experience that frontier life was infinitely complex and not reducible to formula. Consider: I was the child of an apostate Mormon and an apostate Catholic, which suggested that the religious culture of the frontier was far from simple. Across the street from me lived a prosperous miner who made his cross on all documents because he could not write, whose wife could

not read, and who did not send his children to school till
the town forced him to. He was the type-frontiersman of
many thinkers. Yet the book in which I was taught to read
was a Pope's *Iliad* of 1781, and, chanting the couplets
while I played with the miner's children, I was a laboratory
specimen of frontier relationships which no literary or academic formula could express. One of my grandfathers was
an English mechanic turned farmer, another was an Italian
cavalry officer turned commission merchant. I played with
the sons and grandsons of Hawaiian princes, Scandinavian
murderers, German geologists with dueling scars, Irish
poets, Spanish mathematicians, French gamblers, Virginia
slaveowners, Yankee metaphysicians — of men who came
from everywhere, who had every conceivable tradition,
education, and canon of taste and behavior. On Memorial
Day one ancient hung the Stars and Bars on his front door
and mounted guard on it in butternut; the King's birthday
was celebrated three doors away; a pastry cook made a
Dauphinist of me at ten; down the street Kriss Kringle was
venerated instead of Santa Claus; in the next block manuscript letters of Emerson created a whole ritual of behavior; beyond that house a fiercely silent dignity protected
a national but locally unmentioned disgrace. Here, God
knows, was none of that deadly uniformity of thought,
habit, belief, and behavior which books about the frontier
diagnose *in absentia*. I grew up in a culture much more various than I have found anywhere else.

Such a society could have no such coercive singleness of
opinion, no such absolutism, as the books describe. Quite
the contrary: it could survive only by the utmost latitude
of thought, expression, and personal behavior. We learned
to sing "What was your name in the States?" and we sang
it in derision, but it had a meaning which the community

taught us to respect. We learned that what a man thought about God, the government, the banks, the social revolution, women, sex, alcohol, or the Dauphin, Kriss Kringle, or separation for Ireland was most definitely his own business and not subject to our own views. More, we learned that what he did about them was, within the farthest possible limits of community elasticity, even more his business and not ours. We learned this from our parents and ourselves and from the daily practice of our community. The frontier had lapsed just so far that the lesson was not occasionally italicized by gunfire. We learned, in short, that the frontier had existed as a community, and could have existed, only by the constant exercise of the freedoms, individualisms, and eccentricities which the absentee critic finds it never had.

I may say too that we saw these conditions end. As my generation grew up, industrialism and megalopolis made us their benefactions. Luncheon clubs arrived, and Chautauqua, the Y.M.C.A., the syndicated press, booster movements, the hysterias and compulsions of wartime and prohibition, and the liberal point of view and national prosperity. We had been boys in the despotic uniformity of the intellectuals; we did not know what uniformity was till their Utopia gathered us in.

At the same time a boy who had once risen from bed at three of a spring morning with an arctic wind blowing out of the canyons, to irrigate his grandfather's fields with icy water at just such times as the community chose to allot — such a boy understood another widely denied quality of the frontier. For the books have struck the frontier paradox and solved it exactly wrong. They find that the frontier rigidly suppressed individualism in personal opinion and behavior, whereas frontiersmen could live together only by virtue of a greater latitude in such matters than any other part of America permitted. And they find that the frontier enforced an even greater individualism in economic and governmental affairs, whereas the very conditions of frontier life in the desert imposed coöperation. When glacial water seeped down my boots in a canyon wind at hours dictated by the water commissars, I was working in the earliest tradition of the pioneers, locally sixty-five years old and ninety years earlier than Mr. Ickes. Who but the economic individualist was the proverbial victim of frontier violence? It would be unfair to allude to the stage-robber and the horse-thief; but surely the rustler, the claim-jumper, and the fraudulent homesteader were lynched by coöperative effort; surely the stock-detective, the wolf-hunter, and the fence-rider were agents of a frontier economy in which the individualism of the critics had small part. How indeed did a frontier community exist at all except by means of a close-knit coöperation? Especially, how did a frontier community in the desert exist?

The first job I ever held for any length of time was in a land-title office and it took me deep into territorial organization. I found the intricate network of a coöperative system. Not the coöperative merely, for the frontier had its share of communistic experiments which went the way of all communisms and, it may be, left some skeptical deposit on the minds of Westerners. Even Mormonism, whose coöperative society ruled in the name of God by a superior hierarchy, a privileged class, is a practical answer to the enigma of government, had once quaintly investigated communism. There in the records I digested was the United Order of Enoch and its melancholy teachings, with the Prophet John Taylor instead of Stalin to correct its economics. But in the routine of business I had to master the water laws, the grazing laws, the mining code — I had to re-create the frontier's coöperative reduction of chaos. Do not wonder if I have, in print, sometimes suggested that metropolitan authorities on frontier life go and do likewise. Or if I commend to them such casual items from frontier journals as this: "To-day our water committee waited on Stark and Stevens and told them to close up their dams until they come into the agreement." With its entry of a week later that Messrs. Stark and Stevens, kulaks of rugged frontier individualism, have been liquidated.

Well, Ogden of those days was the damnedest place. We were really *fin de siècle*, we were the frontier's afterglow. We saw that glow fade out. We stood, as it were, on a divide, and also we went down the other side. In the class of 1914 at the Ogden High School there were three girls each of whom had one pair of silk stockings. By the class of 1918 there was no girl who had ever worn cotton stockings to the school, and the town had broken out with something that looked like a bucolic variant of the Junior League. Children of parents who had been conceived in cottonwood lean-tos, with their older brothers looking on, had suddenly become a plutocracy with a mistaken belief that they were a fashionable caste. But the sagebrush débutante is without interest to history and is hereby abandoned to literature, which so far has left her out.

The Plundered Province

I

THE Westerner remains a bewildering creature to the rest of the nation. Socially he has never fused with the energetic barbarian that for many decades symbolized the Middle Westerner to the appalled East. Politically, also, he has remained distinct from the Middle Westerner, to whom our cartoonists allot a more genial grin, a better-filled-out frame, and a neater suit of overalls. To cartoonists, the Middle Westerner is the Dirt Farmer and he lives in the Corn Belt and, except occasionally, he is admitted to be a person of some consequence. On the contrary, it is established that the Westerner is gaunt, ragged, and wild-eyed; also he is a mendicant and rapacious. Under one arm he clasps a concrete dam or a bundle labeled Government-Built Hard Roads. Other labels dangling from his pocket announce that he has grabbed a lot of pork. They allude to Reclamation Projects, Forest Reserves, Experiment Stations, Grazing Acts, the Desert Land Act, Crop Surveys, Home Loan

Banks, and similar privileges. Sometimes, with a quaint candor, they mention Land Grant Railroads, and nearly always a caption informs the reader how much Massachusetts paid in Federal taxes and how many miles of concrete in Idaho were laid by the sum. The mendicant's mouth is open: you are to understand that he is bawling for more Privilege and Paternalism. This is his routine appearance when the cartoonists are merely amused, are even willing to tip him a dam or two for the sake of quiet as you would give a child a nickel to go play somewhere else. When, however, the spectacle of human greed dismays the artist the Westerner ceases to be a mere beggar. Gaunt and wild-eyed still, he now rides a whirlwind or rushes over a cliff, invariably dragging the Republic with him, and the lightning round his head is labeled Socialism, Bolshevist Daydreams, or National Bankruptcy. Instead of being merely a national pensioner, he is now a national danger.

This is the symbolism of the Westerner in our metropolitan press — the national wild man, the thunder-bringer, disciple of madness, begetter of economic heresy, immortal nincompoop deluded by maniac visions, forever clamoring, forever threatening the nation's treasury, forever scuttling the ship of state. And yet, a queer thing: a mere change of clothes gives him a different meaning on quite as large a scale. Put a big hat on his head, cover the ragged overalls with hair pants and let high heels show beneath them, knot a bandana round his neck — and you have immediately one of the few romantic symbols in American life. He has ceased to be a radical nincompoop and is now a free man living greatly, a rider into the sunset, enrapturer of women in dim theaters, solace of routine-weary men who seek relief in woodpulp, a figure of glamour in the reverie of adolescents, the only American who has an art and a literature devoted wholly to his celebration. One perceives a certain incompatibility between these avatars.

The land he inhabits has a further symbolism. The West is the loveliest and most enduring of our myths, the only one that has been universally accepted. In that mythology it has worn many faces. It has meant escape, relief, freedom, sanctuary. It has meant opportunity, the new start, the saving chance. It has meant oblivion. It has meant manifest destiny, the heroic wayfaring, the birth and fulfillment of a race. It has, if you like, meant what the fourth house of the sky has meant in poetry and all religions — it has meant Death. But whatever else it has meant, it has always meant strangeness. That meaning may serve to reconcile the incompatibles.

Much energy has been spent in an effort to determine where the West begins. The definitions of poetry and the luncheon clubs are unsatisfactory: vagueness should not be invoked when a precise answer is possible. The West begins where the average annual rainfall drops below twenty inches. When you reach the line which marks that drop — for convenience, the one hundredth meridian — you have reached the West. And it is a strange country.

The first part of its strangeness is that it was the last frontier to fall. The American migration leaped across it and in part returned to it from beyond, Californians and Oregonians invading it eastward from their region of plentiful rain. It lingered on invincible after all other frontiers had disappeared, into a time when pioneering was only a memory already shimmering with the rainbow of the never-never. The pioneers' grandchildren were now citizens of orderly manufacturing towns, and when they read of to-day's happenings over the hill they necessarily thought of them as belonging to grandfather's romance. It must clearly be a strange country where the legendary saga of redskins and first-fruits was still going on.

It was strange too in that the westward-making Americans, when they came to their last frontier, found that what they had learned on the way there would do them little good. They were the world's great frontiersmen. The whole continent had been frontier, and in subduing it they had learned an exquisite craftsmanship, an exquisite technique, round which much of the national culture had formed. Yet four fifths of their travel had lain among trees, and the forests had conditioned their craftsmanship. Was not the first chapter in the heroic legend called "The Cabin in the Clearing"? The roadways through the wilderness were forest-fed streams down which produce could be floated to market and up which the pioneers could make their way by canoe. It was a hard labor, but the very core of American significance was that its results were certain. A man made a clearing with his axe, raised his cabin, fenced his fields, and grew old in security. During the last fifth of the westward journey craftsmanship had had to be somewhat modified, for the Americans had reached the prairies. Yet the problems here differed in degree rather than in kind, for the rivers were still navigable, there was wood for fuel and for the cabin and the fences, and the pioneers could count on even greater security, since this was the richest land in the world. But when they reached the West a craftsmanship refined through more than two centuries, and now felt to be a hereditary way of life, was simply useless.

There could be no cabin in the clearing, for there were no trees to clear and no logs to shape into walls: the pioneer's axe, his greatest tool, was as ineffective as its prototype of the smooth-flint age. The rivers ran contrariwise, most of them ran too shallowly to float a barge or even a canoe, ran brackish water, and in summer sometimes did not run at all. The redskins of the forest had been cruel, pestiferous, and obstinate, but they had never been a match for the Americans. Whereas the mounted Indians of the plains for many years exercised a boisterous superiority over their invaders, easily dominating them because of superior equipment and superior adaption to the land's necessities. Even the fauna gave the pioneer problems his legendary technique was not adequate to solve. Bear and venison were not to be butchered in the dooryard but had to be followed over the horizon and perhaps could not be met with at all; and the buffalo, the West's beef, had had no precedent in the forests. Not only the fauna was unfamiliar — the tight-fisted land would not grow most of the crops which the pioneers had grown to the eastward, would grow little dependably; and nothing at all except under methods radically different from anything the East had known.

It was a strange land, and all its strangeness came from the simple arithmetic of its rainfall. A grudging land — it gave reluctant crops only. A treacherous land — its thin rain might fail without reason or warning, and then there were no crops at all and the pioneer, who had been ignorant of droughts, promptly starved. An inventive land — besides drought it had other unprepared-for plagues: armies of locusts and beetles, rusts and fungi never encountered in the forests, parasites that destroyed grains and cattle which had been habituated to an Eastern climate. A poisoned land — it was variously salted with strange earths which must be leached away before seeds could germinate. And in the end as in the beginning, a dry land — so that all problems returned to the master problem of how to get enough water on land for which there could never be water enough. In sum, conditions that made unavailing everything that the pioneers had learned, conditions that had to be mastered from scratch if the last frontier was to be subdued.

And, therefore, the final strangeness of the West: it was the place where the frontier culture broke down. The pioneer's tradition of brawn and courage, initiative, individualism, and self-help was unavailing here. He could not conquer this land until history caught up with him. He had, that is, to ally himself with the force which our sentimental critics are sure he wanted to escape from: the Industrial Revolution.

Professor Webb's fine book, *The Great Plains*, catches the era in the actual process which can only be alluded to here. The country had no rivers for the transportation of goods — so settlement had to await the railroads. It had, except for the alpine regions, no forests. The pioneer might cut sod or mold adobe bricks for a shanty, but he could not fence his claim until industrialism brought him barbed wire. The Plains Indians were better equipped than he for the cavalry campaigns that had to be the West's warfare — so the Industrial Revolution had to give him repeating rifles and repeating pistols, especially the latter. So far as the Winning of the West was a war of conquest, victory waited upon the Spencer, the Winchester, and especially the Colt. And always the first condition: to grow crops where there was not water enough. The Revolution's railroads had to bring westward the Revolution's contrivances for deep cultivation, bigger and tougher plows, new kinds of harrows and surfacers and drills, and its contrivances for large-scale operations, new harvesters and threshers, steam and then gasoline group-machines which quadrupled cultivating power and then quadrupled it again. Finally, the problem of the water itself. The axe-swinging individualist had farmed his

small claim with methods not much different from those of
Cain's time. The Western pioneer could not farm at all until
the Revolution gave him practicable windmills, artesian
wells, and the machinery that made his dams possible. When
he crossed the hundredth meridian, in order to be Cain at
all he had first to become Tubal-Cain.

II

The West, then, was born of industrialism. When the age
of machinery crossed the hundredth meridian the frontier,
which had so long resisted conquest, promptly came under
the plow. But industrialism has other products than machines. Drawn to his heritage partly by advertising, which is
one of them, the pioneer found prepared and waiting there
for him the worst of all: financial organization.

In one sense the California gold rush won the Civil War,
and that has its importance for history; but a greater importance is that it developed a mechanism for the exploitation of
the West. The inventive men who devised ways of prevent-
ing gold-washers from retaining any outrageous profit from
their labors slipped eastward into the true West with a perfected system. From 1860 on, the Western mountains have
poured into the national wealth an unending stream of gold
and silver and copper, a stream which was one of the basic
forces in the national expansion. It has not made the West
wealthy. It has, to be brief, made the East wealthy. Very
early the West memorized a moral: the wealth of a country
belongs to the owners, and the owners are not the residents
or even the stockholders but the manipulators. Gold, silver,
copper, all the minerals, oil — you need not look for their
increase in the West, nor even among the generations of
widows and orphans thoughtfully advised to invest in them

by trust companies. The place to look for that increase is the trust companies, and the holding companies.

All this was demonstrated by the mines even before the Westerners arrived in force. The demonstration was repeated on a magnificent scale by the railroads, which added refinements in their ability to loot the Westerner directly as real-estate agencies and common carriers. Meanwhile the Government, the press, the whole nation were expediting the rush of settlement. It was *Zeitgeist*, by God! The continent had to be occupied — a bare spot on the map was an affront to the eagle's children. The folk migration, now in its last phase, was speeded up. Manifest destiny received the valuable assistance of high-pressure publicity. Congress, even less aware than the rail splitters that this was a strange country, helped out by passing, during fifty years, a series of imbecile laws which, even if no other forces had been working to that end, would have insured the West's bankruptcy. To inconceivably stupid government was added the activity of the promoter, who in the West had his last and greatest flowering as a statesman. Able to invade the last wilderness after fifty years of frustration, the migrating folk settled on the West like locusts. And they found finance — the finance of the East — waiting for them.

The catch phrase is "a debtor section." This was not, let me repeat, a problem of shouldering an axe and walking into the forest. The country had to be developed with the tools of the Industrial Revolution, and these cost money. The fencing, the wells, the canals and dams, the windmills, the gang plows, the cultivators, the tractors had to be paid for. The pioneers have been a debtor class all through history, and the Westerners as debtors differed only in having to pay more. What distinguished them from the rail splitters was the fact that history had got ahead of them. They had to pay for the development of the country because the financiers were there first, whereas on the earlier frontiers that development had paid for itself.

Costs are not always apparent on the surface. The financing of an expertly wrecked and re-wrecked railroad may be like the salesman's overcoat — you don't see it on the expense account but it's there just the same. The railroads have been made symbolic; but in comparison with some of the other devices of exploitation their watered capitalizations, rigged bankruptcies, short- and long-haul differentials, and simple policy of getting what they could seem social-minded and almost sweet. There were the water companies, the road companies, the land companies, the grain-storage companies. There were the mortgage companies. There were the banks. All of them learned from the mines and railroads, improving on instruction, and all of them looted the country in utter security, with the Government itself guaranteeing them against retributive action by the despoiled. There was also the Deacon Perkins formula which, because it contains the basic principle, will suffice to describe the whole process.

When money was easy, Deacon Perkins got three per cent. for it in his little back-room bank at East Corner, Massachusetts. When money was tight, he raised the rate to three and a half or four per cent. So from a thousand East Corners, a thousand Deacon Perkinses each sent a nephew West, trusting him just so far as it was impossible to find further legal safeguards. Then borrowing from his own bank at three or four per cent., the Deacon had Nephew Jim lend it in the West at twelve per cent. I say twelve per cent. but it was more likely to be sixteen or eighteen per cent., and in the newest districts it went to two per cent. a month. If Nephew Jim wanted to kite the rate a little by charging his client a commission for getting the loan, that was his own affair and had nothing to do with the system, which was concerned solely with the spread in interest rates, East and West. A good many Deacon Perkinses got rich on the system. A good many of them also got into the real estate business; but, with both Government and tradition sending the come-ons West in a steady stream, it was an easy business to get out of with another profit. The point, however, is that this system, a little complicated by the law of corporations, was precisely that of the manipulators. They were Eastern corporations and they financed themselves at two per cent. in order to charge twenty per cent. interest against the West, over and beyond the profits of trade, finance, monopoly, combination, and the normal increase of development. They had learned how to make the country pay. Their system was automatic and self-adjusting, an excellent system — for the East.

Besides taking over the country, then, the East added direct usury. The customary justification has mentioned empire-building — this tax was merely the fee which the strong men, the leaders, assessed for opening up the country. The explanation sounds sufficiently like that of other empire-builders, who got theirs without risk of loss, to sound convincing; and it probably satisfies the principles of imperial expansion in the textbooks. It has not, however, had a wide popularity in the West. The Westerner has seen palaces rise on Fifth Avenue and the endowments of universities and foundations increase with a rapidity that establishes the social conscience of his despoilers. The water company that took a mortgage on his farm grew into a bank, joined a network of interlocked pilfering agencies, changed into a holding company, and ended as an underwriter of railroad bonds and a depressant of farm prices in the interest of someone's foreign trade. In his whole country no one has ever been able to borrow money or make a shipment or set a price except at the discretion of a board of directors in the East, whose only interest was to sequester Western property as an accessory of another section's finance. He has contributed to those palaces and endowments just precisely what his predecessors in the pioneering system were enabled to keep for themselves. Meanwhile, the few alpine forests of the West were leveled, its minerals were mined and smelted, all its resources were drained off through the perfectly engineered gutters of a system designed to flow eastward. It may be empire-building. The Westerner may be excused if it has looked to him like simple plunder.

Meanwhile the *Chicago Tribune*, the *New York Times*, and similar organs of his despoilers have maintained their amusing howl about those Federal taxes. Look how New York and Illinois, Massachusetts and Pennsylvania, contribute fifty- or a hundredfold to the national treasury, and look how their money is commandeered to build roads and maintain bureaus in the begging West. So long as this appears to be mere cynicism, the West enjoys the show, having had an experience that begets an enjoyment of cynicism. But sometimes the spokesmen seem really to believe what they are saying, seem really to be protesting against a form of confiscation, and then one hears above the sage the sound of prolonged and acid laughter.

III

So far as there is any theory in the politics of sectional warfare beyond the simple one of "them who can, gets," it is this: that the plundering of one section for the benefit of another is justifiable if the prosperity of the second spills over enough to compensate the first for what it has been robbed of. The theory sanctioned the tariffs, trusts, and service charges that the dominant East used as implements of exploitation. Since, however, the West flouted theory by going and staying bankrupt, it has for fifty years been customary to supplement the theory, which may be described as the horse-feathers school of thought, with occasional bakshish. The West has sometimes been tipped a fractional per cent. of its annual tribute in the form of Government works or social supervision. This bakshish is what the Eastern press so regularly laments, and yet it is the time-honored way of dealing with agrarian unrest. Throughout history, governments have found it expedient to buy off the farmers when they grow troublesome, in order to sell them out at a profit later on. East of the hundredth meridian the agrarians have satisfactorily responded to that method. It has failed in the rainless country because the manipulators took too large an equity to begin with — they set the empire-builder's fee too high. The West has never had enough to come back on. It is the one section of the country in which bankruptcy, both actuarial and absolute, has been the determining condition from the start.

Newspapers are practising relativists. A proposal to widen the scope of the horse-feathers policy has always been statesmanship. If you are a creditor seeking by tariffs or mergers to expedite the plundering of the West you become *ipso facto* a person of patriotic vision. If, however, you try to slow up the rate of exploitation, you are just an anarchist pushing the Republic over the cliff in the name of Utopia. Fair enough, but at least it may be explained that the cartoonists are wrong about Utopia. The West exists only by rigorous adaptation to a realistic climate. It has no vision of perfection and has been unable to sprout belief in planned economies. Millennial visions in America are native to areas of forty inches annual rainfall or above. Nevertheless, the accepted symbol is accurate: throughout its existence the

West has produced much of the agitation known in the East as "radical" and has wholeheartedly supported all it did not produce. Most notably, schemes to debase the currency. Greenbackery, bimetallism, proposals for the cancellation of mortgages, for the reduction of usury, for even more direct methods with debt — all of them have either been born in the West or have had their apogee there. Nothing can exceed the horror of a banker who owns the mortgages or receives the usury or has participated in the mergers at which the reduction would be aimed. He knows that the Republic would be brought down by the collapse of its cornerstone, the sanctity of property; and in his way he is quite right. Only, the Westerner in his madness has experienced the fall of the Republic. It was property private to him that proved to lie outside the churchyard. The Republic crumbled fifty years ago, about the time a bank took over his first coöperative water-company, and his radicalism consists of inability to see wherein lies the heinousness of trying to get back some part of what was stolen from him at the muzzle of a gun.

The late flurry of doom, which agitated literary folk and frightened customers' men and young communists, anticipated a revolution so vague that one could make out little except that it would be bloody and soon. The prospect was stimulating but uncorrected by the historical approach. Agrarian revolutions in America, as I have pointed out, have always yielded to simple bribery, and our political revolutions have been hamstrung by the more economical method of enlisting their leaders on the side of the virtuous. If American history shows anything, it makes clear that revolution by means of the class struggle is inconceivable. The one revolution that did come to actual warfare in America was a sectional revolution, and it is likely that any new one would take the same form. If the nation weakened sufficiently, conceivably it might split along the cleavage-lines of the sections. (Perhaps intrasectional revolution could then follow the classics. While the united soviets of the steel country marched out to liquidate the kulaks of Western Pennsylvania, we might find General Dawes's minutemen arming themselves with castor oil to extirpate the La Follettes, take over the coöperative creameries of the Green Bay region, and exile the last Socialist councilman of Milwaukee.) The prospect of such fission would not appall the West. When empires crumble it is the provinces that go first, and the plundered province would slide into the sea with a perceptible exhilaration. Imagine repossessing the mines, the oil, the power lines, the cattle ranges and the wheat fields — imagine going into the first conference of independent sections prepared to bargain as proprietors, not as tenants or peons! The West could correct the interest-spread and realign the tariffs on a basis of realism. It could demand something more than the *pourboire* of a dam or some hard roads. Conceivably, Massachusetts and Pennsylvania would learn something from federated bargaining that they have omitted to infer from Federal taxes.

This, however, is a virtual movement, an economic pipe dream kin to the editorials in liberal journals but unrelated to the actual pressures exerted by people who are carrying on economic struggles. The West has no hope of such a dissolution, being able to estimate the strength of chains from their weight. It anticipates neither a breakup of the American economy nor any substantial readjustment of its part in that drainage system. It can fight the battle only on the terms laid down. If you can't win the campaign you try to win the individual engagement; if you can't reduce the salient you make a sortie against a limited portion of the front line. Reversal of the intersectional system is beyond hope, no return to the West of its equity in the nation is conceivable. In effect, no matter how the exterior alters, the East will go on producing protected goods for the West to buy in produce which the East's protection has depreciated. The West cannot modify the conditions but will continue to make sorties against the front line. The equity is not recoverable, but here and there the forced debt may be in part reduced. Cartoonists may as well dig in for a long winter; the West will remain radical. Necessarily, it will always be shoving the Republic over the same old cliff, bellowing one or another insanity. The actual form of insanity will change with chance and opportunism, but the force behind it will remain constant, a desire to rob the robbers of some fraction of their loot. That is part of the West's strangeness: it has always had an inexplicable hankering to get back its own.

Those of its spokesmen who resisted purchase have always been regarded as near relatives of the wild jackass. This too has an irony of its own, considering the politicians who have been the West's governors when they have not been simply the agents of its despoilers. With the greatest kindness, Congress has frequently taken time off to help the West develop institutions fitted to its conditions. Amiable thinkers, who had the traditions of the well-watered country to guide them, produced a series of inconceivable stupidities for the formation of the West — and had the power to convert stupidity into law. Hence another part of the West's strangeness; its lawlessness. Quoting Professor Webb: "No law has ever been made by the Federal Government that is satisfactorily adapted to the arid region."

The West soon realistically phrased the Homestead Act under which the Government invited occupation: Uncle Sam bets you a hundred and sixty acres that you'll starve in less than five years. It was a safe bet and all alterations made in the odds were just as safe. Two only of such alterations need be mentioned. Congress, perceiving a generation too late that the country could not be farmed but might be grazed, authorized patents fully one-tenth the size of the minimum that would permit grazing. But that was enlightened vision compared to another bounty — one of Pennsylvania's little gratuities to Wyoming — under whose terms the Westerner might occupy his land provided he would grow trees on it. God's forestry had not been that ambitious, but it was just lawlessness that withheld the West from complying. The Homestead Act itself provided for units of settlement that had made forests and prairies productive but just one-eighth the size required in the region of thin rain.

The Westerner had his choice. He could become a social producer by occupying and developing the country illegally, in flat defiance of the law, or he could become a social charge by obeying the law and pauperizing himself. He did both. Survival in the West has been won at the price of actual or constructive illegality; beyond the hundredth meridian, the basic social institutions have always been beyond the law of the land, which catches up with them slowly and only in part. And of course, Governmental stupidity coöperating with promotional skin-games, hundreds of thousands of Westerners have failed in their pioneering efforts. These bankrupts form the unlovely finale of the westward wayfaring, the squalor in which the folk movement ended. Brought West by *Zeitgeist* and advertising, they were asked to make the country produce what it could not produce and to do the job under regulations that doubled the grim humor of the farce. They are the West's paupers, victims of the East's advertising campaign for unearned increment; and both Government and the East have forgotten them except as exasperating dependents who must be fed at someone's expense. Probably at the expense of the land-grant railroads or those Federal taxpayers in Pennsylvania.

Government's prodigal stupidity abetted them throughout. They were brought to a country unfitted to produce the crops they were asked to grow — a country which, under the conditions Congress laid on them, could support them at best only two years in five, and one year in five would wipe them out altogether. It was among these foreordained victims of a country which Congress could not understand that Pennsylvania's *pourboires* were expended. Here the dams and canals were built and the whole stupendous asininity of Reclamation enacted. God couldn't grow trees in this country but Congress would.

So now, after sprinkling those taxes on the alkali, Congress, we hear, proposes to buy back the land and let the alkali have its turn at reclamation. The dams and canals built, the generations bankrupted, the land is discovered to be what the maps label it, desert. It was, we are told, sub-marginal land all along. This discovery, in view of its history, is hardly of this world — belonging rather to the cosmic reaches. But let it go: the West is a strange country.

IV

Remember that this sub-marginal land, the sage and greasewood of the West's ultimate barrens, witnessed the end of a historic process. The rainless country was the last frontier, and in its poisoned areas, without dignity, the wayfaring Americans came to the end of their story. Reclamation is a shining image of something or other — aspiration, it may be, or futility. Confronted by the last acres of the tradition and finding them incapable of producing, the Americans wasted millions trying to enforce their will on the desert. The impulse and the glory of the migration died hard but, when the desert was conceded to be desert in spite of will power, they died at last, in something between pathos and farce. So here ends ingloriously what began gloriously on the Atlantic littoral, below the falls line; and the last phase of the westward wayfaring has the appearance of a joke.

Yet, this having always been a country of paradox, there is something more than a joke. Before that ending the Westerner learned something. Implicit in the westward surge, both a product and a condition of it, was the sentiment that has been called, none too accurately, "the American dream." It is a complex sentiment not too easily to be phrased. The plain evidence of the frontier movement, from the falls line on, indicated that there could be no limit but the sky to what the Americans might do. The sublimate of our entire experience was just this: here was a swamp and look! here is Chicago. Every decade of expansion, every new district that was opened, backed up the evidence till such an expectation was absolutely integral with the national progress. There was no limit but the sky: American ingenuity, American will power, American energy could be stopped by nothing whatever but would go on forever building Chicagos. It was a dream that, in the nature of things, had to be wrecked on reality sometime, but in actual fact the West was the first point of impact. Just as the pioneer had to give up his axe and learn mechanics when he crossed the hundredth meridian, just as he had to abandon his traditional individualism, so he had to reconcile himself to the iron determinism he faced. In the arid country just so much is possible, and when that limit has been reached nothing more can be done. The West was industry's stepchild, but it set a boundary beyond which industrialism could not go. American ingenuity, will power, and energy were spectacular qualities but, against the fact of rainfall, they simply didn't count. The mountains and the high plains, which had seen the end of the frontier movement and had caused the collapse of the pioneer culture, thus also set the first full stop to the American dream. Of the Americans, it was the Westerners who first understood that there are other limits than the sky. To that extent they led the nation. It may be that to the same extent they will have a better adjustment to the days ahead.

There at least, and not in the symbolism that has attached to them, is to be looked for the national significance of the West. They learned adaptation: they built their institutions, illegally for the most part and against the will of their plunderers, in accordance with the necessities of a climate that rigorously defined the possible. It was the necessities of the mining codes that first gave the clue of collectivism, and these codes were the nucleus round which the commonwealths coalesced. The law of real estate in part and the law of water rights in entirety followed this lead; the axe-swinger's individualism, in the desert, yielded to an effort much more cooperative. There was no other way in which the land could be occupied; this was determinism, and the Westerners accepted it, and not even their manipulators could do much against the plain drift of necessity. To the dismay of bondholders and cartoonists, the West is integrated collectively. It will stay that way while climate is climate. That also may be a portent for the nation whose dream has receded.

Looted, betrayed, sold out, the Westerner is a man whose history has been just a series of large-scale jokes. That comicality has helped to form the image which the dominant East has chosen to recognize. But it is not altogether a comic image. The wild-eyed figure of the cartoons attests to a certain Eastern uneasiness, and there is always the strangeness of the chaps and sombrero. It is wise to end on that strange-

ness. For the romantic clothes are only occupational garments, a work suit, the sign of the Westerner's adaptation to
the conditions of one of his trades. Their true symbolism is
not romance but intelligent acceptance of the conditions.
The American dream was ended, but cattle could be grazed
in this country, and these were the best outfit for the job, so
he put them on. Thus dressing himself, he has become a romantic symbol to people who live in areas of greater rain; but
do not be fooled. He is a tough, tenacious, overworked, and
cynical person, with no more romance to him than the
greasewood and alkali in which he labors. He is the first
American who has worked out a communal adaptation to his
country, abandoning the hope that any crossroads might become Chicago. The long pull may show — history has prece-
dents — that the dispossessed have the laugh on their conquerors.

Old Jules

BY MARI SANDOZ

~~~~~~

THE *Atlantic Monthly* prize for non-fiction goes to the biography of a pioneer in the sand-hill country of north-western Nebraska. A strange, violent, treacherous, and only partly subdued country, it is fittingly symbolized by this Swiss medical student who shared its violence and treachery, was never subdued, and was part madman and part genius — as perhaps he had to be in order to master the land of his choice. With the scars of terror and adoration plainly visible in her book, the daughter of Jules Sandoz, whom he flogged more to give his own manias an outlet than to secure the utter submission he demanded, and who lost an eye saving his cattle from a blizzard, has written his life without passing over a single wart and has achieved something between a dirge and a Gloria.

I am afraid for this book. The prize award will get it publicity and flattery, but how well will it be understood? It is a magnificent job and Miss Sandoz has come close to making it, as she says she wanted to, the biography not only of her father but of the upper Niobrara country itself. That is just the trouble. It is achingly, glaringly necessary to get the High Plains written about and understood, to force a realization of them and their place in our culture and our problems on the national mind. But Miss Sandoz is a native and a literary artist and, I suspect, disqualified on both counts. For her book has been smoked and weathered in the reality, and the way to call the attention of metropolitan readers to the land they beautify is to import a tabloid reporter and let him slap them in the face. Miss Sandoz, the native, mentions a blizzard that drove fine snow through the walls of a soddy till it popped and sizzled on the stove. The only way to make that carry meaning in the East would be to have Graham McNamee do it on the Ex-Lax hour. Her accents and rhythms, her assumptions, even her vocabulary, are alien. When she speaks of a blowout, the customers will wonder if they had tires in the middle 'Eighties, and if they manage to attach any meaning to nigger-wool it will probably be as a brand of tobacco. The movies have informed them that sheep are bad medicine to the nesters but they don't know why, and as for burning chips, they know there aren't enough in all the clubs on Fifth Avenue to roast one turkey. I say, so far as true books about the West are concerned, the customers are spinach and want more of the same.

Well, this is how. It is a high country with an average annual rainfall of between ten and twenty inches, or from a fourth to a half of what you people are used to. The soil is good, when it isn't poisoned, but nobody has ever found out for sure just what it's good for. There are about four destructive hailstorms (stones from the size of a pea to the size of a pretty big apple) between the last and the first frosts and any of them may mean the end of this year's crop. There is a warm wind in the late winter, very hopeful and deceptive, and a hot wind in the summer that burns up crops like a blowtorch. Yes, and it's still a good plan to plow and trench against fire. In good years the water level rises and the hopeful rush in, get a crop or two, borrow to buy more land and make a killing. Then the droughts come for two or three years and the bankrupt limp out again, leaving a lot of dead, more insane, and still more maimed and crippled. And slowly those who stay, aren't killed, and refuse to be licked, somehow contrive to lick the country. They find the varieties of plants that will survive, they plaster the house and put in a bathroom maybe, they pay off the mortgage sometimes, and it is a little easier to maintain the urban economy on the littoral, and the earth is more productive than it was.

Old Jules Sandoz brought his manias and his violence with him — the country didn't give him either of them but plentifully fertilized both. He was an educated young man and he had an idea: to get more people out here, get the ground broken and the crops coming in, raise up a civilization. He was a doctor, an expert shot, an orchardist and a paranoiac, and it turned out that he had to be all four in order to survive. A couple of playful jokers dropped him sixty feet down the first well he dug and crippled him for life, but Walter Reed, on duty against the Sioux, saved his foot. He drove one wife crazy and two more only saved their sanity by running away, but he found a fourth who could endure him. She tried to kill herself only once, she learned to swing at him with anything at hand when he beat her, and she finally got so that she could exercise a feeble and intermittent control over him. She bore him six children and brought them all up without a doctor — though Jules weakened when he was past seventy and finally died in a hospital.

He fought the country and he fought nearly everyone in it. He quarreled, went to law, was sued and jailed, led the vigilantes against his enemies, beat his children constantly

and once or twice made a pass at shooting them. He had the
energy of all conquerors. He wouldn't be licked. It was a cat-
tleman's country when he came; he made it a farming country. By sheer, dominating fury of will power he held the
nesters together, brought in more of them, filled up the gaps
made by death and desertion, kept them aligned against the
big outfits, and finally won out. He "located" their land for
them in spite of gunfire, terrorism, subsidized judges and the
inertia of sheer worthlessness. He never bathed, he changed
his shirt only when there was a new schoolteacher, and his
children's shoes were made of several plies of denim overalls
or of gunny sacking bound round their feet with baling
wire. But he was a realist rooted in the earth, a Panurge and a
Falstaff in one, and he had a genius with plants that even
the Government came to recognize. He made the land produce wheat and corn and, what was a Grade A miracle, magnificent berries, vines and fruits. He was always in debt but
his fences spread wider and wider. And, under the blast of
his energy, so did his neighbors' fences. They brought the
country in and there it is.

The great virtue of Miss Sandoz's book is that you can see
it happening. It is all there: the soddies and the dugouts and
the lean-tos, and the bugs in them; the prairie fires, the bliz-
zards, the cattle that die in the snow and perfume the spring
months but fertilize the ground; the rattlesnakes, the great
flights of geese, the grouse, the wolves, the coyotes, the jack-
rabbits; the pretty girls, the men who get them in the bushes,
the childbirths without doctors that age them, the savage
labor that cripples them; the children who are wild as fauns,
do a man's work at ten or twelve, but live in paradise; the annual yield in insanity and the murders and suicides that stem
from it, all of them handsomely increased after a bad winter
or a drought summer. And a good deal more: the loafers and

the weak and the maladjusted, but also the victors; the will
to build and plant and stay; the community that will not be
denied, rent by feud or fraud but a living organism, a practical communism, a force that becomes in the end irresistible;
the slow achievement of free men building, in the unlikeliest
places, a commonwealth that stands.

There is a good deal of America in *Old Jules*. It is,
heaven knows, an enthralling story. But it is more than that,
and much deeper. It is an experience in citizenship.

EXPANDED FROM *The American Mercury*, JANUARY 1930

The Centennial of Mormonism

A STUDY IN UTOPIA AND DICTATORSHIP

〜〜〜〜〜〜〜〜〜〜〜〜〜〜〜〜〜〜〜〜〜

I

*A*UTHORITIES disagree about the exact date of the withdrawal from the Christian Church of the divine authority once vested in it. Corruptions of its spirit, misuses of its gifts, and perversions of its doctrine following the death of the last Apostle suggest to some that God then took back His holy priesthood. Others set other dates but all agree that by the fifth century the Church was altogether heretical and the ministry of Jesus, more properly called the Dispensation of the Meridian of Time, had come to an end. From that time forth no one held the keys of the spirit, no priests had authority to perform the ordinances of God, and no church had the organization, ritual, sacraments, government, theological authority or legal succession that God had established. During that period, which is known as the Great Apostasy, the Church of God was altogether absent from this earth. The whole world labored in darkness. Everyone was a heretic.

Mathematical computation establishes April 6, 1830, as exactly eighteen hundred years after the Resurrection of Jesus. On that date, in fulfillment of prophecies contained in Holy Writ, God restored His Church, reëstablished the holy priesthood and the ordinances of salvation, and in doing so opened the Dispensation of the Fullness of Time. On April 6, 1830, therefore, the millennium began.[1] For this was the final Restoration: henceforth the keys and the priesthood would never be withdrawn, and the orderly working out of man's salvation would continue without interruption to the full establishment of the Kingdom of God. The Restoration was clearly the most important event in human history, and its date is obviously more significant than that birthday of Jesus from which heretical Christendom reckons its time.

The scene divinely appointed for the Restoration was an obscure village named Fayette, between Lakes Seneca and Cayuga, near the edge of settlement in New York State. Since 1830 it has been remarkable for nothing whatever, and at that time it was a primitive settlement surrounded by semi-wilderness, a mere dot in the expansion of frontier New York State that followed the construction of the Erie Canal. But the last and greatest of God's prophets happened to be staying there at the time. Ten years before, when the prophet was just short of fifteen years old and while he was living at Palmyra, a similarly primitive community, Jehovah and Jesus Christ had appeared to him and informed him of his consecration. Thereafter he had been in communication with the Angel Nephi (whose name later became Moroni) and with many other personages of heaven — archangels such as Michael, prophets such as Elijah and John the Baptist,

---

[1] In the Church, as elsewhere in American thought, the exact meaning of "millennium" is disputed, and consequently the date of its beginning is variously given. The strictest canonical interpretation, however, is that the millennium began with the Restoration.

and the Apostles Peter, James and John. Nephi had conducted him to a hill near Palmyra and shown him the secret
repository of certain miraculous sheets or "plates" of gold,
which contained a record of the Church of God in America.
This was a history of certain Israelites who, in two different
migrations, had left Jerusalem, had colonized the American
continent with great cities, and at last had fallen from grace
and degenerated into the Lamanites, erroneously spoken of
as "Indians." Nearly three years before the Restoration, the
prophet had been commanded to take the plates from their
hiding place. Since then he had translated them (from a
language known as "the reformed Egyptian") by miraculous means. The translation had been finished and was being printed at Palmyra, as *The Book of Mormon*, when the
Restoration occurred.

The Restoration was less dramatic than a number of events
that had preceded it. The setting was the house of Peter
Whitmer, who probably came from frontier Pennsylvania
but about whom practically nothing is known. Two members of the Whitmer family were present. So was Oliver
Cowdery, a native of Wells, in frontier Vermont, who had
been the prophet's amanuensis. So were two brothers of the
prophet. Joseph Smith, Junior, the prophet himself, was the
sixth. It was just such a group of countrymen as might gather
at a crossroads store to discuss the price of mink skins or the
rumors about Andrew Jackson that filtered through the
backwoods from Washington. After prayer and blessings,
Joseph and Cowdery ordained each other as elders of the
Church of Jesus Christ of Latter-Day Saints. It was a simple
ceremony, consisting of no more than the laying-on of
hands and the pronunciation of the appropriate words. But it
brought back to the world the priesthood that had not existed here since the defection of the apostolic church. And

with that priesthood came "the keys of authority and the power to bind, to loose and to seal on the earth and in Heaven, according to the commandments of God and the revelations of Jesus Christ." Thus simply did the millennium begin.

That was the actual Restoration. Following it, the six members of the true Church blessed the sacrament and partook of it. The Holy Ghost was poured out upon them. Some prophesied, all praised the Lord and rejoiced exceedingly, and the prophet Joseph received a revelation from Almighty God. This exaltation began a period of miracle in the restored Church. As new elders were ordained and as converts were made through the surrounding countryside, all the gifts of primitive Christianity were displayed. The elders healed the sick and the blind, they conversed in the holy languages of Heaven, they suspended the operation of natural laws, they had prophetic visions and they raised the dead. All this had been predicted, not only in Scripture but in the revelations of Joseph, and so they confidently began the proselyting that was to make Mormons of all mankind.

Only one who is unacquainted with American history will find anything amazing in these scenes, or think it strange that God should select an ignorant frontier-drifter, dowser and treasure-hunter as His greatest prophet and a handful of backwoodsmen as the first elders in His restored Church. The year 1830 was well past the halfway mark in our national Pentecost. The breakdown of Calvinism and the rise of the evangelical churches, the subdivision of sects that followed the Great Revival, the repeated outbreaks of hysterical phenomena that created the "burnt-over district," the spread of expansive humanitarian ideas and their degradation by the vulgar — all these encouraged American Protestantism to work itself out to its logical extremes in a territory peculiarly favorable to their development, frontier New England and New York. In the ten years preceding 1830, the True Church of Christ had appeared or reappeared many times; it would reappear many times again in the next twenty years.

A secret expectation that the terrible Day of the Lord would occur within the living generation had, of course, crossed the Atlantic in the *Arbella* and even in the *Mayflower*. Belief in it had, however, formed no part in the Puritan teaching and its occasional irruption among the mystical or the hysterical had been curtly dealt with, so that it found little expression except as a hypothesis elaborated in occasional, abstruse metaphysical works. Nevertheless the mystical and the hysterical exist in all churches and this idea, with its corollary of the establishment of the Kingdom of God, could be easily aroused by such a ministry as George Whitefield's. In fact, millennialism probably became an effective idea in America as a result of Whitefield's preaching; at least, the fires which he lighted never died out. It remained, however, for the mutilation of his ideas and the Wesleyan conflagration on the Kentucky frontier to bring on an era of apocalypse

The passage eastward of the Great Revival occupied a number of years — and it fertilized the soil with piety, religious argumentation and nervous disease. There is no way of estimating, and probably no likelihood of overestimating, the amount of supernaturalism that flourished in the burnt-over district during the first thirty years of the Nineteenth Century. It affected, of course, various orders of intelligence. On the lowest level it produced such squalid ventures in theophany as the one which William Dean Howells described in *The Leatherwood God.* But the same energy found expression on higher levels, and millennialism was not the only shape it took.

For years before the establishment of Joseph Smith's church, for instance, Alexander Campbell had been proselyting among the border Presbyterians and Baptists with a theology based on the literal interpretation and application of the Bible and growing steadily more concerned with the Second Coming of Christ. At the very moment when the True Church was restored at Fayette, William Miller completed the fifteen years of mathematical analysis which enabled him to determine 1843 as the year of Christ's return. Miller was then living in Hampton, New York, a few miles from the Vermont border, and a year later, in 1831, God not only spoke to him out of the heavens, commanding him to make his results public, but also sent a messenger to open the way. In that same year, 1831, another great revival flared up from the embers of the old one. Onondaga Lake makes the third point of an equilateral triangle whose other points are Fayette and Palmyra, and the skies above Onondaga filled with battalions of angels. At Putney, Vermont, young John Humphrey Noyes labored to resist the spirit and did resist it through one protracted meeting, but before long he too was hearing God speak. From Onondaga to New Haven to Putney, by way of Brimfield, spread another doctrine that had been debated in the Puritan metaphysics but now had acquired living force: Perfectionism, the idea that living men might attain sinlessness and might thereafter dwell in the Kingdom, as Saints. This doctrine was also part of the Shaker creed. The Shakers antedated Pentecost and in fact had originated in England. But they too made their greatest gains at this time, they too lived as Saints, they too were the Church of Christ, and it is not without interest that Joseph

Smith had lived in a New Hampshire town where one of
their communities was established.

These, it should be made plain, are only a few of the religions generated in the New England hills and the lake
country of New York during the days of our apocalypse.
Sects rose, flourished or did not flourish, divided, were amal-
gamated with larger bodies, broke up from dissension or the
failure of grace, were snuffed out. An anonymous French-
man had already remarked that although America had been
able to devise but one soup, it had invented a hundred religions. His was a moderate estimate. Some subtlety of climate,
racial stock or social organization on the frontier of New
England and New York made the air fecund. A circle described on a radius of one hundred and fifty miles around
such a center as Pittsfield, Massachusetts, would include the
birthplaces of ninety per cent. of the American sects and of
an even greater percentage of their prophets. Many prophets before Joseph Smith revealed God's will within that
circle, and many more came after him.

But if there was nothing singular in the Restoration and the
ensuing birth of the Church of Jesus Christ of Latter-Day
Saints, there has been something very remarkable in its survival. When on April 6, 1930, the sixth successor of Joseph
Smith, Prophet Heber J. Grant, addressed his flock in Salt
Lake City, his voice went out by radio to Latter-Day Saints
all over America and the seven seas besides. And the prophet
Heber, announcing that the first century of the millennium
had been rounded out, could show that the promises which
God made to the prophet Joseph, alone of all His promises
during the Pentecost, had been fulfilled. Pentecost had been
over for nearly ninety years, and of it only the Mormon
revelation had completely succeeded. The Saints had come
into the inheritance promised them, their rivals had fallen

away, their enemies had been trodden under foot or converted into business partners, their wars were ended forever, Israel was secure, the stake of Zion had been driven fast.

Consider. Of the scores of True Churches that the four millennial decades produced, hardly a handful remain to-day. Of that handful, all but two or three are so insignificant that only specialists have ever heard of them. The Shakers still faintly exist, a few decrepit men and women tottering about the farmsteads that were once pleasant in the sight of God, but in a few years more the last of them must die.[2] The Adventists, in various schisms, still retain enough vitality from the visions of William Miller to operate sanatoria and preach the wrath to come, but they are miserably poor and affect no one. The Church of Christ Scientist, which flowered with the same planting though it was only indirectly Pentecostal, has achieved a social prominence beyond any other, but it has passed its zenith. The rate of increase slows down, revelation is closed, and mighty interior strains threaten collapse. Alexander Campbell's church has some five times as many communicants as Mother Eddy's, but the stigmata of a True Church have long since faded from them, they show few vestiges of Pentecost, and they are to-day hardly distinguishable from the Methodists or the damned. Here and there along the Great Lakes or the Ohio, in interior Missouri, Iowa or Texas, the student will find other microscopic survivals of the True Churches that came down

[2] Celibacy was the Shakers' blunder. Of all the American religions the student finds theirs most charming. They had a serenity beyond any other sect, they lived quietly and in the respect of their neighbors, through their orchards and nurseries they greatly improved American horticulture, and they raised the handicrafts to a greater excellence than any of their rivals. Theirs was a genuine communion and a formidably successful communism. If they had provided for its preservation by other means than proselyting, they might have had a strong influence on American culture.

from the heavens to the high places of New England during the generation of the striving — but they are wretched and pitiful. They came in sudden glory, the sky opening to the immemorial thunderclap, the awful Voice proclaiming that the hour had struck and summoning all kindreds, tongues and people unto judgment. They end with a group of gray-beards kneeling while a priest of the eternal mysteries prays for a miracle that will pay off the mortgage on the meeting house.

Why has one True Church survived while scores of others have perished? What in the Mormon revelation has made it victorious over its myriad competitors? The answer is intricate, not to be glibly pronounced in these few pages. But one may shorten it somewhat by setting down an axiom: Mormonism is a wholly American religion, and it contrived to satisfy needs which are basic with a good many Americans and which none of its competitors managed to supply. Otherwise, one may be sure, 1930 would have found it as dead as the creed of the Icarian communists who took over its deserted city at Nauvoo.

II

The 1870's were the great decade of anti-Mormon agitation among the Protestant churches. As soon as the Union Pacific was built missionaries swarmed westward to the Kingdom of the Saints, and swarmed eastward again to write books denouncing these uncouth, godly, and rather prudish folk as sinners of an imperial magnificence. What the missionaries could not stand was polygamy, as dull and heaven knows as laborious an institution as humanity has ever evolved, and the scores of books they published painted Mormonry in lurid colors that exhibited both their authors' skill at concupiscent fantasy and their total failure to use their eyes. The tide receded when Methodism had its way and, in the 'Eighties, Acts of Congress finally began the suppression of polygamy. When Mormonism again broke into popular literature, in the first decade of this century, it was as big business and a target of the muckrakers. Although several professional Mormon-baiters flourished as late as the World War and one (I believe) still roams the far Chautauquas, and although evangelical congregations deep in the canebrakes still occasionally raise funds to cure the Saints of lechery and free their houris, the surge of the 'Seventies has never been repeated. America will crusade no more against polygamy.

Unhappily, the pornographic bilge then written settled the ideas of the general public. So far as that public thinks of Israel at all, it thinks of sinister, bearded men who have taken fearful oaths to destroy the United States Government, who are Sons of Dan (Destroying Angels) and so slip out of town by night to do a little murder for the faith's sake, and who maintain harems of luscious girls snatched from their true loves or kidnapped from the Gentiles.[3] Not years of patient publicity work by the Saints, not the regiments of Mormons whom Reed Smoot put into the Civil Service, not even the appointment of a Mormon to the Chairmanship of the Federal Reserve Board and the publication of an article about him in *Fortune* has been able to alter this conception in the least. The fact that the Mormons are polytheists and will eventually be gods ought to provide

[3] At all levels of intelligence, education, and travel, Utah means Mormon and Mormon means polygamist. A dozen times a year I am asked, in good faith, if I have more than one wife, and I think I have never had a dinner-table conversation about Utah or the Mormons that did not arrive at the present (mythical) practice of polygamy within five minutes. It is all a little trying to a Utahn, especially one who was brought up in the Church of Rome.

an attractive popular symbol, but seemingly to the Americans at large they will be polygamists forever.

At least the public view has some basis in fact, for the Saints did practise polygamy for many years. Whereas the treatment of the Mormons by our intellectuals has never been contaminated by fact and is a mass of complete nonsense altogether divorced from reality. My profession requires me to read all the books that explain America to itself (I study the *genre* in "Thinking about America" in this volume), many of them discuss Mormonism at some length, and I have never yet encountered in them any statement of fact that would hold water or any interpretation that made sense to a person who has lived among the Mormons and studied their history. You will find some beautiful ideas about the Mormons in the books of our liberal thinkers, but you will find no idea that touches the reality at any point. Let the rhapsodic Waldo Frank serve as a type-specimen. When Mr. Frank wrote *Our America* he apparently had not heard of the Shakers or the Oneida Community (or, so fas as I can see, any of the sects or communities that grappled with the problems he was discussing), but he was sure that Mormonism was an attempt to achieve a more expansive, more dynamic spiritual expression — by means of echolalia and polygamy. Polygamy is susceptible of several explanations, but to call it a deliberate effort to solve any question, whether spiritual or sexual, is a blunder possible only to a man who has read nothing whatever in Mormonism and knows nothing whatever about its contemporaries in Pentecost. And when Mr. Frank calls Mormon doctrine a revolt against Puritanism he not only reveals his complete ignorance of Mormonism but calls into question his knowledge of Puritanism — on which his book was based.

The public may be excused for misconceiving Mormonism, and it is the nature of the intellectuals to derive their ideas about anything from contemplating the imperatives of their own souls. But there is no acceptable explanation of the long neglect of the Saints by scholarship. The only aspect of Mormonism that has been adequately treated is the doctrinal one, and even here the student has to dig his information out of many professional journals, no single inclusive treatment having yet appeared. Apart from the doctrinal aspect, everything is rudimentary, infrequent and mostly wrong. The story of the Mormons is one of the most fascinating in all American history, it touches nineteenth-century American life at innumerable points, it is as absorbing as anything in the history of the frontier, it is probably the most important chapter in the history of the trans-Mississippi frontier and certainly the most varied, and it is treasure-house for the historian of ideas, institutions and social energies. Yet no qualified historian has ever written a comprehensive treatise on Mormonism,[4] and very few have even written monographs on minute aspects of it.

Search the indexes of historical publications and you will find stretches of many years when no title relating to Mormonism is listed. You will come out at the end with a handful of brief articles, some of them about the Reorganized Church and other heresies, most of them by antiquarians writing for local historical societies, and practically all of them devoted to specialized, unimportant inquiries. It is an absurd and even shameful condition, and it indicates a rich opportunity for young historians who want to make a splash in their profession. Economics and sociology, however, have done even worse. A complete bibliography of articles by

---

[4] On the main (Utah) body, that is. Milo M. Quaife's *The Kingdom of St. James,* a history of the Strang heresy, is authoritative and complete.

qualified scholars would not fill this page. Yet Mormonism is the only large-scale social experiment in American history that has lasted a hundred years, it developed institutions of its own of the utmost complexity and the greatest interest, it defied many of the social and economic trends of the nineteenth century, and it is a perfect field for social inquiry, since it is sharply differentiated and securely fenced in. That it has been so long ignored is a disgrace to sociology.[5]

Clearly we cannot answer our question about the survival of Mormonism by appealing to scholarship. The immense literature about Mormonism is even less helpful.[6] Hardly more than a dozen books are worth the time of a serious student, and of these only four or five have much to tell him. W. A. Linn's *Story of the Mormons* remains the best history of the Church; it is invaluable, but it was written thirty-five years ago, before the history of the frontier had been investigated, and it is the work of a man who had no historical perspective. M. R. Werner's *Brigham Young* has a much better grasp on American history, but Mr. Werner did not master the Mormon point of view, was not able to look at the Church from within, and so seriously misconceived his subject at vital points. A more recent book, *Revelation in Mormonism*, by George B. Arbaugh, is in some ways the most sagacious treatise on the Church ever written. In spite of the fact that Mr. Arbaugh is committed to the untenable thesis that *The Book of Mormon* is based on Solomon Spaulding's novel, his book will be indispensable to students from now on. But even he studies Mormonism in a vacuum, quite with-

[5] This deficiency may soon be repaired. For several years there have been rumors of a thorough study by a grandson of the prophet Brigham, who is a qualified sociologist.

[6] A Mormon exegete claims that more has been written about Joseph Smith than about any other American except Lincoln and Washington. That is certainly not true but it suggests the size of the literature.

out relation to the frontier or to the Pentecostal years. The best way to understand Mormonism is still to read its holy books and its periodicals, and the best way to answer our question, to determine why Mormonism has survived, is to read the sermons of Brigham Young.

III

I have said that the answer to that question is complex, and even a superficial outline of it invokes vital forces of history. Such an outline would mention: the frontier environment in which Mormonism arose and developed and in which it took refuge at the time of its greatest crisis; a succession of powerful leaders, not all of them in the Presidency; a series of historical accidents whose outcome might well have been otherwise than it was, but whose issue has attested God's providence to generations of the Saints; the inclusiveness of the Mormon doctrines, which managed to incorporate most of the beliefs agitated during the Pentecostal years and provided a rebuttal to those it did not incorporate; and the martyrdom of the prophet Joseph.

Of these, three forces are much more important than all the rest, the frontier environment, the martyrdom of Joseph Smith and the leadership of Brigham Young. There is in fact no intelligent way of looking at Mormonism except as a frontier movement. It began as a frontier religion, it developed as a frontier social organization, and the institutions which it has evolved and which are what has survived as Mormonism, could be brought to a vigorous maturity only on the frontier.

I have already suggested how the burnt-over district was ripe for the sickle. It had been evangelized to a turn, it had been sown with the seeds of religious hysteria, marvels and

miracles and supernatural manifestations were its daily bread,
it heaved with millennial fervor. Talk of the terrible Day of
the Lord, of the Second Coming of Christ — of literal interpretation of the Scriptures, of reversion to the primitive
church, of the renewal of revelation and apostolic gifts —
was as common, as much a matter of course, as talk to-day of
the next war or the imposition of the sales tax. And now came
a religion which restored the primitive Church of Christ,
stood foursquare on a literal interpretation of the Bible, re-
opened the channel of revelation, announced the coming of
Christ, provided a harbor against the imminent Day of
Judgment, and practised apostolic gifts. More than that, it
resolved a speculation which was as old as Protestantism in
America,[7] (having been tirelessly debated by the Puritans)
and which was a living issue in the New York country of
Indian antiquities and recent Indian wars; it identified the Indians as descendants of a migration from Jerusalem, and so
ended an ancient mystery and harmonized it with the American heritage and the frontier experience. And even more: it
was a magnificent catch-all of the dogmas and doctrines
which had agitated the devout ever since the Great Awaken-
ing and which had most actively flourished on the frontier.
It was at once millennial, restorationist and perfectionist. It
combined in one daring blend the frontier's three favorite
avenues to salvation: salvation by the Last Judgment, salvation by return to apostolic Christianity, and salvation by perfect and present identification with the will of God. It had
a determinism as tough as any in Calvinism; it had an opti-

---

[7] And which had been vigorously renewed in the last fifteen years before *The Book of Mormon*, the theological arguments being reinforced
by scientific thinkers. The most notable item of a large literature is
Elias Boudinot's *A Star in the West*, published in 1816. For other items,
see Woodbridge Riley, *The Founder of Mormonism*. Note, however,
that *The Book of Mormon* does not identify its Nephites and Lamanites
as the lost tribes.

mism as attractive as any in Arminianism. Its name tells most of the story: the Church of Jesus Christ of Latter-Day Saints. It was the Church of Christ, now restored. It was restored in the Latter Days, just before the Last Judgment. And its members were Saints: they were becoming perfect.

But although such a mélange of doctrines and such a confusion of theologies, eschatologies, and metaphysics, or their acceptance, are hardly conceivable apart from a frontier society, that is not the most important part of the frontier's conditioning. What the frontier did was first of all to provide the necessary recruits for and toleration of the original Church; then to provide the opposition necessary to transform the Mormon feeling of peculiarity, of being a people chosen of the Lord, into a coördinated body of sentiments which animated the organization and social system that grew up; then to enormously step-up the power and fervor of those sentiments by persecuting the Saints and martyring their prophet; and finally to provide a distant, secure refuge where the system could expand unmolested till it was strong enough to repulse every attack made on it. If you alter that sequence of reactions at any point, the survival of Mormonism becomes inconceivable.

For it must be understood not only that frontier society supplied the illiterate, the credulous and the dissociated to whom Mormonism first appealed, but also that almost from the beginning Mormonism ran counter to sentiments, ideals, institutions and ways of life that were fundamental forces of the frontier. These were not so much the religious teachings: there was room enough and toleration enough for any vagary that got into the Mormon creed until polygamy violated an ancient taboo. Rather they were economic, and especially social. The difference can be seen as early as Kirtland. The Mormon real-estate speculations and wildcat banking of that period could have occasioned no such antagonism if the peculiar people had not also been a unified people. Ohio at that time was, heaven knows, well acquainted with both activities. But the Mormons could bring to them the communal and corporate power of a society governed by one man who was answerable to no one but God and who was little short of omnipotent in the management of his people's property.

The principle thus established was proved to the hilt in Missouri and Illinois. Into Mormonism, by way of the Disciples of Christ and Robert Owen's experiments and a dozen agitations, had come those principles of communistic association which were, in the Forties, to give a new channel to the evangelical energies that in the Thirties had gone to the production of sects. The United Order, or Order of Enoch, was established by revelation from God as early as 1831, and was the immediate cause of the friction in Missouri. This communism did not last long and the Mormon practice of coöperation was fluctuant and changeful. But at the minimum, and in spite of dissension and occasional rebellion, the Mormons were much more coöperative, much more united for their own purposes under a single control, than any society with which they came in contact. The Middlewestern frontier of those years is the classic frontier of Turner: the frontier of individual effort. Its coöperation was purely neighborly and, beyond roof-raising and township road-building, its entire force was against combinations, and especially combinations in real-estate development and finance.

The Mormons thus encountered the strongest energy of the time head-on. The two kinds of society could not exist side by side; they were necessarily at war and it was necessarily a war of extermination. The Mormons antagonized the Missourians and Illini, of course, by the overbearing smugness that characterizes every chosen people, and disgusted them with outlandish terminologies, doctrines and ceremonies. A more important offense was their political unity, the certainty with which their leaders could turn any election, and thus secure any privileges desired, by voting thousands of men as one. But the decisive offense was the economic power that could be wielded by a coöperative hagiocracy — a people who held a great part of their wealth in common, undertook collective enterprises, excluded the ungodly from their businesses, and obeyed the orders of their leaders. The frontier could not tolerate it — and did not tolerate it. The sixteen years of the Missouri and Illinois settlements were marked by a continuous hostility which was institutional at bottom though expressed in religious terms, which frequently flamed into mobbing and lynching, and which ended in expropriation and expulsion. Those years proved conclusively that Mormonism could not exist in the American system.

But also they were of first importance in that they confirmed the Mormons to themselves. Attacked for peculiarity, singularity and coöperation, they became more peculiar and singular and their group effort became more vigorous. Their system evolved and developed and the fiery sentiments that gave it vigor were tremendously increased. They experienced the unifying force of persecution. To this period must be traced the characteristic Mormon state of mind, that of the Lord's chosen persecuted by the children of evil. It was reinforced for seventy years. The Mormons were, in cold fact, systematically opposed (if with uneven intensity) by their neighbors, by the other churches, by rival businesses, and by the national government down to the Edmunds-Tucker act of 1887, and on past that till a typical hotel-room bargain grafted the minority report of the Smoot Investigating Committee on the policy of the Republican Party, and so recognized the importance of the modern Church and ended persecution forevermore. Throughout all that time the Saints had a sense of present martyrdom, and it was the most important single fact about them, the strongest single force in their survival. They have it to-day, though the occasion for it has been over for a full generation; they will have it for many generations to come.

And of this, the most decisive element was the actual martyrdom of Joseph and his brother Hyrum. That it came when it did come and was not delayed for as little as two years more is one of the providential accidents I have mentioned. For there were already portents of dissolution. Joseph's megalomania had produced a formidable rebellion, in the Church which up to then had sustained no rebellion — it was the immediate cause of the events that ended in his murder. He was giving unmistakable evidence of psychic disintegration and it seems certain that his Church must soon have broken up into warring sects, which is the historic outcome of Protestant heresies in America. But the Carthage mob rose at exactly the right time. The blood of the martyrs became once more the seed of the Church. Thereafter the Mormons were not only a persecuted people: the seal of blood sacrifice had been put upon their faith.

The frontier at once rendered its final, indispensable service. No matter how unified the Mormons might be, it had been proved that they could not exist in the increasingly complex society that was developing in the Mississippi Valley. Brigham Young took Israel to the Far West and so saved it. He probably hoped to escape from American jurisdiction — the Mormon sentiment here was ambivalent and pragmatic, prepared to profit from either patriotic service or expatriation — but that was a subsidiary consideration. Mexican or American, the desert would, and did, secure isolation.

At more than a thousand miles from the frontier of settlement, the Mormons were safe from opposition. Their isolation slowly yielded to the expansion that followed the discovery of gold in California and was ended by the building of the Union Pacific. But the twenty-two years thus gained were enough. In the occupation of the desert, in the increased coöperation necessary to survival there, and in the freedom from outside interference and the opportunity thus secured to deal in its own way with internal dissent, the Church perfected its organization and worked out the way of life that has survived.

Mormonism was an outgrowth of religious and social movements on the New York frontier, which stemmed from the New England frontier. It was given its shape by conflict with the Middlewestern frontier. And it survived by adjusting itself to the conditions of the Rocky Mountain frontier, in the isolation which was essential to it and which could have been obtained nowhere else.

IV

Students have always regarded the personality of Joseph Smith and the authorship of *The Book of Mormon* as the crux which must be solved in the history of Mormonism. They are related problems but the second is much less important than the first. What is significant about *The Book of Mormon* is not its authorship but its acceptance by thousands of people as an addition to Holy Scripture. Furthermore, that acceptance, though the basis of the appeal which Mormonism originally made, was already losing its importance by the time the Saints reached Utah. Since then the Church has venerated its Bible but, in the main, has paid little attention to it: it is there for the doctrinally inclined and the apocalyptic, but Brigham Young believed that the building up of the Kingdom on this earth was more important than the inheritance of the splendors promised hereafter — and he held the Church to his belief. Even in Smith's time, moreover, the immediate revelations of *The Doctrine and Covenants* were more accommodated to the needs of the Church than *The Book of Mormon*, and they have retained their priority. The *Book of Mormon* was a storehouse of arguments for proselyting among the other sects; it has had only a small influence on the development of the social institutions which resulted from that proselyting.

The question of its authorship, however, is inseparable from one's explanation of Joseph Smith. No interpretation of the first prophet of Mormonry has been satisfactory throughout, and none ever will be. Vital evidence is lost in the obscurity of his early life, and there is no way of appraising with absolute finality the evidence that exists. One hypothesis, of course, accounts for everything, is a complete explanation of the known facts, and contains only such small contradictions as must appear in all analyses of human affairs. You may decide that God sent an angel to prepare Joseph for his mission, that Joseph translated the golden plates and organized the Church under divine guidance, and that *The Book of Mormon* is a record of actual events on this continent which was written under the same infallible direction that Joseph received. That is the Mormon explanation. It does not satisfy me.

Once you have discarded that hypothesis, you get into difficulties. The opponents of Mormonism have usually adopted one almost as simple: that Joseph was a complete and consummate charlatan, that his story of his visions was a cumulative imposture, and that the Church resulted from a conspiracy which was deliberate at every step and which used the imposture of the visions and the plates as a basis for one more elaborate still. Other hypotheses, however, suggest themselves. Joseph may have been sincere and self-deceived: his visions may have been the delusions of insanity and *The Book of Mormon* and the framework he gave the Church may have issued as a whole from a psychosis. Or he may have been partly sincere and partly a charlatan: he may have suffered from delusions and, at the same time, been forced to amplify and organize them in cold blood as a result of the momentum which they created.

I have studied the available evidence and arguments, and only the last of these hypotheses has ever seemed tenable to me. I cannot believe that so elaborate a conspiracy as the first one assumes could be maintained or could succeed. And I cannot endow Joseph or Sidney Rigdon, who is sometimes credited with the villainy, with such heroic powers of imposture. They are inconceivable as geniuses of imposture, and the success of such an imposture on such a scale is also inconceivable. It would be unique in history, a greater miracle than the descent of Jesus Christ in Fayette. Nor is a finding of complete sincerity as the result of unvarying delusion any more acceptable. There is too much evidence against it and in theory also it is absurd. The line between religious ecstasy and religious insanity is sometimes impossible to determine, but it seems impossible that anything which was altogether on the wrong side of it could endure and prosper for the fourteen years of Joseph's life following the establishment of the Church. In fourteen years, if he were not in some degree a religious leader of sound mind, he must certainly have been recognized as a religious madman. We are forced to assume both insanity and lucidity of mind — in some proportion and rhythm of alternation which can never be precisely determined.

The Solomon Spaulding theory, the one usually adopted
by those who accept the hypothesis of complete imposture,
is ingenious and persuasive but, I think, untenable. According to this story, Sidney Rigdon, an unfrocked and conten-
tious minister of the Disciples of Christ, who had been an
ally, but had become an enemy of the Campbells, stole or
otherwise came into possession of a historical novel in manuscript by the Reverend Solomon Spaulding. The novel, called
The Manuscript Found, purported to be an account of the
emigration to America of certain Israelties and was strikingly like the narrative thread in *The Book of Mormon* — so
strikingly that when the latter was published many of
Spaulding's friends and neighbors recognized the source.
Working on this manuscript, alone for the most part though
sometimes in collaboration with Joseph Smith, Rigdon in-
corporated in it his controversies with the Campbells and all
his doctrinal, ecclesiastical, eschatological and economic notions.[8] For reasons which remain unintelligible in any interpretation of them ever made, instead of establishing his own
church on the basis of the book thus produced, instead of
making himself the prophet and governor of the ideal society
which he had conceived, he somehow selected Joseph Smith
as the best instrument to achieve his ends. Then, working
secretly with Joseph over a period of nearly four years, he
prepared the detailed imposture that followed.

This theory asks us to believe that Rigdon's notorious
subservience to Smith was not only voluntary — and he was
a man of intense ambition — but even a fundamental part of

[8] To meet various criticisms, champions of the Spaulding theory have
modified it till in the modern version Rigdon is supposed to have borrowed only the proper names and the outline of the story, and to have
written *The Book of Mormon* himself. If Rigdon, why not Smith? Besides, the weightiest evidence for the theory is the assertion of Spaulding's friends that they recognized his style and mannerisms.

the scheme. That is a pretty stiff assumption, but that a conspiracy could have been kept secret which involved not only Smith and his family and a number of his neighbors, but also such unknown go-betweens and assistants as Rigdon's activity must have required, is a much stiffer one. And, even disregarding the assumptions, the evidence is unsatisfactory. *The Manuscript Found* has never been exhibited, our knowledge of it comes entirely from affidavits made by people many years after they were supposed to have heard it read, and the discovery of another and quite different manuscript by Solomon Spaulding (though it does not overturn the hypothesis) is an awkward fact to explain away. Worse still, no description of it in any detail has ever been offered. Modern students have analyzed it at such great length and so minutely that they seem to have had the written page before them as they wrote. But what they have had, and what they have so ambitiously analyzed, is only a few general statements about it — vague to an extreme and made long after it was written. But the most awkward fact is the inability of anyone to prove that Rigdon and Smith met before *The Book of Mormon* was published. The affidavits which support the theory of their collaboration are too vague, ambiguous and contradictory for history to accept. And the Mormons have had no trouble in controverting them with affidavits, quite as plentiful and rather more specific, which prove the opposite. At this distance there is no way of choosing among affidavits.

Moreover, the hypothesis of Rigdon's priority cannot be harmonized with what we know of Smith and fails to explain his dominance, which is established when the Church makes its appearance and grows steadily more marked from then on. Mormon testimony and Gentile accusations agree that from the first he was the personal, despotic leader of his sect. The fact that, crazed or sane, sincere or hypocritical, he had a dynamic faculty of leadership is proved beyond dispute; it is the one fact that no one has ever challenged and the only one which can explain the early rise of the Church. Other facts must, of course, be taken into account, especially the development of a supporting oligarchy, but that the oligarchy was only a supporting one and completely accepted his dominance is clearly established. His ability to win men and to control them was responsible for the Church. Nothing suggests that this vigorous leadership rested on an oblique and secret control by Rigdon; nothing suggests that Smith was capable of accepting such control. On the contrary, he seems to have used Rigdon for his own purposes from the first, freely at all times, disdainfully a good part of the time, and sometimes contemptuously.

The appearance of this essay in *The American Mercury* marked the first time that Joseph had ever been pronounced a paranoid. The finding has been accepted in the only general treatise on Mormonism published since that time,[9] and in more specialized articles. It has been vigorously disputed by Mr. Arbaugh in the book previously referred to. No one knows better than I the unreliability of retrospective diagnoses or could be more reluctant to explore the past by means of a psychological instrument which requires the response of a living subject in order to be verified.[10] But the nature of the evidence makes any interpretation of Joseph Smith unverifiable, and history must use an unsatisfactory instrument when all others fail. Moreover, the psychological instrument is most satisfactory when, as here, we are dealing with clearly aberrant behavior. The psychoses, which show themselves in

[9] Harry M. Beardsley, *Joseph Smith and His Mormon Empire*. Boston, 1931.
[10] See "The Skeptical Biographer," within.

obvious insanity, are on a different basis for history than the psychoneuroses, whose end-product in behavior cannot be even qualitatively determined. A finding that Caligula was crazy can be checked against experience; a finding that Jefferson's philosophy of state originated in his aggression toward his father is uncontrolled.

Suppose a man tells you that he has seen and conversed with God the Father, Jesus, various personages of the Old and New Testaments and various angels and archangels. He has been attacked by demons and other supernatural if vaguely described beings. Unearthly messengers visit him daily, supernatural portents attend the smallest details of his daily life, the heavens are always opening to give him guidance and new truth, and he has acquired knowledge approaching omniscience as a limit and power approaching omnipotence. He has been selected to reëstablish the Church of Jesus Christ which was withdrawn from the earth eighteen hundred years ago, every act of his life is divinely inspired, he is set apart from all other men as the repository of truth and the channel of revelation. His behavior over a period of many years forms a pattern which accords with these assertions, and as time goes on his eccentricity intensifies. . . . What do you decide? That he is just a gifted liar? More likely, I think, that he has delusions.

Take a single incident. When, in 1834, Israel's outpost in Missouri was being harried by "mobocrats," Joseph organized Zion's Camp. As general he led this expeditionary force of about two hundred armed men from Kirtland, Ohio, to Missouri. As prophet he revealed to them the Lord's intention to avenge the injuries inflicted on their brethren, destroy their enemies and pour out His wrath on the unrighteous. The revelations steamed with apocalyptic frenzy. Angels accompanied the expedition and miracles attended it, but it never came to grips with the enemy and the Almighty's vengeance was deferred to another day. Few undertakings so grotesque can be found in American history as this attempt to overcome an entire State with a handful of extemporized militia and the promises of God. As the act of an impostor, be he never so vainglorious, it is inconceivable. It can be read only as an enterprise that began in delusion and when forced to meet reality was compensated by the delusional promises which God at once vouchsafed Joseph.

It is characteristic of the mental construction which psychiatrists call the "paranoid reaction type" that the personality is transformed rather than impaired. It is organized in support of certain dominant ideas which cannot meet the test of reality, but the mental energies involved need not be in the least diminished. Native shrewdness, intelligence, will power, logic, imagination, whatever qualities you will, may be retained — and in fact may be given a complete harmonious expression in the service of the dominant ideas. Paranoia is a great mother of achievement. The paranoid is essentially the man who will not down, who will go on, who will be heard — whom no opposition and no derision, discouragement or failure can deprive of his belief in his mission. As one psychiatrist has remarked, much of the progress of the human race has been a by-product of paranoia — paranoids whose obsessions are socially useful are simply called "geniuses." In the eyes of history, however, not everyone who has heard God speak is a genius.

The finding that Joseph Smith comes somewhere within the wide limits of the paranoid reaction type does not attempt to appraise the degree of his insanity nor the regularity and duration of its attacks. That its rhythm was uneven, that for long periods he was free of it, that at other times his delusions did not affect his behavior apart from the dominant ideas — all this seems to me to show plainly in the record. But that some form of the paranoid constitution is the explanation of him seems necessitated by all the available facts.

Anyone who will read a standard treatise on psychiatry and bring it to bear on the biography of Smith must be struck by the amazing agreement of the two. I quote from Henderson and Gillespie, *A Textbook of Psychiatry*,[11] a paragraph which shows some of the correspondences: —

He [Kraepelin] defined "paraphrenia systematica" as characterized by the extremely insidious development of a continuously progressive delusion of persecution to which later are added ideas of exaltation, without disintegration of the personality. This condition is usually ushered in by sensitiveness and irritability, with ideas of reference. Gradually the persecutory ideas are more freely expressed, and are of the most varied nature. [From bearded Spaniards to the Prince of Darkness.] After a period of years auditory hallucinations begin to show themselves, and, to a lesser degree, hallucinations of the other senses also occur. [God speaks from the heavens or in dreams, and then is materialized in blinding light.] Gradually the ideas of persecution may be replaced by ideas of grandeur. Some patients, for example, make claim to large sums of money [or, perhaps, to an ability to find them by means of a peep stone], and others show erotic trends, believing themselves sought in love by titled people [or, perhaps, instructed by God to marry a number of wives]. The patient's idea of his own importance rises higher and higher [he may see himself as prophet, seer, revelator, translator, mayor, lieutenant-general, and President of the United States] and finally he may identify himself with God [or invent an ascending series of divinities through which he is to progress, all of them greater than the God whom this world knows]. Notwithstanding the deteriora-

[11] Third edition, London, 1932. The passage quoted is on page 231. Chapter X, "Paranoia and Paranoid Reaction-Types," should be read entire.

tion of judgment that such ideas would suggest, the mood does not show any disorder *per se*, but remains appropriate to the disordered ideas. The general intellectual faculties of the patient are well preserved, and the patient's capacity for work may not be interfered with. The condition is slowly progressive, the delusions and hallucinations becoming more definitely fixed; but usually the personality is well maintained.

Joseph's autobiographical account of his youth and of the events bearing on the establishment of the Church was unquestionably doctored to fit the needs of propaganda. Nevertheless it seems to me that it tells an authentic story and is in the main a dependable outline of what he supposed had happened to him. Certainly it records the development of a paranoid delusion. His grandfather and certain of his brothers showed symptoms of emotional instability, which he may well have inherited.[12] Be that as it may, he was a typical product of the burnt-over region, moody, fantastic, acutely sensitive to religious unrest. This sensitiveness increased with the onset of puberty and the young Joseph is a type-specimen of the "seeker." (Is it necessary to point out that a strong anxiety about salvation is not incompatible with an enthusiastic yielding to sin?) His unrest is fed by the revivals and protracted meetings of the countryside. At this time the delusions of persecution appear which are attested not only by Joseph's own account but also by the many stories which the early opponents of Mormonism gathered to prove him a charlatan. (They are especially marked in the early versions of the story which developed

[12] Advocates of the Spaulding theory rule out the evidence of Solomon Mack's autobiography and Lucy Smith's sketches of the prophet and his ancestors. It is not suggested here that they are historical records, but surely they prove the frequency of miracle and hysteria in the Smith and Mack households, and surely Solomon Mack was not assisting the imposture of a grandson who was less than five years old.

into his account of the finding of the gold plates.) Presently, and as the sequel of a revival, he experiences both auditory and visual hallucinations. Diverse and unrelated at first, they are eventually systematized into an image of himself as an instrument of God's will with all the accompanying paraphernalia of gold Bible, revelations, visions, prophecy and priesthood.

Neither the delusions of persecution nor those of grandeur ever left him, though the psychic necessity for the former decreased as the progress of his Church provoked actual persecution. His lust for ritual and masquerade, for military panoply; his epaulettes, sabres, gaudy uniforms, ornate religious symbols, secret and esoteric societies, dreadful oaths; his pleasure in resounding titles and in the civil offices which he conferred on himself; his lieutenant-generalship in the Nauvoo Legion, his climactic fantasy of himself as President of the United States — is not the total inconceivable except as a paranoid syndrome, organized in obedience to the fundamental drive of his nature? Mark too the progress of his identification with God till in his last years we get the resplendent but unintelligible doctrines of the creation and evolution of worlds, the myriad phases of godhead, the eternally orgasmic divinity begetting universes of itself upon itself. Is this development comprehensible as anything but the frenzy of a psychopathic personality at last delivered into stark insanity? I think not, and I think that the intensification of all his other delusions at the same time supports the finding. Whatever periods of quiescence and even complete lucidity he may have experienced before, his last two years were an intensifying mania. As the text I have quoted suggests, the personality was well maintained but the delusions and hallucinations were fixed — and progressive.

Two other data which support the finding of paranoia

must be mentioned: Joseph's sexuality and his faculty of authorship. Probably no religious sect or social experiment at that time could develop very far without experimenting with the marriage relation. The period had seen the Rappites, the Shakers, Nashoba and the Oneida Community, as well as a score of less ambitious doctrines of love feasts, spiritual wifery and free love. The air was vibrant with revolutionary ideas, and polygamy makes its appearance in Mormonism at the very moment when this interest is most intense in the nation at large. Mormon polygamy, in fact, shows a typical vulgarization by ignorant and inferior people of an idea that on higher levels could work out in such an experiment as John Humphrey Noyes's "stirpiculture." That is what Mormonism did with all the ideas it appropriated — one must constantly think of it as a mechanism by which the forces at work on upper levels of American intelligence were accommodated to the understanding of the lowest level. Nevertheless, although some experimentation with marriage was probably inescapable, the experiment actually made was polygamy and it was initiated by Joseph. That he was highly sexed appears in all accounts that have come down. One need not accept the "hundreds" of seductions that are charged against him by Gentiles and apostates: the record of his marriages accepted by the faithful and the accounts printed by his widows are enough.[13] His vigor is as obvious here as elsewhere. One need not suspect that it was pathological but he was conspicuously gifted. It was part of the paranoid syndrome.

So was his literary activity. Many a paranoid seizure ex-

---

[13] I have never seen in print any allusion to an ancient legend of Gentile Utah that Joseph was castrated at Nauvoo by someone — never named — whose wife he had seduced. My father heard it in Utah as early as 1878. Its usefulness, as well as its consolation, to the embattled Gentiles is obvious.

presses itself in ink, many paranoids write compulsively and voluminously,[14] much of the world's literature and a great part of its "experimental" literature flows from this obsession. In the midst of an incredibly active life — a life filled with ruling thousands of subjects besides speculating in land and money, rearing temples to the Lord, maintaining a huge propaganda, developing the organization of the Church and settling hundreds of civic and religious disputes — in the midst of all this, Joseph still had time to emit countless pages of prose. The stream never ran out; to the day of his death he was vilifying his enemies, recording miracles in his autobiography, and setting down fresh gospels and epistles from on high. The paranoid faculty for seizing all the flotsam of thought and converting it to the support of the dominant obsession appears in everything he wrote.

It seems to me that all this evidence requires us to decide that Joseph Smith was a paranoid. It is possible, of course, to accept this finding — which accounts for the establishment and constitution of the Church — and still believe that he did not write *The Book of Mormon*. It is true that he may have assimilated the work of other hands to the needs of his delusion and given the vague body of vision a skeleton which someone else provided. As I have said, the question will never be settled. My opinion is, as I have expressed it in the article on Smith in *The Dictionary of American Biography*,[15]

[14] Sometimes attaching a symbolic meaning to the colors of the inks and the instruments with which the writing is done. Cf. Joseph's corruption of the Urim and Thummim.

[15] Well acquainted with the evidence already, I made another study of it before writing that article. Until then I had leaned toward the belief that Smith must have got hold of the Spaulding manuscript, whether through Rigdon or someone else. One had to swallow the difficulties of that theory or those presented by Smith's known ignorance. I adopted that idea in the earlier version of this essay, but I hereby withdraw it. We must be as skeptical as possible, and such a theory must be supported by much more evidence than has been found. My final opinion is that the evidence for the Spaulding manuscript is in-

that *The Book of Mormon* was in the main Smith's own composition, though he may well have had the collaboration of the associates who were his amanuenses, bankers and witnesses. Nothing that is known of him is incompatible with this opinion. It is claimed that he had neither the intelligence nor the education to write such a book — yet his known writing makes an equal or greater bulk, and it is as imaginative and as literate. Nothing in *The Book of Mormon* is foreign to his known interests or to the common emotional and intellectual preoccupations of the country in which he grew up. Woodbridge Riley's examination of its autobiographical material is persuasive.[16] When conclusive proof is lacking, history must adopt the simplest hypothesis that will satisfy all the known facts without controverting any of them. We must believe that *The Book of Mormon* was the work of the man who is called its "author and proprietor" on the title page of the first edition. It represented the impact of frontier religious speculation on a mind fixed in the paranoid cast. Thus did the aspiration of Puritan divines find a squalid expression on the Hill Cumorah, and thus did the vision of the Kingdom of God broaden down till humble minds could recognize in it the City of the Saints.

For, whether or not Joseph Smith was the author of *The Book of Mormon,* he was the author of the Church of Jesus Christ of Latter-Day Saints. Mormonism was, doctrinally, ecclesiastically, socially and economically, an evolution, a changing product of many influences, a resultant of many

sufficient and unacceptable, and that Joseph's later, and proved, writing indicates that he was capable of writing *The Book of Mormon.*

[16] If easily disposed of by the assumption that Smith's autobiography was a systematic lie composed on no basis of fact and utilizing *ex post facto* material which someone else had already put into *The Book of Mormon.* That is a very helpful assumption when you are proving the Spaulding theory, but the facts do not justify it. And logic texts call the use of an assumption to prove itself argument in a circle.

interacting forces. The structure and organization of the
Church at the time of Joseph's death were far different from
what they had been when God revealed them in 1830, and
in that change the collaboration of the oligarchy that
formed round the prophet was probably as important as the
pressure from the outside world. Such men as Rigdon,
Young, Taylor, Snow, Phelps, Hyde, the Pratts, Kimball,
Marks, Page and Wight unquestionably had a part in establishing the bonds and constraints that held the Church together, contributing earthly expedients and initiating or
clarifying the doctrines that rationalized them. The functions of Rigdon as exegete and Young as chief fiscal officer
were of absolute importance. Nevertheless these men were
banded together in support of Joseph's vision, and it was
his energy and leadership that made them effective. The
Church that existed on June 27, 1844, when Joseph was
martyred at Carthage jail, was the personal creation of a
prophet of God.

V

Joseph Smith proclaimed the millennium. Vision and
proclamation, however, were not enough. The actual
achievement of millennium had to wait for Brigham Young.

Smith's birthplace at Sharon, Vermont, is marked by fine
landscaping and a monument which we are told with
Mormon unction is "the tallest single piece of polished
granite in the world." At Whitingham, some seventy miles
away, you will find no landscaping, no caretakers, no re-
cital of earthly accomplishments and heavenly splendors.
You will find only an unkempt hillside, a space marked off
with barbed wire, and a small white marker which looks
like a tombstone and is carved with one of the world's
most poignant inscriptions. "Brigham Young," the stone

says, "born on this spot, 1801. He was a man of much courage and superb equipment." The historian finds it in his heart to agree. But, he thinks, Brigham is worth more commemoration than that.

The two shrines express the judgment of the Mormons on their first two Presidents. But in the eyes of history not Smith but Young was Mormonism's great man. In 1844, at the time of the martyrdom, the Church was an astounding phenomenon in size, vigor and persistency, but no more astounding than several other fruits of Pentecost. It was, for instance, no more vigorous than and nowhere near so large as the Millerite church, which at that moment was, in a mounting frenzy, awaiting the coming of Christ on its second, more accurately determined Day of Judgment. Furthermore, all the indications are that Mormonism had reached its apogee under Smith, was passing it, and must soon have broken up in factions whose contention would have destroyed it. Apostasies were becoming common and the Church might not have been able to survive many more so hostile as that of John C. Bennett. That vigorous opposition from within was at last possible had been proved by the rebellion of the Law brothers and the publication of *Expositor*. The Church could not have coped with many more such revolts — and more would certainly have come. Also it seems certain that Smith himself had entered a final period of psychic disintegration. The fires had begun to consume him; if he had lived much longer he must soon have been recognized as mad. A few years more would have seen Mormonism going the way of its competitors, division by mitosis, internecine warfare, bankruptcy, disillusionment and decay.

The death of Joseph and the succession of Brigham did produce a number of schisms — and some of them issued from the very feeling that would have begotten them if Joseph had lived, a belief that he had wandered from the path of inspiration, betrayed his priesthood and made necessary a reversion to the tenets and practices of primitive Mormonism. Seven or eight factions split off from the parent stock, under the leadership of various Apostles or of prophets suddenly appearing from the ranks with credentials from God. These doubled by division in the course of a few years, and all told over twenty Mormon churches arose, several of which still exist as organizations or as unorganized millennial dreams. The largest of these was formed by the combination of several which believed that succession to the Presidency should be in the hereditary line of Joseph. As the Reorganized Church of Jesus Christ of Latter-Day Saints ("Josephites," to the Utah Mormons), it was held by the courts to be the legal and true Mormonism. The courts, however, were out of touch with history. Mormonism survived in the main body of the Saints, whom Brigham Young took to Utah. Observe that, after he got them there, only one schism occurred. It was small, momentary and absurd — and it was handled with Brigham's deftness.[17]

Young's succession marks a decisive change in Mormonism, one which must be understood for it is finally important in the answer to our original question. Whatever else Smith was, he was primarily a prophet, a religious leader, a man drunk on God and glory, his head swarming with giddy visions of the end of the world and the prolifera-

---

[17] It was headed by the prophet Joseph Morris. (The "false prophet" alluded to by Jonathan Dyer in the first essay of this book.) Morris had revelations from God and produced sacred books by inspiration. So did most of the prophets of the other schisms. Those of James J. Strang are the most interesting, and his Kingdom in Wisconsin and the islands of Lake Michigan is much the most picturesque of the heresies.

tion of Mormon triumphs through all eternity. Young was primarily an organizer of the kingdom on this earth, an administrative and executive genius of the first order, the greatest colonizer in American history. Under Smith the Church was a loosely coördinated body dedicated to a hodgepodge of dogma so preposterous that the mind rocks contemplating it, a compilation of the worst idiocies that had marked the American Pentecost, a fermenting yeast of nonsense — a mere millennial sect in which the social energies that were to save it were obscured, slighted, left to chance and the conditioning of Gentile opposition. Under Young it became a religio-economic social system, based on coöperative enterprise, subordinating religious ecstasy to practical achievement, utilizing the energies and sentiments of religious faith for the production of collective wealth — and thus winning its fight against the opposition of Protestant America, the national government and the main current of the nineteenth century.

Young troubles the biographer with few subtleties and no ambiguities. He was born four years before Smith in an even more remote and primitive Vermont valley, of the same racial and religious stock. Like Smith he wandered widely through interior New York, and he was living in the vicinity of Palmyra and Fayette when the Church was founded. He had a strong interest in religion — in the burnt-over district he could hardly have escaped having one — but it was entirely intellectual, free of the soul-searching, agony and dementia of the twice-born Smith. He was a Methodist when the new Bible came to his hands a few weeks after it was published. He studied it for two years, argued with its missionary expositors, and was baptized into the faith in the spring of 1832. What he asked of religion was literal interpretation of the Bible, applicability to daily life and a guaranty that millennial glory could be achieved by hard work. Mormonism satisfied his requirements. He accepted the divine inspiration of Smith and the doctrines and destiny of the Church. That conversion settled all problems and his faith was never thereafter assailed by doubt.[18] It is absurd to suspect him of insincerity or charlatanism. He accepted Mormonism in its entirety, and it required of him only to serve its interests. He did so in the one way he understood, the one way for which he was fitted.

In 1844 there was little to suggest that this glazier, house painter, farmer and handyman could succeed where Owen, Fourier, Cabet and the rhapsodic Yankee experimenters failed. Nevertheless he had already rendered the Church invaluable service. He had proved its most successful proselyter and had headed the English mission, which ever since has been the most important recruiting-ground of Israel, sending all told more than one hundred thousand converts to America. And his assumption of its finances had given the Church such fiscal stability as it possessed. He was forty-three. The death of Joseph provided his opportunity. Campaigning to make Smith President of the United States when the prophet was killed, he reached Nauvoo six weeks after the assassination. He found the Church in a condition of collapse, harried by the Gentile mob, stunned by the murder of its prophet, leaderless and threatened with disintegration. He proved that he was the strongest personality among the Mormons in a series of dramatic moves which saved the organization and restored the hopes of the faithful. Israel rallied. The small, schismatic sects broke away, followed by Young's magnificent denunciations, and the

[18] This summary of Young's religious experience is based on his own statements in sermons. I see no reason for questioning any part of it. His sermons, published in the *Journal of Discourses*, are the most important documents of Mormonism.

Church, its fervor immensely increased by the martyrdom, united behind the man who showed it the way to endure. And from that moment the student perceives a consciousness of what it was doing and what it intended to do that Mormonism had never had before. Essentially, Smith did not know: he was moving only toward glory. Young knew: he was moving toward survival on this earth and power which would protect Israel from attack.

The expulsions from Ohio and Missouri, which were now reinforced by expulsion from Illinois, had shown that Mormonism could not exist in the American social organization. Young accepted that teaching. One of the original missions of the Church had been to convert the Indians, and from time to time Smith had vaguely promised or threatened to remove it to the Far West, in spite of the fact that its ordained gathering place in the last days must be the site of the Garden of Eden, in Jackson County, Missouri. Young carried out the removal. In doing so, he saved Mormonism.

Just why he selected the valley of the Great Salt Lake cannot be determined. At Independence the Mormons had been in touch for many years with the fur traders, who knew intimately every square mile of the intermountain region. Frémont's reports and other Government publications, as well as books by travelers, unofficial explorers, and big-game hunters, were available. Young may even have had a report on Deseret by an expedition of his own.[19] The valley was Mexican soil when he started for it, though

[19] The literature of the West contains an occasional allusion to a Mormon party which is said to have been in the Salt Lake valley in the summer of 1846, a year before the advance party of the emigration got there. I cannot identify it or prove that it existed, and Rosamond Chapman, who has made an investigation for me, can go but little farther. Note also that, in 1847, Mormons who had gone to California by ship may have come eastward through the valley and joined Young before he got there.

it came under American jurisdiction two years later, and separation from American control was a lively desire. It was known to be the most fertile part of the Rocky Mountain region, but was barren and unattractive, and its unattractiveness made it fully as valuable to the Saints as its fertility, since it would keep the Gentiles from following after Israel. It was well off the road to Oregon by which the main emigration of the decade moved westward; and the favored route to California, whither emigration was just beginning to turn, branched from the Oregon trail far to the northwest. Deseret, the Territory-to-be of Utah, was in fact the obvious place, if not the only place, for the Saints to go. Brigham selected it in a clear understanding of the needs of his enterprise. He counted on profiting from trade with the Oregon migration, and though he could not foresee the gold rush which would occupy California, he understood that, after a sufficient period of isolation, Israel would profitably advance with the western expansion of the United States which he now joined.

Giving the established technique of emigration a religious nomenclature, in the only revelation that he ever issued, Young took his Church to Utah. He broke no new trails [20] and faced no novel problems (a migration almost as large moved to Oregon at the same time, and numerically greater ones had preceded him), and the enlistment of five hundred Mormons by the Government for a march to California provided financial help without which he would certainly have been delayed at least a year. His success lay principally in building up the spirit of the Saints, convincing them that

[20] Mormon historians used to claim that the "Mormon Trail" along the north bank of the Platte was used for the first time by this emigration, but it was in fact well marked and had been frequently used. While traveling it, the Mormons met several parties coming east along it.

they were in fact leaving Egypt for the land of Canaan and the new day, keeping them at a pitch of religious fervor which, in the end, welded them into an instrument magnificently fitted to his hand. For this two years' journey to Canaan established Young's mastery. The last opposition collapsed or was rooted out; the westward migration confirmed the docility, obedience and malleability of the Saints, and made Young a more effective dictator than Smith had ever been.

The fact that he issued no more revelations is significant. Smith had produced a communication from God at the slightest exigency — to close an awkward argument or to get someone out of town for a few weeks while the prophet explained celestial marriage to his wife. Young made it clear that he retained the power of revelation; but his failure to use it, while asserting that God inspired his activities, set Mormonism in a new form. Progressively, as time passed, he discountenanced all the Pentecostal gifts that had flourished so tropically for sixteen years. He managed to stamp out private revelation altogether — if the President refrained, doubt was easily cast on the inspirations of the humble — but the other gifts of the spirit were not so easily suppressed. Prophecy, visions, speaking in tongues, and the interpretation of signs, dreams and portents had been so long the daily bread of Israel that in spite of the skepticism and denunciation directed at them from the pulpit they maintained an illicit, sub rosa existence, and in fact have continued down to the present. Young steadily opposed them but was forced to yield to the outbreak of evangelical frenzy known as the "Reformation," when, after deflation and crop failure and the hand-cart emigration which was his most serious blunder, the old apocalypse flared up. The doctrine of blood atonement (sacrificial murder as absolution for sin) appeared during this communal hysteria, and the passions then aroused were responsible for the infamous Mountain Meadows massacre.[21] This period, which ended in Young's nominal submission to the Government when Albert Sidney Johnston's expeditionary force arrived, was the most serious crisis that he ever had to face. How far he shared the fierce sentiments of his people it is impossible to determine. He could not have been altogether free of them, but he conducted himself with a wary understanding of what was happening. His genius for leadership is nowhere shown more clearly than in his ability to convert even this aberration to his own purposes (and in reality turn dissatisfaction with the priesthood into community penitence), make the Church more than ever responsive to his will, and emerge from conflict with the United States even more unmistakably the master of its fate.

In thus closing revelation and turning the Church from the very practices on which it had been founded, Young's doctrinal position was clear. With the mission of Joseph Smith the gospel and priesthood had been restored. Israel now had the fullness of truth: its obligation was to build up the Kingdom. Build it up here and now, preparing the glories of the future by making sure of the possessions of the present. This interpretation of prophecy preserved Israel — and it contains the whole personality of Brigham Young.

[21] A party of Gentile emigrants traveling to California were slaughtered by Mormons, only a few young children being spared. The act must be understood as an end-product of many months of religious excitement begotten by famine, panic, and the threat of invasion. Israel was harrowed by its own soul-searching, the wrath of the Lord had been made manifest, and the priesthood had been inciting the Saints against the Gentiles — an expedient made sufficiently familiar to this age by European dictatorships. Young was not directly responsible for it and was genuinely horrified when he learned of it — for reasons both of humanity and of statecraft. Nevertheless, as I say in *The Dictionary of American Biography*, he must be charged with the constructive responsibility of all dictators.

He could understand salvation by works and the attainment of eternal glory by means of earthly diligence, but he had no interest whatever in metaphysics. Having once accepted the vaporizings of Joseph, he devoted himself to providing a mechanism to perpetuate them. "Live your religion" was his unvarying counsel to the Saints. And by "Live your religion" he meant: take up more land, get your ditches in, make the roof of your barn tight, improve your livestock, and in so doing glorify God and advance His Kingdom. At least four fifths of his sermons are altogether free of dogma, and though he did embroider a few variations on Joseph's themes, he did so with a humor that reads suspiciously like parody. He let his assistants satisfy the need of the Saints for doctrine. Orson Pratt, Orson Hyde, Jedediah Grant, Heber Kimball, C. C. Rich — it is in the sermons of such men that you will find the rhapsodies on celestial glory, the planet Kolob or the polygamy of Jesus which fed that insatiable hunger. Brigham was more interested in irrigation, freight transport and whether a wife in Israel could rightfully require her husband to construct a stand for her washtub.

But if the Apostles worked in the service of hermeneutics, they also had a much more important role. "Young's greatest achievement was his transformation of a loose sacerdotal hierarchy consecrated by Smith's revelations to apocalyptic duties, into a magnificent fiscal organization for the social and economic management of the Church. . . . Accepting Smith's priestly system, he made it a social instrument and to this realistic revision the survival, the prosperity and the social achievements of Mormonism are due." [22] Under Smith the priesthood had been a system of stairways and corridors through the crazy-quilt glories of the Mormon apocalypse,

[22] My article on Young in *The Dictionary of American Biography*.

a secret society with robes and passwords and magic rituals
that at first was like nothing on earth or in the Bible but
began to imitate Masonry when he and his lieutenants joined
the lodge.[23] It was essentially a series of cabalistic "degrees,"
attended by litanies and tableaus, through which one rose
by piety and divination. Under Young, however, the priesthood became the commissioned and noncommissioned staff
of the social army. They were the great and the small leaders
of Israel, the channel of direction and control, the over-
seers, the department managers, the adjutants, the deputies
and the police. They were the nervous system of a coöperative enterprise in the occupation of the desert and the development of a commonwealth. Young established them in
that function, which they retain to-day. That is the change
of phase that he gave the Church; it is the principal part
of what has survived as Mormonism.

The occupation of Utah must be understood as the accomplishment of a coöperative society obedient to the will
of a dictator. There was precedent and technique for the
system of city-building which Young initiated as soon as
he reached Utah. Smith and his counselors had received
divine advice on planning cities — the engineering of God
corresponding to blueprints drawn by the communistic experiments in New England. There was also precedent and
technique for the system of irrigation which Young began
on the very day of his arrival in the valley of Great Salt
Lake. But there was neither precedent nor existing technique for the colonization of the desert. Young's genius
shows clearly in his immediate and unhesitating attack. The

[23] Because they then initiated the Saints wholesale and because their
ceremonies were really a parody, they were expelled from Masonry.
I understand that since then no Mormon has been received into a
Masonic lodge.

word is exact: he retained the theological idiom but the investiture was military.

The positions of strategic importance, the only parts of the desert where settlement was possible, were the mountain valleys and the plateaus at their mouths which are watered by the streams that flow down them. Young occupied these positions as rapidly as possible, some of them during the first year. Parties under the command of proved leaders and assigned the right proportion of trades and handicrafts, with every man's duties allotted him, were sent out to form "stakes" which were branches of the settlement at Salt Lake City and were supported and directed from that headquarters. In the course of a few years such colonies were set up in every fertile valley of what was to become Utah and a good many in Idaho, Wyoming, Colorado, Nevada, Arizona and New Mexico as well. Israel also maintained outposts at positions of actual military importance — desert water holes, river crossings, and mountain passes through which either emigration or punitive expeditions must move. As a result the Saints acquired a monopoly; they owned practically all the valuable real-estate in the intermountain region.

Such social planning was effective because it was done at the muzzle of a gun. The colonization of the desert was quite impossible to individual endeavor.[24] It could be financed only by the collective wealth of the Saints. It could be initiated, carried out and maintained only because there was a central authority capable of commanding absolute obedience and able to suppress any dissent that might arise. The Church had become a coöperative body managed by

[24] Observe the national Government's half-century of assistance to settlers elsewhere in the desert. You may also observe its failure.

a dictator (and a developing oligarchy) who had absolute power deriving from the authority of Almighty God. Only that formula could have succeeded.

Young cut off everyone who rebelled — he had to if the interests of the group were to be served, if the group was to survive at all. He tolerated no interference from Gentile America — framing, flouting and terrorizing the Federal officials who were sent to Utah, terrorizing and sometimes murdering the private individuals who got in his way. Almost at once he became a national ogre, vilified as a tyrant who suppressed all the liberties and privileges of the American system. The line of cleavage, with the line of hostilities, however, is the line of group pressure. Dictatorships do not arise and cannot endure except in the service of group needs. Mormonism ran squarely against the main currents of nineteenth-century American life — and naturally the collision generated heat. What seemed to be a religious warfare, Methodist America upholding the principles of Christianity and Mormonism those of a barbarous Asiatic heresy, was in fact a warfare of economic systems and social organizations violently opposed to each other. Mormonism was a true dictatorship. But the word should be quite neutral. To the Gentile United States it seemed an intolerable tyranny, un-American and repulsive, exploiting religious faith and depriving the faithful of every value that gives dignity and worth to human life. To the Mormons, however, it not only had divine sanction but was the only means of preserving the way of life for which they had endured persecution and unimaginable hardship, had sacrificed their fortunes and were prepared to sacrifice their lives. Dictatorship was a form conditioned by group ideals, group desires and group efforts.

The country thus occupied had to be filled up. Every

immigrant who could be brought to Utah would increase
the wealth of Israel. The Church already had an effective
proselyting system which covered both the United States
and Europe, of which Young himself had organized the
richest field, the British Isles. He now increased both the
extent and the effectiveness of the mission system. He was
engaged on a large-scale real estate development. The promise of land which his missionaries held out to the tenant
farmers and city unemployed who proved to be their best
prospects was an even more effective bait than the heavenly
glories which the Church assured them. Note also that these
classes had the native docility which the Mormon system
requires. Missionaries were sent as far afield as Australia,
Africa and the Sandwich Islands. They made converts
everywhere but the only field which proved comparable to
Great Britain was the Scandinavian countries, whose croft-
ers were a dispossessed class.

Immigration, like colonization, was financed from the
common funds. Young devised the Perpetual Emigration
Fund by means of which converts who could not pay their
own way might be brought to Zion on their notes of hand.
Converted abroad, you paid your own fare to Utah if
you could afford to. If you could not, the Church would
lend you enough to buy passage to America. Arrived at an
Atlantic or Gulf port, you found work if you could and
earned a grubstake to take you West.[25] If you could not
get employment, the Church would also charge against you
the expense of transportation to Zion, add you to one of its
emigrant trains, and employ you on public works in Salt
Lake City when you got there, till your proper place in
Zion could be determined. In any event, you were effectively indentured to the priesthood.

[25] See "The Life of Jonathan Dyer," within.

A convert's control of his own movements had a proportional relationship to the wealth he brought with him. In theory all the possessions of every Saint were consecrated to God under the direction of the priesthood. The theory could be enforced, however, on only the poorest or the most enthusiastic proselytes, and the wealthiest were certain to be given the freest choice and to begin their service farthest up the scale of spiritual evolution. Every effort was made to utilize the talent and training of the converts, and they were sent wherever the best use could be made of them. But since Zion was overwhelmingly agricultural, many a man who had never seen a plow was ordered to the fringe of settlement and spent his life breaking desert land to crops. Again, only a despotically governed coöperative society could enforce a regimentation that got results.

Young thus established his commonwealth on a landed base and gave it a solidity that has never been endangered. In doing so he had to restrain the Saints from developing the great mineral wealth of Utah; he understood what he was about and the loss of the mining country to the Gentiles was an inconsiderable price to pay for stability. He also understood the debtor status of frontier communities — he had spent his life in contact with that reality. His effort to give Israel financial independence accelerated the development of a totalitarian state. There can be no doubt that, granted the terms of his religious conception, Young understood the principles of autarchy.[26] The cost of freight transport by ox team from the frontier (the Missouri River, until the Union Pacific started to lay track) was of itself a powerful conditioner; the drainage eastward of Mormon

[26] The economist who will investigate this question will find a wealth of supporting detail, from a managed currency and efforts to prevent the export of capital down to a purified alphabet to prevent contamination by foreign ideas.

money was even more powerful. He embarked on a policy of home manufacture to supplement his colonizing policy. Manufacture of every conceivable kind was undertaken and though some of the experiments (notably smelting and beet sugar) were premature, an amazing success attended it.

Here enters, however, the force which, after Brigham's death, was to bring Mormonism considerably closer to the main stream of American development than it had ever been before — the force which tangentially allied the Church with the currents it had opposed. To support an agricultural colonization with the common funds did not create a division of interest between the Church organization and the people. The people were the colonization. But to support manufacturing and mercantile enterprises in private hands with those same funds [27] or to put the Church itself into either was at once to make possible a division of interest between the people and the organization. It was an irretrievable first step in a change from coöperation to corporate control. The Church thus set up financial bodies, banks, corporations and holding companies which had access to and were in part supported by the common funds, and whose interests were frequently opposed to those of the Mormon people. The step was taken in behalf of Young's vision of coöperative self-sufficiency. But he paid in loss of coöperative unity for what he gained in independence from Gentile finance — and in the end Israel had to make terms with that finance. He understood what was happening and his revival of the United Order, the communism which had been tried under Smith, was an effort to reverse the trend. Doc-

[27] The basis of them has always been the tithes, a ten per cent. income tax and in theory also a capital levy. No accounting of them, or of the other financial property of the Church, is ever made. At Annual Conference an aseptic report is made on expenditures for missions, Church edifices, and charitable organizations.

trinally the United Order was the system which the entire Church must some day embrace.[28] But the other energies were too strong and the communism could make no headway. Young left it, perhaps a little wearily, to perish by itself, and his successor destroyed it. He had himself evoked the force that killed it. Endeavoring to deliver Mormonism from exterior debt, he had started it on the path to conformity.

In leaving him, it is convenient to list a few of the parallels between Mormonism and the European dictatorships. The Mormons had their Aryan myth: they were a chosen people and were destined, after conquest, to dominate mankind. Dedication to that destiny implied their saying "Liberty, we spit on you," and cheerfully accepting a rigorous and sometimes savage discipline in which the individual counted for nothing against the group. Opposition to the priesthood has always been as inconceivable as individual defiance of Hitler or Stalin. The Saints are privileged to "sustain the Presidency" by a free show of hands in affirmative vote: they believe, precisely as the Russians under the new con-

---

[28] The revelation which originally established it has never been countermanded, and the Saints have always had a vague expectation that it must someday be obeyed. During the last few years that expectation has grown livelier. I greatly regret that I am not qualified to discuss the effects of the depression on Mormonism. What most impresses one from a distance is the revival of the old millennial fires. Israel has had a contrite heart and the gifts of the spirit have flourished. There has been a widespread, if not officially indorsed, belief that the Last Days have begun. World-wide upheaval, wars, rumors of wars, famine, drought and sun spots have been interpreted (as they have been all through Mormonism's century) as the fulfillment of Joseph's prophecies. When Mr. Marriner Eccles was summoned to the Treasury Department the matter was clinched — Joseph having specifically foretold that in the Last Days a Saint would be called to save the nation. There seems to have been a reversion to a much more active coöperation, leading in the summer of 1936 to the Church's withdrawing all its people from national relief. Granted enough disaster, it is easy to imagine the restoration of the United Order — with, however, the hierarchy in absolute control.

stitution believe, that they are exercising the democratic right of the franchise. Effective government required the use of an Ogpu: the Sons of Dan may never have existed under that name, or any of the other names given them in the Gentile literature, but Brigham had an efficient secret police who kept him informed and, on occasion, disposed of a Saint or a Gentile who stood in his way. Effective government, too, required a sedulous attention to Israel's young. Brigham developed and his successors have maintained a succession of schools, classes, clubs and training corps which operate on the children of the Saints from the age of three until they are admitted to the priesthood, and which condition their reflexes as effectively as the corresponding institutions of Russia and Italy.

Furthermore, a steady necessity was the perpetuation of and appeal to the persecution-neurosis: Israel has always been told that every man's hand was against it, that it must always work unanimously toward the righting of that wrong, and that any faltering would insure victory for its enemies. Appeal to that sentiment has also provided the Presidency with a screen for failure and a canal to carry away from its activities whatever curiosity or resentment the Saints might feel. The "Reformation" under Brigham was a blood purge which got rid of some of the inconvenient and united Israel against the world outside, forty years of Gentile agitation against polygamy served him and his successors in the same way, and the appeal is just as useful to the hierarchy to-day. The mumbo-jumbo of a ritual symbolizing the common aspirations, and the infinite gradations through which every Mormon is always ascending, correspond to the steps of mythical promotion and reward which Italy, Russia and Germany extend to the orthodox and faithful. State works have supplemented the central

economy, religious courts have usurped some of the functions of civil courts (in varying degree, at various times)
and have permitted a convenient secrecy and disregard of
legal forms, excommunication has served the immemorial
purpose of banishment, and the tests of orthodoxy have
always been shaped to reveal economic, political and even
intellectual nonconformity. And finally, Mormonism re-
peats the experience of all absolutisms: a dictatorship must
rest on the interests of a ruling class and comes to be a
mechanism by which an élite exercises power over a society.

VI

No one may say whether Brigham Young could have
maintained his power if he had broken with the oligarchy
which he came increasingly to represent. Probably he could
have, for during his lifetime it did not completely crystal-
lize and its interests had not been differentiated from those
of the Church as a whole. His rule was personal and he
could probably have maintained it, even in his last years,
against the hierarchy as effectively as he did against the
United States Government. He was, however, the last of
the personal dictators, and after his death Mormonism entered a new phase. It remained a coöperative society but
the coöperation was now governed by an oligarchy instead
of the prophet, it was governed in the interest of the élite
that had arisen, and that interest was sometimes opposed to
and even exploitive of the interest of the people who composed the society. Mormonism was developing not in the
direction of Rochdale, New Harmony, the Oneida Community, Brook Farm, the United Order or the Kingdom of
God — but in the direction of Standard Oil.

The coalescence of a ruling class was inevitable. Any

kind of government, any kind of colonization, any kind of social planning implies leadership and control, and as the profits begin to come in they must flow through the channels established. Along with the profits there are opportunities, perquisites and privileges; they must be used by someone; they end by being used by those who are in the best position to use them and have the most shrewdness and the greatest capacity. Already in Joseph's time a hierarchy of useful, superior and ingenious men had formed round him. They composed the Quorum of the Twelve Apostles and the other sacerdotal bodies of the Church. Converting them to administrative duties, Young chose his leaders from this caste or speedily admitted to it those outside whose talents signified their fitness. This hierarchy was the nucleus round whom the ruling class crystallized. The process is functional in human institutions.

When a Mormon speaks of "the hierarchy," he refers to the General Authorities. They are: the First Presidency, consisting of the Prophet and his two Counselors; the Twelve Apostles, who are the principal administrative officers, the vice-presidents, so to speak, in charge of plant, production, distribution and sales; the Seven Presidents of Seventies, the executives through whom the authority of the First Presidency is exercised over the Saints, the heads of the organization which is the nervous system of Israel; the Presiding Bishop, who is the Treasurer of the Church, and his two Counselors; and the Presiding Patriarch, an honorary office hereditary in the Smith family and charged with only sacerdotal duties. This, however, is merely the official framework. The true hierarchy is composed of those families which have achieved wealth through the development of the Mormon system, and those whose service to the Church has been conspicuous or whose talent for fiscal or religious administration is marked — augmented in every generation by such newcomers as may conspicuously qualify in any of the requirements. It is largely a hereditary class, but the avenue of accession is kept open. It remains devout, lives its religion and derives its vigor from that of the religion it lives, but its interests have always won when any conflict between them and those of the Mormons as a whole has appeared.

The title of President includes that of "Prophet, Seer, Revelator and Vicegerent of God on earth," but before the Prophet Heber lists those heavenly distinctions in *Who's Who in America* he records that he is president of Zion's Coöperative Mercantile Institution (the firm which Brigham organized to defeat Gentile competition), the Utah-Idaho Sugar Company (carrying with its corporate alliances control of the beet-sugar industry in the United States), Zion's Savings Bank & Trust Company, the Utah State National Bank, and the Beneficial Life Insurance Company — and director of the Union Pacific Railway Company. The list shows the final emphasis and values of Mormonism, but it merely hints at the economic power that is vested in the hierarchy. That power is absolute over the business and finance of Utah, it has a great and probably decisive influence throughout the intermountain region, and it has working alliances with the countrywide network of finance. It is a banking system, a manufacturing system and an interlocking directorate. The Church, for instance, is said to own more stock in New York Central than the Vanderbilts, it holds directorates on other railroad boards, it dominates the manufacture of beet sugar, and through such manufactures as those of salt and woolen goods it is linked with many national interests. In such matters the Church is the hierarchy. And the hierarchy is a holding company.

The history of Mormonism after Brigham Young is the story of the process which brought the hierarchy into this relationship with the system of commerce and finance that triumphed in America after the Civil War, while retaining the coöperative system from which its power flowed and maintaining the sentiments which animated that coöperation. There is no need to tell that story here. The decisive period was that between the Woodruff Manifesto of 1890, which put a stop to polygamous marriages without impugning the doctrine of polygamy, and the adoption by the United States Senate in 1907 of the minority report of its Committee on Privileges and Elections which confirmed Reed Smoot. During that time the Church learned not only that it must outwardly conform to the requirements of the American system but also that it would lose nothing by doing so.

The generation which had known the prophet Joseph in the flesh died out. Whatever memories of hardship in Utah might remain, the agonies of Missouri and Illinois became only a tradition. Meanwhile the businesses of Israel had prospered and, since the United States could seize them, had made Israel vulnerable. The Edmunds Act and the Edmunds-Tucker Act which supplemented it did in fact confiscate Church property. They also, in flagrant violation of the Constitution, disfranchised polygamists and attached a test-oath to the franchise — gelding and gutting the organization of Mormondom and threatening it with complete destruction. They signalized the intention of the Government, after fifty years of compromise, to bring the Church into conformity. They were directed at polygamy, but in the background was much unresolved matter, such as terrorism of the Gentiles in Utah, political exploitation, disregard of political and legal forms, and Mormon attitudes toward the tariff, the wool and hides industries and corporation law which the party in power could not approve. Well, Israel's fire had sunk somewhat and Israel had learned wisdom. This time not life but property was at stake — so the dreadful oaths to avenge the murder of Joseph and Hyrum, to destroy the United States, to make the ground smoke with the blood and bowels of the Gentiles, were quietly laid away. The new generation of leaders heard but impatiently the grandsires who preached fidelity to prophecy even though it should destroy the Church. Israel capitulated to the United States, has never violated the bargain then made, and has had no reason to regret it.

Splendor dies with that hardheaded decision. On June 26, 1858, the United States Army under command of Albert Sidney Johnston entered Salt Lake City in order of battle. It came to assert the sovereignty of the national Government and to raise the flag above a capital where, up till then, only the banners of heaven had been acknowledged. All morning long the troops filed through the city, but the mirth of drums and bugles floated down empty streets. Here and there the military might see a Gentile watching this assertion of the nation's will, but they saw no Saints. The only Mormons in Salt Lake City that day were hidden in designated houses, and they had torches and inflammables with them. Mormonry itself, thirty thousand strong, was miles to the south, waiting with Brigham Young to see what terms could be made. Just so far would he go, just so much would he yield to the children of evil — and no more. By God he would make no peace endangering Israel — and by God he didn't. If he had had to, Salt Lake City would have been burned to the ground, all Zion besides would have been laid waste, and Brigham would have led his people on one more migration. Into the badlands of the

Virgin and Colorado Rivers they would have gone, and there the Kingdom would have been set up among the desert peaks and would have resumed its ancient warfare with the damned. That was the stature of Brigham when, all expedients failing, he had to face submission and decide Israel's fate. He won. The United States submitted.

Things went otherwise in 1890. Israel's wealth was saved. Polygamy was postponed to the celestial state, the Saints were arbitrarily assigned to Democratic and Republican Party organizations, the Endowment House was torn down (as a pretty symbol), and the path to Reed Smoot's Senator-ship opened straight ahead. Personal leadership waned. George Q. Cannon was the last great leader of the Saints and, working through the figurehead prophets Taylor, Snow and Woodruff, he was neither President nor a per-sonal dictator. Cannon's oldest son, Frank, was much the most brilliant mind of the younger generation. He played a leading part in the preservation of the Church and the shift to a new basis following the Woodruff Manifesto, then he rebelled against the hierarchy, was cut off and became the most despised apostate of Mormon history. By that time the government of the Church was openly vested in the hierarchy. Reed Smoot rising to power in the Republican Party, becoming chairman of the Senate Committee on Finance, consulting with his peers to force the nomination of Warren G. Harding — Reed Smoot is the perfect image of modern Mormonism. Or, if you like, the Vicegerent of God's directorship of Union Pacific. The flight of the angel Nephi, the sacred repository of the Hill Cumorah, the temple of God reared secretly by night in the looted city of Nauvoo, Joseph Smith's visions of the Terrible Day and his murder in Carthage Jail — came in the end to a treasurer's signature on a dividend check. God had brought His people into the glory promised them. His house, it was already recorded, had many mansions; of them the one that had proved most durable was the countinghouse.

The inescapable word on polygamy may be spoken here. It must be thought of as an experiment that failed. The Gentile literature has enormously exaggerated its importance. The institution was fastened on the Church by Joseph's mania, working aberrantly on this current agitation as on so many others. It was certain to fail. Polygamy is not adaptable to American *mores* and is especially unfitted to an agricultural society. Its preservation through so many years was a considerable handicap, holding back a development that would have proceeded more rapidly without it. Young could not be expected to get rid of it: he himself was a polygamist and so were all his lieutenants. He deliberately used the opposition it aroused outside Zion to keep alive the persecution energies of the Saints, and that realism represented the best he could do. Polygamy was, moreover, a caste privilege. Only the well-to-do could afford it, a fact of importance in the linkages that gave the hierarchy power. The Saints defended it as a vital part of a religion revealed by God Himself, as they defended baptism for the dead and the multiplicity of gods. But they did not, and could not, practise it very much. The modern Mormon rationalization of it as a device to take care of surplus women is absurd, for there were never more women than men in Utah. It affected only a small part of Israel at any time. The most reliable estimate ever made indicates that at the most active period only four per cent. of the marriages in Utah were polygamous. I believe that the estimate is too high, perhaps as much as fifty per cent. too high. Polygamy would have fallen of its own weight long before it did, if the Gentile agitation had not kept it alive.

It was falling of its own weight when the Woodruff Manifesto ended it.[29] It was on its way to join the Deseret alphabet, the United Order and the fiat money of Deseret which was the only currency in history to be secured by the promises of God.

VII

Theologically, Mormonism is a creation of the American Pentecost. Philosophically it is a solution of a problem which American thought has grappled with for three hundred years: how to identify spiritual grace with the making of money. It is interesting to observe that, whereas Mormonism is a complete materialism, Christian Science, a complete idealism, came to the same successful issue. Mother Eddy provided a means of vulgarizing, of adapting on the lowest level, a mysticism whose highest level may be seen in Emerson and Jonathan Edwards, and in her world-swallowing metaphysics there is no material existence, no external reality, no objective good except cash. In the Mormon metaphysics everything is real and has an objective existence — even "spirit is matter but more finely divided" — but real things compose an ascending gradation whose climactic value is material prosperity. Dozens of sects, scores of philosophers, tried to give that principle implements of expression. The mechanism which developed under Joseph Smith and Brigham Young has a certain permanent importance in the history of thought.

---

[29] There was a thin trickle of secret polygamous marriage for some years after the Manifesto. Then toward the beginning of the century the hierarchy became afraid that the loyalty of its members might be affected by the new alliances with the Gentiles. At that time, according to a Utah rumor of long standing, it required all of its members who were not polygamists to secretly marry plural wives. If that is true, it was the last flare-up of any importance. The Mormons to-day are as monogamous as the Presbyterians.

The mechanism required was one which would utilize religious energy for financial ends. Psychologically, religion is an energizer, an emotional stimulus: it gives its possessor life more abundantly. Mormonism succeeded in harnessing that power for profit. Briefly, this is the solution: a coöperation of energized believers working in the name of God for an earthly Kingdom that will persist into eternity, and commanded by an oligarchy of superior persons whose authority is absolute because it originates in God and can be vindicated, whenever necessary, by revelation.

The Kingdom must actually be sanctified in the present, so that the believer may keep a lively sense of grace from day to day. And it must extend into eternity, so that he will always have a stimulus to greater exertion. He must, that is, be laboring in an industry that is both temporal and eternal, that advances him on earth and in heaven. Also, he must have a lively awareness of fellowship with others who are set off with him as a people chosen by God and, for greater effectiveness, persecuted by the Gentiles. He must hold a priesthood not given to those outside the law, so that he may always be aware of his superiority, but it must be one not completely conferred on himself, so that he will not unthriftily waste time in doubt or self-satisfaction but will always press on to advance through the infinite series of degrees open to him. Granted a society of such believers, granted such a lesser priesthood working toward a common end and controlled by a greater priesthood which has absolute power and immediate communication with God — and the result is not only great wealth but also a religion which satisfies a need that has been constant throughout American history.

That religion has had the fullest expression it is likely ever to have, in the pleasant valleys of Deseret which Israel is content to occupy in place of the lost Missouri Eden. Jens Christopherson, newly arrived from Norway and set to forking out his bishop's barn, participates in glories that no Gentile will ever behold. Ahead of him are dozens of steps which will take him farther and farther into the blinding light; till he dies he will be penetrating deeper into God's mysteries. He cannot so much as shingle a woodshed without adding to his spiritual stature, and when his daughter learns how to bake a cake without eggs she confers more glory on him. He goes on in splendor, his priesthood developing as his savings account grows — and as his priesthood develops it creates increment for Zion. And Reed Smoot, progressing from Henry Cabot Lodge's yes-man to the Senate chairmanship that allowed him to write tariffs favorable to Israel's industries, has always walked in the same glories, and in the greater ones of the Melchisedek priesthood. No step that Smoot took in the service of Israel's debentures was without immediate reward in the eternities, for you cannot build up the Kingdom of earth without also building it up in heaven. And Reed Smoot, if he lives long enough, will come into the greatest glory of all. The manipulator of tariffs and nominations will, by that fact and along that path, become Prophet, Seer, Revelator and Vicegerent of God on earth, holding the keys of the spirit and the mysteries and gazing into the awful secrets of all time to come. By the quarterly dividend ye shall come to know God: Mormonism is Jens Christopherson plus Reed Smoot.

VIII

But historically Mormonism is the fulfillment of a social ideal, the fructification of a social myth, the achievement of Utopia. It is what happens when Utopian dreams work out a free society. It is the actual resultant of the theoretical forces, the vision realized, the hope given flesh. It is the reality which the dream creates. That is its importance. And that is why it justifies study, these days of vision and desire . . . remembering that Robert Owen's vision perished, that Fourier and Cabet are only footnotes in the dream book, that Ballou and Lane and Brownson and Ripley and hundreds like them went down to dust while Joseph Smith's Utopia reached the golden shore.

What is Utopia when you get there? Make no mistake about it: the Mormon Utopia is a great deal. Brigham Young founded a state in the desert, the Mormons developed a culture there, and as states and cultures go they are good ones. The state at least is better than the American average — Utopia is above the median line in civics, which, I take it, is what our prophets promise us. Nearly any statistical index you may choose — literacy, school system, good roads, public health, bank savings, *per capita* wealth, business solvency, ownership of land free of incumbrance, infrequency of divorce or infanticide, infrequency of crimes against persons and property — will show that the Saints are better off than the average of their neighbors. And the state has always taken care of its poor. Poverty there has always been, but it has not been hopelessness. Israel has remembered its persecutions and so has helped the widowed, the orphaned and the dispossessed — it has managed to watch over its own. It has preserved great inequalities of wealth and has been forced to institutionalize its charity as thoroughly as the capitalists and the damned — but that merely says that Utopia remains outside security. On the other hand, the Church has developed agencies for finding the gifted, the useful, clearing the way before them, and bringing them to a better functioning in Israel. The agencies and

the institutions are there, and the priesthood is there, over-
seeing the people, going among them and counseling them,
sharing their problems, working with them toward the
answers.

That, heaven knows, adds up to an impressive total. But
there is something that counts much more: the Saints are
members one of another. They form a community with
recognized objectives, in the realization of which every
member has an active part. They share the effort and they
know that they have a value in the result. Before them is
the ideal which they are helping to realize; around them is
the culture which they have helped to shape. The slightest
of them has more identity of his own because he is identified
with the great society and with its dream. Here is the fellowship of common endeavor, the sense of sharing a social
vision, the communion of men bound together in a cause —
that is gone from the Christian Church and from the modern
world. It is what Stalin and Hitler and Mussolini have tried
to invoke; it is what ardent and generous and despairing
people hold out as our only hope, our only defense against
chaos. The Saints have had it from the beginning and they
will never lose it.

Yes, Utopia exists in the Wasatch valleys. And its idiom
is completely American. This is the fulfillment of our
prophets' dreams. So let us see some of the conclusions it
indicates. Utopia, then, can be achieved. How?

The first conclusion: that not Brook Farm but Mormonism is Utopia, that not Charles Fourier but Joseph Smith
brings it about, that not the highest level but the lowest
level is its absolute condition. Mormonism was first embraced by the illiterate and the inferior, has been recruited
from them ever since, and is held together by a body of
belief that can satisfy only the most rudimentary minds.

Destroy that body of belief, alter it in the least particular, and Utopia will sink and vanish. The Mormon ideology springs from dogmas not only preposterous but actually revolting to the intelligence. In order to share the common effort of Utopia you must accept as holy books some of the most squalid creations of human thought, you must receive as God's messages to mankind the delirium of insanity, you must believe that ignorant and stupid fools had the answers to all questions and were the channels of all truth. You must believe that Reed Smoot trading votes with Boies Penrose and Murray Crane was in touch with ineffable justice and the light of the world. You must believe that the president of your life insurance company is guided by the Holy Ghost, that the cashier of your bank is a son of Abraham and has his father's access to immortal truth, that the Socony man who sells you a quart of oil gazes down the eternities. You must believe that you yourself have kinsmen on the planet Kolob and will some day be a god begetting on a herd of brood-goddesses an infinity of other gods who will fill intergalactic space with new worlds to increase your glory. You must dedicate yourself to an organized body of damned nonsense so beyond-conceiving idiotic that a mind emancipated enough to embrace the dogmas of the Holy Rollers is forever immune to it. Touch that belief at any point and you have severed the aorta — Utopia will topple in fragments. Utopia is not dedication to the humanitarian vision of George Ripley; it is dedication to the hallucinations of Joseph Smith. The vision perishes, it is the vertigo that endures.

And if Utopia is a rigid selection of the inferior it is also a ruthless destruction of the individual. What European dictators have been practising for twenty years has always been the practice of the dictatorship that maintained Utopia.

It is, of course, an American Utopia — it has had to do but little murder in the faith's name, has used no castor oil, has flourished its knives but infrequently and then with a native humor. But at moments of crisis it has had its purges and proscriptions — and day by day the priesthood is there, with powers not only of excommunication from eternal glory but of boycott, espionage, monopoly, price-cutting and the big stick. Refusal to "sustain the Presidency" in any way is inconceivable. The Saint in business "accepts counsel" — that is, does what the priesthood tells him to do — quite as inevitably and as thoroughly as he does in matters of doctrinal orthodoxy. There has never been a time when any Mormon's business, politics and mind were not as completely at the disposal of the ruling hierarchy as his belief in miracles. Utopia can tolerate unorthodoxy in behavior or in idea no more than it can tolerate disunion in belief.

This implies that the culture of Utopia, though it be vigorous, must be conformable and mediocre. What has Israel produced? Business men, politicians, bankers and men gifted in the elaboration and propagation of doctrinal idiocies. Its genius finds expression in that kind of man; its élite are a business élite exclusively. Its scholars, scientists, artists, thinkers, all its infrequent talent, it has plowed back into the Kingdom. In Utopia the fate of the superior person is tragic. Consider an anthropologist set to vindicating *The Book of Mormon*, a musician condemned to write cantatas celebrating the flight of angels above Cumorah, a logician who must resolve the contradictions of *The Doctrine and Covenants*, a sociologist who must rationalize polygamy, a poet whose lyrics must idealize the Word of Wisdom's prohibition of hot tea. In Utopia talent must string along or it must get out. Actually, not much agony of this sort has been caused. Israel is the Kingdom, not the spirit, and has given irrigation to America, not arts and letters. To the Kingdom, not the spirit, such talent as arises devotes itself. The soprano comes back to Zion to drill "primary" in singing "Come, Come, Ye Saints." The painter, if the priesthood has been unable to turn him altogether from his vagary, comes back to do a mural of Joseph and the angel Moroni on a blank wall in the chapel of the Twelfth Ward. It is that, or it is get out. The sensitive, the intelligent, the individual, all those not gifted for the increase of kine, have always got out, for Utopia is death to them. They have not been numerous: the élite reproduces itself in kind.

Again, the classless society must inevitably develop a privileged class. Remember that Mormonism is a society of just men in process of being made perfect. It is, that is to say, the exact fulfillment of the common dream out of which it sprang, which launched a hundred experiments in liberty and equality. It is George Ripley, Robert Owen and Charles Fourier making good their vision of a common endeavor and a common life wherein each should contribute according to his ability and have according to his need. The liberty Utopia has is the freedom to conform, the equality it has is a common privilege of "sustaining the Presidency," and though each contributes according to his ability, each has — whatever he can get from the system that supports the hierarchy. The great society is one organized to advance the interests of the ruling class. All that a century of vision and labor has accomplished is to give that class a resounding title and make it more secure. Whatever benefit the humble Saint may get from the system comes to him and by the permission of his masters as the largesse. He serves God and will profit exceedingly thereby when he is dead; he serves the hierarchy and profits thereby as may be when the dividends and the sinking fund have been taken care of.

Finally, Utopia does not alter the shape of things. What is Mormonism in the twentieth century? A grotesque ideology, a set of coöperative institutions strictly limited and managed in support of an élite, and, beyond that, effectively an identification with industry and finance. Martyrdom, years of suffering, the colonization of the desert and the dream of millennial justice come out by the same door as any private enterprise in stock-jobbing. Utopia begins by calling down the lightning and the Terrible Day on the corrupt system of the Gentiles, and for some time it dances the carmagnole; but the bloody oaths fade out and the Prophet, Seer and Revelator sanctifies the World War and announces with the power of inspiration that God has blessed the United States, on which the earliest prophet invoked His eternal wrath. At arm's length you cannot tell Utopia from anything else. It has blended with the map, it has joined hands with the damned.

There it is: what has actually survived from the Newness and the Striving. That is the way the dream and the word are made flesh. Mormonism is the millennium that comes through. This is what Utopia is. Now that the heavens open again and voices speak once more out of the thunder and the whirlwind, now that the vision reawakens and the heart lifts, answering . . . it is worth scrutiny and meditation.

FROM *Harper's*, MARCH 1932

New England: There She Stands

I

IN August 1927 I resigned my assistant professorship and undertook to support myself by what Ring Lardner has probably called the pen. Implicit in the change was a desire to live in some more agreeable community than the suburb of Chicago that had been my residence for five years. Since I carried my pen with me, I might live in any place on earth that pleased me. I might have gone to Montparnasse or Bloomsbury, Florence or the Riviera or Cornwall. I might, with respectable precedent, have chosen New Orleans or San Francisco. I might have selected one of the Westchester or Long Island towns in which writers are commoner than respectable men. I didn't. To the consternation of my friends, I came to Cambridge, Massachusetts.

The choice at once expelled me from a guild to which for eight or nine years I had impeccably belonged, that of the intellectuals who have right ideas about American life. For, of course, according to those right ideas, New England was a decadent civilization. It was no longer preëminent in America. Its economic leadership had failed so long ago that hardly a legend of it remained. Its intellectual leadership had expired not quite so early perhaps but, nevertheless, long, long ago. Its spiritual energy, never lovely but once formidable, had been degraded into sheer poison, leaving New England a province of repression, tyranny, and cowardice. At the very moment of my arrival Mr. Heywood Broun announced that all New England could not muster a half-dozen first-class minds. Mr. Waldo Frank had explained that nothing was left this people except the slag of Puritanism—gloom, envy, fear, frustration. He had explored the wasteland and discovered that practically all new England women suffered from neuroses (grounded in the Denial of Life) and contemplated suicide. Mr. Eugene O'Neill had dramatized a number of Mr. Frank's discoveries and had added incest to the Yankee heritage. In short, the guild had constructed another one of those logically invulnerable unities to the production of which it devotes its time. New England was a rubbish heap of burnt-out energies, suppressed or frustrated instincts, bankrupt culture, social decay, and individual despair.

In the month of my arrival there was a vivid confirmation of these right ideas. At Charlestown two humble Italians were executed because the ruling class did not like their political beliefs. The Sacco-Vanzetti case completed the damnation of New England: the right ideas were vindicated. Well, it helped to focus my ideas about the society to which I was returning. Six years earlier I had served on a committee which solicited funds for their defense. I believed them innocent of the crimes for which they were executed, and I held that any pretense of fairness in their trials was absurd. But several inabilities cut me off from my fraternal deplorers of this

judicial murder. For one thing, I was unable to feel surprise
at the miscarriage of justice — unable to recall any system of
society that had prevented it or to imagine any that would
prevent it. I was unable to believe that any commonwealth
was or could be much better constituted than New England
for the amelioration of a class struggle. I was unable to believe that any order of society would alter anything but the
terms in which social injustice expressed itself.

These inabilities added considerable force to my immediate, private reasons for desiring to live in New England.
The private reasons were very simple: I wanted to use the
Harvard College Library. I liked the way New Englanders
leave you alone. I had lived in the West, the Middle West, the
South, and New York, and knew that the precarious income
of a writer would assure me more comfort, quiet, and decent dignity in New England than anywhere else in America.
But these personal motives were buttressed by generalization. As the great case had shown, I profoundly disbelieved in
the perfectibility of Society. Societies, I believed, would not
become perfect and could not be made perfect. The most to
be hoped for was that, as a resolution of imponderable forces,
as an incidental by-product of temperaments and interests
and accidents, a way of living in society might arise that was
somewhat better than certain other ways. And, because I had
lived in New England before, I knew that accidental by-
products of the Yankee nature had given New England an
attractive kind of civilization. I did not believe in the perfect
state but, like Don Marquis, I knew something about the
almost-perfect state. It had somehow begun to be approx-
imated in New England.

Two simple facts had conditioned it. For one thing, as my
former union announced, leadership had departed from New
England forever. That meant, among many other things,

that the province was delivered from a great deal of noise and stench and common obscenity which are inseparable from leadership in America. It meant that the province was withdrawn from competition; and this implied a vast amount of relief, decency, and ease. But there was something more. In that fall of 1927 Mr. Ford Madox Ford was writing a book whose title expressed the hopefulness of hundreds of thousands of Kansans, Texans, and Californians: *New York Is Not America*. Maybe it isn't; as an apprentice Yankee I am not interested. What has been important in the development of the almost-perfect state is that New England is not America. The road it chose to follow, from the beginning, diverged from the highway of American progress. By voluntary act the Yankee, whose ancestral religion was based on the depravity of human nature, refrained from a good deal that has become indispensable and coercive in America. Thus delivered and refraining, there was space for New England to develop the equilibrium whose accidents had produced a species of almost-perfect state.

So Mr. Mencken's laboriously assembled statistics have recently made clear various superficial ways in which the burnt-out, frustrated, and neurotic province must be called the foremost civilization in These States. And as I write, Mr. Allen Tate has just explained a difference, not quite clear to me, between regionalism and sectionalism. I do not quite understand the difference, but I do make out that it's now orthodox and even virtuous to be sectional. . . . I am encouraged to apply for a union card. The Yankees and I seem to be in good standing again.

II

In New England the mills idled and passed their dividends. The four-per-cents decayed. The trust funds melted. Outside, the American empire was conceived, was born, and attained its adolescence. Its goods and capital overspread the earth. Detroit was a holy city. The abolition of poverty drew near, and the empire's twilight flared in murky scarlet. Then it was October, 1929, and midnight. . . . Novel paragraphs worked their way into a press that had long ignored the section it now reported. Business was sick, but New England business, we heard, wasn't quite so sick. Panic possessed America, but New England wasn't quite so scared. The depression wasn't quite so bad in New England, despair wasn't quite so black, the nightmare wasn't quite so ghastly. What the press missed was its chance for a pretty study in comparatives. How, indeed, should hard times terrify New England? It had had hard times for sixty years — in one way or another for three hundred years. It had had to find a way to endure a perpetual depression, and had found it. It began to look as though the bankrupt nation might learn something from New England.

Some time ago I drove over December roads to the village in northern Vermont where I spend my summers. Naturally, I called on Jason, who is my neighbor there. Evergreen boughs were piled as high as the windows outside his house; the first snow was on them, and its successors would make them an insulation that would be expensive in the city. Piles of maple and birch logs had grown up back of the shed; they would increase through early January, for they are the fuel that Jason burns all year round. Under the floor of another shed was a pit that held potatoes, cabbages, and beets. Emma, who is Jason's wife, had filled her pantry with jars of home-grown corn, string beans, carrots, and a little fruit. She was making bread and doughnuts when I arrived. We had them for dinner, with cabbage, some of the string beans, and a rabbit stew. Jason had shot a couple of rabbits, and

Emma explained how welcome they were. They didn't get much meat, she said; the deer Jason killed a few weeks before had been a life-saver.

I stayed the night at Jason's, slept on a feather bed, ate a breakfast which included doughnuts and pumpkin pie, and came away with a dazed realization that I had visited a household which was wholly secure. There was no strain here; no one felt apprehensive of the future. Jason lives far below "the American standard," yet he lives in comfort and security. He is so little of an economic entity that he can hardly be classed as what the liberal journals call a "peasant"; yet more than anyone else I know, he lives what those same periodicals call "the good life." He has lived here for fifty years and his forebears for sixty more, coming from more southerly portions of Vermont where the breed had already spent a century. During that time the same liberty, tenacity, and success have formed a continuity of some importance.

Jason owns about seventy acres of hillside, sloping down to an exquisite lake. He considers that, in view of his improvements, he would have to get two thousand dollars for the place if he were to sell it. Part of it is pasture for his horse and cow. Part of it is garden; enormous labor forces the thin soil to produce the vegetables that Emma cans. The rest is wood lot, for fuel, and sugar bush for Jason's one marketable crop. The maples produce, in syrup and sugar, an annual yield of from one hundred and fifty to two hundred dollars — about one half of all the cash that Jason handles in a year. A few days of labor on the roads bring in a little more, and during the summer he does odd jobs for such aliens as I. His earnings and his one crop bring him perhaps four hundred dollars a year, seldom or never more, but frequently less. On such an income, less than a fifth of what Mr. Hoover's Department of Commerce estimated to be the minimum capable of supporting an American family, Jason has brought up his children in health, comfort, and contentment.

There are thousands like Jason on the hillside farms of Vermont, New Hampshire, and western Massachusetts, and there have been for three centuries. They have never thrown themselves upon the charity of the nation. They have never assaulted Congress, demanding a place at the national trough. Wave after wave of clamor, prayer, and desperation has crossed the farmsteads of the midland, where the thinnest soil is forty feet deep and the climate will grow anything; but from this frigid north, this six-inch soil sifted among boulders, has come no screaming for relief. The breed has clung to its uplands, and solvency has been its righteousness and independence has been its pride. The uplands have kept their walls plumb, their barns painted, their farms unmortgaged. Somehow, out of nothing at all, they have taxed themselves for the invisible State. The district nurse makes her rounds. The town roads are hard. The white schoolhouse sends its products to the crossroads high school and on to the university. The inspector calls and tests the family cow; State bulletins reach the mailbox at the corner. The crippled and the superannuated are secure.

One of Mr. Mencken's incidental revelations provides a succinct, if vulgar, summary of the statistics that verify it; if you want to be listed in *Who's Who in America* your first step should be to get yourself born in Vermont, and three of the next five best birthplaces are New England States. More briefly still: here are people who have mastered the conditions of their life. With natural resources the poorest in the Union, with an economic system incapable of exploitation, in a geography and climate that make necessary for survival the very extreme of effort, they have erected their State and made it lovely. They have forfeited the wealth and advertisement and glamorous turmoil of other sections, but they have preserved freedom and security. The basis is men who must make their way as individuals, but the communism of the poor exists also. If Jason falls ill he will be cared for; if his one crop fails his neighbors will find food for his family; if he dies his widow (who will never be a pauper) will find the town putting at her disposal a means of making her way. . . . I cannot imagine a change in the social order that would much alter this way of life. I cannot imagine a perfected state that could improve upon it.

These were hard times, I said to Jason. He agreed, ramming cheap tobacco into his corncob pipe. Yes, hard times. Nothing to do, though, but pull in your belt and hang on. Some folks thought it might be good to move ten or fifteen miles north, over the line into Canady. But on the whole, no — not for Jason. He and his pa had made a living from this place for seventy years. He couldn't remember any times that hadn't been hard. He went into a discussion of Congress, so much more intelligent, so much less deluded by wishfulness than those I listen to in literary speak-easies in New York. This lapsed, and he began to talk at his ease, with the undeluded humor of his breed. It is the oldest humor in America, a realism born of the granite hills, a rock-bottom wisdom. He was an un-American anomaly as 1931 drifted to its close in panic and despair — a free man, self-reliant, sure of his world, unfrightened by the future.

He has what America, in our time and most of its past, has tragically lacked — he has the sense of reality. The buffalo coat he wore when we looked at his sugar bush is in its third generation in his family, having had I do not know how many owners before it strangely reached New England from the plains. I do not know how long it is since Emma bought a union suit, but I am sure that need dictated its purchase, not fashion or advertising. Here are rag rugs she has made from garments whose other usefulness was ended; here are carpets that were nailed long years on her grandmother's floor. The pans above her sink date from no ascertainable period; she and her daughters will use them a long time yet, and no salesman will ever bring color into her kitchen. Jason has patched and varnished this rocker, and Emma has renewed its cushions innumerable times. The trademark on Jason's wagon is that of a factory which has not existed for forty years. Jason does not know how many shafts he has made for it; he has patched the bed, bent iron for the running gear, set new tires on the wheels perhaps ten times. Now he contemplates putting the bed and shafts on the frame of an old Ford and will move his loads on rubber tires.

A squalid picture, a summary of penny-pinching poverty that degrades the human spirit? Not unless you have been victimized by what has never deluded Jason and Vermont. To this breed, goods, wares, chattels, the products of the industrial age, have been instrumentalities of living, not life itself. Goods are something which are to be used; they are not the measure of happiness and success. While America has roared through a prosperity based on a conception of goods as wealth-begetting waste, while it has pricked itself to an accelerating consumption that has progressively lowered quality, while its solvency has depended on a geometrical progression of these evils, the granite uplands have enforced a different standard on their inhabitants. Debts, these farmers know, must eventually be settled. It would be pleasant to wear silk stockings, but it is better to pay your taxes. It would be nice to substitute a new car for the 1922 model that came here at third hand, but it is better to be free of chattel mortgages. It would be nice to have steak for supper and go to Lyndonville for the movie. But at four hundred a year and with the granite knowledge that one must not live beyond one's means — well, rabbits are good food, and from this cannily sited kitchen window sunset over the lake is good to look at.

Neatness, my guild assures us, proceeds from a most repulsive subliminal guilt. Maybe; but these white farmhouses with their scrubbed and polished interiors are very lovely. Also the peasants are the enemies of beauty in our day, but somehow their houses invariably stand where the hills pull together in natural composition and a vista carries the eye onward past the lake. Their ancestral religion told them that the world is a battleground whereon mankind is sentenced to defeat — an idea not inappropriate to the granite against which they must make their way. By the granite they have lived on for three centuries, tightening their belts and hanging on, by the sense of what is real. They are the base of the Yankee commonwealth, and America, staring apprehensively through fog that may not lift in this generation, may find their knowledge of hard things more than a little useful.

III

Since we do not believe in perfect states or in the beautiful simplicities, composed by right ideas, it would be silly to expect the Yankee to be a complete realist. He has ideas about himself which are almost as romantic as those the intellectuals have developed about him. He considers himself a cool, reticent person, dwelling in iron restraint, sparse of speech, intensely self-controlled; whereas he has no reserve whatever, indulges his emotions as flagrantly as a movie queen, and at every level, from the upland farms to the Beacon Street clubs, talks endlessly, shrilly, with a spring-flood garrulity that amazes and appalls this apprentice, who was born to the thrift of Rocky Mountain talk. He thinks that his wealthy burghers are an aristocracy, and the burghers, who share that illusion, consider their mulishness a reasoned, enlightened conservatism of great philosophical value to the State. He thinks that his bourgeoisie possesses a tradition of intelligence and a praiseworthy thirst for culture; whereas it has only a habit of joining societies and a masochistic pleasure in tormenting itself with bad music which it does not understand and worse books which it cannot approve. He thinks that he is set apart in lonely pride to guard the last pure blood in America; whereas he has absorbed and assimilated threescore immigrations in three centuries. Recognizing his social provinciality, he thinks that he is, nevertheless, an internationalist of the intellect; whereas his mind has an indurated parochialism that makes a Kansan's or a Virginian's seem cosmopolitan. That is what is important about his mind.

Nevertheless, he is fundamentally a realist, and these illusions are harmonious in the Yankee nature. Accidental by-products of that nature, of these qualities as well as more substantial ones, have produced the Yankee commonwealth, the almost-perfect state.

Let us begin with Cambridge's dead end streets, which Mr. Lewis Mumford was recently commending. Mr. Mumford, who agitates for the perfected municipalities of the future, had been looking at Brattle Street, Concord Avenue, and the little streets that wander off them but end without joining them together. He believes that cities must be planned so that quiet, safety, and seclusion will be assured their inhabitants. In the automobile age, highways must be constructed for through traffic, while the streets on which people live must receive only the necessary traffic of their own cars and those which make deliveries to their houses.

Our little dead end streets accomplish that purpose perfectly. They are safe and quiet and they seem to Mr. Mumford a praiseworthy anticipation of the machine age. They aren't that, of course. Their landscaped crookedness represents the wanderings of Cambridge cows and the strife of Yankee heirs when estates were settled. They come to dead ends not because a prophet foresaw Henry Ford, but because some primordial Cambridge individualist put up a spite fence or fought a victorious court action against the condemnation of his property. Similarly, though modern highways allow locust-swarms of cars to approach Boston, its downtown streets will never experience Fifth Avenue's paralysis. Yankee mechanics, going homeward across marshes, laid them down; a convulsion of nature could not straighten or widen them, and accident anticipated Mr. Stuart Chase's omnipotent engineer who would plan the almost-perfect city.

I cannot praise some aspects of the Yankee city. Such ulcerous growths of industrial New England as Lowell, Lawrence, Lynn, Pawtucket, Woonsocket, and Chelsea seem the products of nightmare. To spend a day in Fall River is to realize how limited were the imaginations of the poets who have described hell. It is only when one remembers Newark, Syracuse, Pittsburgh, West Philadelphia, Gary, Hammond, Akron, and South Bend that this leprosy seems tolerable. The refuse of industrialism knows no sectional boundaries and is common to all America. It could be soundly argued that the New England debris is not so awful as that elsewhere — not so hideous as upper New Jersey or so terrifying as the New South. It could be shown that the feeble efforts of society to cope with this disease are not so feeble here as elsewhere. But realism has a sounder knowledge: industrial leadership has passed from New England,

and its disease will wane. Lowell will slide into the Merrimac, and the salt marsh will once more cover Lynn – or nearly so. They will recede; the unpolluted sea air will blow over them, and the Yankee nature will reclaim its own.

Consider one civic flowering of the Yankee nature on a lowly level. The Yankee has always done his major sinning in distant places. A century ago waterside dives across the world welcomed the roistering of Salem fo'c'sle hands, who in due time came back and married Prudence or Priscilla and took up a hillside farm, argued conservatively in town meeting, and joined the church. The righteous-enough have called this hypocrisy. Still, it made the hillside farms peaceful, and if we must go to New York for our conspicuous sinning to-day, Boston is thereby preserved from speak-easy life. Do not misunderstand me: the thirsty wayfarer need not suffer, and I shall be happy to supply addresses to visitors. But there is no place where you can entertain a New Yorker as he entertains you when you visit his home town. No ritual of introduction and recognition, no transformed brownstone fronts with bars and murals and ten-dollar Clos Ste. Odile and fifteen-dollar Berncasteler Riesling, no stratified social order following the geography of streets and the mechanization of amour. Boston throws its parties at home. The loss is perceptible but the gain is tremendous. Drinking retains the decency, the personality of private hospitality, which is something; and the social implications of the speak-easy do not exist, which is far more. A city in which there are practically no speak-easies. A city in which one does not eat and drink or meet one's friends or conduct one's love affairs at Jody's place or Number 47. A community life conducted without reference to the obligations of speak-easy entertainment. . . . Problems of noise and expense, of stridency and nerve-fag and disintegration, of extravagance and display and impersonality, have been solved by a Yankee trait that avoided creating them.

But take the Yankee nature at a higher level — the sense of the community. I know a Middle Westerner who, graduating from medical school with distinction, came to Boston to study under a great surgeon. He has finished his work now and is going to begin practising. He considered Chicago but has finally determined upon New York. The rewards of distinction are highest there. Not Boston — oh, not by any means. Boston fees are ridiculously small, and Boston specialists neglect to capitalize their skill. They waste time in free clinics, in research laboratories, on commissions for the investigation of poliomyelitis or rheumatic fever or cancer or glaucoma — all highly commendable for the undistinguished, the rank and file, but very foolish for the truly great, since they may treat millionaires. My friend will be, when his chief dies, America's leading surgeon in his specialty. So he goes to New York — and, I think, something about the Yankee commonwealth is implicit in that decision. . . . In Chicago a member of my family required the services of a specialist. The doctor grumbled about treating the family of a college teacher, whose trade proclaimed his income, but there was something about ethics and the Hippocratic oath and so he took the case. He did his work hastily, botched the job and, after inquiring the exact figures of my income, charged me one fourth of a year's salary and said he would write off the rest to charity. So in due time a Boston specialist had to do the job over again and spend more than a year in treatments which, because his predecessor had bungled, required close individual attention and the long, costly technique of the laboratory. His fee, though my income had quadrupled, was one fifth of the Chicago man's and, because the case was a problem rather than a potential fee, he performed the cure. He had the obstinacy of Boston doctors, the conservative notion that medicine is a profession of healing and not an investment trust.

The Yankee doctors are citizens of the invisible state. The drug list of the Massachusetts General Hospital is about one fourth as long as that of the Presbyterian Hospital in New York; medicine has its fads as often as architecture, and the Yankee mulishness avoids fads. But the researches go on, and students come from all over the world, and somehow these obstinate physicians fail to lose their preëminence though they lag mightily behind in the possession of Rolls-Royces. Citizenship shows up in them, and New England witnesses what America has not seen for a long time — the wrath of doctors, spoken in public places, against abuses. Yankee foresight carries them into the slums, where they lose money but forestall plague and, incidentally, relieve suffering. Yankee geniality makes them friends of their patients, and we of the little bourgeoisie find that the terror of disease is allayed for us so far as may be. . . . I smoke a cigarette with the pediatrician who, at five dollars instead of twenty-five, pays a monthly visit to my infant son. I mention group medicine, now much discussed, and he explodes. "Hell! If I find a tumor in your gut [the Yankee tang] shall I send you to Smith because he's the best gut-opener in Boston, or shall I send you to Jones because he's in my office?" A problem in sociology receives its Yankee dismissal, and the pediatrician departs for the East End, where he manages a foundation that promotes the respectable adoption of foundlings. It keeps him from the golf course, and his waistline thickens; but he must maintain his citizenship in the Yankee commonwealth. Or my furnace man develops a queer pain, and I send him to the head physician of a great hospital. He is kept in an observation ward, where for some weeks all the resources of the laboratory are applied. Finally an operation is performed, and he goes to a camp in Maine to recuperate. No medical man receives a cent, and the hospital fees are paid from a fund created in 1842 to care for the moral welfare of canal-boat men. He will continue to tend furnaces for a long time yet. But what, I wonder, would be done for him in a perfect state — Mr. Swope's or Mr. Hoover's or Comrade Stalin's — that the almost-perfect state has failed to do?

It is this Yankee citizenship that has created, upon the granite base, the Yankee commonwealth. Our governments are corrupt — not uniquely in America or history — but somehow they govern. Racketeers exist but somehow they do not take over our municipalities. Fortunes are made from city contracts, but somehow our garbage is collected and our streets are swept. Sojourn in Philadelphia or New York and then come back to Boston — see order in place of anarchy, clean brick and stone in place of grime, washed asphalt in place of offal. Babies starve in Yankee slums and rachitic children play round the statues of our great, but not so many nor so hopelessly. The citizens have no hope of perfection, and Mr. Hoover's abolition of poverty found few adherents among them; but, as Mr. Mencken's figures show, they have made the start. Something toward a solution of the problem of how to live in decent cities has been here worked out. . . . Another friend of mine, a lawyer, possesses a divided self that beautifully exhibits the Yankee commonwealth. Professionally he creates trusts for the protection of his clients' heirs, and conscientiously forbids the trustees to invest in the securities of Massachusetts corporations. State socialism, he is sure, has fatally encroached on their profits. Then, the business day over, he enthusiastically pursues his lifelong avocation — agitating for labor and pension laws that will more drastically cut down those profits.

Clearly, this is not Utopia, but it is a citizenship, and it glances toward the almost-perfect state.

IV

Drive southeastward from the Vermont uplands toward Boston, through a countryside where the white steeples rise across the not accidental vistas of village greens. It is here that, while the empire roared away elsewhere, the Yankee learned the equilibrium of his estate. Here is the New England town, the creation of the Yankee nature, which exists as something the empire has forever passed by. There are no booms here. The huntsmen are up in Chicago, and they are already past to-day's high-pressure drive in Kansas City, but in New England who can ever share an expectation of bonanza again?

Here are the little mills that squatted beside a waterfall and for some generations sent out their trickles of stockings and percales. Manchester and New Bedford, Lowell and Lawrence absorbed them in the end, and now these places go down in turn before the New South. So the little mills close up; shreds of belting hang from their pulleys, and bats emerge from windows that will never again be glazed. Dover is only a pleasant place which had an Indian attack once and has a handful of beautiful houses now. Orford ships no products southward, but the loveliest mall in America drowses under its elms, undisturbed when the wind brings across the Connecticut the whistles of the railroad it would not suffer to cross its borders. The last tall masts have slipped out of Salem Harbor, and Hawthorne's ghost is more peaceful in the Custom House than ever those living ghosts were among whose dusty papers he found an initial bound with tarnished gold. Here are fifty inlets once resonant with hammers pounding

good white oak, once uproarious when new vessels slipped
down the ways. They are marshes now, and the high streets
of Portsmouth and Newburyport remember a life once rich
in the grain and wholly free of the repressions Puritans are
supposed to have obeyed. And down their high streets will
never come a procession of real estate men, promoters, financiers, and fly-by-nights.

America is rachitic with the disease of Bigness, but New
England has built up immunity against the plague. It is impossible to imagine Concord tattooing its lowlands with
white stakes, calling itself "Villa Superba: The Sunlight City
of Happy Kiddies and Cheap Labor," and loosing a thousand
rabid salesmen to barter lots on a Vista Paul Revere or a
Boulevarde de Ye Olde Inne to its own inhabitants or suckers
making the grand tour. There have been factories, of a kind,
at Easthampton and Deerfield for a hundred years, but their
Chambers of Commerce will never defile their approaches
with billboards inviting the manufacturer of dinguses to
"locate here and grow up with the livest community in God's
country." Pomfret or Tiverton or Pittsfield will never set
itself a booster's ideal, "One Hundred Thousand by 1940."
Bigness, growth, expansion, the doubling of last year's quota,
the subdivision of this year's swamps, the running round in
circles and yelling about Progress and the Future of Zenith
— from these and from their catastrophic end, New England
is delivered for all time.

Here, if you have a Buick income, you do not buy a Cadil-
lac to keep your self-respect. You buy a Chevrolet and,
uniquely in America, keep it year after year without hearing
that thrift is a vice, a seditious, probably Soviet-inspired assault on the national honor. The superannuation of straight-
eights and the shift from transparent velvet to suède lace are
not imperatives. You paint the Bulfinch front; you do not

tear it down. You have your shoes pegged while the uppers remain good. You patch the highway; you do not rip it out. . . . The town abides. No Traveler's Rest with an arcade of self-service hot dogs and powder puffs will ever be reared on the Common. The white steeples rise at the far end, and the white houses of the little streets that lead into it are buried in syringa and forsythia, hollyhocks, Dorothy Perkinses, and the blooms of rock gardens. Soap, paint, and Yankee fanaticism have made an orderly loveliness not to be found elsewhere in America. The town is beautiful, and something more. Boys toss baseballs on the Common, infants tan themselves in safety, dogs conduct their tunneling and exploration. The Common and its tributary streets are quiet. Beneath the exterior, an efficient organization deals with the problems of the community; the townsman contributes his share but mainly he lives here, uncrowded. There is time; there is room; there is even, of a kind, peace. A society is here founded on granite. No one supposes it is perfect. It is not an experiment; it was not planned by enthusiasts or engineers or prophets of any kind. But out of the Yankee nature and the procession of blind force somehow dignity and community decency were here evolved.

The New England town, that is, has adjusted itself to the conditions of its life. It is a finished place. Concord was Concord when Newark was a pup, the song almost says; and Shirley will be Shirley when Great Neck is swallowed up. The butcher sells meat to his townsmen; he does not attempt exports to the Argentine. The turning-mill makes cupboards and cabinets for the local demand; it does not expand into the gadget business, and so throws no families on the town when next year's fashion demands gadgets of aluminum. Mr. Stuart Chase went to Mexico to find a community whose trades supported one another in something like security. He found it, but recorded his hope that some day the Mexicans would have dentists and bathtubs. In our imperfect way, we could have shown Mr. Chase his desire. The butcher's boy grows up to be a butcher, not a merchant prince; and meanwhile his teeth are taken care of and he bathes in porcelain, though while the white tub continues to hold water he will not bathe in something mauve or green that reproduces motifs from a Medici tomb. He has no hope of unearned increment when a hundred thousand shall have come to Shirley in 1940, but he has sunlight and clean air, quiet, a kind of safety, and leisure for his friends. You will not find him in Los Angeles — and the perfect state could offer him nothing that is denied him in Shirley.

New England is a finished place. Its destiny is that of Florence or Venice, not Milan, while the American empire careens onward toward its unpredicted end. The Yankee capitalist will continue to invest in that empire, while he can, so that the future will have its echoes from the past, and an occasional Union Stockyards, Burlington, or United Fruit will demonstrate that his qualities are his own. But he, who once banked for the nation, will never bank for it again. The Yankee manufacturer will compete less and less with the empire. He will continue those specialties for which his skills and geography best fit him, but mainly he will be a part of his section's symbiosis. To find his market in his province, to sustain what sustains him, to desire little more, to expect even less — that is his necessity, but it implies the security of being able to look with indifference on the mirage that lures the empire on. The section becomes an economic system, a unity; it adjusts itself in terms of its own needs and powers.

The desire of growth and domination is removed from it — and with the desire is removed also their damnation. It will tranquilly, if aloofly, observe whatever America in the future does and becomes, but it is withdrawn from competition in that future. Almost alone in America, it has tradition, continuity. Not a tradition that everyone can admire, not a continuity of perfection, but something fixed and permanent in the flux of change and drift. It is the first American section to be finished, to achieve stability in the conditions of its life. It is the first old civilization, the first permanent civilization in America.

It will remain, of course, the place where America is educated, for the preëminence of its schools and colleges must increase with stability, and the place which America visits for recreation and for the intangible values of finished things. It will be the elder glory of America, free of smoke and clamor, to which the tourist comes to restore his spirit by experiencing quiet, ease, white steeples, and the release that withdrawal from an empire brings. It will be the marble pillars rising above the nation's port.

Or if not, if the world indeed faces into darkness, New England has the resources of the Yankee nature. They are not only the will to tighten one's belt and hang on. They contain the wisdom of three centuries whose teaching was, finally, defeat. They contain the dynamics of a religion which verified experience by proclaiming that man is depraved, that his ways are evil, and that his end must be eternal loss. Religion develops into the cynicism of proved things, and the Yankee has experienced nothing but what he was taught to expect. Out of this wisdom, in his frigid climate, against the resistance of his granite fields, he built his commonwealth. It was a superb equipment for his past; it may not be a futile one for our future.

Thinking about America

~~~~~~

I

DURING the War vaudeville managers were accustomed to save a weak act by appealing to the dominant sentiments of the time. A team of ham acrobats or a group of badly trained seals were coached to come into their finale brandishing the Stars and Stripes. When a mind reader, a hoofer, or a whisky tenor seemed unlikely to make his own way the orchestra was cued to play the "Star-Spangled Banner" at curtainfall. Universally effective during wartime, the practice has by no means lost its value now, and it may be supposed that the empiricism of theater managers represents a sound principle of psychology. It does. The flag is irrelevant to acrobatic skill and the "Star-Spangled Banner" has no relation to a hoofer's art, but relevancy and relationship are supplied by the logic of sentiment. Because the flag and the anthem symbolize to the audience certain sentiments which they possess, they promptly identify those sentiments with the performers, and so break into applause. Thus stated, the principle is seen to be one of the most useful in the literary world.

The first chapter of a book which has been widely recommended to college freshmen is called "The Origins of the American Mind." Halfway down the first page the author states his intention of finding those origins. In the course of the book he finds them, describes the American mind in detail, and on the basis of his description proves many interesting theses about the history and civilization of the United States. But the title of the first chapter states a fallacy that vitiates the whole book, "The Origins of the American Mind." It seems not to have occurred to the author that his book was dedicated to a description of something which does not exist, or that his analysis of the non-existent can have no meaning. For, of course, there is no such thing as the American mind. The phrase represents to any given person merely a group of his private sentiments, and though it may be used to symbolize those sentiments for people who share them, it is barren of meaning to people who do not. Its meaning, that is, does not derive from any objective thing but depends on the logic of sentiment, precisely like the applause that greets a ham actor waving a flag.

The fallacy is elementary but, because it has been so widespread in contemporary thinking, it may be examined at some length. If we set out to demonstrate the existence of the American mind we may, of course, establish it by definition, a procedure to which no objection may be made. We may say, for example, that we shall consider Benjamin Franklin a representative American, and that we shall call minds which are like his American minds, those unlike his being necessarily non-American. We may now make generalizations about the American mind and they will be unexceptionable so long as we hold rigidly to our definition — we

must say nothing about the American mind that is not true of
Franklin's mind. But now we think of one of Franklin's
contemporaries, Jonathan Edwards, who was quite as characteristic an American as he. It, therefore, seems desirable to
enlarge our definition to include Edwards; but since two
minds could not readily be more different than his and Franklin's, our definition becomes untrustworthy. It can justify
few generalizations, and any statement we may make on the
basis of it is likely to be challenged on the ground that,
though true of Edwards or of Franklin, it is not true of the
other one, and is, therefore, untrue of the American mind.
But J. Hector St. John Crèvecœur, a contemporary of Franklin and Edwards, was a characteristic American, and so was
Samuel Adams, and it is clear that their minds cannot be
called similar to each other or to those already included in
our definition, or to either of them. If the definition is expanded to anatomize these four as the American mind it has
already become almost meaningless, since what must be disregarded is much greater than what they can be shown to
have in common. What can be said about the American mind
on the basis of these irreconcilables? Nothing with certainty
and very little with sense. Add now such characteristic
American contemporaries as Count Rumford, Lorenzo Dow,
Thomas Jefferson, Daniel Boone, Benjamin Rush, Thomas
Paine, Alexander Hamilton, John Sevier, Robert Morris,
Hugh Henry Brackenridge, William Findley, James Mc-
Gready, John Hancock, Mother Ann Lee, John Singleton
Copley, Aaron Burr, and Manuel Lisa. All generalization has
ceased to be possible; the common characteristics of these
persons, from which the American mind is to be derived,
are so purely formal that nothing can be said except that
they were all bipeds and spoke more or less similar dialects
of English. To select a few characteristics of some of them

and to ignore the opposite characteristics of others would be farcical. Yet analysts of the American mind ask their fiction to harmonize such disparate Americans as these, and then extend it backward to cover the colonies for a century and a half, and require people who quarreled endlessly with one another to agree for the sake of sweet hypothesis. Thereupon, this essence having been distilled, they find it capable of reducing to a unity of indigenous American characteristics such intelligences as Emerson and Henry Ford, Brigham Young and Abraham Lincoln, Kit Carson and the late Gamaliel Bradford, Willard Gibbs and Frances E. Willard, Francis Grierson and Thomas A. Edison, Henry James and Mary Baker Eddy, Ulysses S. Grant and Henry Adams, Bronson Alcott and Jesse James, Andrew Mellon and Eugene V. Debs, John Humphrey Noyes and Commodore Vanderbilt, Charles A. Lindbergh and Julia Ward Howe, Jefferson Davis and Babe Ruth and the Fox sisters and Henry George and Edgar Allan Poe and John D. Rockefeller and William Lloyd Garrison and Jim Bridger and Emily Dickinson and Theodore Roosevelt and Mae West.

What any two of these minds have in common for the distillation of a national mind is enormously diluted when any third one is added, till a generalization about any six of them is worthless. The American mind thus comes down to the human mind; but it was in an effort to distinguish from the latter what was unique in the former that the original effort was made. Here the logic of sentiment begins to operate. Since the heterogeneity of the Americans cannot be reduced, the phrase "the American mind" corresponds to nothing real; but it is given a subjective meaning by a very simple mechanism.

The person who goes in search of the American mind has certain sentiments about it and, usually, wants to say certain things about it. The phrase represents those sentiments, and he selects from America or the Americans whatever corresponds to them and dismisses the rest. That selection and dismissal make the phrase a symbol, and to personify it requires but a short step beyond. Personification having occurred, the phrase has a life of its own and one may reason about it as if it were an entity, as if it really existed. Although there is no such thing as the American mind, the searcher may think beautifully about it. The abstraction is in accord with his sentiments: when he says something about the American mind he is really saying "Certain aspects of America or of certain American minds, which I prefer to consider, excluding those which differ from or contradict them, fulfill my ideas of what the American mind should be." The assertion is disarming, but it would serve as a warning that what he alleges about America is subjective — which is why it is never made. It shows that appeal is being made not to objective fact, to history, sociology, or psychology, to the United States and its inhabitants — but only to similar sentiments. Whoever has such sentiments about those selected aspects will probably applaud as the curtain comes down. But a person who does not share them, together with one who is thinking objectively about America or the Americans, will find himself trying to find meaning where no meaning is possible. To such a person the search for the American mind, whether accompanied by the "Star-Spangled Banner" or the "Internationale," will be only an annoying kind of nonsense.

II

For many years the search for the American mind — and such similar personifications as "the American point of view," "the soul of America," and "the American experience" — was a prerogative of politicians, clerical spellbinders, and foreigners, especially Englishmen, on tour. About 1914, however, a number of literary critics, feeling confident that an acquaintance with a number of American novels and essays gave them authority about the past, undertook to re-write American history in accordance with their sentiments. Their apprenticeship, observe, had been served in literary criticism, a profession in which impreciseness of idea is a virtue and a generalized sentiment is much better than a fact. It followed that the history they wrote was an "interpreta-tion," a search for symbols that could be personified.

It would be unsafe to generalize about the literary mind, but the books of these critics are tangible data and subject to analysis. They reveal a group of curiously disparate senti-ments which, nevertheless, have in common a desire to pro-ject their prejudices on the past in the shape of general ideas. In addition, they have in common an invincible ignorance of the history they are endeavoring to rewrite. Ignorance is not a satisfactory equipment for a historian, and it is not helped much by disdain of the methods and material of history. The literary historian practises intuition as a method of research. He has frequently announced his superiority to facts and customarily dismisses as a pedant the historian who insists on saying nothing that facts do not justify. He prefers truths — poetic perceptions, guesses, and beautiful notions.

He prefers, that is, the literary idea. His criteria are those of literary criticism, of fantasy and poetic necessity, not those of the objective world. The symbol is the final authority. When Mr. Mumford, for instance, symbolizes his sentiments about the Middle Ages by remarking that their world went to hell when people began to hang clocks in steeples, he is within the privileges of a poet. The idea has much senti-mental force and suggests a great many pleasing and persuasive if somewhat indefinite emotions: in literary criticism, therefore, it has absolute validity. But when a writer forsakes literary criticism in order to make statements of fact about the past he must meet other criteria than those of pleasure and persuasiveness. For the past is a fact of experience. The events that happened during it actually happened and, within varying limits, are recoverable. A statement about it is worth nothing, is worth less than nothing, if it does not correspond to the recoverable facts. When you set out to write history, no poetry however beautiful and no sentiments however commendable can be substituted for statements of fact.

Such literary ideas about America may be illustrated, on a simple level, by Mrs. Mary Austin's doctrine of occupational rhythms. Mrs. Austin feels deeply that the rhythms of our daily lives must have a formative effect on our minds and so on our speech and writing. It is a pleasing idea, and so in the domain of literary criticism it is valid. But the logic of sentiment projects it into the area of fact. The "must be" of poetry becomes the "has been" of history. Lincoln at the dedication of the Gettysburg cemetery, Mrs. Austin says, "fell unconsciously into the stride of one walking a woodland path with an axe on his shoulder." To illustrate the rhythm of that stride forming the rhythm of speech, she quotes from the peroration of the Gettysburg address, setting it off as follows: —

> It is rather for us
> Here to be dedicated to the great task
> Remaining before us;
> That from these honored dead we take
> Renewed devotion to that cause
> For which they gave the last full measure of devotion.
> That we here highly resolve
> That these dead shall not have died in vain;

> That this nation under God
> Shall have a new birth of freedom.

It is probably pedantic to wonder why the rhythm of one of Lincoln's occupations should form this speech to the exclusion of his experiences as a storekeeper, flatboatman, lawyer, and politician, and to inquire just how the axe on the shoulder is discernible or how the path is shown to be in the woodland. It is not pedantic, however, to point out that in her quotation Mrs. Austin twice departs from the text of the speech [1] and that one departure alters the rhythm, nor is it pedantic to bring what she says to the test of fact. If the passage means anything outside of poetry, it means that the quoted words have the same rhythm as a man walking. It means that his steps mark the accent of the lines. Well, anyone who cares to make the experiment will find out that they cannot be walked.

Mrs. Austin goes on: —

Thus the rail splitter arrives at his goal with the up-swing and the down-stroke: —

> That government of the people
> For the people
> By the people
> Shall not perish from the earth!

And the axe comes to rest on the chopping log while a new length is measured.

[1] The accepted text of the Gettysburg address, the one which is usually reprinted to-day and the one which Mrs. Austin appears to be quoting, is Lincoln's sixth manuscript copy — sent to the Sanitary Fair at Baltimore. It reads "for us to be here dedicated," and "we take increased devotion." The quoted words are unchanged in all the other manuscript copies that still exist and in the only accepted transcript of the speech actually made by a listener at the time of its delivery.

Mrs. Austin here achieves the triumph of misquoting the best-known line ever written by an American.[1] If this means anything it means that logs can be chopped or rails split to the quoted lines. But they cannot be — either by an amateur or by a woodsman. And if they cannot be, what happens to Mrs. Austin's beautiful idea? This I think: it retains its power of evocation as poetry, but in the domain of fact, into which she projects it by discovering the rhythms of woodchopping in the Gettysburg address, it is utter nonsense.

That is a comparatively simple projection of a literary idea into history, but it shows the process clearly. Because it is beautiful (*i. e.*, because it accords with certain sentiments) it must be true, and because it must be true, therefore it is true. The same process appears in, for instance, Mr. Lewis Mumford's discovery of the Golden Day in American life. This is an effort to find a place and a time in American history which please the discoverer (accord with his sentiments), so that by describing them he will be able to express his dislike of other portions of that history. It is a selective, *a priori* undertaking. By ignoring all parts of the past, all sections of the country, and all Americans that contradict his thesis, Mr. Mumford easily satisfies the requirements of his Golden Day. But it is the Golden Day of Mr. Mumford, not of America, for his analysis disregards all that cannot be harmonized with the thesis. So far as it is history at all, it is a history of Mr. Mumford's sentiments — which are interesting but should not be mistaken for the United States. Mr. William Aylott Orton, on a similar subjective quest, has recently identified another Golden Day in American history. The most interesting aspect of his discovery is the fact that his Golden Day ends just before Mr. Mumford's begins. The

[1] Quoted from *The American Rhythm*, 1923. In 1930 a second, enlarged edition was published: the quoted passages are unchanged.

Regionalists of the South have also produced a Golden Day — in a time and a society antipathetic to both Mr. Orton and Mr. Mumford. . . . It is a characteristic of objective fact that when people refer to it they can, whatever their sentiments, agree on a description of it. No one can object to a critic's writing his emotional autobiography in terms of the United States. It is not autobiography that is objectionable, but the attempt to pass off autobiography as history.

All these literary efforts display a hunger for unity. They are efforts to impose order and simplicity upon an obstinate multiplicity, and their authors are incorrigible monists. The realities of the American past refuse to form coherent sequences, being full of contradictions, disparate elements, eccentric and disruptive forces that war on one another, events and tendencies and personalities that cannot be reduced to formula. Against this multiplicity the monist makes headway by sheer violence of personification. He has his words, his symbols, the embodiment of his sentiments, and by treating the words as things, he is able to perceive a subjective order in the data that refuse to arrange themselves. Mr. V. F. Calverton's effort to force American history into a Marxist commentary on American literature is at once regrettable and absurd. Regrettable because history has not yet adequately studied the inter-class and intra-class struggles in America and their amazing shifts, and could use more analysis from even the simple Marxian formula than they have yet received — and Mr. Calverton thus disregarded a promising opportunity. Absurd because, though engaged in a work of history, he decided to remain within the area of his preconceptions. He was content, that is, to write his history by *a priori* deduction from a half-dozen phrases. Simplification enabled him to reduce the complex and inharmonious class and sectional interests of three centuries to

a simple article of faith, the Marxian Class Struggle. Personification enabled him to make such phrases as "bourgeois
ideology," "bourgeois philosophy," "bourgeois conception
of life" crush the disorderly into order. They are subjective
phrases; they symbolize Mr. Calverton's sentiments but are
barren of meaning. What is "bourgeois"? What is it, especially, when applied to the expansion of a nation across a
continent through three centuries? Mr. Calverton asks us to
assume that the "ideology" of a Salem shipowner of 1800
is reconcilable, even identical, with that of a Charleston factor of 1700 and that of a San Francisco stockbroker of 1900.
This monster of contradiction, even, is not enough, and we
are required to believe that frontiersmen of all sections and
all periods, although mystically opposed to this ideology, also
share and condition it. Well, by convention or agreement,
we might permit the phrase to stand for one of them and so
avoid fallacy, but a statement made about America in terms
of them all can only be preposterous. In three centuries
America has contained not one but fifty bourgeoisies, and
their interests, on which their "ideologies" primarily depend,
have mostly been in violent conflict with one another. To
identify one with another, to detect a fundamental agreement
among them is to make an irreparable blunder. It is to be
struck blind to the realities of history, and to lose the objective world in the delusions of faith or fanaticism.

Mr. Calverton's survey, chasing bourgeois ideology
through American history by means of American literature,
appeared only a few months after Mr. Ludwig Lewisohn
had hunted another personification through the same covert.
Mr. Lewisohn's quarry was the Puritan, and the Puritan
turned out to be a person whose sexual behavior and philosophy Mr. Lewisohn could not bring himself to admire. The
two books may well signify a change in critical fashions. A

good many literary critics before Mr. Lewisohn had denounced America in the name of the Puritan, but it was difficult to get them to agree about the nature of their prey. The Puritan was alleged to be so many incompatible things that he had identity only in the logic of sentiment: he was whatever, at the moment, you happened to dislike in American history. Very possibly, that burden of symbolical cliché may have permanently shifted to the bourgeois ideology. The literary lynching of the Puritan, and especially of his sexual timorousness, Mr. Calverton decides, dealt chiefly with myth. . . . Yes. And the bourgeois ideology?

III

Another of Mr. Calverton's phrases is "frontier individualism," which brings us to the favorite personification of the literary historians. Discovering the frontier something more than a generation after legitimate historians had exhaustively surveyed the facts about it, they have given it a fundamental place in their systems. It has proved possible for historians to arrive at a few generalizations about the frontier. But it has proved possible only by means of a long study of an almost infinite number of facts. When a historian speaks of the frontier he refers to those facts, whereas in the mouth of a literary historian the word means only another projection of his sentiments precisely like "the American mind." It means, that is, another simplicity, another unity — which is to say one more distortion of history.

Let us examine "frontier individualism," a cliché which Mr. Calverton received from a long line of critics. Such a word as "individualism" is dangerously vague; it cannot possibly be qualitative but only at best, and doubtfully, quantitative. Yet the literary historian uses it as if it designated a thing as precisely as the "oxygen" or "acid" of chemistry. There were many frontiers and they differed considerably, and to lump them all together as individualistic is to avoid meaning anything. Are we to think of the individualistic enterprise of bear-hunting, or the coöperative enterprise of roof-raising or tariff-fighting? A man may be one hundred per cent. individualistic on land tenure and zero per cent. individualistic on water rights: is he an individualist or an advocate of community coöperation? The frontier which expropriated Spanish land grants, riparian rights, and the grazing privilege would seem to be notably less individualistic than the one which enforced the right of preëmption. If piratical laissez-faire was characteristic of some frontiers, coöperative enterprise, and even communism, were quite as characteristic of other frontiers. What does the phrase mean? Clearly, whatever sentiments it symbolizes.

The method is to annihiliate by a personification whatever contradicts the literary historian or diminishes the effectiveness of his thesis. Thus the birth of a demi-urge: the "pioneer," a person who went West and created the frontier. To the critic he was one kind of person, a quite simple kind. It is a kind, however, that changes with the nature of the critic's aversions; so that the pioneer who for one analysis is a Rousseauian conducting "an experimental investigation of Nature, Solitude, the Primitive Life," is for the purpose of another a Puritan (a Calvinist, a believer in a completely antagonistic set of ideas) who is in search of the only good that religious people recognize, financial gain. He goes West because he is "unadjusted" or "maladjusted," because he is an economic misfit, because he resents authority or cannot stand discipline, because he is driven to escape reality, because he is under a compulsion to "revert." It turns out, too, with the happiest results, that he is coarse, hard, extraverted, unintelligent, devoid of imagination and culture, resentful and contemptuous of everything he does not understand. He is a pretty accurate summary of the critic's phobias. And he wears well, for throughout history he does not change.

It would be a mistake to expect complexity in the society which so simple a person creates. The life of the frontier, we are told, "is life at a rudimentary animal level, a life that does not rise above the latitude of the spinal column." Frontier society was "an infantile society, infantile in its homicidal impulses, infantile in its mental development, infantile in its humor . . . infantile, in fact, in most of its tastes and interests and preferences." Observe with what assured ease the critic reduces to unity the greatest confusion of cultures, nationalities, and races in modern history, diffused over one of the largest national areas and most diversified geographies in the world, subject to change and circumstance through three centuries. This is literary intuition, and it asks us to suppose that on the frontier, climate, geography, wealth, commerce, and occupation produced no differentiation. All races, all degrees of intelligence, all individual variation, that is, and all the differences of religion and private interest and group effort and civil war were overcome by some process of mystical disintegration. If you remember that, elsewhere in the literary scheme, the frontier is inhabited by a race of obstinate individualists, you are to submerge the recollection in the realization that the logic of sentiment recognizes no contradictions.

One might inquire whether infantile is not an apt adjective to describe a mind which finds chaos so singularly unified. From any point of view such a description of the frontier is naïve; from the historian's point of view it is incomprehensible. A historian does not speak of the frontier's "tastes and interests and preferences." He sees the frontier as many different places in many stages of development, inhabited by many different people with many different kinds and degrees of culture, intelligence, racial tradition, family training, and individual capacity. He cannot speak of the life of the frontier, for he knows many kinds of frontier and many kinds of people living many kinds of lives. He cannot call any of them infantile, for he does not assume that people lapse to an infantile level when they move to a place which a literary critic happens to dislike. He sees many kinds of civilization, many kinds of education, many interests, many institutions, many forces. He deals, that is, with a complexity, with a constantly changing, extremely intricate set of relationships. When he thinks of Timothy Flint, publishing Byron and Shelley and reviewing French politics in his magazine, while the swamps of frontier Cincinnati were still undrained, he does not lump him with a *mangeur du lard* on Black's Fork and say that their mental development was infantile. It is beyond the reach of his integrity to assert that both the squatters of Bayou Tensas and the Chouteau family of frontier St. Louis lived at a rudimentary animal level. In most of the frontier explorers, many of the frontier politicians, many of the frontier teachers and inventors and parsons and organizers — in Ashley and Jedediah Smith, in Jackson and Benton and Lincoln, in Judah and Sutter and Brigham Young — he fails to find evidence of the infantile mind. He does not ignore such a frontiersman as Francis Grierson, or the biography of his neighbors which Grierson wrote, when he considers the spiritual squalor of the frontier. He does not ignore the commonwealths and social institutions which the frontier built when he considers its failure to rise above the level of the spinal column. . . . The frontier is not a person to him; it is a relationship among many variables, and his analysis of it must be complex. To select any one or any group of those variables and to ignore the rest is as ignorant, or as dishonest, as to describe the soil of the frontier as clay or its rock as sandstone. Clay and sandstone, rudimentary animal life and infantile mental development were there — as elsewhere in the known world. But a report which confines itself to either is unusable as fact and childish as judgment.

Ignorance or dishonesty — it is an unpleasant dilemma. Happily, we need not impale the critic on either of its horns, for there is another explanation. His ignorance of history, of course, tends toward maximum, but his profession is the better key to him. He comes to history from the criticism of literature, an activity in which success is attainable by means of sustained thinking. If you sit down and think about a literary problem it will eventually yield. It is because he tries to apply this combination of intuition and introspection as a historical method that he produces his grotesque results. His frontier is just one more unity, another personification, a cliché like "the American mind," significant only as an embodiment of his sentiments.

Method and results are summed up in a passage which one of these critics devotes to the coarsening effects of the frontier on the pioneer, in which he quotes an English traveler's reflections. After looking at the frontier, this traveler decides that man is more virtuous when subjected to culture. He supports his declaration by mentioning the wild strawberry which is insipid in flavor, wild peaches which are tasteless as a turnip, and wild roses which have little or no scent. No historian, I imagine, believes that an analogy from botany is worth much as historical judgment. But such an analogy as this one is a splendid literary idea and so it is irresistible to the literary historian. It is striking and picturesque — it must be true. But even so, it would have been wiser to investigate. For, whatever tasted like turnips on the frontier, wild peaches did not. Peaches are not indigenous to America: there is no such thing as a wild American peach. And the traveler could not even have tasted an "escape"; for if it was frontier, there had not been time for trees to escape from cultivation, and if there had been, the escaped peach does not ripen. Also, some varieties of wild roses have a strong, distinctive perfume. And finally, the wild strawberry has more flavor than the domesticated varieties — which have achieved size, color, texture, and stability at the expense of flavor.

These are facts, the inconvenient data to which the literary historian is superior. The first of them is available in all histories of American horticulture, in all botanies, in most general histories, and even in the encyclopedias. The other two are more accessible still, facts of experience open to everyone who has ever walked across a hillside in June. But the English traveler's literary ideas, exactly opposite to the facts, were persuasive — and they served the critic's purpose. Why, then, should they be verified? His sentiments, in this instance, require wild strawberries to be tasteless, and that ends the matter. He has found a symbol, he has projected his resentments and dislikes. He has written a portion of his autobiography, and the facts of history, an objective pursuit, seem to him trivial and pedantic. They are irrelevant to his higher truth, and, besides, they provide him with no mirror in which to find himself.

IV

These historians divide into sharply differing schools of thought. Each of them has identified and isolated these various phantasms — the American mind, the Puritan, the frontier, the bourgeois ideology, and a good many more. Each one can identify them to the last watermark, and invariably

they turn out to be a summary of the sentiments and prejudices for which the school stands. They are never, by any
chance, the same for two different groups, and so there is
much warfare in the name of heresy. With that term the
somewhat puzzled onlooker at last gets on familiar ground;
it gives him a key to the controversy and he knows what to
expect. He recalls another, earlier argument equally endless
and fundamentally the same. Substance, essence; generation,
creation; emanation, incarnation; *homoousion, homoiousion*
— over these words other generations fought the same battles.
Our historians of the intangible are the Fathers, the School-
men, Eusebius, Athanasius, Peter Abelard, William of Cham-
peaux. It is only an accident of time that has them searching
for the American mind — they are metaphysicians, they
are theologians, and they pursue the *nous* through material
that differs only in appearance from that which their predecessors treated. They work on a plane altogether separated
from the desire of the earthbound for ideas that correspond
to something in the real world. With the history that is the
past of men, ideas, and events they have only a formal relationship: it is the springboard from which they dive into
dogma and system-making. Their significance is primarily
that of the unconscious mind or, if you like, of the soul, not
of logic. And Miss Gertrude Stein, who is the Sibyl of this
age, supplies a description of it. Miss Stein found occasion
to tell Bertrand Russell that a knowledge of the classics was
not essential in the United States. She has Miss Alice B.
Toklas thus report her: "She grew very eloquent on the disembodied abstract quality of the American character and
cited examples mingling automobiles with Emerson and all
proving that they did not need Greek." That is the method
of literary history in America. It is very eloquent. It deals
with disembodied abstract qualities and with such spectral

shapes as the American character. It mingles automobiles with Emerson. And it proves a lot.

It is an attractive and no doubt entertaining pursuit, but it belongs somewhere within the wide, elastic boundaries of literature. Nearly everyone enjoys metaphysical debate, many of us derive great profit from it, and for many people it is the most important thing in the world. Only, metaphysics is not experience, and the philosophy of history is not history. It is nice to be told how imaginative people wish the past had arranged itself or how they can arrange it on their own behalf; but that information differs in important ways from the past. It would, therefore, seem desirable to hold our literary historians to a responsibility at least as strict as that which we try to exact from manufacturers. No code of fair practices in thinking beautifully about America seems practicable; there is no way of insisting that the vendor shall beware. But he is constantly misbranding his product and selling it as something different from what it is, to the possible damage of the consumer. For fraud of that sort neither generous emotion nor sheer ignorance would excuse a manufacturer of canned ham. Why should it excuse the manufacturer of history?

There is an eternal, fundamental, and irreconcilable difference between fantasy, any kind of fantasy, and fact. The fantasies of the literary historian are frequently beautiful and nearly always praiseworthy, but they are a form of protective or of wishful thinking, a form of illusion and even of delusion, and they must be constantly denounced as such. The past of America is immensely complex and immensely at war with itself. No unity exists in it. Its discords and contradictions cannot be harmonized. It cannot be made simple. No one can form it into a system, and any formula that explains it is an hallucination. The person who wants to understand it must enter upon a tedious, rigorous, and almost end-less labor. Without that labor, and without a mind both able and willing to distinguish between the thing that is and the thing that is desired, nothing profitable can be said about our history. With them, nothing whatever can be said that implies simplicity, unity, or beautiful ideas. For that reason, or some other, literary historians have unanimously declined the labor, preferring the *must be* and the *ought to be* to the cold fact. Theirs is the easier method — to think it out. Doubtless that results in comfort of a kind, and in certainty. But also it is a fantasy. No one can object to it as such, but it should be labeled.

FROM *Harper's*, JANUARY 1933

The Skeptical Biographer

I

SOME years ago a new biography of a famous American was published. Most of the subject's life, including behavior of public importance, was explained as the result of the subject's impotence, here for the first time diagnosed. The biographer offered no evidence for his discovery but made the diagnosis by psychoanalyzing what the dead man had written and may be supposed to have said. Evidence exists, but was not mentioned by the biographer, that on two different occasions women were forced to defend themselves against sexual assault by the subject of the biography. There is also in existence an autograph letter written by his wife, whose virtue there is no reason to suspect, in which she tells her mother that she has just had a miscarriage. . . . Another recent biography also diagnoses impotence. Acknowledged and proved descendants of this impotent man are alive to-day. The biographer had neglected to investigate his subject's relations with his slaves. . . . The personality and entire career of an American woman have been explained as the result of a frustrated love affair. Three biographers have identified three different men as her lover. Two of them must necessarily be wrong, but it happens that all three are. She had no love affair. . . . Several studies of Walt Whitman present him as a homosexual. Another study finds that he was "a-sexual," that he was incapable of feeling sexual love. The same evidence is open to all biographers of Whitman.

Classify the foregoing specimens as simple ignorance. What happens in biography when simple ignorance is ornamented by guessing? Well, there is "Ethan Brand," a moral fable by Nathaniel Hawthorne. It has played an important part in two recent biographies, one of Hawthorne, the other of Melville. The lesson of the story is that a search for the unattainable leads to disaster. According to both biographies, Hawthorne wrote it to rebuke if not to repel his friend Melville. He made Melville the hero of "Ethan Brand" in order to discourage Melville's demands for perfect friendship, to indicate to him the folly of metaphysical absolutes, and to assert the boundaries of propriety. This, you will understand, was all very regrettable. It illustrates the Puritanical inhibitions of Hawthorne's nature, and they imply the Philistinism of American life and show that America is hostile to artists. Also, the publication of "Ethan Brand" deeply wounded Melville and helped to bring on the (supposed) despair that kept him silent for a good many years. But "Ethan Brand" was published several months before Hawthorne and Melville met for the first time — before there was any friendship between them, before the famous letters were written. Furthermore, it was written several years before it was published, and had existed in Hawthorne's notebooks for some time before it was written. A little work in a library would have revealed the facts of publication to either biographer, and it would seem fair to require both to be familiar with Hawthorne's notebooks. But, in a condition of ignorance, the guess that the hero of the story must be Melville was too attractive to be resisted.

What, then, about the lighthearted omission of evidence? In a life of General Grant the biographer tells a story which he says is significant, one which was first told by a member of Grant's staff..While a great battle was raging, while hundreds of men were being killed, Grant saw a teamster flogging a horse. He was horrified, and violently rebuked the teamster. And what, for the purposes of the biographer's thesis, does this tale establish? Why, that Grant was insensitive to human suffering but could be horribly upset by the infliction of pain on a horse. He was, says the biographer, a "zoöphile." Perhaps. But a member of General Robert E. Lee's staff tells an exactly similar story about Marse Robert. Was Lee also a "zoöphile"? If he was, just what does the word mean? The biographer must have read the Confederate version. (If he hasn't he has read less about the Civil War than a man should read before he writes a life of Grant.) If the behavior is significant enough to diagnose zoöphily, wasn't he under an implicit obligation to tell us that Lee behaved in exactly the same way? Or was he?

The next step takes us to the distortion of evidence for special effects, to "creative" biography. The term, in our time, has meant the work of Mr. Lytton Strachey, with Maurois and Ludwig following his plow, and after them some seven thousand inconsiderables diluting Strachey to the hundredth attenuation. Mr. Strachey had an enormous reading knowledge of history and literature, a knowledge which tended toward pedantry and preciosity. He possessed also a talent for irony and a prose style of great distinction. For a while he wrote literary criticism, an activity in which uncontrolled speculation is virtuous and responsibility is almost impossible. Then, turning biographer, he published *Eminent Victorians*, and from that moment the minds of dead men have yielded up their secrets to anyone who cared to reach for a pen.

A Strachey biography is an adult form of art, and anyone who happens to know something about its subject may derive from it an intense esthetic pleasure. But God help the man who comes to Strachey ignorant and desirous of learning the truth. Mr. Strachey was not in the truth business. In his last book, to be sure, he was content to be guided by fact — the facts about Elizabeth and Essex were sufficiently sardonic and perfumed and paradoxical for his purposes — but it was not his last book that inspired the seven thousand. His Queen Victoria has very little in common with the actual maiden and wife and widow of Windsor. His Chinese Gordon could never have worn a uniform; his Florence Nightingale is only a series of epigrams about a nurse, and not even that much links his Doctor Arnold with the master of Rugby. These portraits are enormously entertaining. Strachey's pyrotechnic method overwhelms the reader, and his flashes of insight are hardly to be equaled outside of great poetry. But if they are brilliant portraits, they are also studies in deliberate deception. One reason for reading biography may be the desire to know the truth about its subject. Is it a valid reason? Has it any bearing on the conduct of a biographer?

Finally, an inquiry into motives may be made — the motives, that is, not of the subject but of the biographer. It was Mr. Woodward, I believe, who suggested that certain historical personages should be "debunked." So the seven thousand promptly took his tip, and if he had overthrown Parson Weems, he had only set up the *Daily Graphic* in his place.

For some years biography in America seemed to be no more than a high-spirited game of yanking out shirt-tails and setting fire to them. In "The Life and Times of" anyone, you might be sure before you began to read that the life would prove to be ridiculous, the time barbarous, and both corrupt. Genius was mere disease (though few biographers had read widely enough to quote Nordau). Reputation was just publicity. Sexual aberration or incontinence was to be taken for granted, and with it cowardice and venality in public life, cowardice and hypocrisy in private life. Our ancestors were far more vigorous than we, it developed, for they could play the villain's role, whereas we are only victims of circumstance. And always the clothes they wore and the way they decorated their houses were, to us emancipated, simply preposterous. The debunker has never lost his astonishment at those silly clothes. . . . But the man who starts out to write a debunking biography has notified us that he is either a special pleader or a charlatan. He has something to prove. His purpose is not to find out and report the facts of history; it is to argue *ex parte*. He is not a judge. At best he is a prosecuting attorney; at a lower level, he is a kept detective; at the lowest level — one fairly common in recent years — he is the man who designs "composographs" for a scandal sheet. His art may solace his own needs, it may pay him pleasant royalties, it may even entertain intelligent people in moments which they would otherwise waste listening to tenors. But it has nothing to do with fact or integrity, and so it is not biography.

A historian was discussing Mr. Lewisohn's *Expression in America* with a prominent literary editor. He took exception to one of Mr. Lewisohn's chapters on the ground that it rested on statements of fact which he, having recently investigated them, knew to be altogether wrong. (That Mr. Lewisohn, a critic, had taken them in good faith from a recent biography establishes one of the obligations of a biographer.) The editor listened courteously but shook her head. The facts didn't matter, she said, for "It's a very interesting interpretation." The historian was obstinate. It didn't matter how interesting the interpretation might be, he asserted — the facts were wrong, and since they were wrong, the interpretation was wrong also. But no. The lady kept on shaking her head. Not only was the interpretation interesting; she would commit herself to calling it brilliant. . . .

Has a biographer this privilege? Should he refrain from making statements of fact until he has found out what the facts are? Or may he be ignorant of his subject so long as he makes an interesting interpretation?

Asking the lady's forbearance, I think he may not be. Biography differs from imaginative literature in that readers come to it primarily in search of information. The man who reads "The Life and Times" wants to learn something about the life and times. He wants to know how this particular person was entangled with the world, what the conditions of his life were, what they did to him, how he dealt with destiny, what he overcame, what overcame him. He desires this knowledge not only because of the curiosity that is our simian heritage but because he too is entangled and hopes for wisdom. Conceivably, something of his knowledge and wisdom will depend on what he learns from his biography. It is a jigsaw piece to be fitted into his picture of the world. Some of his decisions, some of his behavior, will in part depend on what the book tells him. Multiply him by a sufficient exponent and you have the next generation — part of whose knowledge of the world will be derived from biography.

It seems both precarious and absurd for a biographer to add unnecessarily to the ignorance and misinformation with which they will have to deal.

II

Literary people should not be permitted to write biography. The literary mind may be adequately described as the mind least adapted to the utilization of fact. It is, to begin with, much too simple. The novelist, the dramatist, the poet or the critic selects vivid phases of experience and coördinates them in such a manner that they give us an illusion of the whole. The significance, the ultimate value, of the process resides in its omissions. But biography cannot simplify and must not omit. The experience with which it deals is not simple. A novelist may invent a motive or a situation of magnificent simplicity; but that is fiction, and the motives and situations of fact are not simple but complex. The novelist deals with social organization only so far as he sees fit; but the subject of a biography was part of a web so intricate that only an objectification beyond the reach of fiction can comprehend it. The mathematics of a complex variable are forbidden to the literary mind.

That mind is also habitually, even professionally, inaccurate. Accuracy is not a criterion of fiction, drama, or poetry; to ask for it would be as absurd as to appraise music by its weight or painting by its smell. Hence the literary person is horribly inept at the practice of biography, whose first condition is absolute, unvarying, unremitting accuracy. He is subject to credulity — a reliance on intuition, on appearance, on rumor and conjecture and sheer imaginative creation. He is sometimes unable to read accurately and is nearly always unable to report what he has read. Some years ago a literary critic, writing the life of a novelist, dem onstrated that he could not even read his subject's books. He ascribed words and actions of characters in them to other characters; he erred in summarizing the plots of books; he asserted that events happened in them which did not happen, which were even specifically denied; in general, he appeared unable to report either the geography or the events in them as they really exist. This form of illiteracy is buttressed by another defect in accuracy, unwillingness to turn a page. One grows weary of seeing passages quoted from letters, journals, and notebooks in support of ideas or sentiments which the next manuscript page, usually the same entry, categorically denies.

The literary mind, furthermore, is naïve. That is its charm. From this unspoiled freshness, this eager willingness to believe, this awe and wonder, the world's poems and romances are woven. But it disqualifies its possessor for biography, which requires an all-inclusive skepticism and a cynicism that are best cultivated in human intercourse. The artist is usually a simple, home-loving person, given to nerves or paternity or the cultivation of some bourgeois hobby. He has little experience of the great world and none at all of the world of action. He knows nothing about the conditions of practical life, the way in which members of trades and professions and businesses must conduct themselves. He is ignorant of even rudimentary organization, business, military, political, diplomatic, economic, or religious. He could not conduct a horse trade, a sales drive, a senatorial campaign, an order of battle, or a revival, and usually has never observed one. Yet when he essays a biography of Napoleon, Saint Francis, Roscoe Conkling, or Jay Gould he must not only master these mechanisms but must also understand their laws. In a novel or a play the problem is simple: he may brood about Napoleon till his own special talents invent something that will give us an illusion. But it is not illusion that biography demands — it is fact. The literary mind can imagine a world for Saint Francis but it cannot deal with the actual, the factual, world of Saint Francis. It succumbs to fantasy, which is its proper medium. It is effective when it is evolving a world out of its own inner necessities, when it is creating its own material and data. But that is why the literary mind has worked so much stupidity in biography. We do not want illusion there, however convincing — we want reality. We do not want invented facts, created motives, phantasmally generated problems solved by intuition. We do not want anything whatever that imagination, intuition, or creation can give us. We want facts; and the literary mind is incapable of finding them, understanding them, and presenting them.

That is why the literary biographer has been victimized by preposterous methods. Unfitted to understand the nature of fact and bountifully endowed with credulity, he has relied on preposterous instruments for the ascertainment of fact. Most notably, in the last decade, on psychoanalysis.

An acquaintance with the terminology of psycho-analysis gives the literary a means of transcending their limitations. It shifts the field of biography from the empirical world where the subject mingled with his fellows, lived, worked, struggled, and, it may be, loved. In that world there are all sorts of dark places, mysterious bare spots about which nothing can be found, lacunæ, ellipses, conflicts of testimony and narrative, contradictions in evidence, insoluble problems, and sheer chaos. The lay biographer, denied the resources of Freud, must deal with these as best he may — by the swink of a never-ending labor which terrifies his slumber with the dread that he may have missed something, and which enables him in the end to say only "*a* is more probable than *b*." Labor and nightmare are spared the amateur psychoanalyst. He needs only the subject's letters and diaries, his books and speeches if he wrote any, the more intimate letters of his friends, and an earlier biography. Not all of these items are indispensable: much brilliant work has been done on the basis of the last alone. The external world is to be disregarded; the amateur Freud will devote himself to a far richer field, his subject's mind. He has, for the exploration of that field, an infallible instrument. It is the celestial virtue of lay psychoanalysis that it can make no mistakes. The amateur will never stub his toe on the discouragement of the biographer — he will never find that no evidence exists on a question he is trying to answer, or that the evidence which exists is insufficient. All of his subject's mind is of one piece and all his life is a unity, and so anything that is desired can be recovered from anything else. And if he finds a conflict of evidence, that too is simple. The principle of ambivalence tells him that all evidence means the same thing.

Thus, a lay psychoanalyst finds that the political philosophy of Thomas Jefferson was a product of Jefferson's infantile revolt against his father. He then says: "It is significant that Jefferson's antipathy to his father was so infantile and deep-seated that it was scarcely ever raised to consciousness. He frequently speaks of his father in his writings in a reverential and awe-inspired attitude. This, of course, made the disguised and substituted forms of outlet for this repressed revulsion all the more vigorous and extreme." Observe the assurance with which, a century after Jefferson's death, the amateur analyst speaks of his repressions. He passes a judgment that a professional analyst would not have felt qualified to make until he had spent two years in intimate association with the living man, chasing those repressions through a hundred disguises, each one unlike the last and all unlike what Jefferson had written. Any earlier or easier judgment, or a judgment derived by any other procedure, he would denounce as what it is: absurdity and charlatanism. Jefferson did not know what his infantile repressions were or what form they took, and no professional analyst can ever know, for Jefferson is dead. But our biographer knows.

The amateur begins with a set of necessities to which his subject must be fitted. The science he has acquired from a month's reading — more often from a couple of popular outlines — gives him a number of patterns and a series of keys. He knows before he begins that Diogenes, Brutus, or Cleopatra must have had this complex, or, if not, then that one. He knows in advance that inhibition must have been responsible for something, under-sublimation for something else, over-sublimation for still more. He knows that one kind of behavior indicates a form of sublimated anal erotic interest, another kind, oral eroticism. The indices of Sadism are given on page 114 of Tridon, those of masochism in the third chapter of Hinkle. The Œdipus complex (the amateur's modernization of original sin) may be expected to show itself in one of certain catalogued ways. It will produce such other universals as the castration complex. These in turn will work out, sometimes through other complexes, in behavior whose meaning and symbolism have been carefully charted. There remain such beautiful and versatile instruments as the death-wish to explain any chance fragment that might seem incommensurable with the rest. Or if something is still left over, the biographer has the blithe freedom of dropping Freud and picking up one of Freud's murderously incompatible opponents. Perhaps the unin-

terpreted residue of Cæsar's unconscious had better be
treated in the light of Jung's types, which are beautifully
systematic and have recently been doubled for American
use.[1] Few biographers, however orthodox in their use of
Freud, have been able to refuse the help of Adler's "*Minderwertigkeit*" — fewer still have used it to mean what
Adler means. It is a reasonable expectation that few will
hesitate to marry the death-wish to the birth-trauma when
an adequate exposition of the former works into the outlines.

The rabbit, observe, has been hidden in the hat. There
remains only to pull it out with a smile of reassuring omniscience. It is obvious how unnecessary are the researches
and verifications of the biographer. Conversations which
no one ever recorded can be reproduced and explained. In-
terviews which no one ever witnessed can be described.
Documents long since vanished from the earth can be
materialized and interpreted. The method cannot make
mistakes: it is, in literary hands, infallible. You have what
the dead man wrote, what it is said he said, and what some
people have said about him. Your method dissolves all
doubts, settles all contradictions, and projects the known
or guessed into absolute certainty about the unknowable.
You wonder, perhaps, what Diogenes said at the grave of
Keats or where Apollonius was and what he did on a
certain fourth of July? If you are a historian you examine
all possible sources of information and if you find no information, you report "I don't know." But if you are an
amateur analyst, to hell with uncertainty. You have discovered that Diogenes possessed a mother fixation as the
result of jealousy before his second birthday (evidence of
what was in the mind of a child twenty centuries ago does

[1] James Oppenheim: *American Types.*

not exist, but no matter), that he had a mania for overripe plums as the result of an incestuous admiration of his sister, and that his Id and Ego were abnormally at peace with each other. What, therefore, must Diogenes have said on the specific occasion? Where, therefore, must Apollonius have been? Obviously, where he must have been is where he was.

That *must* is the mechanism of psychoanalytical biography. It is the invention of the biographer, his deduction from an *a priori* principle. It has no relation to the subject of "The Life and Times." It does not tell us what did happen. It tells us instead what must have happened. Biography proper is not concerned with the *must* but only with the *did*. Between them is a sheer gulf which no theory can possibly bridge. Psychoanalysis cannot come into effective relationship, into any relationship, with a dead man.

Professionally, it does not try. The physician to diseased minds is engaged in a process whose aim is therapeutic — empirical. He practises an art whose entire condition is the mutual association of living minds. His technique requires a constant interplay of a myriad variables, a constant shift and adaptation, a constant accommodation and reëxamination and reinterpretation — all of which are impossible to biography. Psychoanalysis is dynamic or it is nothing. The professional must deal with phenomena which his trade-jargon calls Displacement, Conversion, Resistance, Transference, and with similar psychic energies which perish when the patient dies. These phenomena never engage the attention of a biographer: no dead man exhibits them. The amateur does not hesitate to dispense with them. He has his pattern, his clues, his guidebooks, and they are enough. As the result of his skill, they create his patient for him.

The result may be, as our literary editor insisted, an interpretation in the highest degree entertaining. It may be a brilliant exposition of its author's sentiments or his talent for denunciation or his exhortatory power. When produced by an intelligent man it may approximate the art of the detective story, whose clues are also invented and whose deductions are also made to fit. But it exists always on the left side of a fixed line. On the right side of that line are the materials of biography. The findings of psychoanalysis, any findings whatever, belong forever on the left side, with guesses, improvisations, fairy stories, and mere lies. The obligation of a biographer is to find facts. When he employs psychoanalysis he cannot arrive at facts but only at "interpretations," which is to say theory, which is to say nonsense.

III

Honesty in biography is a gradation. In a way, the most dishonest is the most honest, for its nature is most easily perceived. The late Senator Lodge's life of Alexander Hamilton, for instance, is clearly an item in Mr. Lodge's lifelong effort to prove that the Republican party was the heir of both Federalism and God. It may be described as political pro-bunking biography. Most biographies by recent converts to Marxism are easily recognizable as products of generous emotion, tracts, acts of faith, studies in the propagation of a religion. The works of convert-ites, out of whom much matter is to be seen and learned, have always a legitimate use, when they have been recognized as such. More difficult are the products of prejudice, which also make a gradation. Least offensive are those like Henry Adams's life of John Randolph. One knows what an Adams would be forced to do with a Southerner who had expressed his dissent from the Adams conviction that the family beliefs were indistinguishable from God's will. Not many advocacies are so easily corrected — notably the recent swarm of lives of Civil War notables, most of which are really passionate attacks on or defenses of political, economic, or sociological theses. The iridescent rhetoric that played round these same notables two generations ago was, effectively, more honest.

In every biography ever written certain passages are printed in invisible italics, the involuntary emphasis of the biographer which springs from his emotional, intellectual, religious, economic, political, social, and racial prejudices. The reader has a problem in moving points. A conscientious biographer will have faced the same problem and made what adjustment he could. There would be no occasion to state here the bald platitude that a biographer must have integrity, if fashion had not permitted it to be ignored. A reader may accurately estimate a biographer's integrity by the force of his refusal to depart from verifiable facts. The disciplined biographer will say, in effect, "Here are the facts I have found. Anyone who is interested in testing them may consult sources *a*, *b*, *c*, and so on." If for any reason he cares to enlarge on his facts, he will give unmistakable notice that the discussion is shifting to a different plane. He will say, in effect, "I infer from *a* . . . ," or "*b* leads me to guess," or "my hunch is," or "it may be, but I can't establish it." He will supply actual italics.

There remains the biographer whose dishonesty is deliberate — or who, to designate him more charitably, practises a flexible art. So many recent biographers have been novelists turned rancid, so much success has rewarded fiction mislabeled biography, that the technical devices of novel-writing have usurped the place of factual instruments. There is, for instance, "incorporation," a method now almost universally employed in lives of writers, orators, and others who committed anything to paper. The biographer selects something from the subject's written works, his essays or his novels or his diary, and without quotation marks sets it down as part of the subject's thoughts on a given occasion. The ideas, the emotions, and the phraseology of the diary thus becomes the content of the subject's mind. Passages written years later than the time indicated, or years before it, have been used to illustrate states of mind widely different from those indicated by the context. Passages widely separated in time have been combined. Highly important phrases or sentences have been left out, so that the meaning of the passage has been vitally changed. Such misrepresentation of the defenseless dead is dishonesty of the rankest kind, but the device is dishonest no matter how carefully employed or how rigorously controlled. It is not accountable. Between what a man thinks or feels and what he writes about it, especially what he writes creatively or polemically or for purposes of self-analysis, there is likely to be a difference that no skill or selection or representation can reconcile.

The device, however, enables the biographer to assert something about his subject's mind, as psychoanalysis also enables him to do. For the same reason a different kind of biographer employs another method of fiction. He enters his subject's mind and reports what he finds there. This is a novelist's instrument, whether it reports merely "Diogenes thought . . ." or extends farther toward the "interior soliloquy" or "stream of consciousness" of the postwar novel. From Queen Victoria to Lord Byron, from Herman Melville to Boss Croker, how many dead people have confided to us thoughts they could never have set down in a private journal? They have been presented to us with an accuracy of reporting that catches the minutest syllable of their minds. The reason why this method of fiction is illegitimate in biography is, however obvious, worth noting at length.

A character in fiction is invented — made to order. The requirements of fiction are served if his creator succeeds in making us believe in him, in giving us an illusion that he really exists. When the thoughts of Tristram Shandy or Molly Bloom are reported to us, we receive the thoughts of phantoms and the only necessity is that they shall seem to be real thoughts. The interior soliloquy of Molly Bloom is not the actual content of a mind, for Molly Bloom never lived. It is the possible content of an imagined mind. It is only one of many possible sequences of thought, any other of which would conceivably give us as convincing an illusion. It succeeds when that illusion is created.

But Molly Bloom is one kind of person and Queen Victoria is another kind. Swann and Charlus, Clara Middleton and Carol Kennicott are imaginary persons, whereas Nathaniel Hawthorne, Julius Cæsar and Catherine the Great really lived. The biographer who tries to tell us what they were thinking at any given moment must work in the domain of historical fact. At that moment Hawthorne was thinking one thought or one group of thoughts and no other. With all the resources of art and science, research, imaginative sympathy, and sheer good luck on his side, no biographer can recover it. Have you ever stood at the bedside of a dying person and wondered what images were flickering across that fading mind? You stared into a mystery which no biographer could ever penetrate. He can guess, he can "interpret," he can invent. He can build a beautiful and convincing illusion for us, but it is only a possible, an unconditioned mind that he gives us, not the actual mind of a person who lived in the world. If he presents it as "interpretation" he is a novelist. If he presents it as fact he is a charlatan.

But, I am told, the biographer has the testimony of his material. He has a letter or an entry in a journal. His subject has actually written, "I was greatly moved. I thought that . . ." and so on. For the most part "interpretative" biography derives its stream of consciousness from the biographer's own mind, but even when it uses intimate personal documents it remains invention. No man unassisted can recover the past of his own mind. He can say "I was grief-stricken" or "I was overjoyed." He can describe his thoughts and emotions with general nouns — anger, delight, ecstasy, melancholy, discouragement, despair. Sometimes he can recall images, metaphors, or curious preceptions of the exterior world, but even here he is almost certain to be victimized by creative reminiscence. The biographer may write "Cæsar wrote Pompey that he thought . . ." or "Margaret Fuller wrote in her diary that she felt . . . ," or even "Melville believed that he had once thought . . ." Such statements may be statements of fact. But such a statement as "Cæsar thought . . ." or "Margaret felt . . ." is just guesswork, just theory, just nonsense.

Still, the rebuttal runs, a biographer is entitled to "interpret" his subject. The point of view of the literary editor already quoted sanctions him to transcend the limitations of fact. That transcendence being sanctioned, he is free to re-create his subject's mind. Excuse me: he is not. The interior of his subject's mind is forbidden him by the nature of reality. He may tell us what the subject has said or written about his mind, but he may not on his own authority make any statement whatever about the immediate content of that mind. He cannot know what is there, he can only guess. Any guess whatever is a clear warning to his reader. When he makes it, he departs from fact and enters theory. We will not dispute about words: you need not follow me in calling a guess dishonest. But certainly it is theoretical — and if theoretical, then contingent, inexistent, and mystical. And, therefore, improper to biography.

IV

And the moral? The moral is: Back to Lockhart, back to Froude, back to Morley. Back, in short, to Victorian biography. For the great Victorians, however timorous in refusing to call fornication by a ruder name, had as biographers an invincible integrity. They acted upon an implied contract, they accepted obligations to the reader. They assumed that the reader's interest was in the subject and not in the biographer; wherefore they resolutely submerged their own personalities. They assumed that biography dealt with fact; so they refrained from guessing. They assumed that fact-finding requires accuracy; so they checked their dates and titles, verified their quotations, and abstained from reporting what they had never seen or heard or read. They assumed that re-creation of their sitter's thoughts was impossible; and they sacrificed the God's-eye view. So one may read their biographies in the assurance that he is not being deceived, whether through ignorance, guesswork, special pleading, or deliberate fraud. Such confidence would have its value, these gloomy days.

It would imply, I am afraid, the disappearance of the literary from biography and the occupation of the field by historians, students, and analytical searchers after fact. We should lose a great deal of beautiful writing; for most historians and most scholars appear to write with something

between a bath sponge and an axe. But we could accept
that loss in gratitude for the loss of beautiful thinking as
well. There would be no more "restitutions" — the journal-
ist's discovery that Andrew Johnson had his points twenty-
five years after the historians had done him justice would
be spared us. There would be no debunking of great men
about whom no one acquainted with history had ever believed any bunk. We could pick up the life of a Civil War
leader confident that the colonels would not be called gen-
erals, that armies five hundred miles apart would not fight
battles of which history has no record, that Chattanooga
would not be fought in 1864 or Vicksburg surrendered
on the wrong side of the river. In that Era of Accuracy the
Shenandoah Valley will not be a prairie; they will not mine
gold on the Comstock; Jesse James will not ride to the
attack on Lawrence at the age of nine; Robert Burns will
not die when Washington Irving is three; Mrs. Hale will
not write to Rufus Griswold thirteen months after his
death; Rouen will not contain rival cathedrals; John Keats
will not read a translation of *Oberon* that Southey did
not write. Biographers will know who was President of the
United States in any given year. When they describe the
appearance of Charles Dickens during his 1842 visit to
America they will not take their data from the reports of
people who saw him on his second visit a quarter-century
later. There is hope that they will master the fashions of
the past and refuse to seat Edgar Allan Poe on an antimacas-
sar. There is hope that they will quote the titles of books
as they were written, even that they will learn to find out
when they were published. A vision now wholly chimerical
may be fulfilled: American biographers may become acquainted with the more salient facts of European history
and literature. Still, if a contemporary American historian

can misdate the Regency by forty-six years, it would be romantic to ask the merely literary to know who wrote *I Promessi Sposi*, to understand the difference between an abbé and an abbot, or to identify the author of *The Wanderings of Cain*.

But accuracy will be only a lesser glory of that great dawn. When we read about Uncle Billy Sherman we shall not be told of an infantile fixation which the biographer has deduced from the letters to Joe Johnston before Atlanta. John Greenleaf Whittier's dislike of slavery will not spring from a sense of guilt acquired in his fourth year, which intense brooding in the night watches has revealed to the author of the life and times. Jay Gould's manipulation of Erie will not be symbolic of his erotic reveries and, though we search wonderingly, we shall not read an interior soliloquy which Andrew Jackson aimed at the twentieth century on the eve of New Orleans. Psychoanalysis will retreat from biography to the consulting room, where it belongs, and to the literary speak-easy, where thereafter it will have to compete with the Revolution. With it will go all the other instruments of amateur psychology – they are worthless in biography. They have been eloquent helps in the production of absurdity. They have given the half-educated a feeling of profundity. They have comforted a good many wishful, believing minds and softened a harsh world for the tender. All this is probably a social service, an accessory to the public welfare; but let it go.

We should forfeit much amusement if these things disappeared, but the loss would be compensated. The republic of letters would gain in dignity. Something of its vulgarity springs from our permitting gentlemen in the service of causes to lie ignorantly about dead men. In an honest world the Rosicrucian, the Humanist, the Marxist, the Fascist, the politician, the economist, the regionalist, the evangelist — in short, the doctrinaire — would be required to conduct his propaganda in the open. In such a world the lecturer to adolescent girls would be required to report accurately on what he reads, and told that a generous spirit is not in itself enough for the perception of facts. He and all the hopeful minds of which he is symbolic would be, in a tradition of integrity, forbidden to misrepresent the past, no matter how beautiful their motives.

What about the "interpretation"? Well, it has a valid place as the most intelligent of literary guessing games, and something more. Given an alert mind and some horse sense, a "psychographer" may contrive a stimulating essay. It must remain an interpretation of the unknowable in terms of the author's personality, but if the author is a distinguished person it may be a fine art. It may be a vehicle for wit and malice and good writing, of which the world can never hold enough, and an expression of literary talents which find no other form well adapted to them. Mr. Gamaliel Bradford wrote the "psychograph" in its most legitimate form. He was too disciplined to offer the pompous fiction of a Maurois or a Ludwig as history. He had too much Victorian integrity to plead a cause, and he refrained from the delicate distortion of plain fact that constitutes the art of Strachey. The same integrity made him notify his reader, on nearly every page: This is what I think or suspect or infer. But his interest and his field can be observed in the word which worked into so many of his titles, the soul. It is an honest interest, a legitimate field. But just what is it? Biography knows nothing about the soul.

Biography is the wrong field for the mystical, and for

the wishful, the tender-minded, the hopeful, and the passionate. It enforces an unremitting skepticism — toward its
material, toward the subject, most of all toward the biographer. He cannot permit himself one guess or one
moment of credulity, no matter how brilliantly it may illuminate the darkness he deals with or how it may solace
his ignorance. He must doubt everything. He must subject
his conclusions and all the steps that lead to them to a cor-
rosive examination, analysis, and verification — a process
which he must hope will reveal flaws, for if it does he has
added one more item of certainty to his small store. He has,
apart from such negatives, very little certainty. His job is
not dramatic: it is only to discover evidence and to analyze
it. And all the evidence he can find is the least satisfactory
kind, documentary evidence, which is among the most
treacherous phenomena in a malevolent world. With luck,
he will be certain of the dates of his subject's birth and marriage and death, the names of his wife and children, a
limited number of things he did and offices he held and
trades he practised and places he visited and manuscript
pages he wrote, people he praised or attacked, and some
remarks made about him. Beyond that, not even luck can
make certainty possible. The rest is merely printed matter,
and a harassed man who sweats his life out in libraries,
courthouses, record offices, vaults, newspaper morgues, and
family attics. A harassed man who knows that he cannot
find everything and is willing to believe that, forever
concealed from him, exists something which, if found,
would prove that what he takes to be facts are only ap-
pearances.

From this quicksand and mirage he will derive facts.
Only a few of them are unmixed fact, free of misunder-

standing, misinformation, and plain ignorance. The rest he will grade in a hierarchy, and arrange them as their nature, value, and validity make necessary — not as some wish or religion of his own would like them arranged. In the end he can say, "*A* did this, and I think he did that, and for the rest I am ignorant and refuse to guess." This is the act of judgment, and it contains three different stages, each one of them serviceable to his reader — who will use them, according to their degree, in his acquisition of knowledge. When he has said this much, the biographer has done his job. He will say, "*A* did this," but he will not try to say why. For that is speculative, the gate that lets the motive in, and with the motive enter all the guessing, hoping, and chicanery that have debauched his profession.

His result lacks brilliance. It is without the certainty of the ignorant and the psychological — the certainty that is the unmistakable hallmark of the theorist's cocksureness. It is without the ingenious nonsense of the interpreter. It is without the invective of the debunker, without the contrived, humanitarian unity of the hopeful, without the passion of the generous. It is without teaching, without preaching, without hope for a better world: altruistic desire does not come into it. It will not make life seem easier to optimists and has no bearing on reform or revolution. It is only an intelligent man's efforts to deal with facts. It is a faulty, imperfect picture, a blurred image, an uncompleted map. But such as it is, it is trustworthy: it looks toward reality. It establishes part of a pattern, makes out some lines of the obscured page, recovers something from the past. Like other controlled and tested knowledge, it is usable. It is an accounting, the settling of a stewardship. Momentarily, mists have partly blown away and the North Star, though blurred, has been visible. It is an effort in the direction of truth. Such an effort has a value that no ignorance, however brilliant, and no wishfulness, however kind, can offer in competition with it.

What the Next Hour May Bring Forth

HIS Excellency the President of the United States is formally memorialized, and the Honorable the Senate and the Honorable the House of Representatives of the United States, in Congress assembled, are petitioned:—

In order to avert the dangers and destructive violence that must ensue until, after a series of convulsions, a different order shall be established: — To execute measures on behalf of society as a whole that will effect an orderly transition to the Power Age, utilize the potentialities of the Economy of Abundance for the liberation and security of mankind, and establish what the petitioner does not hesitate to call paradise within a calculated period of ten years. . . .

There is no need to examine here the *whereases* on which the petition is based. Repetition has made us all letter-perfect in their details, and the reader may be assured that the petitioner has mastered the findings of science, engineering and economics. He analyzes the process and acceleration of technological unemployment. He describes the violent revolutions that must follow the development of new mechanical inventions. He sets forth a laborious, orderly and detailed study of the new energies at the disposal of mankind — which, he points out, have rendered man-power obsolete, which if intelligently used can raise the standard of living incalculably higher than it has ever been; but which, if their management is bungled, can plunge the world into another barbarism. Declaring that complete autarchy is both desirable and unavoidable for the United States, he points out the catastrophe that will follow any delay in its establishment. For some European nation may beat us to such an organization and may then militantly turn upon us the engines with which we have neglected to supply ourselves.

Our petitioner lists some of the benevolences now within the power of science and engineering, if society will but provide mechanisms for coöperation and distribution. Agriculture is to be collectivized and so completely mechanized that only a few need labor at it, and they so lightly that the working day will consist of minutes rather than hours. It is also to be made independent of weather and seasons. Artificially produced climate will ripen crops in soils which are not dependent on nature's stupid whim but have been mixed to order in the chemical laboratory. For transportation we shall have a system of rationally located express highways paved with a vitrified substance superior to any surface now in use — one of the innumerable new materials at the disposal of the modern engineer. Along them will travel vehicles of a size hitherto undreamed of, at a speed currently regarded as fantastic. It is unlikely that these vehicles will be geared to climb grades, for the highway engineer may call upon energies sufficient to level mountains. The new materials include fabrics which may be hardened or dissolved into fluids as required, which are produced in sheets of paper- or rayon-like substance of any length or thickness or softness, and which may be compounded to last a lifetime, or to be thrown away after one use like paper napkins.

Yet it is in megalopolis and the housing of earth's children that the new age shows most brightly. Our petitioner assumes pre-fabrication, quantity production and interchangeable parts as axiomatic. He suggests the possibilities latent in new cements, vitrified building materials, glass bricks, flexible glass and plastic woods which may be dyed and molded. He thinks of such accessories as mechanical dishwashing, private elevators, and selective and even therapeutic air-conditioning as commonplaces within the expectation of everyone. But he goes beyond. With such materials, temperatures, and energies available as are now easily produced, why pre-fabricate a house? Why not mold it as a unit — why not indeed mold it as an enormous unit, capable of domiciling several thousand families, a city in itself? Super-apartment-houses up to two hundred feet high are feasible, with vast covered arcades wherein climate may be manipulated at will and the ancient dream of the city in the country may be realized. These units will make possible an entirely new communal life, at once private and coöperative, with all the civilizing forces of a city and all the humanizing forces of a village inside the common walls. Not only may everyone have his own phonograph and player-piano — though television is not yet clearly indicated, a device is announced for the translation of speech into type and its transmission by electricity. With humanity enfranchised by megalopolis, it follows that the normal expectancy of life will rise, and that medicine will be almost entirely preventive — though the promise of a cure for seasickness is consoling. . . . These monolithic edifices will be "neither palaces nor temples nor cities but a combination of all, superior to whatever is known."

They will necessitate, our petitioner clearly understands, an entire reorganization of the social system. He outlines its principles and mechanisms at great length. He agrees with Major Douglas that our present attitude toward labor is economic Puritanism. He borrows the Major's National Dividend, he takes over much of the economics popularized three years ago by Technocracy, and perceives unemotionally that education, art, and amusement will have to be controlled by the State in its own interest. He sees that to reconstitute society you must begin with the organization of group-pressures, and like the Communist Party, the Townsend Plan, and Tammany Hall he concentrates on the neighborhood infiltration of ideas and the house-to-house canvas for Utopia. The plan can be completed in the United States, which has the best natural endowment, in ten years. That being done, we shall be organized to extend our universal paradise over Europe in only six years more. There will be no poverty by then, no wealth, no need for the accumulation of property. The profit-motive will evaporate, there will be no urge toward self-interest, and international competition will disappear, taking war with it forever. It follows that intemperance and all bad habits (such as lying and cheating) will also disappear. There will be, even, no marital disagreements, in the great dawn. Children will achieve an adult education by the age of ten. We shall be able to remake the intellect and distribute it to all members of the race, develop universal benevolence, and free mankind at last for the cultivation of its spiritual gifts. This is the "unavoidable revolution of the human condition that must take place, in consequence of the progress of human intelligence."

Mr. J. A. Etzler then admonishes the Senate and the House: "The fate of the world is thus depending from your decision." The body he is addressing is the Second Session of the Twenty-Second Congress. The President to whom he speaks is Andrew Jackson. His petition is dated, "Pittsburgh, February 21, 1833."

Mr. Etzler's essay is a movement from the known to the mathematically implied, an adventure in extrapolation. The dewy morn of the industrial revolution was all about him, as he sat there where rivers meet which the revolution has recently proved itself unable to control and gazed westward from the frontier to the Great American Desert where, he felt, his first monoliths would best be constructed. Its energies could be caught in algebraic symbols and then put through the maneuvers of an engineer's vision. If his intoxication became rhapsody and if he extrapolated mathematics to sheer fantasy, why enthusiasm is endemic among engineers — and time has been on his side. An addict of Science Service's communiqués from the front line comes upon an old acquaintance on nearly every page, and one's cup runs over when he meets the vegetable "glutinations" for outer and under wear which Mr. Howard Scott's followers were to invent just exactly one hundred years later. Sometimes, in fact, Etzler is far too conservative. His minimum time for the passage from the Atlantic to the then uncolonized Pacific is between three and four days, and the currently fantastic speed at which his queer vehicles are to travel the modern highways is forty miles an hour. We have bettered both speeds without attaining his paradise, without even developing the "union of a few intelligent men who do not judge before they examine" which was to bring in the dawn.

The prophetic slide-rule, the truth is, stood in its own

way. Etzler could see clearly the cloud-capped towers on the horizon, but he refused to concern himself with the unforeseen, and so he missed not only the middle distance but even the very foreground at his feet. Two years after Joseph Henry had begun to experiment with the galvanic telegraph, Etzler weaves it into his scheme, but his electricity goes no farther than that. His monoliths are lighted by gas, his railroads run exclusively by steam as railroads ran when he was writing, and his vision sees no omen of the storage battery. For storage, in fact, he has to fall back on precisely those reservoirs of kinetic energy which Professor Furnas was predicting just a few months back. His floating islands (which are still much dreamed about) move by mechanical energy recovered from waves and tides, and so do his land vehicles, which one visualizes as a kind of apotheosized cable-car traveling gigantically along a line of sunken cams and cogs. He was on fire with vision, but that radiance blinded him to the internal combustion engine.

There were, that is, ambushes on the way to Jerusalem, new forms of energy which were to switch his whole program down a spur track back of the dumps. His system of harnessed waves and tides, his mile-long batteries of windmills and clusters of mirrors which were to transform solar energy into steam, his blueprints of nightmare steamengines made of cement and ratcheted balance wheels and compensating conversion-machines — well, it was completely rational, the next hour or two made it preposterous, and though parts of it still trouble the sleep of prophets not a single item has ever come about. The road led straight across an open plain. But some protective coloration hid from the prophetic eye gasoline, the dynamo, electromagnetic waves, the vacuum tube, the high-frequency transmission line, the portable motor, the propeller and the machine-press. Not to foresee them proved something of a mistake. Though *The Paradise within the Reach of All Men* was first-rate as diagnosis, it was, as prognosis and program, a complete bust.

About the system of social reform that was geared to it lingers not only the aroma of miracle that attends all paradises, but also the purer miracle of scientific mysticism. The idiom of Etzler's age shows in his proposal for organizing Utopia as a joint-stock company. That was the way you went about preparing the Kingdom, in the Thirties and Forties; and a respectable series of visions, including Brook Farm, proposed to alleviate man's lot and renovate society for the greater glory of God by means of corporate consolidation. That antique idiom slides easily into our own of yesterday, to-day and to-morrow when Etzler proves conclusively that an investment of twenty dollars in New Jerusalem will multiply itself one thousand times within five years. For of course he was also something of a promoter and stock-salesman, as most dwellers on the high place seem to be, the blue-sky laws of common sense yielding easily to vision. There was nothing wrong with his diagnosis, and there seldom is — diagnosis is the simplest process of sociology. No one can quarrel with Etzler's fact or figures: you must grant his premises as you must grant those of his lineal descendants in these days. And, granting them, you are constrained to accept every step by which he moves upon his paradise, for all are rigorously logical and supported by mathematics which you can check for yourself.

It is proved, and it did not happen. Three things stood in the way. First, it was extrapolation, which is precarious. Second, mathematics allowed no leeway for the unforeseen, which is catastrophic. And third — Mr. Etzler mentioned in 1833 a slight impediment to his remodeling of society.

"Man," he tells us, "needs not to eat his bread in the sweat
of his brow, and to pass his life in drudgery and misery, except he perseveres in his mental sloth and forgoes the use
of reason." That, however, is no more than an irritant and
may be disregarded. "The accomplishment of [our] purposes requires nothing but the raw materials for them, that
is to say iron, copper, wood, earth chiefly, and a union of
men whose eyes and understanding are not shut up by preconceptions. . . ." Yes. No more than that has ever been
required. And will the local papers please copy.

Ten years after Etzler's date-line a copy of the second
English edition of *The Paradise within the Reach of All
Men* came for review to the hands of a Yankee in whom
enthusiasm had been winter-killed. Later on Henry David
Thoreau was to set down a conviction, induced by long residence in a center of enlightenment, that "if anything ail a
man, so that he does not perform his functions, if he have a
pain in his bowels even — for that is the seat of sympathy —
he forthwith sets about reforming — the world." He had
not quite reached that impatience when he came upon Etzler: He said that the *Paradise* was "transcendentalism in
mechanics" but he was willing to examine it, and in fact
discussed it so heatedly in Concord that he got embroiled
with Emerson. He acknowledged that the times were out of
joint. On the authority of his friends he understood that
the world had "asthma, ague and fever, and dropsy and flat-
ulence and pleurisy" and was "afflicted with vermin." Nevertheless, he decided, the trouble with Etzler was precisely
that he tried to meet the condition head-on. He tried "to
prescribe for the globe itself," and Thoreau could accept no
prescription of that scale. He asked leave to doubt and to
reject — for two reasons. "We are never," he said, "so visionary as to be prepared for what the next hour may bring

forth." And, "You may begin by sawing the little sticks, or you may saw the great sticks first, but sooner or later you must saw them both" — and the slight impediment mentioned above was one of the sticks that must be sawed. Though a surveyor and a handicraftsman, Thoreau lacked both science and social vision. He was not gifted with belief. Etzler's vision came down to a promise that man's will would yet be law to the physical world and that man should "no longer be deterred by such abstractions as time and space, height and depth, weight and hardness." With firm courtesy, Thoreau repudiated all such projections of the known into the much-desired, and would buy no shares in paradise. He was a sad cynic, and the prophets of his day prayed over him in vain. But after ten times the prophet's ten-year plan for the production of Utopia, somehow it is the cynic that the light falls on. Etzler dreamed greatly, but Thoreau was right.

The Absolute in the Machine Shop

THE Townless Highway designed for efficient automobile traffic which Mr. Benton MacKaye once envisioned and the scientifically planned and sited cities to complement it which frivolous engineers enjoy sketching for us will never exist while Utopia remains on the far bank. They would require, as a preliminary, a cataclysm that would destroy the present economic system and the greater part of its wealth. They would also require a nation sufficiently regimented to scrap its whole plant and begin again from scratch. Granted that development in the direction of that New Jerusalem is desirable, progress toward it can come only in part, very slowly, and as the resultant of forces which are certain to move at best tangentially to the dream. No such obstacles, however, stand in the way of that other vision of engineers, the Absolute Automobile, the motor car designed with reference to nothing but mechanical efficiency and styled in complete conformity to the principle of functionalism. Few economic forces oppose this eidolon and neither politics nor theology taboos it. And still, after thirty years of fanciful sketches and detailed blueprints that have familiarized us with its potentialities, the Absolute Automobile does not appear. Why?

By one of those linkages of emotion which makes sociology the most fascinating of the sciences, a desire for this kind of automobile has somehow become associated with the liberal faith. A good many people who yearn for the democratization of industry or the suppression of the opium traffic have come to believe that the teardrop car is a step on the way to their objectives and in fact inseparable from the good life. Such people commonly explain the non-appearance of the Absolute Automobile as one more villainy of the profit system. The manufacturers, we are invited to believe, have conspired to deprive the public of its right to cheap, efficient and long-lived automobiles and to the beauty which such cars might have. Unhappily, no social phenomenon is so simple as that. Such a conspiracy does not exist, and the dream would probably be nearer if one did. For it would remove some of the present barriers, if only minor ones, and under the profit system the manufacturers would still be quite willing to make any kind of machine they could sell. No, the trouble with the Absolute Automobile, as with so many other attempts to rationalize society, is that it is complexly impossible. The conditions of the problem itself are one insuperable obstruction, and the habits and desires of the public are another. Finally, it seems likely that engineers are no more rational than the rest of us when they go mystical, and that an absolute in motor cars is as phantasmal as an absolute in biochemistry or dry-fly fishing.

To begin with, it is possible to define mechanical efficiency, in a product which has so many different functions as the automobile, only by selecting limited ends. Even then the materials out of which an automobile is made and the purposes to which it is put impose conditions that may become contradictory. After a certain amount of improvement you reach a reciprocal equation, and further improvement in one direction must be compensated by an unfavorable result elsewhere. Thus the use of lighter materials cuts down weight and so upkeep-expense, but it also impairs stability and comfort, and this loss can only in part be made up by changes in design. Again, increased efficiency in the transmission and application of power permits the use of less powerful engines — but at a sacrifice of acceleration, flexibility, and certainty of control. Likewise from the point of view of the consumer, longevity may be a very doubtful virtue. The progress of mechanical invention may be haphazard under the present conspiracy but under any system it will go on, and a long-lived car may be obsolete before it is worn out. The British practice of building for a century machinery which Americans build in the knowledge that its optimum expectation of life is ten years has proved a serious handicap to British industry. Similarly with automobiles. Compared to the cheapest car of 1935, the best-made car of 1920 is inefficient.

The attitude of the buying public is a final determinant and will remain one. It is most discouraging. The actual user of a car is a poor authority on its efficiency and commonly he is very little, if at all, interested in it. Fuel costs, for instance. The average driver has no accurate and little relative knowledge of them, and the occasional one who is aware of them is more wishful than realistic. He has no means of accurate measurement, no formula to adjust the variables, no means of controlled experiment and nothing to confine his guesses within a fifty per cent. margin of error. Most men buy a new car on the basis of satisfactory experience with another of the same make, the advice and experience of friends, or wholly irrational grounds. The values which they consult leave efficiency quite out of account. They want, so far as they can phrase their desires, reliability first of all: a car that can be depended on to start in all weathers, to get where it starts for, regardless of road conditions, and to operate in its day-to-day function with a minimum of trouble and repairs. If a car runs satisfactorily and reliably, they don't much care how inefficiently it may run. After reliability, safety, comfort and currently fashionable styling — perhaps in a different order — all come before efficiency in the scale of effective values that determine the sale of automobiles.

It is also true, as with many other products and institutions objected to on theoretical grounds, that the practical efficiency of the conventional automobile exceeds the requirements of the public. Its engine, its brakes and its general "roadability" are superior to the demands put on them. No matter how far it may fall short of the eidolon, it is a magnificent machine. That being so, the consumer does not consider potential gains which, for the most part, he does not understand. Besides, such gains are, to an amazing degree, merely theoretical. At the customary speeds, for instance, streamlining the body will not materially improve performance — and that being so, the fact that someone drove a car backward more efficiently than it could go forward is irrelevant. Similarly, the increased efficiency to be obtained from mounting the engine in the rear and similar proposed improvements is so generalized as to affect the consumer not at all. Their principal bearing is on the ultimate exhaustion of the gasoline supply. The average driver is about as interested in that as he is in the revolution of binary stars.

Some people think he ought to be interested in it. And right here enters the mysticism to which one type of engineer, and a whole species of pseudo-engineer, is prone; enters

as a theory of mechanics, takes out papers as a theory of social aims, and marries a theory of esthetics. Because any
given problem of mechanics can be satisfactorily solved in
only a limited number of ways, it is assumed that some in-
herent necessity of that problem dictates one ideal design
of the eventual machine, and that other designs are therefore
against God. The corollary is then drawn that this design
should be forced on the consumer in society's interest. That
is bad logic and a defiance of experience. Then, for no stated
reason, it is assumed that beauty in a machine is a result of
leaving it naked in its one ideal form: a mowing machine is
beautiful because it has no lambrequins or scrollwork on it,
and the native loveliness of a pneumatic drill is evident till
someone hangs antlers on it to make it resemble something
else. That is absurd, and even if it were true it would be,
so far as automobiles are concerned, irrelevant. It leaves the
subjective factor quite out of account, which in esthetics is
fatal. A good many hearts have been sincerely grieved because the automobile of commerce still shows signs of having descended from the farm wagon — is still not styled in
accord with an ideal functional form. What is that form,
and why should the automobile assume it? No matter what
the styling, the car as a machine for transportation is doing
its job more efficiently than the unexacting human race asks
it to — its esthetic quality, then, depends on how it pleases
the eye. Chairs, which are machines to facilitate sitting, may
please the eye in radically differing ways, and so may automobiles — even those with a whipsocket on the cowl and a
mud-scraper just outside the driver's seat. About all we can
say with assurance is that a lot of people like the looks of
a lot of different cars, and that this esthetic satisfaction has
been known to change and is likely to change again. One
manufacturer says flatly that streamlining is purely a prob-

lem of styling, with all the neomania and neophobia that fashion implies, and he is probably right. It may be that people ought to find the design of an Absolute Automobile beautiful. But when *must* and *ought* get into esthetics, you are about ready for the police arm. ·

With the most charitable intentions in the world, then, the enthusiasts are lusting for a familiar reconstruction of the human race. Practically all visions of perfection imply dictatorship, ever so kindly in intent but, to be effectively kind, backed up by mustard gas. You can force the manufacturers to make the Absolute Automobile and the public to buy it by legislation or decree, if you have the military on your side. For the automobile is involved with social energies: dent the equilibrium at one edge with a teardrop car and it will bulge somewhere else with street rioting and the crash of kings. There is a chance that you may emerge with a car of ideal efficiency and design, but it is absolutely certain that you will also come out with a new organization of society — and if the whipsocket and the oil-wick headlights aren't on the automobile they will appear somewhere on Congress, the Constitution, or the Council of Soviets. Society and the human race operate on a resultant, on the minimum useful level of efficiency, with a motor in front because that's where the horse used to be and a high seat like that in the king's coach, which can be pretty uncomfortable on a corduroy road and looks absurd on a modern highway. Here and there its operation rises above that minimum usefulness. The excess, like the reserve power of the engine, is velvet; the public is glad to have it, when the public thinks about it, but can't be induced to catch fire from a suggestion that the amount of velvet can be enormously increased. That potential increase, on the other hand, inspires the mystical engineer. He concludes that the public are fools and the manufacturers villains who betray them. The next step is simple, pious, and self-sacrificing: to raise a howl for the machine guns, streamlining, the Kingdom of Heaven, and some blue-prints that will guarantee efficiency and give the race the good sense it ought to have.

This suggests why, to one kind of devout mind, the most indispensable job in the world is so abhorrent — politics. Such a mind sees the politician as a manufacturer under the profit system in conspiracy to rob the public. Well, maybe he is; but that is accidental, subsidiary and after the fact. His primary job — it is the same whether he is a Fascist, a Commissar, a Jacksonian Democrat or a school trustee in Ward Seven, and he loses it if he doesn't do it effectively — is to maintain the operation of the most complex and im-portant machine that exists at the minimum level of useful-ness. The moment he boggles that job, the moment operation falls below that level, there is hell to pay for the rest of us. Such a level may permit a glittering embroidery of gadgets but its fundamentals are stability and flexibility, repair, re-modeling, and extension — in all of which the actual users of the machine are profoundly uninterested. A politician is a man who somehow, by instinct or intelligence, by guess or by God, by a faculty for human contraries and the old Adam and plain graft, keeps the myriad variables working together at the minimum level — and so allows us to get over the road in a model which is always obsolete and has never had the efficiency or the beauty of an absolute. From a thousand drafting-rooms issue loud yells for efficiency and beauty, and an unending series of blueprints exhibiting ideal designs. But the same barriers stand in the way: the conditions of the problem, the limitations of the materials, and the attitude of the consumer. So long as the machine runs satisfactorily the buyer doesn't care how inefficient it may be, and his preference in styling never consults the ideal. As for the politician, he works in the machine-shop, not the drafting-room. With the best will in the world he can take from the blueprints only an occasional spare part that fits his needs for emergency repair, looks odd in the old model that is still running, and tends to reduce the ideal form to caricature.

Which may be just as well. The history of thought displays a long series of ideal designs for society. Lined up in time's Smithsonian, they look pretty quaint. Even the absolutes of the drafting-room, the Townless Highway to Utopia, may be a function of fashion, along with the whip-socket on the cowl.

The Well-Informed, 1920-1930

~~~~~~~~~~~~~~~~~~~~~~~~~~~~~~~~~~~~~~~

I

THROUGHOUT the summer of 1920 Mr. Gibson's girls coquetted in the pages of *Life* with only the slightest possible change, sartorially, from their flirtations of 1910. Their skirts billowed at the hips and narrowed at the shoe-tops, above which everything was conjectural. A heroine of Mr. Coles Phillips' had to trip and fall down in order to display the lustrous calves which would soon be Mr. Phillips' principal charm. Bathing girls everywhere, even in the advertisements, were skirted and stockinged: not a single one-piece suit was chronicled. Coiffures remained voluminous. On August 19, however, *Life* perceives an omen. The caption of its cover is "What Next?" and the design presents a hussy at the country club. Her golf skirt terminates no more than eight inches below her knees. Under a wide hat, her hair is bobbed. A culminating nastiness exhibits the omen, for the hussy holds a cigarette in one hand and her lips form smoke rings. . . . The cover is drawn by Rea Irvin.

Life had not yet ratified the revolution in manners which, four months earlier than this cover, Mr. Fitzgerald had announced in *This Side of Paradise*. Meanwhile the *Nation*, a vehicle of optimism, recognized a temporary interruption to progress in the debates then current between Senator Harding and Governor Cox, but felt that not even these could much longer delay the triumph of enlightened public opinion. It admired a permanent third party of great promise for liberalism which was led by Mr. Parley P. Christiansen of Utah. Mr. Bertrand Russell, who was still writing books rather than prefacing anthologies, told the *Nation's* subscribers that a trip to Russia had cooled his enthusiasm for communism.

Mr. Sinclair Lewis had forsaken *The Saturday Evening Post*. His new novel, *Main Street*, attracted wide attention to his talent for mimicry and burlesque. It fitted nicely with Mr. Anderson's *Winesburg Ohio* of the year before and produced a suspension of critical intelligence. Before long it had been joined by *Miss Lulu Bett* and other derivatives from Miss Cather and Mr. Howe. Mr. Carl Van Doren forgot *Huckleberry Finn, The Story of a Country Town, Zury, The Damnation of Theron Ware*, and the short stories of Mrs. Freeman and Ambrose Bierce. He announced that American literature, belatedly, had revolted from the village. Unlike most of his colleagues, however, Mr. Van Doren remembered his reading before long, and, in some embarrassment, made amends.

In January a magazine had removed from Chicago, which Mr. Mencken would soon declare to be the literary capital of the United States, to New York, which was the literary countinghouse. The intention of the *Dial* was to conduct a revolution in literature. Its preferred material, however, was poetry, and though American poetry had spent the past five years experiencing a renaissance, its revolutionary fervor now slackened. Fewer tumbrils were drawn about the streets, not so many furies knitted beside the guillotine and though Miss Lowell's work went on, the new Spoon River proved more brackish than its predecessor. Mr. Robinson, Mr. Frost, and Miss Millay remained inattentive to revolution, and the *Dial* dedicated itself to the performance of another function. It inherited the mission of *The Seven Arts* and became the rostrum of people for whom Mr. Harold Stearns promptly found a benignant label. These were, though the adjective was imperfectly descriptive, the Young Intellectuals.

They had been vocal for some time. Mr. Van Wyck Brooks had announced the passing of American pioneering materialism. That atrocity came to an end, he showed, not long before the war broke out in Europe in 1914. The date may have signalized the graduation from college of the Young Intellectuals, equipped with Professor Carver's theories about the economics of the Group. Or it may have coincided with the publication of Mr. Brooks's *America's Coming of Age*, one of the decennial abstracts of Emerson's "American Scholar." At any rate the Young Intellectuals had existed, in 1920, for about six years. They had developed, during the war period, a pattern of beliefs; and especially in the postwar year, 1919, had found conversation and the press sympathetic. That year, too, had given them a minor culmination in *Our America*, by Mr. Waldo Frank, whose English style had not yet swallowed its tail. Nevertheless, they did not achieve complete expression until *The Ordeal of Mark Twain*. The book affronted the Philistines, but it was discovered that their number had amazingly decreased. The intellectual were charmed, but Mr. Van Doren wondered whether Mr. Brooks really understood Mark Twain and whether this brilliant denunciation of American economics might not be irrelevant. He was shouted down, for the book had found a new playground for the intellectual in the reinterpretation of American history, and it had provided, in the words of Mr. Stearns, "a genuine Freudian analysis of Mark Twain's unconscious motives."

The works of Sigmund Freud blossomed tropically in America in 1920, and for the first time had a genuine circulation among the intellectual. They had been discussed in American learned journals since the middle Nineties. They had slowly found their way into the possession of medical schools, psychologists, and psychiatrists until by 1909 it was possible for Dr. Freud to visit America in the capacity of prophet. The visit multiplied his disciples and produced translations of his writings. By 1919 a good many hundred psychoanalysts, at least one in every hundred of whom was trained for his craft, were scattered about America; the Freudian dogmas were being taught in college courses; and American variants of the system flourished. Very few of the Freudian ideas, however, had worked into conversation; they reached popular art through the adventures of Craig Kennedy, in fact, before they colored the discussions of the intellectual. The reason for this delay was the quality of the translations. The German of Dr. Freud and his expositors was mysterious enough, but his translators accomplished marvels by rendering it into an English darker still. In 1919, however, Mr. André Tridon began his series of explanations, which brought a comfortably diluted version of Freud within the capacity of anyone. He seminated imitators by the long ton. The presses of America, throughout 1920 and the succeeding three years, produced an endless succession of explanations of the Freudian psychology.

American conversation now had most of the themes that would occupy it through the next ten years. The well-informed entered another decade of the Newness, which was to gleam with hope and resound with the pursuit of certainty. There were enormous numbers of them in America and they created a golden day for publishers. For every one of them felt that he could acquire merit by reading a book.

II

The *Dial's* business manager was probably the most literary ever possessed by an American magazine. In 1930 he looked back on the by then extinct activity of the Young Intellectuals, the course of which may be charted by two of his books. In 1924 Mr. Gilbert Seldes gathered his *Vanity Fair* articles into a volume called *The Seven Lively Arts*, and, before a creation of Picasso's, felt that "the significant and overwhelming thing to me was that I held the work a masterpiece and knew it to be contemporary." When Ernest Boyd quoted the attitude he was widely supposed to be alluding to Mr. Malcolm Cowley, but this was Mr. Seldes and his book pointed the attitude at vaudeville clowns and jazz bands. The figure of Charles Chaplin emerged, a sort of superior Duse, and Krazy Kat was clearly an important creation. The attitude was amusing but behind it one perceived the awful tensity of significance. It required four more years for Mr. Seldes' maturing emotions to produce *The Stammering Century*, the first book by a Young Intellectual that did not misrepresent America. Two years later, as the decade ended, Mr. Seldes appraised the history of the Young Intellectuals and decided that it was a case history. The movement, he concluded, was a product of unstable nervous systems.

The hypothesis is illuminating but too easy an explanation. The frequency of nervous disorders was probably no greater

among the chosen than in the country at large. We are
forced, as with all American thought, into metaphysics. The
Young Intellectual, in the great majority, inherited the moral
ideas of Jews or of New England Puritans — so nearly identical, as Barrett Wendell pointed out, that one name will do
for both. He was an American, and hence much given to
idealism. He had been brought up in democracy. He had
acquired a set of economic principles, themselves derived
from religion, a set of political dogmas, and a suspicion that
art was immoral unless it tried to effect economic justice.
His type characteristic, in fact, was that he had his ideas in
sets. There were right ideas and wrong ideas, and right
ideas were linked in a pattern. If you had the right idea *a*
about Whitman, then *ipso facto* you had the right ideas *a'*
about state socialism, *a''* about the deportation of Reds, and
a''' about sexual freedom. His mind had been shaped in
the shapeless religion called Liberalism. He therefore found
literature merely a convenient approach to the remaking of
America. Literature was seldom an art to a Young Intellectual: it was a kind of politico-economic machinery whose
function was the reformation of society.

A good many years before him, Bernard Shaw had described his end: the fate of a man who sees life as it is and
thinks about it romantically is despair. The Young Intellectual thought about life romantically: his religion told him
that if he got enough votes and statutes, founded enough liberal schools, supported the good life with enough righteousness, felt intensely enough, conversed enough, and wrote
enough books, the world would shape itself to his visions.
Of late he had begun to see life as it is. The war had shown
him that his system of ideal economics and politics had no
correspondence in experience, but America was never deeply
involved in the war and he did not emotionally realize the

lesson. Peacetime America now supplied the realization, and the books of the Young Intellectual recorded his despair. They were phenomena of insufficient sophistication, of optimism betrayed, of religious fervor pitifully wrecked on fact. They formed an immense repudiation of America, which had wounded him. He professed to be revaluing civilization antiseptically, toward a finer culture. In fact he was exposing his naïveté.

Criteria were badly scrambled. Regard, for instance, the purely literary appraisals of such writers as Herman Melville and Emily Dickinson, which, originating among the Young Intellectuals, have broadened down until they are now the common equipment of the well-informed everywhere in the land. Melville's centenary brought him to the attention of the intellectual. They welcomed him with intense emotion, not as the author of *Typee* and *Moby Dick* but as an artist whom American materialism had frustrated. Thousands of feverish pages exploited the virtue of this symbolism, which was the more piquant in that Melville had suffered the same obsession with metaphysics that betrayed his rediscoverers. Even at the end of the decade realism about him is impossible. If a critic should suggest that Melville quit writing because his mind grew sodden with religious symbolism, that *Pierre* met exactly the reception it merited, or that *Moby Dick* was sprinkled with moony nonsense, he would be screamed out of the reviews. They are still subject to opinions about Melville conceived by thinkers who were really objecting to the Dawes Plan or expressing their disenchantment with the Republican Party. Emily Dickinson seemed likely to share Melville's destiny. The intellectual canonized her because she withdrew from the abhorrent spectacle of Philistinism and repression in America. She retired to her garden and the retirement clearly signified that

America destroyed its artist. This symbolism rioted at large till Miss Taggard ventured to suggest that it might be more intelligent to think of Emily as a poet than as a victim of the Ford plant at River Rouge. Sanity thus returned, but the opinion that any line she wrote must be fine poetry because Mark Twain had made money from his books had filtered down to the well-informed, among whom it remains unalterable.

In 1922 Mr. Harold Stearns brought the Young Intellectuals to their highest phase. For *Civilization in the United States,* indeed, he had to go outside the movement, the chosen not being competent in all departments of this inquiry — whose purpose was to ascertain the complete truth about America once and for all. The limitations of the Intellectuals' experience explained the presence of Mr. Mencken, Mr. Nathan, Professor Chafee, Mr. Taylor, Mr. Macy, Professor Lovett, Professor Spingarn, Mr. Boyd, and Mr. Ring Lardner. And the presence of these aliens gives the book some worth to-day. The effort was to discover the unified system that would completely describe American life, past and present, and attain certainty; the achievement was a system whose components, brilliant, tawdry, or irrelevant, swallowed one another. The effort was that absurdity of optics, a lens whose angle of view is 360°; the resultant was a cyclorama of selected images each one crazily distorted in relation to the rest. A few of the chapters were permanently descriptive: Mr. Mencken's, Professor Chafee's, the by then familiar spectacle of Mr. Ernest Boyd patiently correcting the education of critics. And though some of the others were mere nonsense, some were vastly illuminating. It was the major effort that failed. The parts warred furiously on one another and logic could make nothing of the debris. If *a* was true, *b* could not be; no position in space existed which both could occupy at once. What the religion of the intellectual required was certainty, and the major effort to attain it had failed. Tidemark was reached; the movement retreated down the beach. Issuing a papal malediction, Mr. Stearns sailed for Paris.

The activity of the Young Intellectuals, though it had not existed on a plane of stern reality, had been sincere and sometimes brilliant, and had succeeded in telling much truth. For purposes of conversation among the well-informed, who cannot sustain general ideas, this activity, however, had to be vulgarized. The framework existed: postwar America was prosperous but abhorrent, materialism and repression were functions of Puritanism, a conspiracy to strangle truth and art and to brutalize amour plainly existed, and it was possible to understand the world if you practised the psychological inquiries of Dr. Freud. To commensurate these incommensurables required but one further hint from the upper intelligence. This was inadvertently and much to his horror supplied by a professor of American history. Mr. Arthur Schlesinger felt that his profession required a statement in general terms of its first generation of realistic research. In 1922 he provided the statement in *New Viewpoints in American History*. It was not intended for the vulgar, who, nevertheless, received it with cries of orgiastic surprise and stampeded down a steep place to the sea. The little red schoolhouse, then, had lied to the well-informed! The vulgar are incapable of general ideas: the adulteration of Mr. Schlesinger's book can be observed in the procession of what were curiously called debunking biographies. The production of such a work required little material and less effort. You brought together a copy of the official biography of the subject, a volume of *Godey's Lady's Book, Civilization in the United*

States, and one or more of Mr. Tridon's journeyman pieces. Biography thereupon wrote itself. Mr. Tridon's exposition of ambivalence satisfactorily dissolved evidence, and Mr. Schlesinger had suggested that history was bunk. You might track down the Civil War till its origin was located in the formation of a women's organization which first existed in 1867. You might show the blight on your subject's career in his repudiation by a friend who did not hear of the subject till eighteen months after the repudiation was in print. You might psychoanalyze documents that never existed, reproduce conversations never recorded or suspected, and derive the unconscious motives of your subject from your inner sense of what must be right. No matter. You pointed out the Œdipus complex and told the whole truth about your subject when you named him a hebephrenic, an extravert, a manic-depressive, an invert, or a zoöphile.

III

A Burgundian peasant of the thirteenth century knelt before a splinter of bone, besought any convenient saint to remove the mark of scrofula from his child, had seen the Virgin at nightfall when a spring miraculously sweetened, sprinkled holy water to avert the malice of devils, and had measured with his fingers the footprints of the true God in a neighboring boulder. There was somewhere a sequence of relationship from these ideas to the religion of Augustine, Aquinas, and Abélard. Exactly the same relationship existed between the conversational certainties of the early 1920's and the psychology of Sigmund Freud.

The well-informed were now expert in their Freud. They had read a book. That made them competent in the interpretation of phenomena and all but infallible in the solution of insolubles. The good Tridon had made every sofa a consulting room. Confession and absolution are sacraments in all religions because they provide an easily invoked pleasure. The charm of popular Freudianism was the gusto of revelation plus economy. No effort whatever was required to arrange the world in a pattern and explain its inhabitants. Both proved susceptible to two dollars' worth of reading matter.

Even Tin Pan Alley explored the unconscious and the amours of Coney Island profited, but the serious labor was sustained on the level of the well-informed. The two dollar book, without temporizing, laid truth bare. The American Radiator Tower rose skyward to an accompaniment of understanding smiles, and the pleasures of architects were sympathetically perceived. The lens focused informatively on everything one had been taught. Folklore succumbed, then religion, then philosophy — by means of history, which the biographies were making plain. The law, business, and politics followed. In a moment of extravaganza, Mr. Simeon Strunsky noted a scandal in Euclid and reduced the *pons asinorum* to the Œdipus complex. He supposed he was writing burlesque, but the folk accepted his findings and geometry was now classified as a neurosis. Still, what chiefly made psychiatric conversation pleasurable was its personal utility. F.P.A. grew *ennuyé* and protested in a ballad "Don't tell me what you dreamt last night for I've been reading Freud," but you were fortunate if your friends confined their explanations to your dreams. The wary threw away all of their cravats that had a reddish tinge and antiseptically devoted themselves, in public, to the other sex. Shrewd women received each other only behind doors closed to common scrutiny. The income of pet-stores fell off, for the possession of dogs or parrots was a symptom;

if the *Minderwertigkeit* was not indicated then the master-slave complex was, or at least a partly sublimated impulse to murder your wife. Penitentiaries, we came to understand, might be made into solaria when we learned to convert our sadists into surgeons or butchers.

The objective was sanitation: to reveal one's sex-life together with the traumas that had kept it short of the ideal. At table and in corners matrons charted the symptomology of their Messalina complexes, for the pleasure of gentlemen who reciprocated by describing the events that had warped them to a lifetime of fetichism. The investigation of sexual inversion had the brisk novelty of mah jong. It was no longer necessary to invoke self-expression as a motive for promiscuity; the heroines of fiction had shown the way to consider it a defense against neurosis. Conversation thus became the largest part of what the *Nation* called *Our Changing Morality*, with preface by Bertrand Russell. The effect of all this on manners was doleful, but psychiatrists, both quack and legitimate, were enabled to become two-car conscious. The stage profited from The New Freedom, and the revues glorified inversion in ways that Shakespeare's androgynes had been unable to invent. In what is called the legitimate theater, the well-informed saw conversation actually built up into drama. They may have imperfectly distinguished between *Pleasure Man* and *Desire Under the Elms*, but the esthetic judgments of the educated have seldom been trustworthy.

Behaviorism flared up, a conditioned response to the unconscious. It was gorgeous for a while, then lapsed into the possession of experimental schools for infants, being stilled by the folk's ability to ingest it with Freud. It proved possible to blend Freud, Jung, Adler, and Watson in a satisfactory system. The inferiority complex made great progress among the educated, who perceived its utility and merged it in the

Œdipus complex without a smile. You classified your friend according to the nomenclature of Jung and further explained him on the basis of Œdipus coiled in the inadequacy-feeling, sub-vocal speech coöperating handsomely with the censor. Meanwhile hypotheses became entities and terminologies acquired objective existence. To the well-informed the castration complex had exactly the same spatial existence as the spirochete and could probably be stained with eosin; the censor had the same organic structure as the gall-bladder and was as susceptible to surgical exploration. A neurotic fantasy had the same etiology as a case of typhoid fever. When you studied a friend's phobias and reduced them to a pattern which you derived from the experiences of his infantile libido, you were as objective as a clinician, dealing with measurements as factual as temperature, blood-counts, and X-ray photographs.

Popular Freudianism, in fact, was another search for certainty which ended, like most of its American analogues, in the infinitely unconditioned domain of symbolism. Step by step it marched on metaphysics, where it merged with the infinite. Its infinity, and not its destruction of social taboos, was in fact its fascination for the well-informed. It was intended to make all things clear — to bathe every phenomenon in brilliant light, to answer every question with complete certainty. Now, certainty, so far as science is concerned with it, is only accuracy of description, and accuracy of description is attainable for only a few things and for them only at the cost of stupendous labor. Whereas the educated demand certainty about everything and cannot patiently abide labor. Psychology was not a description: it was an explanation, an interpretation. It armed the well-informed against doubt. It explained the world. It identified itself with metaphysics, telling the folk what was real. It was a form of religion. A limitation in its capacity finally slew it, but for a while it was, as a religion, tremendously successful.

Its success explains why the irruption of biology at mid-decade was unfruitful. Dayton, Tennessee, did indeed call to the attention of the well-informed a department of science which their college courses had not included. Publishers hastened to supply reading matter, but the movement flopped. The educated learned that evolution was something more than a quandary associated with the length of the camelopard's neck, but biology never caught on. Perhaps it was on too high a plane: Darwin fared more happily than most of the great dead, for his biography came to the hands of Mr. Bradford and Mr. Ward. But mainly it failed because biology did not mature its metaphysical seeds. It was too limited. Its field was the earth, whereas the folk are most at ease in the universe. Its data were the animals, among them man, whereas the folk, in America, prefer the farthest reach of thought. It occupied itself with concreteness that left no room for the infinite. And the biologists were not "pure" scientists and so expressed an aversion to finalities. Their object was description; they achieved it as nearly as might be and then pointed out the gaps they had left. The folk will tolerate no gaps. They rejected biology, which refused to express any certainty about man's fate. It was hence inferior to psychology, which chased certainty through the dark vastness of the unconscious and left the soul open to the winds from beyond the stars. Yet the limitation of psychology was that its metaphysics, too, was earthbound — that its hands did not tightly grasp the universe, that it did not look far enough beyond the stars. Science had not yet provided an adequate religion for the brighter people. Then, as the decade ended, revelation came back. From beyond the stars.

IV

The *Nation* announced the permanence of Mr. LaFollette's third party in 1924, and though it admired Al Smith in 1928, felt that the time had come for a permanent third party under Mr. Norris. In 1930 it still believed that the Americans might yet add a cubit to their statutes. Skirts had gone up till the female knee and much else ceased to be a matter of conjecture; then they had reverted to the level of 1910 and the design of 1890. Corset factories once more paid dividends. Bathing costumes had shed their skirts and stockings, and in reverence to the spectrum below λ 390 $\mu\mu$, their backs also. Nevertheless hostesses spoke of beginning dinner on time and the Junior League feared that manners might have decayed. The girls investigated a notion called Humanism which, they understood, had something to do with decorum. Mr. Sinclair Lewis, who had spent the decade revolting from the village, the metropolis, the medical profession, Abercrombie and Fitch, and the ministry, now profited from a Swedish chemist's desire to encourage the art. He commended the European admiration of his works and talked, without much conviction, rather like Harold Stearns.

No Young Intellectual was anywhere discernible. Literary controversy occupied itself with Aristotle, for whom the academic performed an *auto-da-fé* and whom the non-academic denounced as a sort of Frederick Taylor. The politico-economic criticism of literature had completely vanished, except for Mr. Michael Gold's disparagement of Mr. Thornton Wilder as an instrument of capitalism. The *Dial* had found literature unsusceptible to revolution and had died. A journal without a noble cause had meanwhile appeared; the *American Mercury* was a channel of civilization.

So was the *New Yorker*, whose attitudes hid no tensity whatever and whose drawings gave the nation a new idiom.

In all this there was little comfort for the well-informed, whose conversation requires hypotheses. Oswald Spengler's elegy on the dispossessed Junkers seemed promising; its interminable vagueness ought to have held room for the infinite. But history, even the philosophy of history, is earthbound, and it proved unfeasible to leap from the declining West into the eternal sunrise of metaphysics. Science seemed to be muffing its job. Yet in 1925 Professor Whitehead had already brought tidings of beautiful ideas beyond the galactic system. Professor Eddington's Gifford lectures were available in 1928. The next year Sir James Jeans performed a clarification of Eddington, and in 1930 dived from their common springboard into the infinite. The folk now had their desire; and science, as the decade ended, revealed to them a completely satisfactory pattern of ideas. It was metaphysics, it was symbolism, it could not be understood, and its locale was the universe as far as thought could reach. At last, therefore, it must be certainty.

In ten years conversation had progressed from American Philistinism to the limits of knowledge. The irresistible attraction of this new metaphysics is the folk's complete inability to understand it. No language existed for the communication of Abélard's celestial physics to the Burgundian peasant. A language does exist for the communication of twentieth-century mathematical physics to the multitudes of its converts but none of them have learned to speak it. In order to syllabify a page of Eddington or Jeans one must have mastered at the very least the calculus of differentials and integrations. Mastering the calculus requires something more than exposure to instruction in it — requires its use, quite apart from projects, as a method of thinking. As the books of mathematicians go through multiple editions hardly one in five thousand readers has this elementary preparation. Yet the calculus is no more than an alphabet of the mathematics through which physics organizes its data. Physics is a science which operates on the highest level of the intelligence, and the newspaper headlines which announced in 1923 that probably less than a dozen men in the world could understand Professor Einstein's work approached realism. That permits the culminating beatitude of the well-informed, who now joyfully construct systems out of ignorance uncontaminated by any comprehension whatsoever.

An intelligent use of the critical appraisals of American civilization attempted by the Young Intellectuals following 1920 required an encyclopedic knowledge of American history — a greater knowledge than the appraisers themselves possessed. Yet the lack of it in no way deterred the well-informed from building misconceptions, misstatements and sheer guesses into systems which had a dazzling glitter. An intelligent understanding of the psychology of the unconscious required years of clinical experience and a slow integration that nothing but constant observation could supply. Did not the Master denounce lay analyses and insist that to understand psychoanalysis one must be psychoanalyzed? Yet the folk sublimated one another's conflicts and created metaphysical systems out of sheer nothing. Likewise an intelligent understanding of mathematical physics requires years of apprenticeship in mathematics and years of habituation to laboratory apparatus of whose existence, even, the general are unaware. Yet conversation, which enjoyed American materialism and the Œdipus complex with equal enthusiasm, now faces the 1930's with a chromium-plated terminology and the ideas that beautiful words invariably generate. And there is empirical proof that a new religion has been organized: the itinerant lecturer has added astrophysics to his repertory.

Reading matter has advanced to three dollars a volume but the sofas that once commended the flight of artists to Paris, where no materialism existed, and later dealt shrewdly with infantile fixations, which obviously did something or other to people, now occupy themselves with gravitational instability and the Doppler effect. Somehow, minds virgin of physics are excited about the FitzGerald Contraction, frames of space, main-sequences on the Russell diagram, monomarks, binary systems, continua, and the nebula M_{51} in *Canes Venatici*. Dinner-table scientists who have never seen a spectroscope and to whom any page of formulæ, say a fragment of Willard Gibbs's statement of his phase-rule, would be far more unintelligible than so many Maya carvings, deduce the bearing of Minkowski's calculations on the problem of evil, and sternly deprive causality of its possible relationship to knowledge. The mathematics of a complex variable is wholly beyond their grasp but they reject the Newtonian physics, have defined reality, and are working out the implications for ethics of this astrophysical metaphysics. . . . What we behold is, of course, the familiar dualism: the vulgarization of ideas and the search for certainty. The folk are incapable of general ideas and if Professor Eddington cannot sometimes prevent himself from seeing red electrons and gray protons, the well-informed feel quite sure that the neighborhood druggist can sell them a pound of entropy. They know that atoms are events, that energy is music, and that Whitehead has rebuked Calvin and made freedom of the will an honest woman once again. For, perceive, God is a mathematician and somewhere in this vertiginous scheme of the unknowable certainty abides. In the simultaneity and probability of the electrons or at a temperature of thirty-six million degrees where the nuclei are naked, a man may be sure of himself. Metaphysics has chased the absolute to the boundaries of the universe and, beyond the stars, the sofas are content.

It was thus that the Burgundian peasant accommodated the true essence of God to his capacity. Till the inconstancy which is our simian heritage has displaced physics with anthropology or spiritualism or economics in 1935, the well-informed will elaborate their religion of what cannot be understood. They will exert these gaudy rumors to explain their impulses, justify their conduct, reconstruct their societies, and give meaning to their laws and institutions. No doubt priests will arrive to harmonize this advance in piety with worthy portions of the discarded creeds, so that we shall see Virgo preyed upon by Philistinism and uncover the havoc of Œdipus among the electrons. That is the way of popular religions, and the scientist who finds his hypotheses creating chimeras among the folk should betray no surprise at the corruption of prophecy. It is an amusing spectacle — mathematics, the remote and dispassionate summary of inert data, invoked for the interpretation of human folly which is warm and live. It has the great virtue of suggesting that any idea is fully as valid as any other, and that the opinions of a man about subjects in which he is entitled to no opinion whatever are rich with comfort. To shift the interest of sofas and dinner tables to a different inquiry may mean a loss in color or intensity. Paleontology, the class struggle, or statistics — whatever next occupies the art of conversation — may be less sprightly in the propagation of ignorance. And — a consideration which should have some force in time of depression — it may cost five dollars a volume.

FROM *Harper's*, SEPTEMBER 1927

The Co-Eds: God Bless Them

I

NOT long ago a man with whom I had roomed at college came to visit me and during his stay expressed a desire to observe me perform as a teacher. The motive that prompted him was no doubt malicious, but it was quite forgotten before he had sat through his first class. For he and I had gone to one of those monastic Eastern colleges where few women ever get past the visitors' gallery at the commons, and now for the first time he was seeing co-education. I expected him to say something appropriate about the lecture I delivered, for I had talked about Coleridge, and Professor Lowes's book was hot from the press; but he seemed to have forgotten that I had been any part of the hour's diversion. As we strolled across the campus he tried vigorously to reduce to order the confusion that his experience had brought him.

The first coherent idea that he voiced was, "Good Lord! I was expecting a college, not a sample room. That front row! It looked like the hosiery window at a spring opening or the finale of a Vanities first act. What do you teach 'em, dancing?"

A moment later, "Educational patter from the little ash-blonde: 'Does a poet know what he is writing or does he just tap the subconscious?' That's what happens when you expose a predestinate chocolate-dipper to Psych A."

And then, "How can a man teach with a roomful of beautiful girls listening to him? Do you expect the men to keep their minds on Coleridge? And you can't be ass enough to want girls who look like that to handicap themselves with an education."

Later still he settled matters to his satisfaction. "Don't tell me you even try to teach 'em anything. You've got a living to make, and you merely elect to make it talking about Coleridge to a chorus of ravishing girls who all their life long will continue to associate Coleridge with henna and *Narcisse Noir*, and who merely use your classroom as a convenient place to pry luncheon-dates out of susceptible males. It's an old delusion that you can educate women. You're not fool enough to think that even one of that ballet has any idea that Coleridge wrote poetry, or what poetry is, or gives a damn, anyway. Sure! I saw 'em putting down pages of notes. You'll give them A when they come back to you on the final."

It was all very amusing. It reminded me forcibly of the day, some five years before, when I faced my first co-educational class. The offer of the position had reached me on a desert ranch, where I was working for my board and where even the pittance the Dean offered me seemed munificent. I traveled two thousand miles and bolted from the train-shed directly to a room containing thirty-five freshmen who were waiting to be told what to do for their first college assignment. I was on the rostrum before I fully realized that Atlantis was, after all, a co-educational university; and the sight of "that front row," crammed with new fall creations and shiny with French-nude stockings, appalled me. For the moment I wished myself back in the Idaho desert, untempted by an instructor's salary fully half as large as a milkman's, eating mutton three times a day, and rejoicing in the only beard I have ever owned. I was not long from the Eastern college, you see, and I knew all about the higher education of women. I knew that Middle-Western universities were contemptible from the point of view of scholarship (the knowledge had been confirmed by my being hired to teach at one). I knew that girls went to such places primarily to find husbands who didn't live in the old home town. I knew furthermore that women didn't belong to the class of *educabilia*, which included in fact only a distressingly small percentage of males. And I knew, finally, that most women didn't pretend to take education seriously and that the few who did were not only esthetic atrocities but also the most saddening numbskulls to be encountered anywhere by a vigorous mind.

To be sure, several of the graduate schools of my own university admitted women; and there was a regulation whereby students of a neighboring women's college might very occasionally enter an undergraduate course. That I had been in a philosophy course which one of these rare specimens attended probably contributed to my idea of her sex's mentality. She was so homely that we called her "The Pure Reason," and she was eternally interrupting the professor's lecture, no matter what it concerned, with the stern question, "Is that reconcilable with Kant?" She was miserable whenever his language descended to intelligibility, and her distress at his mild, unworldly witticisms so saddened him that he gave them up altogether.

I could not see, after a desperate glance, anything corresponding to The Pure Reason in my first class. Quite the contrary. There were fully as many men as women in that class, but I was not aware of them. I could see only women, and they were all staggeringly beautiful. It could not be possible that such stunning girls would even pretend to take an interest in intellectual matters. They were undoubtedly a frivolous and giddy crew who would ogle me out of passing grades and coax me into letting them go free of assignments, and chatter and make up their faces during my most solemn flights. The room seemed oppressive with femininity, and I was quite sure that such an atmosphere, however favorable it might be to nature's designs for the perpetuation of the race, was frost and blight and mildew to that orderly discipline of the mind which I considered education.

Well, one learns, and I wonder now that in the moment of shock I did not recall the empirical fact that nine tenths of the truly wise people I had known were women. Even if I had, at that stage I should doubtless have contended that wisdom was something apart from education, some derivative from the nebulous function which is called intuition.

Before long, however, I began to realize that not all my pupils were beautiful, and with that first discrimination began a series of readjustments which quite reversed most of my preconceptions. The whole point of this article, which is a recantation, is my discovery that the greater part of the education which the modern college manages to achieve, in the intervals between endowment campaigns, football championships, and psychological surveys, is appropriated by the very sex who presumably do not belong to the *educabilia* at all.

The women, these scatterbrained co-eds, are better material for education than the men and readier at acquiring it, and are also the chief hope for the preservation of the values which were long declared to be the ideals of liberal education.

II

Here I must take one or two stipulations. It must be understood that I speak entirely in generalizations, having no space to take account of exceptions, and that I generalize about the average student, not the exceptional one. To judge the colleges on the basis of the superior student — two per cent. of the enrollment — would be foolish, and to attempt a differentiation between superior men and superior women would be more foolish still. Above a certain level of intelligence there seems to be little fundamental difference between the sexes, so far as their work in college is concerned. The tendencies with which I am now concerned are those of the mass, the undistinguished young folk who are the backbone of the colleges; and I am speaking of the tendency, not of any given individual who may oppose it. It must also be understood that I am generalizing from my own experience. I have checked it so far as possible by the experience of others, but without much finality on either side. A publicly expressed opinion on this subject is rare, since it exposes one to the headlines and editorials of the press, the recriminations of a dean who is harassed by officious associations, and an avalanche of letters from the nation's cranks. It is easier to get a privately expressed opinion but it is also more likely to be conditioned by the accidents of the week. The Kappa weeper may have cried Professor Smith out of a passing mark for a sister half an hour before he defies the whole University Club to find him one co-ed who ever did a lick of work. Or Professor Smith may have married his brightest senior and so wedded an idea that the co-eds, as a sex, comprise the upper three fourths of the intellectual scale, to the complete exclusion of the men.

The first observation is that the old debate is over, and the old problem of what aim a college education should have, if not solved, is at least settled forevermore. Even ten years ago the battle between the humanists on the one hand and the vocationalists on the other was still vigorous. Its outcome though unmistakable was not yet achieved, and the dwindling but vigorous defenders of liberal education showed no signs of panic. To-day, after ten years that have telescoped a century of evolution and have left the American colleges completely bewildered, hardly even the tradition survives. Not more than eight colleges in the country even pretend to champion the old ideals or to adapt them to postwar problems; and of those that do pretend, the loudest-voiced has done more to injure the cause than any dozen of its most Rotarian rivals.[1]

By and large, the American college is now a training-school. It is engaged in preparing its students for their vocations. It is a feeder for the professional schools, on the one hand, and for business, on the other. Primarily it provides training for salesmanship. In the mass, young men come to college to learn how to sell. In the mass, they are not interested in the kind of education that is generally called liberal — or humanistic or cultural or intellectual. The man who comes to college to-day is not there to grow in wisdom, or to invite the truth to make him free, to realize his fullest intellectual possibilities, to learn the best that has been said and thought, or to fit himself to any other of the mottoes carved above his college gates. He is there to get through

[1] The reservation was not loud enough. Permit me, in 1936, to exempt from this and the following paragraph the leading universities, including the noisy one. And permit me to apologize for public nonsense.

the prerequisites of a professional school or of business. In either case he is righteously intolerant of all flapdoodle whatsoever that does not contribute directly to the foreseen end. Anything which undertakes to make him more efficient he will embrace with as much enthusiasm as he has left over from "activities" which are the organized hokum of college life. Anything else — be it anthropology or zoölogy or any elective in between — he will resent and actively condemn. He'll be damned if he's got time to waste on wisdom — or knowledge — or truth and beauty — or cultural development — or individuality — or any of the other matters with which the colleges used to be concerned.

One who speaks to the college man of a different kind of education meets not the derision his opponents might have cast on him before the War, but an incomprehension, a complete failure to understand his language that is a thousand times more conclusive. Such an outcome was inevitable from the moment that the higher education became democratic, and its original momentum dates from the establishment of State-supported universities. But whereas, in spite of its democratic power, the really powerful authorities were opposed to the development as late as 1917, those same authorities have been since then its most enthusiastic leaders. Where the ideals of liberal education still survive they are cherished by aging and solitary men who can never head an educational body or sit on a president's throne. The administrations have gone over wholly to the popular cause. Recently the President of one of our largest universities said flatly to his faculty, "The students are our customers and we must give them what they want." [1] His language was more forthright than

---

[1] If the reader will interpret the earlier part of this paragraph in the light of this incident, he will understand how a generalization can be made enthusiastic. I chose to forget that there are colleges and colleges.

that of most of his peers, who adopt the terminology of
Service, but unquestionably he expressed the philosophy
of most of them. With this policy in the throneroom the
faculties in general whoop up the process. Ask any college
teacher which departments have their budgets ratified without a murmur of complaint. Ask any department head what
courses he must stress to the trustees who guard the purse-
strings. Ask anyone what the dominant ideas of his campus
are and what professors are picked for the key positions in
the faculty committees. The colleges have gone out to give
the student what he wants. And what he wants may be defined as courses that are thought to provide training in efficient salesmanship.

This is, however, education from the point of view of men.
The women — those lovely co-eds whose stockings so disturbed my friend — are another matter. In the mass, they see
no need to prepare themselves for law or dentistry and feel
no call to become expert at selling. Their lives still have room
for the qualities that education once dealt with. They have
time for wisdom — and knowledge — and truth and beauty
— and cultural development — and individuality. That is
why they are so significant for the future if society has any
use for liberal education and expects the colleges to have
anything to do with it.

III

The canons of liberal education — if I correctly interpret
its champions — may be summarized as receptiveness to new
ideas, freedom from prejudice or other emotional bias, in-
sistence on factual or logical demonstration of everything
presented as truth, ability to distinguish between appearance and reality developed somewhat beyond the naïve faith
of the uneducated, refusal to accept authority or tradition as

final, and skepticism of the fads, propagandas, and panaceas that may be called the patent medicines of the mind. To abbreviate some centuries of definition still farther, the liberally educated man is supposed to possess an intelligently discriminating mind. The avenues by which this desirable possession may be acquired need not be scrutinized here. It suffices to remember what attributes have been considered the desiderata of liberal education and to estimate their relative distribution between the sexes in the colleges of to-day.

According to ancient theory, women's judgment is swayed by emotional considerations to a far greater extent than that of men. The daily routine in the colleges quite controverts the theory. It is the men, for instance, who die for dear old Rutgers. Here at Atlantis we have just emerged from a period of athletic failure which has given me an excellent chance to observe the passions in their natural state. I have seen many men in tears because the football employees of Utopia, that university of poltroons, had walloped our own; but I have never seen a co-ed leaving the stadium other than dry-eyed. The bales of themes that have rolled in upon me demanding a sterner athletic policy, bigger salaries for bigger fullbacks, in order to vindicate Atlantis as the best college in the world, have been without exception the work of men. The idea that the worth of a college is to be judged by the success of its football team is a man's idea. So is the idea that Atlantis is the best college in the world. A man is not satisfied, it seems, unless he can assure himself and the world at large that the college he attends is clearly superior to all others: a co-ed does not bother her mind with such infantile rationalizations.

As with football and world-leadership, so with the other functions of the college. Some years ago a newspaper, during a dearth of excitement, discovered the foul taproot of Bolshevism and the dead hand of Lenin (its own phrases) in an Epworth League at Atlantis. The organization that promptly had itself photographed kissing the Stars and Stripes, to prove Atlantis free of that moral plague, was a fraternity, not a sorority. The parade of patriotic youth carrying posters that damned all Bolshevists to the American Legion was entirely male. Male, too, were the petitions praying the President to redeem Atlantis before the world by expelling the Epworth League — they originated and circulated among the fraternities. So jingoism widens out: the co-eds think, the men throb. It is not enough that Atlantis is the world's-champion university with the loveliest campus and the most modern gadgets from the school of education. America, as the nation that is graced by Atlantis, must necessarily be immaculate, inimitable, and in all ways supreme.

Every year passionate organizations in the colleges pass hundreds of resolutions condemning the un-American conduct of some hapless professor who has suggested that the English plan of government is better than the American plan, that the Germans have a better civic policy, that the French eat better cooking, that a Japanese has thus far done the best research in this or that, that a Portuguese preceded a native Bostonian in sailing round Africa, or that the Mona Lisa is clearly superior to a fire-insurance calendar. Everyone who knows the colleges will recognize the phenomenon as one of the weariest bores of campus life. How many of these resolutions come from co-ed organizations? I have yet to observe one. It was a man, I remember, who refused to find any literary value in the Old Testament — obviously there couldn't be, he said, for it was written by a bunch of kikes.

In my survey of contemporary literature I deal perforce with much fiction and poetry of the day that, in method, is

Freudian, and with much that is behavioristic. In general, the men are antagonistic to it. They object to both Freud and the behaviorists, partly on the ground that they are new, but mostly on the ground that they are unpleasant. The young male is affronted by the public discussion of sex-motives though he is a whale at discussing them in private, and he is much more deeply affronted by behaviorism. Consequently, he does not consider whether they are true, but merely loathes them. Now this is proverbially a feminine response, and it exhibits with admirable clarity one of the crucial functions of intelligence. The person who says, for instance, "I'd hate to think that Freud is right" betrays an essentially ignorant attitude of mind; the seeker after truth has nothing to do with liking or hating and the only intelligent question is, Is Freud right? But this ignorant, or proverbially feminine, response in my advanced class is confined to the man. The dispassionate point of view is invariably that of the co-eds. They do not unthinkingly accept the new literature. They welcome it as an interesting phenomenon, something to be analyzed and appraised without preconceptions. That, I submit, is the intelligent, the educated attitude.

Perhaps a few examples are relevant. It was a man who rejected *Elmer Gantry* because it must be bad art since Sinclair Lewis could not possibly be sincere in such a biased and contemptible book. The tangle of fallacies displayed by this earnest senior was the kind traditionally ascribed to the feminine mind which cannot think impersonally; yet it was a co-ed who in class informed him that a man who differed from him was not necessarily insincere, asked him what an author's sincerity had to do with his art, and criticized *Elmer Gantry* from an intelligent point of view. It was another man who in amazement and disgust pronounced Mr. Anderson's *Winesburg, Ohio* an utterly untrue book, the phantasm of a diseased mind. It was a co-ed who checked off on her fingers the analogues of Anderson's characters whom she had observed in her own home town and named a number of Russian and French novelists who, though respectable in her opponent's eyes, used precisely the same method. It was a man who called Katherine Mansfield "nasty-minded" and found no moral teaching in her work: it was a co-ed who put him in his place. Finally, after we had read *Ulysses* it was the men who pretended to understand it and, without pretense, condemned it utterly — but it was the co-eds who admitted that they could not understand it but found occasional passages of magnificent prose and tentatively accepted the method as valid.

This, however, is all literary criticism. I am, perhaps, betrayed by the limitations of my subject? Not if I correctly observe the adventures of my colleagues. Is the campus stirred by a protest against the atheistical teachings of the zoölogy department? Then the howl is sure to be traced to some embryo revivalist from the Red-Flannels Belt — someone whose sister is not in the least appalled. Does the Dean have to listen for some hours to complaints against Mr. Dash of the history department, who has suggested that economic considerations somewhat influenced the wisdom of the Fathers in 1787, and so is patently subsidized from Moscow? Then the complainant is Bill Juicy, the pride of Sigma Sigma, who would die the death rather than hear Hamilton traduced. At that very moment Alice Apple, with whom Bill has a heavy date to-night, is writing a report for Mr. Dash's class and adding in a postscript that Mr. Dash must be wrong about Jefferson, for Alice cannot believe that even Jefferson could be so consistently high minded as Mr. Dash maintains. Or the large class files out of University Hall where Mr. Circle has been lecturing on Watson's theory of conditioned response. Bill Juicy lights a cigarette and ponders the lecture briefly. It's all a bunch of hooey, for if Watson is right then Bill can't think for himself. And that, in the face of Sigma Sigma's united stand for compulsory military training, is absurd. Bill dismisses Watson — whom he will thereafter associate with a brand of shock-absorbers — and goes to the fraternity house to find out whom to vote for in the class elections. But Alice, who also lights a cigarette as soon as she is screened from the Dean of Women, is also pondering. If Watson can establish his thesis; if those experiments Circle talks about are exhaustive, then — well, it's going to chase Mr. Dot of the Ethics course and Mr. Starr of the Social Progress course into a corner they'll never escape from. H'm — it rather knocks old Dot's idea of the Moral Will into a cocked hat.

IV

In various courses I have taught the wide expanse of English literature from Chaucer to James Joyce, but, apart from the tittering bromides of Polonius, I have found only one sentiment that appealed irresistibly to the male students in the class. That is the declaration in which Pope plumbed the depths of Bolingbroke and dredged up the assurance that whatever is, is right. It is the hoariest and most awesome conviction of the Babbitt mind, and its acceptance by the college youth of to-day is a broadly farcical commentary on our times. Here, I realize, I run counter to the shibboleths of the newspapers, which intermittently grow hydrophobic over a rebellious generation. It would be delightful and encouraging if the newspapers were right, but they are not. The wave of revolution that Mr. Coolidge discerned from afar when Vice-President never broke among our classic halls. How should salesmen-to-be revolt against anything?

If whatever is, isn't right to the last electron, then the future is unsure and efficiency is imperiled. It must be right, and the bozo that says it isn't must be extinguished with the full police power of undergraduate taboos. There need be no apprehension about college men among those shadowy personages who are assumed to be interested in the preservation of the established order, for college men are sound to the core. Beside the conservatism of a fraternity, a Directors' meeting of United States Steel would have a pronounced Bolshevistic tinge. A caucus of the Republican Old Guard is distinctly radical in comparison with the men of a normal American college. They are not only instinctively reactionary, but even consciously so — and with an unctuousness that would appall the editor of the *Wall Street Journal.*

I have just said that this condition is farcical, and to my low, pedagogical mind, which studies the American scene without rancor, it is precisely that. But from another point of view it is pitiful and, indeed, tragic. For youth is the gallant season when the milk bill is of less consequence than certain spears and the glory of dashing oneself against them. Youth satisfied with anything is youth curdled with the hope of selling bonds. There is a time for the slaying of dragons and the pursuit of Utopias. A fair share of revolutionary thought is essential for the full development of intelligence; for soil is made fruitful by plowing, and dynamite in deep-blast charges is acknowledged to be the best means of breaking up the clods and setting free the chemistry of creation. Ideally, college should give young minds four years of splendid intoxication. Made drunk with the freedom of ideas, college students should charge destructively against all the institutions of a faulty world and all the conventions of a silly one. Well, they don't.

My courses in advanced composition are an outlet for the

ideas of students who take them. In five years I have had a number of dissenters. I have had themes that inveighed against war and against marriage, themes that advocated an immediate proletarian revolution in the United States, themes that spoke highly of free-love or anarchy or communism, compulsory education in birth-control or the unionization of the farmers, military despotism or the creation of American soviets. One might focus on these themes — the work of some fifteen or twenty persons — and feel gratefully sure that all was well with the colleges, that such bright if momentary enthusiasms were evidence that college youth remained generous and undiscouraged. I might not dissent from such a judgment, but I must add that of the fifteen or twenty only one was a man.

I do not mean to suggest that the co-eds as a group are radical, but only that the college radical is more apt to appear among them. And I do insist that, as a group, they are more liberal than the men, less terrified by the prospect of social or intellectual change, and less suspicious of novelty. They seem to take for granted that in whatever is there must be, *ipso facto*, a great deal of nonsense. They are willing to examine what is proposed in place of it. The men merely set up a yell for the police or what, intellectually, corresponds to the police.

Above all, they are interested. The college man lives up to the type that has been created for him by the humorous magazines in that he seems perpetually bored. His is not the boredom of cynicism, not even of the callow cynicism of the cartoons, but the boredom that is usually called Philistine. Show him that the principles of Mr. Blank's course in "Business Psychology" will enable him hereafter to close a sale, and he will cast off his lethargy and dig; but through courses in the Greek thought of the Fourth Century or the

social institutions of Medieval Spain he wanders somnolent
and pathetic, a weary, grumbling lowbrow who has been
cruelly betrayed into registering for what rumor held to be
a snap course. The excitements and the ecstasies of the intellectual life are not for him. He has no hunger for those
impractical, breathless, dizzying wisdoms that add stature
to the soul. But the co-eds, whether self-consciously or not,
are really interested in living by the higher centers of the
brain. Education retains, for them, something of its old
adventurousness; and, for them, there is still some delight
to be had in the pursuit of intellectual ends which can never,
by any conceivable means, be turned into commissions. The
sex is proverbially curious — and curiosity is no poor syno-
nym for intelligence. And no doubt another proverbial at-
tribute, stubbornness, is responsible for the other virtue that
remains to be dealt with. Skepticism seems to be indispensable for education, but the college man neither possesses it
nor respects its possession in others. He relies on the com-
mercial honesty of the institution that accepts his tuition:
surely no professor would accept money for saying something that was not true. A textbook cannot lie, and a professor will not. Logic, evidence, experimentation, and verification are all very well, no doubt, but an uneconomic waste of
time. In a pinch, I would undertake to convince a class of
men of nearly anything, merely by repeating many times
that it was so because I said it was so. One does not teach
women in that way. One painstakingly examines all the facts,
goes over the evidence, caulks the seams of one's logic, and
in every way prepares oneself for intelligent opposition. It
may be the devilish obstinacy of the sex. No doubt it is, but
also, whatever its place in the ultimate synthesis of wisdom,
it is the beginning of knowledge.

All this narrows down to one very simple thing. Democracy has swamped the colleges and, under its impetus, college men tend more and more to reverse evolution and to develop from heterogeneity to homogeneity. They tend to become a type, and, our civilization providing the mold, the type is that of the salesman. The attributes that distinguish it are shrewdness, craftiness, alertness, high-pressure affability and, above all, efficiency. There seems to me little reason to believe that the tendency will change in any way. I have not, indeed, any reason to believe that for the Republic any change is desirable. The mass-production of salesmen, we may be sure, will not and cannot stop. But, at least, there is one force that moves counter to this one. The co-eds, in general, develop into individuals; and, in general, they oppose and dissent from the trend of college education. I do not pretend to say whether their opposition is conscious or merely instinctive, nor can I hazard any prophecy about its possible influence on our national life. But if, hereafter, our colleges are to preserve any of the spirit that was lovely and admirable in their past, I am disposed to believe that the co-eds, those irresponsible and overdressed young nitwits, will save it unassisted.

FROM *The Harvard Graduates' Magazine*, MARCH 1932

Grace Before Teaching

A LETTER TO A YOUNG DOCTOR OF LITERATURE

I

MY dear ——y: —

A committee has read the footnotes of your dissertation, has subjected you to three hours of candid questioning, and has certified, in happy issue thereof, its confidence in your fitness to teach English Literature. You have read *The Pearl*, which is more than Shakespeare ever did. You can manipulate Grimm's Law, a proficiency that was not in the power of John Keats. You know more Icelandic than Chaucer knew, more Frisian than Swift, more Gaelic and Provençal than Samuel Johnson. The rigor of your novitiate, your letter to me says, has left you little time to read the great works of English literature, but those gaps you hope to fill during the early years of your professorship. And if you have not read Shakespeare's *Troilus*, you are acquainted with its sources, real and alleged, and are intimate with all the variants of Chaucer's treatment of the pretty legend. You have not had time for the *Apologia Pro Vita Sua* or *The*

Hind and the Panther or the *Journal to Stella*, but, to compensate, you have studiously read every absurd nonentity in the language from *A Treatise on the Astrolabe* and *The King's Quair* to *Madoc* and *Kehama*, from *Polyolbion* and *The Baron's Wars* to the *Olney Hymns*, from *Britannia's Paradise* and *Davideis* to *The Bothie of Tober-na-Vuolich*.

It is a formidable preparation, this four-year apprenticeship of yours devoted to the study of extinct or theoretical languages that embody no literature whatever, and to the reading of books whose interest for scholars is that they interest no one else. But, impressive as it is, your contribution to the world's knowledge obscures it. I allude, of course, to your dissertation "On Some Latin Marginalia in the Manuscript Poems of Gabriel Harvey." By the exercise of almost incredible labor, represented in the completed dissertation by twelve hundred and sixty footnotes and a bibliographical list of nine hundred titles, you have made certain what was heretofore uncertain. You have identified "Chloe" in one of the poems as a certain Mistress Anne Sutton, about whom nothing else is known. You have proved that a libelously descriptive passage cannot possibly have been intended to reflect on Queen Elizabeth's elder sister. You have proved that one of the marginalia in question is certainly in Harvey's handwriting, and that others just as certainly are not — and all the world is at liberty to guess whether, since they were not written by Harvey, they were written by William Shakespeare, Robert Benchley, or St. John the Divine.

That is the addition to the straitly won learning of the world that entitles you to the degree of Doctor of Philosophy and licenses you to begin, in the colleges of America, your painful ascent toward a professorship in English Literature. Your achievement, outside the vested interests of scholarship, is without value. Gabriel Harvey has no importance. Dreadfully dull, indescribably pedantic, prey to the same sort of literary unintelligibility that afflicts his successors in the colleges, he had, during his lifetime, a closet-influence of the kind exercised by certain bigwigs in the profession you are entering. That and no more. In three centuries hardly anyone outside the scholar's pasture ever read him. To-day few scholars, even, read him — which is why you found him, and not someone still more negligible, sufficiently untreated in dissertations to permit your writing one about him. No one will ever read him again; no one can conceivably want to know about him; he is as unimportant as the anonymous creators who compose the statistics about the squash crop that are used to make the columns of country weeklies justify. But you have exposed several of his marginalia, and if ever, just possibly, some aberrant scholar should want to know about them, he may have his library send for your thesis. You devoted to it the twenty-sixth and twenty-seventh years of your life; there it is; and you are licensed to teach literature.

And so, realizing as well as I do how unutterably trivial the whole course of your preparation has been, you write to me for comfort, and, if I have it, encouragement for your future. You employ to describe your studies and dissertation one or two monosyllables in which the frankness of pre-Norman English is apparent. Unhappily, they are less admirable in print than in penmanship, and I cannot repeat them here in my agreement. But they are apt and completely descriptive. For your long philological training and for your dissertation on Gabriel Harvey, there are — remembering that your intent is to teach literature — no adequate epithets except those monosyllables. But in spite of all that, and in spite of the mountainous asininities that still confront you, there is still some comfort. If a man has intelligence to begin with, the training for the Ph.D. cannot vitiate it. And intelligence, with a kind of integrity not disturbed by the Ph.D., will enable you to teach English with the satisfaction of knowing that you have some valid place in the world. As, for your sake, I ask leave to show.

II

I will not waste time repeating the denunciation of the Ph.D. in English Literature that scores of rebellious men have written. Nor will I list some of the mad dissertations recently awarded the degree or now being written for it. All the world knows that nine out of ten doctors' dissertations, or rather ninety-seven out of a hundred, are not worth the time of even the humble intelligences that produce them, still less that of any mature intelligence that might chance to read them. That, I think, is exactly the point for you. In the denunciation of the rebels, the Ph.D. is made a straw man and attacked as if there were something evil in the mere fact of research into the nature, origin, and organic function of literature. Well, I am virgin of any desire to make such research, but to declare that it is evil, antisocial, or destructive art is to write oneself down an ass. The trouble with the Ph.D. is seldom its method or its purpose, but the trivialities to which they are too often applied. The intellectuals object to Mr. Kittredge's method of studying Shakespeare, for instance, apparently on the ground that to know what Shakespeare meant by what he said will forever prevent one from appreciating the splendor of his genius. They object to Mr. Lowes's study of Coleridge on the ground that the writing of poetry is a mystical gestation, to be apprehended only in terms of the Immaculate Conception. They object to the notion that literary creation can be made the subject of any investigation, historical, psychological, or comparative. Now such sentimentality is absurd — more absurd, even, than the concern of an embryo Ph.D. over a misprint on the title page of the twentieth edition of *Pilgrim's Progress*. In this forbidding world we are everywhere surrounded by mystery, which wraps us in the cloak of our own ignorance, and any genuine solving of any genuine part of it is good. An intelligent study of the sources of *Hamlet* (though I shall be vilifying "sources" in a moment) is as legitimate as a study of the Defenestration of Prague or of the behavior of *Drosophilia* under violet rays — and may be made as illuminating to the bewildered gropings of the mind. The mysterious world seems, also, to be deterministic, though the tender-minded thrust against the bars, and if the tortured motility of Coleridge's mind went as far afield as Cotton Mather's commonplace book for the pretty symbols of a poem — then that item, too, can be made use of when we take account of ourselves and our bewildering adventure.

No, my dear ——y, I am not on the side of the intellectuals in this prolonged warfare of the colleges. Rather, if I must choose in that warfare between the professors and the intellectuals, then let me stand with the professors — who do not weep and who, intermittently at least, correct the darling theories of their hearts by referring them to fact. The kind of literary study that has of late been fashionable in America moves me only to contempt. The intellectual reads André Tridon's dilutions of Freud, carefully avoiding Freud's own works, which require intellectual activity, and then writes a book proving that John Greenleaf Whittier was impotent or that Henry Cuyler Bunner should, really, have joined the Mormons. Or he reads Waldo Frank's *Our America*, and reaches a conclusion in four hundred pages that the Oregon pioneers went West each one carrying a copy of Rousseau's

Emile and expecting to find on the banks of the Willamette an earthly paradise constructed for them by the Noble Savage. If the alternative is forced upon me I must choose to stand with John Doe, Ph.D., who inhabits a world where every book has been stolen from every other book, and can supply an occasional fact to support his contention, rather than with Richard Roe the tearful of Provincetown, Peterborough, or Forty-Second Street, who really lives in a world that went to hell when someone hung a clock in a steeple.

But do not, therefore, conclude that John Doe has my admiration. In one aspect, the Ph.D. in English Literature has committed obscenity and aggravates the offense from day to day. That obscenity is the concentration on method without reference to subject and, in that concentration, the creation of a protected caste to which nincompoops may be admitted provided only that they have the degree and from which men of talent will be excluded because they lack it. Whatever isolated exceptions may be urged, the unchallengeable fact is that the way to advancement in the teaching of English is through the Ph.D., and that no one dare dream of teaching college English without it. And that evil begets the specific evils that have produced your letter to me. It begets the dissertation on the marginalia of Gabriel Harvey's manuscript, a contemptible research that has wasted two years of your life. It begets your study of Gaelic and Frisian, a still more contemptible perversion of effort, since these languages have no more to do with the art of literature than with the manufacture of fire extinguishers. It begets, also, the debauchery of scholarship, since the colleges swarm with students who want to study English, since professors must be developed to teach them, since the caste demands such training, and since the subjects to which the scholarly technique can be applied are all but exhausted. If ninety-seven out of a hundred researches are now worthless from any point of view, the time is not far off when ninety-nine out of a hundred will be worthless. The one per cent. remaining will be dissertations in investigation of earlier dissertations, applying a reverent zeal in pointing out absurdities.

In consequence of all this, our English departments are increasingly invaded by young men whose qualifications for their jobs are their certified ability to employ Grimm's law and the four hundred pages they have written revealing the exact moment in which an idea that Voltaire had resurrected from Cyrano de Bergerac entered the writing of a negligible correspondent of James Boswell's. These persons naturally respect the processes that have produced them. The result is that as such nonentities multiply in the department, literature atrophies there. It ceases to be an art, it ceases to have any bearing on human life, and becomes only a despised corpse, a cadaver without worth except as material for the practice of a barren but technically expert dissection. The worst that one can say of this degradation is unprintable — the weak best, that it has some of the minor trappings of a science, such a science as embalming. Increasingly, the English departments convert literature from a living art to an abstract and bastard science. Increasingly, history departments, newly invigorated by the rise of social history, regard literature as an art, and embrace it. Art does not die, in this mysterious world: as it slips away from the laboratories of English scholars, it may accept sanctuary with the historians.

What, my dear ——y, what are you, a newly fledged Ph.D. in English Literature, to do about it? Nothing. You must take the colleges as you find them. The existing order cannot be changed by a young journeyman, and even if it could be, your concern is not with reform but with literature. You have performed the indecencies necessary to your license. Regard them as that, and no more. You have the assurance that though linguistics and source-hunting have enabled many fools to succeed in the profession, they have never harmed a good man. Your four graduate years have disgusted you, perhaps, and given you a saddening experience of human capacity for folly. But they have not damaged your intelligence, only temporarily frustrated it. You have not lost your integrity; you have merely wasted your time.

And after all, however annoying this frustration, the important question is not how you qualified yourself to teach English, but how, once qualified, you are going to teach it. God knows, the immediate problems that face you there are sufficiently important.

III

I ask you first to resolve on forfeiting the respect of half your colleagues in the department. Of more than half, perhaps — for I ask you to decide that you will teach not graduate students of literature but undergraduates. Half or more than half of all Professors of English slight or despise their undergraduate courses. They believe themselves justified of God only when conducting seminars or lecturing to groups of people who intend to teach English in the high schools or go on to the full glory of a professorship. In such courses, scholars initiate the neophytes into the mysteries of the caste, which is no doubt important; parade their technique of scholarship, which is pleasing to the ego; and manipulate the machinery for perpetuation of the caste, which has its justification in foresight. But the result is only the propagation of the caste. Literature becomes merely a bed of fossils wherein men who lack imagination bestir themselves shamefully among the vestiges of what once lived but is now dead.

No doubt earnest souls delude themselves with the notion that they perpetuate the ecstasy of medieval monks glorifying God in discovering His past. The vision, however, is deficient in realism. I repeat, graduate training in English is only the multiplication of pedants. They become college teachers and begin their service in the succession, creating others like them in due time. Or they go out into the sticks and teach in high schools. And the hardest job a teacher of English to college undergraduates has to face is that of giving therapeutic treatment to freshmen whose liking for literature was poisoned in high school. In either case, the attenuation of a living art goes on till the spark dies, the spirit flees away, and there is left only the corpse with pedants busy about it.

I speak perhaps too strongly: but you must remember that I denounce not the great man who is also a pedant, but the machine-made copies of him who possess his learning but lack the intelligence, the imagination, the taste, and the breeding that, in him, illuminate it. These, and they swamp the departments of English, debauch the fair art of literature with a systematic and corrupt intensity that suggests unconscious motives hardly decent to scrutinize. The Goths are among the statuary, the locusts have settled on the wheat.

You must not accept the professorial notion that seminars and graduate courses are a labor for the State, a sort of public-mindedness that is a social virtue. Professors of literature should not pray too fervently for Progress! Progress might consist, some day, in setting a committee to examine this labor for the State. It would find that the graduate training of every other respectable department in college performed a public service, but that graduate English served only its own cult. There might be, in the name of Progress, a new Innocents Day among the sources and the perished

tongues. . . . But with the undergraduate we come back
to real things, to actual values, to living minds, to a genuine
social possibility. If you determine to confine yourself to
undergraduate teaching, you need never have the inferiority-
feeling that assails teachers of English when they compare
their trade with that of his historians, or the biologists, or,
God help us, even the psychologists. You will have allied
yourself with what remains, while the pedants are still but
incompletely dominant, the finest influence in the colleges.
Need I point out that the English department, the better
part of it, performs the function that used to belong to
teachers of the classics? One ancient aim of education was to
acquaint the students with the nature of human life, the
meaning of human experience — in so far as human life and
experience can be made to disclose their significance. To
attempt the consideration of life in flesh and blood. To look
into the souls, if the noun is not too metaphorical, of men
who had lived diversely — in many ways, in many ages —
briefly, in their books. To investigate what great and little
men had made of mystery. To discover that men had faced
the inscrutable and wrung from it a real, if fragmentary,
meaning; had faced chaos and subdued it to a true, if tragically brief, order. To display the continuities of fate and
death, of hope and anguish, of ecstasy and despair, glowing
through fogs of pettiness but glimpsed for a moment. To
learn what shadow man can cast upon eternity and to consider it for one's guidance, one's solace, or one's reconciliation. . . . There is no need to rehearse the degeneration that
brought the classics departments to their present sterility.
They are to-day a sunless attic wherein incompetents out-
number gallant men who fight a cause lost these fifty years.
My point is that the decay was inevitable and that the opportunity to quicken the souls of college students has passed

to the English department. It hovers there still, that opportunity. But it will not hesitate for very long. If you hold to the dissecting tools, the historians, newly refreshed by contact with the world outside the legislatures, will attract it away from you.

You cannot quicken the minds and spirits of young people by teaching graduate students how to pursue a source through forty dubious relationships. The witch-hunt of alleged borrowings, the study of languages never spoken and never read by writers of English, have nothing to do with life. The *a fortiori* asserts that they have, therefore, nothing whatever to do with literature. What is more immediate, only the undergraduates ask for light. God knows, I have written enough doubts of undergraduate interest in education and capacity for it. But so far as the college student of to-day wants education, the desire exists only in the undergraduate body. So far as there is eagerness, so far as there is generosity and aspiration in American youth, they are there. The heaped-up experience of the race, that is literature; and leading young people to be aware of it, that is teaching.

You will not feel the impotence of a man whose life's work is proved worthless before his eyes, if you decide to stand on the side of the humanities. But if you decide to be merely a grave-robber — well, we know the pedants, you and I. The world knows them, too — and the psychiatrists.

IV

The decision to stand for the light will not remove all dangers from your path. It at once forces another choice on you: shall you flirt with popularization? You know the type, for every English department contains at least one specimen, and they are a cursing in the mouths of all men.

We need not analyze them — need not determine whether their uncleanliness springs from the illusion of democracy, or from a sense of inferiority engendered by the ballyhoo of the pedants, or from some still more deeply egoistic motive. By the size of their courses, alas, you will know them, for the worthless and the empty-minded, preferring vaudeville to instruction, crowd happily into classes where they may count on entertainment.

These songbirds have looked too enviously at William Lyon Phelps. Observing a career that is among the most reassuring of the age, they have permitted themselves to be deceived. Mr. Phelps has scholarship; he has also, together with a deplorable fluency in superlatives, enthusiasm and courage and taste and discrimination and a subtle intelligence. The songbird, to duplicate Mr. Phelps, would have to have all these qualities and some inner essence as well, the unknown quantity that makes the personality of Billy Phelps. So far the formula has been impotent: no one has become a Billy Phelps. But dozens of efforts have proved that a faculty for vulgarization has no part in the mystery. . . . They are the nightingales and spellbinders of literature, the performing seals and the comb-players and the royal marimba band. They have conceived too highly the place of the saxophone in modern life. When the undergraduate body decides that their courses are vaudeville, it decides exactly right. I know them! Among their most valuable props are their young sons — and Junior will be quoted in lectures on Shakespeare and in denunciation of the "garbage-can school" of contemporary fiction. "Father," said Junior, after glancing unobserved at *Dark Laughter,* "I think that Mr. Anderson has a dirty mind." The case is proved: out of the mouths of babes comes the wisdom of their fathers. Experience has proved that a little child will always redeem a weak lecture, always retrieve the wandering attention of a class, always drive home a platitude. At a very early stage of their development, you will remember, the movies mastered the same principle.

Junior is merely one item in a systematic debauchery. Whatever motive inspires the songbirds, the result of their labors is a *nach*-Kiwanis corruption of taste, an accessory prostitution of democracy. I heard one of them inform a radio audience that he had complete confidence in the literary judgment of the people who put Calvin Coolidge in the White House. The *non sequitur* is magnificent; also, it necessitates final judgments. The people who put Calvin Coolidge in the White House have decided that *The Winning of Barbara Worth* is a finer novel than *Manhattan Transfer* or *Jennie Gerhardt*, or *The Forsyte Saga* — and the nightingale who sang that roundelay has not, in fact, hesitated to concur. That principle of criticism would pronounce *Uncle Tom's Cabin* incomparably the finest work of art yet produced in America — and the nightingale's published opinion, in fact, dissents hardly at all from that judgment. On the strength of it, Mr. Eddie Guest's *A Heap o' Livin'* is unquestionably finer art than *Tristram* or *North of Boston*, though this particular nightingale has not yet caroled so forthrightly. The people who put Calvin Coolidge in the White House, you must understand, are fundamental in the songster's method and in his aims. They are the people and wisdom will perish with them, and the only legitimate purpose of a college teacher is to confirm their obscenities and to assist in their self-corruption.

He radiates human kindness and geniality and fellowship — all the luncheon-club virtues. Above all, he is reassuring to the young minds before him, minds that may possibly have been disturbed in other classrooms. He makes himself one of them. Let not your hearts be troubled, he says to them, for I will show you that there is nothing in art to trouble anyone. We are all, in Mr. Guest's inspired phrase, Just Folks — all of us, you and I and Junior and Dean Swift. In all the great, in Chaucer and Shakespeare and Milton, was the same clay that we are made of. We shall go adventuring through literature, sailing seas that are forever placid, examining ideas that are but our own prejudices clothed in common words, unendangered by storms or doubts or tragedies. In all literature there is nothing mysterious to the common man, nothing beyond his grasp, nothing to disturb his self-esteem or his unclean protectiveness. Literature is life — he says, corrupting the decency that permits him his trade — and life is what the people who put Calvin Coolidge in the White House believe it to be. Something not so earnest, quite, as it is real — something constructed out of safety and prejudice — something to be protected from faint doubts. He fills his act with biographical chit-chat about the great, telling his hearers that John Keats suffered from weak lungs, as indeed any of us folks were apt to do before the Life Extension Institute existed, but never alluding to Amy Lowell's further notions about John Keats. He displays the sanctities, the trusty platitudes, and proves that all literature defends them. Shelley? Oh, all of us had a revolutionary phase When We Were Very Young: it's nice, if one gets over it promptly. *Gulliver's Travels?* Oh, don't let that sadden you, boys and girls, for Swift was crazy when he wrote it, and look at Nietzsche. The angry ape? Oh, I don't think that is the true Shakespeare — read what Polonius says about being true to oneself. The fleshly school of poetry? Yes, they were daring in their day but time has dealt with them and "The Passing of Arthur" is the true spirit of that age, as Calvin Coolidge's electorate have already shown. Rabelais? The unread classic of male freshmen. Or *Babbitt, Jurgen, Poor White, A Lost Lady, The Apple of the Eye?* That, brother Kiwanians, is the garbage-can school of modern fiction. The true spirit of America is expressed in *So Big.* It proves that honest hearts get their reward, and Junior likes it, and hundreds of thousands of people have bought it. . . . No one who desired to minister to the herd tastes of America has ever failed at his trade. Also, my dear ——y, there is the dog and his vomit, the sow and her wallowing in the mire.

The nightingale (except an occasional specimen who has equipped himself with a tachometer) is at one with the pedant in his distrust of modern literature. I can respect the pedant more, even in the person of a young professor who told me pridefully that he had read no book written later than 1800 and tended to distrust everything later than 1700. His aversion is generally rational, whereas the songbird's, nurtured on the securities of conformable opinion, is only apprehensive. The neurosis I have already pointed out: the sense of inferiority. Much of recent literature challenges the inherited bases of the songbird's life: therefore, all of it is contemptible. Much of it deals nakedly with areas of his mind that a dogma or a fig-leaf should protect: therefore, all of it is base. Much of it impeaches the *gemüthlichkeit* of Just Folks; therefore, all of it should be forbidden in the public interest. None of it has been appraised by generations of academic opinion: therefore, the songbird will reject it all, lest his judgment in any instance be proved, retrospectively, an error.

All of this, my dear ——y, you must avoid. Love of an art dictated your choice of a profession. Do not, then, timorously conclude that art stopped short with the cultivated court of the Empress Josephine. Be sure that life goes on, though Messrs. More and Babbitt feel sure that since, anyway, Rousseau, it has all been an illusion, and that while life goes on, necessarily art must go on too. The fear of modern literature, the rejection of it *a priori*, is basically a lack of intellectual virility. You must have the courage of your hormones: you must prepare yourself to believe that departure from the ways of the fathers is not necessarily evil, that to write otherwise than as Aristotle or Pope or Landor prescribed is not necessarily anarchic, that to find a changing form and a changing content for the expression of a changing world is not necessarily contemptible. The more heartily you love life, the more vividly immortal art will seem to you. There are many mansions — at least the songbird, with his preference for bungalows assures me there are — and to declare that a date, any date, or a theory of ethics or esthetics, any theory, invalidates any of them is only foolish. Modern life surrounds you with its unimaginable vigor, crowds in upon you with all its novelties of experience, presents to your eyes and ears such colors and sounds as no age before us has ever known — a superb pageant of vitality, however deplorable it may be, however basically evil or despair may exist in it. Shall you be afraid to grapple with it? When students come to you asking for guidance in it, will you declare that it is Rousseau or it isn't Lucretius, that 1857 was the last year when art lived, or that life to-day, lacking the approval of Aristotle, should be ignored for a heresy hunt in the ideas of the eighteenth century?

But, of course, you will find that many of your colleagues — all of them, I venture to say, who are worth a damn — if not as deeply learned in modern literature as they are in the correspondence of Ben Jonson, are at least willing to grant its legitimacy. Loving literature, you will have only occasional trouble with them. You will, however, face trouble in the obligation I now venture to set for you. In departments of English, American literature is a poor relation — or rather, on the town.[1] And that is a condition that, whatever subjects you teach, I ask you to fight against. I shall not repeat the declaration, made often enough before Emerson's "American Scholar" and often enough since Van Wyck Brooks's *America's Coming of Age*, that the time has come to legitimatize American literature. The time had come long before Emerson, and I ask you merely to labor for its recognition in the colleges — to help conquer their timidity and renovate their point of view. If valid subjects for the Ph.D. in English literature are about exhausted, those in American literature have hardly been touched. Seemingly, they will not be. In New England, research about the "Concord school" and its contemporaries and about the early Puritan culture is freely authorized. In New York, contaminated by intellectuals who have never read Whitman and never studied Poe, dissertations on either are permissible. In the South, perhaps, you could write one about the Methodist hymns of 1850. But anywhere else a dissertation in American literature must come down no later than 1800. And in all the colleges, East, West, or South, it is far better to study English literature. This condition is an open scandal and I describe it no further. I merely ask you to do what you can do to overcome it. Here is the nineteenth century in America, a period full to overflowing with the stupendous vitality of our race — and the colleges shudder away from it. If the scholar has any duty to society, Emerson

[1] This assertion was already ceasing to be true when written. The study of American literature in the colleges has made steady and amazing progress in the last ten years. The American Literature Group of the Modern Language Association and the trade-journal, *American Literature*, have been the principal forces in this development, but the times have handsomely coöperated. Much, in fact most, of the research in American literature is trivial and absurd. Nevertheless, the fact that it is now legitimate has significance and importance.

defined it for him: it is to increase our awareness of ourselves. If the teacher has any obligation, it is to clarify his students' ideas of their race. Let that be one major effort of your career. I say nothing of the magnificent opportunities open to you in American literature. They are there but whether you shall try to seize them is a personal problem and I am content, for, if the English department doesn't, the historians will. Already they are inside the fence, convinced at last that art is more important in the world than acts of legislatures. They will beat you there, as they are beating you elsewhere, if you are not vigilant.

v

I have described, dear ——y, an English department which drifts placidly toward damnation. As I examine the tendencies in our colleges I cannot speak otherwise. On the one hand, the cheer-leaders and the songbirds pander to the meanest ideals of democracy; on the other hand, the linguists try to make literature an exact science, and devotees of what is erroneously called the historical method try to make it an inexact science, and both are loathsome. It is not, as yet, that the department is dominated by inferior men: the future might seem brighter if that were true. Not inferior men are responsible for the degradation, but mistaken men. They have chosen Baal, of their own will to worship him. The department progressively divorces itself from the art of literature, and in the end, if present tendencies continue, it will formally free itself from art and take an autonomous if minor place among the pseudo-sciences.

Your part is to resist this tendency, to offer no doves to Baal. Simply remember what so many of your colleagues will have forgotten or denied: that literature is an art. That art is a living thing, the expression of a human soul entangled with the world. You are dealing with the imaginative projection of experience — the experience of men in whom desire was once as hot and fear as cold as ever they can be in you. Save only as your machinery of research and your baggage of linguistics may serve to make you more aware of life itself, you must deny and disregard them. They will do far less for your teaching than one moment of perception. You must be yourself a kind of artist — as, indeed, the best teachers of literature have always been poets or novelists or dramatists or philosophers otherwise completed. I do not mean that a teacher of literature is, rightly, a man who would be a poet if only he could write poetry. I mean that the communication of literature to students is a form of the imaginative expression of experience, and is subject to the principles of creation, not to those of dissection. It is an act of imaginative union, the fructification of life for which we have found but one word, and that word art. It is an identification with Shakespeare or Swift or Carlyle, and with the world in which they rejoiced and despaired — not a mechanism to ferret out their sources. The teacher of literature must have the ability to give vitality to experience for the benefit of his students; which is, let me wearily point out once more, a form of artistic interpretation, of creation, of synthesis. If he has that ability, he may call upon the scholarly resources to widen his horizon and to deepen his experience, if he pleases. If he lacks it, even though he surpass in scholarly attainments all his predecessors in the profession, he will be only an empty man spouting irrelevancies from a contemptible rostrum.

Be humble! Dedication to the understanding of greatness is the least fee you can pay your profession. Your job is to help young men and women to understand what great spirits have made of human life. That and nothing else. It is a task that will exhaust your full strength and will leave you, in the end, no more respect for the sum of your life than falls to any of the rest of us.

And also — be arrogant. In all the college, only your department deals with the whole of life. The rest are simplifications, abstractions, arbitrary limitations. There is no obligation for you, through a feeling of inadequacy, to support your courage with a parade of scientific methods as if literature need be made an honest woman by economists or psychologists. There is no need for a protective coloration of linguistics or charted curves, as if you were an anthropologist or a statistician. Grant these other departments their momentary impressiveness, their item in the fads that rise and pass themselves off for wisdom and are swept into the dust heap. You have joined yourself to a stream that has flowed uninterruptedly from the first alphabet. Whatever obsesses the tortured spirit for a moment and then dies, literature does not die; and while man is still bewildered by his destiny, literature will not need the protection of scientists. It is a light in darkness — a feeble one, but the only one that has never yet been extinguished. Remember that — against your competitors. Remember it against your colleagues, too, refusing to let them convert that which is light into a darkness giving off the smell of death. . . . And, perpetually, remind them that art will find its servitors where it will, and need not, for all their learning, submit itself to a Department of English devoted to the embalming of the dead.

Farewell to Pedagogy

I

HE was a Professor of Pretentious Noise, and he was taking his ease at the University Club. This almost Georgian fortress is a sanctuary for jaded pedagogues. When twilight comes up across the campus from the lake you will see them emerging from their offices, stoop-shouldered, astigmatic, a little depressed, and making their way among the elms toward the Club's cushions and hooded lights. There is enough of cerebration in the day's job. These tired men make their living by keeping the gears of the mind always overheated. Therefore, when they seek repose they will not demand intellectual fare. You will find no books at the University Club, and few of the journals in the reading room are profound. All this the Professor of Pretentious Noise took for granted. He was there for comfort, and, in the dusk, he would take a little quiet pleasure reading. So he picked up a magazine. When I came upon him, the veins on his forehead were swollen and he had found treason in the Club. For the journal he had happened upon was that contumacious *New Republic*, and he wondered what wretch had got its name on the budget. He banged his fist. Look here, the sheet spoke slurringly of the Vice-President! Mr. Dawes lived not more than half a mile from the Club, and the Professor had shaken his hand, some years before, when Mr. Dawes organized the Minute Men of America. He was for deporting these damned I.W.W. editors to Leningrad, where they belonged, whence they were paid. He would see that whoever was responsible for the presence here of this vileness lost his job or his membership. He tossed the *New Republic* away and picked up another journal. I asked if he knew this one at all. No, he said, but he had heard his uncle, years ago, speak highly of the *Nation*. I waited happily. In a moment there was a great roar, such a bellow as Professors usually reserve for colleagues who flunk fullbacks. I followed after when he dashed to the secretary's office, where with my own ears I heard his ultimatum. Either the Club would immediately cancel its subscriptions to these two subversive and inflammatory weeklies, or — or by God! the Professor of Pretentious Noise would resign from the Club and then bring suit against it.

Always, of course, there was Prexy. One day he telephoned to a colleague of mine in the English Department. Parents, he said, were complaining about the work that two of my colleague's students were doing. It was, he understood, alarmingly suggestive, and, if the reports were true, even erotic. Would my colleague investigate? Would he, if the charge proved true, move to suppress these activities? My colleague asked the names of the two rakish youths. Just a moment — Prexy had made a note of them. Ah, yes, here they were. Would my colleague kindly make more seemly the undergraduate essays of — George Moore and Oscar

Wilde. . . . I once asked him, looking forward to that Greater Atlantis for which a corps of expensive publicitors was designing slogans, whether the mounting Endowment Fund would give us a university press. I thought of the presses at Yale, Harvard, Columbia, Chicago. One was, I thought, little less than obligatory on the Greater Atlantis, which was to do so much for Scholarship, the State, the Community, and the mail-order houses. He looked at me patiently, understanding that I had the scholar's impracticality. No, he said, no university press ever made money. There would be none at Atlantis. . . . And once he called me in for rebuke. The President of the University of Utah had been offended by remarks of mine about his institution that had been published in a magazine. Displaying the provincialism I had commented on, the President of the University of Utah (and the head of his history department, too) had written, not to me but to Prexy, suggesting that I ought to be disciplined, suppressed, and — the inference was — fired. Prexy was on my side and was only bored by the protest of his peer, but the situation was delicate. Was what I had said true? he asked. I suggested that perhaps I should not have said it if I had not believed so. If it wasn't true, then it was libel, I informed him, and he might write his petitioners to sue me for damages. Ah, yes. Prexy thought and studied and looked at me. Sometimes, he said, sometimes there had been trouble — members of the faculty who had published articles, reports, and other material that, later on, proved to have been, well, not precisely their own work. Could I — that is, did I care to assure him that — that what I had written had been entirely my own?

Not forgetting the Professor, who was also a Dean. He dealt with stirring and vital truths, and he was of the department that more than any other might lead our national thinking into better ways, and his conception of his subject was based on the year 1850, when that subject was sheer romance. He would interrupt his lecture on matters of greater import, I think, than any others we pedagogues deal with and, fixing a stern eye on a man in the front row who was a candidate for honors in his field, would announce, "Mr. Smith, I did not see you at Epworth League last night." He was Professor Blank, but mostly he was Dean Blank. One dared not call him Blank or Mr. Blank. One day a library assistant approached him, a girl who was earning her tuition working at the delivery desk. "I have the book you wanted, Mr. Blank," she said, for she was young and unpractised and knew not the management of the Levites. Without a word to her he marched into the Librarian's office and demanded that the girl be fired. "A woman with no greater sense of academic rank than she has," he said, "is absolutely unfit to be employed by the college."

II

For a thousand years the history of the universities has been the history of civilization. Moreover, the teacher is the elder wise man of the race, nor has his caste ever been widely separated from that of the priest. Always, in any age, pedagogy is a vital, adventurous profession. Always, too, at any moment, it is torn within by discord and self-distrust and the turmoil of the new age that is perpetually coming to be. Reading in the public prints to-day the dirges and pæans of those who are considering the state of the colleges, one is amused to find a prevalent belief that the present turmoil is something new and that the colleges face a crisis which is likely to destroy them. A certain ignorance characterizes those experts in education who make most outcry. Abélard, I remember, complained bitterly that the colleges of his day were overcrowded, and Erasmus after him. Have we forgotten Herbert Spencer's declaration — it might well have been Mr. Dewey's — that the colleges must adapt themselves to the new age or perish? One whole school of modern complainants cast out entirely the whole complex of education, the colleges, the curricula, the faculties, the student bodies: and no one remembers that a diversion of Edward Gibbon's was the writing of autobiography. Nor do I find anywhere among the current Hoseas and Jeremiahs any awareness that they are echoing Henry Adams or Matthew Arnold or Cardinal Newman, or Plato, Zeno, or Epictetus. A bilious onlooker might suggest that one cause of the crisis may be the scarcity of educated men among the faculties.

Nevertheless, it is true that the profession was never in a greater chaos than to-day's and that the problems confronting the colleges were never more difficult. Novel as the idea may be to the editorial writers, no one is quite so keenly aware of these facts as the colleges themselves. Panic, indeed, has settled on them. A great many of them actually confess failure by pausing in the year 1928 to inquire just what their function is. Atlantis, which I have just quitted, was feverish throughout my stay with that very question. With every equinox the Dean of Liberal Arts, or the Department of Personnel, or the Department of Education, or the President himself launched on the faculty a questionnaire asking every teacher to state his conception of the proper aims of the college. It was a great bore, but lightened occasionally by some of the replies. All but a few of them were trite, most of them were dull, and some were asinine. One man, I remember, victimized by the necromancy of alliteration as the writers of advertisements are, summed up the aims of education as Fun, Friendship, Facts, and Faith. There was a great but secret laughter among the juniors of his department, one of whom remarked, with a conception of education that goes back to the time of the Greeks, that a truer statement of them would be Doubt, Disillusionment, and Despair. I do not quarrel with that last definition. Another colleague answered the last questionnaire to this effect: to improve the quality of instruction at Atlantis, which should be one aim of the college, cease bothering us with questionnaires, weed out the fools from among us, get better teachers, and try to see that the students who face us are of a higher type. His was the only realistic moment in the whole incident. If the colleges have reached a situation in which they do not know what education is, if they do not see clearly what their purposes are, if they do not know unequivocally what they should be doing and how they should be doing it, if, in short, they do not understand the present age and their function in it, then indeed they are bankrupt and damned.

Here a digression seems called for. It is a little odd that one must explicitly declare that college professors are, for the most part, able, intelligent, and efficient men. Yet the contrary opinion is so widely held that my solemn declaration must seem iconoclastic to many people. So accepted is the belief in professorial incompetence that the very freshmen who come to be taught that sentences are preferably begun with capital letters or that *a* times *b* equals *ab* are convinced that their instructors are nincompoops and regard them with a contempt it is hardly worth while to disguise. Outside the campuses, the world at large thinks of professors as halfwits. If they are capable of anything, why are they content with five thousand dollar jobs? — so runs the question held to be unanswerable. The fallacy usually takes this form: "Those who can, do: those who can't, teach." Mr. Mencken has printed ten thousand variations of the theme, and that group of extraordinarily dull young thinkers whose only distinction is that they have repudiated Mr. Mencken parrot this particular idea of his with unanimous approval.

The idea, of course, is utterly absurd. If pedagogy had not taught me to avoid generalizations I should be disposed to stand on the exact converse. In contemporary America, it is generally true that those who can't, do, and those who can, teach. Except for the arts, I can think of no intelligent calling whose most distinguished practitioners are not college professors. It is almost literally true that professors are responsible for all that is admirable in the recent progress of law, medicine, surgery, public hygiene, physics, chemistry, biology, and a dozen other activities of the mind. The half-sciences are wholly professorial, so that you will hardly find all told a half-dozen reputable philologists, anthropologists, psychologists, archeologists, sociologists, or economists outside the campus gates. Are not the new colleges of journalism admittedly the happiest omen in to-day's press? As editors and critics are Professors Canby, Krutch, Van Doren, and the late Stuart Sherman noticeably inferior to their unacademic colleagues? Could you refute a man who thought Professors Pound and Frankfurter better lawyers than this great name or that one? Perhaps you are moved to recite the greatness, in our day, of the scientific and scholarly foundations created by rich men, or the research laboratories maintained by industrial corporations, or the more admirable bureaus of the national government. These, indeed, seem a refutation of my statement — till one reflects that they are manned entirely by ex-professors.

No, the pleasant trade of pedagogy (it is pleasanter, I think, than most others on earth — and that fact answers the unanswerable question) is made up of highly skilled men who are highly competent at their business. Its mean efficiency is higher than that of any other profession. Why, then, if this is so, are the colleges now confessedly ineffective? Well, it was to answer this question that I introduce my digression.

In any other profession the incompetent and the brainless settle to the bottom, where they are impotent: and impostors, conjurors, and charlatans are soon placarded as such so that their colleagues may deal with them. But in pedagogy they do not fare that way. They become Professors of Education. Then, in due time, because members of their brotherhood are in control, they become chairmen of the committees that control the college, and then they become Deans, and then they become Presidents.

Let me at once admit that some Professors of Education are both able and aware that their science is preposterous. Let me assert further that here and there you will find one who is actually doing valuable work. I have known a few: I have even known one Dean who was a Professor of Education but who, nevertheless, when the time came, stood firmly on the side of the angels. I hear that he has recently won his battle and has delivered Atlantis from the most serious menace to academic freedom it has had to face. Yes, unquestionably some of the species are good men, but though you may sometimes find good men in stews and hop joints, still you must hold to your judgment of people who frequent such places. And toward the generality of Educators one must urge the teaching of the church toward heretics. They may be charming fellows, now and then, but they are accursed of God and damned, and they shall be run to earth and slain for the glory of God, the salvation of their souls, and the security of the faith.

As a veteran of the colleges, and one who has done his share of soul-searching, I am convinced that the greater part of the

present plight of the colleges is due to this group of uneducated fanatics, crazed enthusiasts, or wilful charlatans who
have, in the last fifteen years, ridden into power. It is they
who have debauched the curricula, violated the chastity of
pedagogy, ravished the academic quiet of sane men, and
created the noise and stink and smoke-screen that envelop
the profession. Borrowing everything that is illegitimate in
several sciences, incorporating with it half a dozen major
sophistries, and begetting upon themselves a thing called
"methodology" and other monsters, they have created what
is known as the Science of Education. There is, their hallucinations have it, a Science of Teaching, a Science of Man-
aging and Governing Universities, and a Science of Classify-
ing, Guiding, and Prophesying about the Young. The sum
of these is the Science of Education.

Inscribing the slogans of this idiotic Science upon their
guidons, the Educators have besieged the Trustees of the
colleges and the public. Now a Trustee is a man who has been
given authority over a college, to shape its destiny and dis-
burse its funds and dictate its policies, for the sufficient
reason that he delivered four counties to the Governor intact
or that he has money enough to make him a prospective
donor of a dormitory or a gymnasium. Or the sufficient reason may be, merely, that he hopes to be Bishop of New
York. He is frequently not a college man, seldom an educated
man, and never a teacher. He is almost always a business
man with a superstitious awe of education — a willing, toler-
ant person who wants to do justly in his position but has
learned to demand things which he calls Facts and Results.
Upon him the Educators descend, mouthing their hideous
jargon, chanting litanies whose terms are pseudo-scientific
neologisms of no meaning whatever. There is a magic in
words, especially for the uneducated. These quack scientists

with their charts, graphs, tests, questionnaires, reports, surveys, analyses, and all the other trappings of their trade —
accessories as gaudy and pinchbeck as those of any other
medicine show — have worked their sorcery. There is, of
course, nothing of science about them, but they have convinced the amiable, ignorant Trustees that there is. They
have taken the element of chance out of education, they
say, so that hereafter there will be nothing unpredictable
about it, nothing mysterious, nothing immaterial or vague
or unstatable in terms of Facts and Results. So they have
captured the Trustees, and, because no advertisement that
promises "You can't lose" or "Cure guaranteed" ever fails
of its intended effect, they have taken in the public as well.
The public, on their assurances, believes that the laborious
and mysterious process of education is to be made, by the
Educators, as simple and effortless as a consultation with a
palmist.

Now they are in the saddle. They control the colleges,
doing with them what their aberrant instincts lead them to
do. Oh, they are not yet quite secure, nor are they unmolested in their madness. But for the time being at least
they grow more powerful. They snow the faculties under
with questionnaires. They harass them with reports and
analyses. They demand increasing portions of their time for
the collection of data out of which spells and incantations
are to be made. They lecture them about the technique of instruction and come more and more to enforce their demands
for it. They select the material for education, they dictate
the processes, and they control the support. The worst
omen of their power is the way in which they are made
Deans and Presidents all over the Republic. Formerly, when
you had to appoint a Dean or a President, you chose a man
who was a great teacher or was otherwise remarkable for

intellectual attainments. A few of those who belong to the great tradition are left us; but as they die or retire their places are everywhere filled by men whose only qualification is one that should forever disqualify them, that they are experts in the Science of Education. What will happen when all of the great tradition are gone from us and Professors of Education have succeeded them? What would happen if we made chiropractors dictators of public-health control, or appointed Justices of the Supreme Court exclusively from among astrologers?

III

The Great Educator was addressing us. "Gentlemen," he said, "the students are our customers, and we must give them what they want."

He voiced the "*credo in unum Deum Patrem*" of the Educators' faith. That way, irretrievably, goes the course of American education. I doubt that, save for five or six institutions (which are exempt, let it be understood, from everything I say), any college in the country would oppose it, if it were stated in terms of vocational guidance. One ponders. The customer of the surgeon might want his lower intestine removed in the hope of realizing Metchnikoff's dream. The customer of the lawyer might want to experiment with his private interpretation of a blue sky law. The customer of the priest might demand his approval of a little private murder for the faith's sake.

The Educators have slain the classics department, but the English department has risen up to preserve those immaterial values known as the humanities. Therefore, the Educators war upon the English department. This second Educator was no departure from the type. "What you gentlemen of the English department must realize," he informed the score or more of us who were gathered to hear him, "is that you are not scientific. You have not rigidly standardized your methods. You do not explicitly state your aims. You have no formula by which to achieve them. How can you expect, then, to achieve them? I venture to assert that there is not here to-night one of you who can tell what the norm of his subject is. And if there were one stated norm here, I know very well that it would differ widely from that which another of you might work out." The Educator denounced us with his eyes and, I swear it on my sword, he then said, "What, for instance, would you say was your norm for the appreciation of Shakespeare?"

And then there was that evening when we gathered to hear still another Great Educator. This one, like so many others, had about him that air of fanatic zeal I have often seen in the prophets who come down from the greasewood slopes of my native state, crying the wrath to come. His eyes were fiery, and he was not in the least of this world but was altogether dedicate to the mad voodoos of his faith. He began to tell us about the psychological tests. Of these tests, pedagogy at large believes that they are harmless, the psychologists that they are an occasional means of grace, and the Educators that they are the Word, the Way, and the Light. This Educator, like all his tribe, was convinced that they were the ultimate key to the problem of making pedagogy an exact science.

He began to tell us of the success that one kind of test, the general intelligence test given to all Freshmen, had achieved at Atlantis. Graph after graph passed under his fingers till the floor about his chair was snowy with reports. I had a sense of the enormous energy expended on this survey and the costly machinery created to perform it. The labor of many men and enough money to maintain a research professorship in the study of diabetes had gone into this single incantation. Gradually the point emerged — if one had skill enough, as we philologists had, to understand the barbarous terminology. The point was this: a magnificent vindication of this test had been accomplished. His department had analyzed the results of that test and had compared them with the grades which the Freshmen had later achieved in college courses. The coefficient of correlation, he said in an awed voice, was .054! On the basis of this test, his department could have predicted, to the power of that coefficient, what any given student would do in his classes — that is, whether he would fail or pass the requirements of the college. The Educator's eyes were those of one who had seen God. The test which was given at such an expense of time, energy, and money, achieved exactly the same result, the same coefficient of correlation, that anyone could achieve with no effort and in one-tenth of a second by tossing a coin. The test occupied three hours. I think that any teacher worth his salt may confidently engage, if he be allowed to talk to a Freshman for one hour, to achieve a coefficient of correlation, bearing on that Freshman's success in his course, of something like .85. Or let him teach that student for three one-hour periods, the time expended on the test, and he will achieve a coefficient of correlation not lower than .965. But that, of course, is what the Educators call the Personal Equation in Teaching.

And, it developed as the Educator passed on from the science of his test to the metaphysics of his ideal, the Personal Equation must be rooted out of teaching. It was, he said, the supreme obstacle to the progress of Educators. For behold, there was now no way of predicting what a given student, *A,* would do under a given Professor, *B.* Professor *C's* methods differed violently from those of Professor *D.* Not only were the methods of teaching one subject absolutely non-interchangeable with those of another, which was a villainy dreadful enough, but even, incredible as it might sound, one man's ways of teaching a given subject were absolutely non-interchangeable with those of another man who was teaching the same subject. Here the Educator was aghast. This intolerable situation wrenched him with rack and pinion, but, incredibly, there was worse to be noted. Not only was there no standardized method of teaching a given subject, but there was not even a standardized body of material to be taught. Jones, teaching English B19, stressed facts that Smith, teaching the same course, ignored or perhaps even denied. White, teaching History 107, preached doctrines that Green denied. In economics, sociology, philosophy, fine arts, and even the sciences (except Education) there was dissent, contradiction, and dispute. And until this incredible folly should be remedied there would indeed be no progress in education but only the blind and fumbling wastage of to-day.

We must, he said, codify, fix, and standardize our corpus of knowledge. We must see that everywhere teachers of the same subject taught the same thing. But, what was far more important, we must see that they taught it in the same way. Fixed, standardized, and scientific methods! — that was the hope of the world. We could not, otherwise, be fair to the student. We could not, otherwise, honestly accept his trade. We could not, otherwise, guarantee him the accomplishment of his desires. There was, also, this still more important angle: till methods were everywhere standardized the Educators could not perfect their psychological tests. We must understand that there was no deliverance from death till those tests should be perfected. Here the Educator confided to us some of his expectations. Some day, when material and methods were standardized, he would relieve us of the Examination

Problem: that is, of all the bother about grades and quizzes and ranking. Some day he would be able to give an entering Freshman a psychological test that would consume no more than three hours. At the end of it he would be able to predict with absolute certainty not only what grade that Freshman would receive in any course under any instructor in the university (provided standardization had been established), but also what his exact ratio of success would be in any branch of human endeavor he might desire to follow. That, we must understand, was the millennium, and when it came all the devils that annoy education would be chained forevermore. But to attain it we must first rigidly codify our material, eliminate all that was equivocal in it, wholly standardize our methods, and weed out from ourselves every atom of the Personal Equation that remained to trouble him.

He was an Educator and, therefore, innocent of the world. He did not know that the kind of education he had set up as his ideal was already available. It was, of course, and any practical man could have explained it more eloquently than he. He could have bought it at any store that dealt in phonograph records, and all his milennium needed further was a constitutional amendment creating a bureau of acoustic standards and making it against God to lecture from a platform.

I have dealt with this Educator at length because his madness is characteristic and his fate significant. Let us suppose that, somewhere in the prairies, a new prophet one day appears. He is clad only in a breech-clout, and his food is locusts and his drink water. He begins to preach a new religion. He preaches, say, the elder deity Anubis returned to earth and ready for the coming of his kingdom. Anubis, the god's new prophet says, has ordained a penance. All those who believe in him must cut off the forefingers of their left hands, must sell their goods and give all to the priests, and must take only one meal in forty-eight hours and that raw. He makes converts — for no religion that has yet appeared in America has failed to do so. Thereupon, emboldened, the prophet makes public the meat of Anubis's worship, having heretofore revealed only the milk. Anubis, it appears, is a jealous god and has commanded the spoliation of unbelievers. They who are faithful shall sacrifice only their firstborn, cutting their throats at the altar of Anubis, but they who have not acknowledged him shall at once perish by the sword, they and all their offspring and their menservants and maidservants and all the increase of their kine. Moreover, the prophet announces, the earth is flat and a comet will destroy it at 9 : 28 P. M. a week from next Thursday, and he who eats white bread is an abomination unto Anubis. . . . What do we do with the prophet? Do we not, acting for the good of society, pronounce him mad and shut him up in the booby-hatch?

I think we do. But the Great Educator whose madness I have described was not shut up in the booby-hatch. Instead, his delusions were noised abroad outside Atlantis, and presently came Trustees bearing incense and sandalwood, and he departed from among us. He was made a college President. And that is what is wrong with the colleges.

IV

Good humor must be preserved. I do not think that the present crisis will yield to any theoretical, idealistic, or practical solution, whether conceived by Professors of Education, by their saner opponents, or by a race of hard-headed, fact-loving pedagogues who may some day arise. The function of the colleges is too completely organic with the interests of the commonwealth to permit much conscious guidance of their development. The complexity of the social organism creates an impersonal determinism that controls the colleges. I think, however, that the current pressure will be eased and the current griefs assuaged by the further course of an evolution that is now discernible. Once the colleges recognize and sanction a condition that already exists and are content to abide by it their problems will be enormously simplified. The condition I refer to is the grouping of the colleges in what may be either a guild or a caste system. Such a grouping is already much more than embryonic: the recognition of it proceeds apace. All that is required is a frank acceptance of it by those that now ignore or deny it.

Already a number of colleges have abandoned their efforts to be all things to all students. Increasingly, I think, economic necessity and the sheer power of numbers will force more of them to do so. It is perhaps true that the desire to participate in fraternity affairs for the purpose of preparing oneself for a political career is as legitimate a motive for going to college as the more ascetic desire for intellectual discipline. But certain colleges — call such a one Avalon — have already announced their intention to limit their students to those who are governed by the latter hope. They say, in effect, if you want education come to Avalon, but if you want student activities go to Valhalla. Similarly, other colleges (it may be, reluctantly) have forever abandoned hope of being national athletic champions. These say to prospective registrants, if your ideal of college life is basking vicariously in the sun of great halfbacks, go to —— (insert the name of the university that has never joined the Big Ten, or, in the East, the one that — but there, there!), but if you are content with other values we will consider you. Such choices as these, and there is more evidence of them than I have hinted at, seem to me to indicate that a selective process is at work.

In the day when that selective process has fulfilled itself there will be various groups of colleges. The group of which Valhalla is representative will devote its energies to the support of such democracy and salesmanship as are now mainly identified with the State universities of the Middle West. Another group, with Avalon for type, will exert itself keeping alive scholarship, research, culture, and intellectual integrity. Another group will soberly prepare its students for the professional schools, another will preserve the country club college to teach the children of the newly rich the amenities of their station, a third will produce vibrant Christian manhood, and a fourth will provide asylum for the Professors of Education. As affairs now stand, the average college is wasting its energy and substance trying to be all these colleges in one, but in the great day that I foresee it will choose one type, or have that type forced upon it by natural selection, and give up yearning after the rest. In that day Avalon will send out no alumni scouts when the football team has been beaten and will hear without a pang of self-reproach the tale of Utopia's new stadium, Valhalla's glee clubs, and courses in radio-announcing, and the vast registration in the department of menu-reading at Yvetot. It will inform those who lust after the specialties of other groups that its endowment in them is but feeble, no more than decently pertains to relaxation, and that those whose interest in them is professional would be wise to register elsewhere. And in that day, too, Valhalla and Yvetot shall be one voice repudiating any more than an amateur curiosity about the intellect. And parents of prospective Freshmen may govern themselves accordingly.

Here, however, I touch upon romance and prophecy, which are wholly the province of the Educators. I seriously believe that some such evolution will take place, and is even well begun. Pending its fruition, however, if I am reproached for offering destructive criticism only, and if anyone demands that I forthwith clear up the present crisis, I have a reply at hand. It is a purely impersonal solution for I am no longer a pedagogue [1] and will neither suffer nor profit by its adoption. I have already written it down herein, quoting a colleague of mine who in his time has done some noble larruping of pedagogical quacks. I repeat it: to improve the colleges, get rid of the fools who roam among them. Begin with the Professors of Education.

[1] It seems right to point out that, two years after the writing of this article, I was again a pedagogue. After seven more years of teaching, I am again saying farewell to the profession.

Another Consociate Family

LET me say that I know very little about Black Mountain College except from reading Mr. Adamic's article. I may seriously misunderstand and misrepresent the college: if I do, I must delegate the blame to Mr. Adamic. I should add that I have been a college teacher for twelve years, five of them at a large co-educational university, seven at Harvard. What I take to be logical objections to "experimental" education may be sheer prejudice; at any rate, I have been offered chairs in three different experimental colleges and have declined them all, each time with increased distaste. I have always distrusted the assumptions and the aims of such colleges, and as my experience increases I distrust them more. I believe that the basic problems of education are insoluble, and though I see no reason why people should not try to solve them, I regard optimism and idealism as unpromising equipment for such efforts. I believe that there is no right way to teach, or even a best way, and no optimum environment for college life — there are only more or less effective ways of *ad hoc* teaching in circumstances so complex and multifarious that it is idle to theorize about them. The conception of an ideal college seems to me preposterous; I cannot believe in such a conception and if confronted with its realization I should probably flee howling.

Mr. Adamic is a layman: his article frequently demonstrates his ignorance of the past and the present of education in America. The "revolutionizing of American education" which he thinks twenty Black Mountain branches would accomplish has been at the boiling point for a century — for two centuries if you recognize the process as religious. It is cyclic and its periodicity could probably be worked out. At any rate Black Mountain is older and less insurgent than he thinks. Nearly everything he mentions has been tried before, even in the same linkages and relationships: all of it has been, if you include the educational sects among the educational institutions. Whether or not it is new, of course, makes no difference; but at least there is a basis in experience for the objections I proceed to voice. For some of the things that rouse Mr. Adamic's enthusiasm seem to me futile, some of them irrelevant, and some vicious.

Let's begin with the simplest, the mixture of physical and intellectual labor which dozens of colleges encourage to-day and which has been a cornerstone for scores of our consecrated groups, from Mother Ann Lee's Shakers on up through Brook Farm to Helicon Hall. Mr. Adamic thinks that rolling roads and picking up cigarette butts give the students "a sense of participating in the vital day-to-day life of the place as a whole." Well, you find that participation in the oddest places. It is the practice in jails and army cantonments, and if dishwashing is a stimulus to communal life we ought not to be so hard on Hitler and Stalin, for they realize this educational ideal in their labor battalions. If a student has to support himself by such work, college teachers usually regard it as a tolerable evil but still an evil. Some of my students wash dishes and tend furnaces; I think they would be better students if they didn't have to. So do the deans and college presidents who are continually trying to get larger scholarship funds. I don't think that the deans and presidents are conspiring against the good life.

It's pretty bad for the students. It's far worse for the faculty. (I understand Mr. Adamic to say that the dividing line is pretty faintly drawn at Black Mountain, but it must exist.) The best use for an astrophysicist is in astrophysics, not bookkeeping. His job is to be a scientist and to teach. The functions of the teacher-pupil relationship, however mystical they may be at Black Mountain, can be better exercised within the limits of his science; if there is anything spiritual in bookkeeping, a professional bookkeeper will be more adept at it than a philologist. No college will ever be free of administrative work. It's best to have it done efficiently, by specialists. Most teachers are bad at it and dislike it and are glad to be relieved of it. Even if they like it and are good at it, any time they spend at it has to be taken from their primary jobs.

And these repeated efforts to give the management of the colleges back to the faculty have always seemed to me a kind of romance. A type-specimen of human absurdity is any college faculty forced, reluctantly and protestingly, to deliberate any question of policy or government. Ask anyone who ever went to a faculty meeting. The Boys don't know much about it, are properly skeptical of those who pretend to, resent being called from the laboratory, bog down in inertia, and are pitifully glad to leave the decision to a committee or a dean. All a faculty needs — more than it usually wants — is a reserved sovereignty, to make sure that nothing will be slipped over on it. It nearly always has that, few attempts to slip something over are made, and fewer still succeed. No attempt has ever been made by any college officer or trustee to limit my freedom of thought, expression, teaching or action, or that of any acquaintance of mine. Such attempts are sometimes made and sometimes succeed, but the total is far smaller than editorial writers believe. The college teacher is about the freest man in the country. Certainly he is freer than the members of any other profession. When you read otherwise you are being misinformed. When his freedom is threatened, he has his own pressure groups, and you can do more for him by solidifying those groups than by giving him a part-time janitor's job.

Mr. Hearst, the American Legion, and all the other ogres combined have done less damage to American education than that hoary wisecrack about Mark Hopkins and a log. Some people like that kind of education, but there are a lot of us who don't. Mark Hopkins is all right at one end of a corridor, the longer the better, if there is a first-rate laboratory or library at the other end. It's nice to have Mark on call when you want him, if he holes up when you don't (Black Mountain's cramped quarters might make that hard to manage), but he is a ghastly bore when he is on hand all the time, and you want a good microscope or some original-source documents oftener than you want Mark. You can frequently find substitutes for Mark or even do without him, but there is no substitute for libraries and laboratories, and the small college, the poor college and especially the experimental college fall down here. Mark can ramble on ever so enchantingly about the web of nature or the class struggle, but you learn about them by investigating them, and that takes equipment, and equipment costs money and isn't to be assembled overnight. For instance, Mr. Adamic's article sent me to a lot of original publications of Brook Farm and the Oneida Community, to verify my impression that I had seen a good deal of Black Mountain there. How many of those publications has Black Mountain got?

Then there is freedom for the student. I don't know what is good for either society or the individual, and no one has yet convinced me that he does. But granted that Black Mountain knows, I can't say that its procedure is an innovation. Let's say that the superior students are one fifth of any enrollment. Most of us begin our teaching on a theory of the more liberty the better for everybody. Year by year we back away from the theory, and the interesting thing is that the pressure which makes us back away comes from the four fifths. They flounder and sink in freedom, and they resent it. My belief is that it doesn't matter what happens to the four fifths, and year by year more of my energy is expended on the one fifth. The trend of the colleges in America is just that. The superior student has complete freedom now, in most places, and teaching-methods, library and laboratory equipment and social environment are all being oriented from him and toward his development. It seems to me that Black Mountain is in a serious dilemma. If it holds to its policy of the cross-section, it must to some degree disregard the superior student. If it concentrates on the superior student, it can't possibly afford the libraries, laboratories and teaching by specialists that he needs.

All this, however, is comparatively unimportant. The pat answer to it is that Black Mountain isn't so much interested in developing students as in developing personalities. And right here is where Black Mountain as Mr. Adamic describes it stops being, in my opinion, merely irrelevant or *vieux jeu* and becomes downright dangerous. It sounds a good deal less like an educational institution than a sanitarium for mental diseases, run by optimistic amateurs who substitute for psychiatric training some mystical ideas that sound non-sensical to me and some group practices that we usually denounce when we find more conspicuous groups indulging in them. This fact does not alarm me. A lot of the "group influence" must be fun, and anybody who wants it is certainly entitled to it. The human organism is tough: it can survive the mayhem we orthodox pedagogues commit on it, which is the insurance policy that safeguards education, and it can survive evangelical psycho-analysis by idealists. But the idealists are monkeying with mechanisms which they are not trained to monkey with and which psychiatrists leave strictly alone except in the gravest emergencies. You do not invade a gall bladder for fun but only when it gets infected, and then you want a surgeon, not a woodcarver, be he ever so artistic and optimistic. As a teacher, I'll stay away from those areas, thanks, and as a father I'll hope that when my children reach college age they won't be interested in fingering themselves that way.

Mr. Adamic talks about "truth" in a large and pretty vague way. I doubt that Black Mountain knows what truth is any better than jesting Pilate did. I don't know what it is, but I do know what these phenomena of "group influence" are; lots of people regard them as the most desirable things in the world, but they make me gag. No matter how suavely contrived, they are the phenomena of evangelical conversion, and we have a lot of them in the colleges. Out in Terwillinger, which I was writing about last month, the Y.M.C.A. invokes them every year with much the same jargon and machinery. The Oxford Group, the Buchmanites, who carry on what seems to me a pretty loathsome activity in the better colleges, are an even more exact parallel. There you have the same mechanism of house-parties, exhibitionism, group pressure, the dark night of the soul, mutual criticism, summons to the more ecstatic life, and rebirth in grace. Pretty dangerous stuff. Usually it doesn't do any harm to the individual, except as exhibitionism and emotional jags may be harmful *per se* and as a state of grace is usually a state of Godawful priggishness as well. But it can do harm. It can increase emotional instability and maladjustment, and it can create them. It can produce hysteria and even insanity: the camp meetings, which use the process in its purest form, are not a fine flower of the good life. Let us prayerfully remember the "burnt-over district" and its effects on American society — the hundreds of consecrated groups and experimental communities, which were also based on a cockeyed psychology and which also multiplied as Mr. Adamic expects Black Mountain to do.

The terminology varies — Black Mountain's is more like Gourdyev's than John Humphrey Noyes's — but the energies involved and even the mechanisms employed are eternally the same. A teacher or a student from Black Mountain could step into any of the Consociate Families of a century ago and, except for the vocabulary, feel perfectly at home. The consecrations of those days didn't prove much — except, maybe, that dedication and hope and idealism are neither an aim nor a process of education, and that phrases like "to experience art as a process which is also life" are mere logomachy. I can't see that Black Mountain proves anything that wasn't known and suspect long ago. And certainly it is part of the renewed Transcendentalism of these days. The long summary of Mr. Rice's ideas which Mr. Adamic gives in his third section is full of echoes for anyone who knows Ripley, Brownson, Alcott, the *Dial* and the *Harbinger*. There is the same call for the second birth of the individual and the regeneration of society, the same mystical ecstasy, the same wild marriage of apocalyptic vision and untenable

psychology — and the same jargon. For if Mr. Adamic understands what he represents Mr. Rice as saying about education
and about the function of the artist in society, I don't and
I doubt that many others can find meaning in it. It may carry
a more direct consolation and inspiration than meaning can
possibly have, but I am not sensitized to receive it and a
good many people must share my lack. I can only say that
its conception of mankind, the world and society is hidden
from me and certainly different from mine, and that, to me,
it sounds like a trance. I have seen that trance a good deal in
our history, and I distrust it. It sounds like Charles Fourier
to me, and Fourier has nothing to say to us to-day. We've
tried him out — why repeat the experiment? In the end he
came to promising that, if his theories were faithfully applied, all the seasons except Spring would disappear and
the oceans would turn to lemonade. They didn't, and Black
Mountain's promises seem to me no more realistic. Fourier's
American followers could interpret a man's character by
putting a line of his handwriting to their foreheads and could
work other mystical miracles, just as some of the Black
Mountain boys and girls can converse by twitching their
eyebrows. But that proved to have not much bearing on the
problems of education, and the phalansteries broke up. Mr.
Adamic expects Black Mountain to multiply, but its predecessors multiplied by fission, by division, and that is the
history of experimental societies and colleges in America.
Black Mountain itself came about by secession: another experimental college split mitotically to give it birth.

George Ripley, one of Mr. Rice's forerunners, stated as
the great object of all social reform: "the development of
humanity, the substitution of a race of free, noble, holy men
and women, instead of the dwarfish and mutilated specimens
which now cover the earth." That is the object that experi-

mental colleges have always had in view. It would be interesting to see some really radical experimenters forego the free and holy and occupy themselves with the dwarfish and mutilated. An experimental college staffed by fanatical realists and fanatical cynics instead of idealists would have a lot less fire but it might have a lot more iron. But you could never get such a faculty together. Teachers like that stay where they are, being bored from within and thanking God for an occasional brilliant student whom they can really help. Such a student doesn't show up very often, but when he does they try to assist his search for knowledge — they don't lead him down into the waters of redemption that he may be born again.

Ann Vickers

BY SINCLAIR LEWIS

WITH good business acumen, the publishers of Sinclair Lewis have brought out in the same fortnight with *Ann Vickers* a small volume in which Mr. Carl Van Doren bestows on him the most unchecked adulation he can have received since the 1902 graduation issue of the Sauk Center High School *O-Sa-Ge*. Mr. Van Doren's book has some sound criticism in it, but you have to clear away a vast debris of emotion to get at it. His primary thesis, that Mr. Lewis is the most thoroughly American of contemporary novelists, can hardly be controverted, and his assumption (which seems to him so axiomatic that he hardly phrases it) that Mr. Lewis is the best novelist of his generation, will not be questioned here. Mr. Van Doren had intimated as much before, but enthusiasm has now so wrought upon him that the comparative detachment of his earlier studies has melted away and his discussion of the novelist becomes something very much like a hymn to the sun. "Mr. Lewis," he says, "has a mind better disciplined than Mark Twain's, and more mental and moral courage." The word, observe, is "disciplined." "Not one of them [Theodore Dreiser, H. L. Mencken, Eugene O'Neill, James Branch Cabell, Edwin Arlington Robinson] has kept so close to the main channel of American life as Mr. Lewis, or so near the human surface." And "not only is he an American telling stories, but he is America telling stories." And, "Even in the Middle West men and women have had to look twice at their own faces in the mirror to be sure that they are or are not like the men and women of Zenith and its suburbs." And finally, "When the actual cities have faded into history, Zenith, with all its garish colors and comic angles, will stand up like a living monument. It will be the hub of the universe which Mr. Lewis has shaped out of the Middle West of his age."

With this more than princely ability to promise diuturnity unto his relics, Sinclair Lewis clearly enters a new phase, as a culture hero or a sun myth. It is all a little amazing to those outside the cult. What's all the shooting for? After all, this is only Doc Lewis's boy, Red, who has been writing novels. Pretty good novels, but not — quite — masterpieces that justify that sort of incense. Mr. Van Doren's book lacks something as critical finality. But the publisher's impulse was sound: it makes a fine blurb.

Yet the appearance of a new novel by the only American who has ever been awarded a Nobel Prize for literature ought to be an opportunity for criticism. For unemotional analysis, for the examination of a number of critical conventions already established, for a consideration of primary purposes and the extent of their achievement. The first step of such an examination would ask an elementary question. Are these six novels, the most vigorous of our time in America, supposed to be satire or realism? Is Mr. Lewis dealing, as realists deal, with the truth of experience in American life, or is he, as a practising sociologist with a fine talent and a burning rage, caricaturing the America of our time with a moral purpose equivalent to Swift's? So far as I know, no one has discussed that question very seriously, and yet it makes all the difference. For if Sinclair Lewis thinks of himself primarily as a satirist, then the brilliance of his achievement is not open to question. But if he intends realism, then his instruments are defective and a large part of the work he has done with them is just grotesque.

Mr. Van Doren, without asking the question, votes for realism. For instance, *Elmer Gantry*. It is, Mr. Van Doren says, "essentially a story, and a classic story, of a false priest who himself committed the sins he scourged in others." But is it? One remembers that the book contains a number of other priests besides Gantry and that they are all kicked about in the same way. One remembers the wholly fantastic distortion of the religious scene. It was written after an intensive study of the American clergy, a study made with the help of expert consultants. In *Elmer Gantry*, as in *Arrowsmith* and *Ann Vickers*, Mr. Lewis constituted himself a commission of inquiry making a survey, a sociological survey. The book sets forth his findings, but one knows that the commission posited its findings before beginning the inquiry, and that would not seem to be realism. As a novel about a false priest, it is intolerably deficient in understanding, intolerably naïve in its consideration of spiritual affairs, intolerably faulty in its presentation of experience. But considered as the work of a sociologist in fiction, a headlong satire of religious hypocrisy and commercialism written by a man who furiously hates them, it is one of the most invigorating books of our time. Similarly with *Arrowsmith*, a study which was also directed by an expert — one who happened to dislike the Rockefeller Foundation. A realistic novel about a bacteriologist would require more subtlety and intricacy of understanding than is ever expended on Martin. (His prayer, which Mr. Van Doren quotes, and his customary state of mind while working at his trade, have caused a bacteriologist of my acquaintance to want — I use his own winning expression — to puke.) But it is a novel of great power and great charm, and those qualities proceed from the satirist's fervor — his hatred of stupidity, his scorn of frailty and time-serving and injustice, and his admiration of heroism and determination. And *Babbitt*. It has made a mould; it has worked its way into the possession of everyone, a complete expression of our time. But not as an expression of the truth about business men, or even about George F. Babbitt, but as an expression of certain sentiments, in this generation, about them.

Or take the "superb mimetic gift" of which Mr. Van Doren speaks, and which every commentator has dwelt on since the publication of *Main Street*. It is perhaps time to inquire whether Mr. Lewis possesses it. If the phrase means anything, it means that he can reproduce with great fidelity the idioms, rhythms, and melodies of actual speech. But can he? At least he never has. Take the "yuh's" and "yarr's" of Dr. Kennicott and the similar alphabetical explosions that signify the exclamations of daily speech. They have never been heard on this earth. Mr. Lewis's use of them has nothing to do with a mimetic gift, but they mightily serve him as a device of caricature, in the depiction of objects of satire whose relatives are the human monsters of Dickens. Take the opening pages of *Ann Vickers*, pages which make unnecessary Mr. Taylor's reminder that Lewis once wrote boys' books. Children have never talked that way outside the *Youth's Companion*. Take the incredible soliloquies of Ann Vickers, of Martin Arrowsmith, of Babbitt, of Carol Kennicott. Take the lightning self-summaries that all Lewis's characters manage to get into every third speech, their flood-tide garrulity, their only half-heard slang, their naïve self-betrayals, their conversational dotting of every *i*. Take the sort of speech, ten thousand times repeated, which enables the satirist to score a point over the realist's shoulder — as when Edna Derby speaks, in "Ann Vickers": —

"Oh, rats, you're so old-*fash*ioned! Why do you suppose we *go* to college? Women have always been the slaves of men. Now it's the women's hour! We ought to demand all the freedom and — and travel and fame and so on and so forth that men have. And our own spending money! Oh, I'm going to have a career, too! I'm going to be an actress. Like *le belle* Sarah. Think! The light! The applause! The scent of — of make-up and all sorts of Interesting People coming into your dressing room and congratulating you! The magic world! Oh, I must have it. Or I might take up landscape gardening, I hear it pays slick."

Very surely, that sort of thing does not show a mimetic gift. But it, with all the other devices I have mentioned, enormously serves Mr. Lewis, in a way that is worth pointing out.

We approach the crux with the interminable speeches, from three to ten pages or more, with which Lewis's characters frequently introduce themselves and into which any of them, any at all, is likely to break without notice or provocation. They dredge up the depths of his nature quite as effectively as any "interior soliloquy." They paint before our eyes whole panoramas of his social class, his genealogy, his history, and his fortune. By sheer power of athletic endurance they create before our eyes the monster whom Mr. Lewis is assailing. But the ingenuous technique offends a novelist. They are not dialogue, they are not speech, they are not even character. What are they? They are an instrumentality of satire, an energetic caricature, a genuinely magnificent method of attack. Their function shows most purely in *The Man Who Knew Coolidge*, where they are perfectly accommodated to the end in view. Elsewhere they succeed or fail in varying degree, approaching cliché. And the cliché of dialogue is only one evidence of a cliché of character which serves for satire but is deficient as realism.

The truth is that Sinclair Lewis is a warring marriage, a divided soul, a novelist and a satirist forever at each other's throats. The virtues of the satirist are the defects of the novelist. He has never yet succeeded in creating a complex character nor, in the best sense of the word, a sophisticated one. He has not given us a person of mature intellect or one in whom the passions of the mind or of the spirit seem credible. When he draws a college professor, he manipulates a cliché from the comic strips with the single-minded enjoyment of Booth Tarkington drawing a silly young dramatist of a later day than his own. If he should draw a duchess, we would be aware of her red flannels. When he essays a scientist we get only Martin Arrowsmith, a Babbitt touched with inspiration, or Sondelius, a study in advance glee-club portraiture, or Gottlieb, an adventure in pure tears. The pastels, the chiaroscuro of personality are quite beyond him. He has made his way through the American scene with a naïveté, a simplicity of point of view, a limpidity, and even a shallowness which it is now time to pronounce invincible. And yet these qualities have enhanced his satire. Simplicity enables him to concentrate his superhuman energy; insensitiveness to chiaroscuro prevents the doubt that would be fatal. He becomes a flaming hate, and out of that hate he has written the most vigorous sociological fiction of our time, in America or anywhere else. Be sure that it is accompanied by a corresponding admiration, which gave us Gottlieb and Sondelius and Ann Vickers, but that admiration too is a simple passion and they also are creatures of simplicity, who exist primarily as channels for the hate directed at the milieu that they struggle against.

Ann Vickers, Lewis's first novel in four years (it appears that he chucked the labor manifesto about which rumors once circulated) makes all this plain. For what has been said above merely announces that Sinclair Lewis was shaped by the Herbert Croly age in American thinking — the pioneer era in Greenwich Village, the days of generous, idealistic thinking about the future in America, the last generation of American hope. He is Randolph Bourne writing novels, and in his novels that liberal hope meets the reality of post-war America and, its eyes opened, goes the way of all optimism. So he turns now to hagiology, giving us a saint of that movement, a nun of the sisterhood most consecrated and most esteemed in that happy noon. Her legend has all the fecundity, all the gusto, all the hate that gave life to the earlier novels. It is Lewis writing, in matters of mere style, rather better than he ever wrote before. It is magnificently informed — instinct with a hundred qualities of the time it deals with that only Lewis could seize and fuse. A comparison is just: the novel partly coincides, in time and intention, with *The 42nd Parallel*, and of the two Lewis's is much more alive, much deeper, and infinitely more aware. Beside it, the work of Dos Passos seems precious, somehow inert, and more than a little flat.

Ann Vickers is a sister of Martin Arrowsmith — simple-minded and single-minded, dogged, undeluded, honest with herself, capable of the tumultuous activity that gets things done in the world. She is a suffragette, a social worker, a "penologist," and finally the superintendent of a prison. Unlike her predecessors in Mr. Lewis's biography, she does not originate in Winnemac, that state which no one who is sensitive to words could have named, but in Illinois. First converted to reform by a cobbler who is a sentimental socialist, she experiments with debating and "leadership" in college, joins a suffrage flying-squadron, and is jailed for biting a policeman, works in settlement houses, has a fling at charity, spends some time as a matron in a Southern penitentiary, and eventually becomes both the head of a women's prison and a national authority on reform, ending by seeing her lover, a dishonest judge, condemned to the system she hates and delivered from it by methods she has denounced. Her story is loosely strung, panoramic, and headlong, like all its predecessors. Ann's is somewhat more biological — in the earlier Lewis novels people seldom went to bed together except in *Elmer Gantry,* and there only meretriciously — but the biology is as simple and unromantic as Ann herself. Passion, even sentiment, as a human motive eludes Mr. Lewis. He is better at hate.

It is hate that has made his earlier novels memorable, and it is hate that provides most of what is good in this one. It is spent lavishly on the politicians and reformers who are to *Ann Vickers* what pastors were to *Elmer Gantry* and doctors and bacteriologists to *Arrowsmith,* and it rises to the finest rhapsody he has yet given us when Ann goes to the State penitentiary at Copperhead Gap. Those pages are Lewis at his purest, most concentrated, most powerful — hurling at our naked nerves cruelty and stupidity, ugliness, graft, bribery, wretchedness, hopelessness, despair. Public attention will probably concern itself mostly with Copperhead Gap — approval and resentment will center there. And yet those pages and the magnificent hatred that produces them are not all. For Ann's career covers most of the thinking that was going on in America during its time. Constantly interrupted by Mr. Lewis's scolding and by his frankly Thackerayan essays on a myriad liberal themes — published separately, they would make a year's output for any Foundation — it does project Our Times, and on the whole more truly than Mr. Sullivan. It is an America violently caricatured by a satirist and further distorted by the lens of the hopeful generation, and yet it is the America we know, more profoundly seen and more vigorously rendered than anywhere else in our fiction.

There you have him. Too unscrupulous a satirist, too defective a technician, too limited by the intellectual and emotional clichés of his generation, too naïve and too earnest, Sinclair Lewis is nevertheless the best novelist of his generation in America. He knows America better than any of the others, and he has conspicuously what they lack, fecundity and strength. Mr. Van Doren is right in calling him masculine. But why be euphemistic? The word is "male." He has extraordinary power, virility, boisterousness, and sheer nervous and muscular energy. They are qualities which dissolve away his shortcomings and which cannot be spared from fiction, these days of anemic invention and querulous estheticism.

Still, he is no sun god. Mr. Van Doren's expectation that *Babbitt* will live on long after Detroit is dust seems to me a little silly. Mr. Van Doren, not I, is responsible for the appeal to Mark Twain who, he feels, had as wide a sweep as Mr. Lewis but was otherwise inferior to him. But *The Adventures of Huckleberry Finn* possesses, besides an infinitely deeper and wiser knowledge of America, a serenity that makes the anger of the Lewis novels seem a trivial and somewhat hysterical yell. In that serenity, not elsewhere, immortality resides. The shadow of a period is already on

Lewis — already he seems, even in *Ann Vickers,* a little shrill. Public preference moves on to novels written with a firmer technique, to themes whose tragic despair goes deeper spiritually than his basic optimism, to methods more rigorous and ideas more skeptical. That, no doubt, is a fashion and will pass, but first it will establish a sense of proportion about Sinclair Lewis. The Detroiters of that day, in their unfallen city, will say truly that he was the finest American novelist of his period, but in that period no American of genius was writing novels.

Exile's Return

BY MALCOLM COWLEY

~~~~~~

MR. MALCOLM COWLEY has undertaken to write the history of the lost generation. He identifies this generation as a group of writers who saw service in the Army, lived in Greenwich Village for a while, expatriated themselves on behalf of the good life, and finally returned to make what terms they could with the America from which they had seceded. It is not clear just how or wherein these people were lost, nor just why an explanation of them is desirable, but *Exile's Return* is an effort to tell their story in relation to the infinite.

Mr. Cowley's book will be an easy exercise for Freudians. Much the most important fact about the generation, the author tells us, was the process of deracination to which it was subjected and from whose effects only a part of it recovered. The mandrake has an important place in art and folklore: uprooting is a symbol of emasculation. The sense of personal enfeeblement, of power and identity lost, is usually associated with the castration complex. When a fixation occurs on the level of that infantile dread, the complex works out in adult life as a fear of impotence and an uneasy search for replenishment or restoration. These often produce what is known as fugue, an impulse toward flight which may be expressed in various ways. Note the "escape" to which Mr. Cowley alludes so often. To interpret it as retreat from an unfavorable environment or even as retreat from one's unprofitable self is merely rationalization: it is a search for personal completion, an effort to recover what the infantile despair held to be lost. It is dominated by the desire for wholeness, and wholeness was first associated with the womb. Suicide, the Catholic church, and communism, the typical fulfilments that Mr. Cowley records, are psychologically identical. These are, remember, literary people. The free-floating anxiety of the castration complex is powerfully supported by their vocational narcism; literature is an exhibitionist phenomenon. Significantly, the lost generation are nostalgic about their childhood. In the slate country or on the banks of the Wabash or north of Boston, before the rape of the mandrake, they were whole. They have not been since, and the compensation of that impairment is their history. If anyone be found who has made an adult adjustment to that early lack, he does not belong to the lost generation.

Psychoanalysis, which the lost generation once devoutly embraced, would thus interpret the data which Mr. Cowley presents. Mr. Cowley repudiates the Freudian dogma, however, and it will be more fruitful to discuss his book sociologically, since he insists on the social significance of the movement. But the moment that this sterner criterion is applied, concealed theorems are revealed. *Exile's Return* at once ceases to be a history of a generation and becomes the apologia of a coterie. Within the guild, there will be writers of Mr. Cowley's generation who dissent from his identification with himself of all literary phenomena since 1917, refusing him power of attorney to speak for them. And outside the guild, literary ideas and behavior are considerably less important than Mr. Cowley assumes. The importance of literary people is chiefly to one another; a fixed difference between the voice of a nation and the manifesto of a house organ must be taken into account.

The literary first, since it was probably the literary whom Miss Gertrude Stein meant when she uttered a phrase that must eventually lose its tragic connotation. There are a good many writers who were of draft-age or below it in 1917 but who nevertheless failed to suffer the uprooting, the frustration, and the despair that Mr. Cowley describes with such eloquence. What, in terms of Mr. Cowley's book, is to be made of them? One may say that they are unimportant writers; one may assert that they have no relation to the true spirit of the times or the genuine current of social and intellectual and emotional movement, or that they are counter-revolutionary phenomena. But such a judgment is flagrantly subjective — it is to define importance or the true and the genuine as what I hold to be important and true and genuine, and that is not at all the burden of Mr. Cowley's book. There they are, distinguished writers who show none of the stigmata of the lost generation and so escape from his generalization. What, for diagnosis, is significant about them?

First of all, I think, that they were not betrayed into megalomania, and second, that they omitted to interpret purely private bellyaches as a universal principle of evil. The lost generation whom Mr. Cowley describes was a group of writers whose sentiments were similar, and these sentiments, which he calls the religion of art, included a necessity to be great artists. These people would Go Beyond. They could create only the immortal. They recognized, to begin with, as Mr. Cowley records, that the cards were stacked against them since all the themes had been used up and all the symbols were worn. Hence a frantic effort to destroy both theme and symbol, carried to *surréalisme* and, it may be, beyond that. Hence a triumph of the castration feeling in the nihilism of Paul Valéry's withdrawal from art. Hence, most revealingly, the impotence that rebuked them when they actually wrote books, when their fantasies were forced to meet the test of reality. Mr. Cowley notes that a surprising number of them did not write books at all, finding it more secure merely to talk about writing them some time later. He should have gone on: he should have noted the astonishing infecundity of those who did. The resolve to abandon the sense of humor might secure them some comfort, blunting their ability to distinguish between sublimity and preposterousness, but in the end not even a solemn decision that they would not be Proust could assuage them. In their religion they had desired and intended to be Proust, and here were books which no fantasy could make out to be more than ordinary books. Therefore they despaired, and it is significant that they interpreted their own despair as the collapse of the moral order.

Mr. Cowley says that eventually, as part of their belated integration, some of them came to write stuff that they could read to their friends. That, in effect, is what writers who did not belong to the lost generation had been doing all along. These had intended to write quite ordinary books. They had, that is, abstained from the religion of art, they were under no compulsion to be great. Their effort was to write as well as they could; they wanted to utilize their experience as honestly as possible in books to which the canons of eternity did not apply. Narcism had in them a lower potential. That fact protected them from frustration and despair. Also it restrained them from identifying their experience with that of the race and the angels. If some of them were mutilated or shellshocked by the war, they tended to conclude that they had had hard luck rather than that the world was evil. If they discovered symptoms of degeneration in themselves, they did not interpret them as the collapse of civilization. There has always been this alternative to the auspices: a hangover can be the result of having drunk too much quite as readily as it can be the vindictiveness of God or the injustice of the capitalist system. Meanwhile, with only moderate self-consciousness, they found a discipline. Few traveling fellowships were granted to them, and their friends were usually unable to lend them steamer fare. They went to work — teaching in colleges, reporting for newspapers, even contaminating themselves with advertising copy. They wrote their quite ordinary books in their time off. Either humor or realism made them reluctant to describe themselves as artists. The same quality kept them from issuing manifestoes, and when they socked the proprietor of a café they were not led to associate the act with the *Zeitgeist*. When they went abroad, they went for pleasure or education or debauch, not to fulfil themselves. They seem, on the whole, to have had a good time during the lost years. When they didn't, they were by no means sure that unhappiness was of itself enough to make them either great or betrayed. And they wrote their books. To say that these are better books than those of Mr. Cowley's coterie would be to repeat the subjective fallacy. But they are books, and they are books of the era but not of the lost generation, and, observe very carefully, Mr. Cowley's thesis has no room for them.

Mr. Cowley expresses the alternatives of the lost generation. It could, in the person of Harry Crosby, follow the cognate religions of art and individualism to insanity and extinction; or, in the person of Mr. Cowley, it could repudiate both religions and finally achieve integration by identifying itself with a social cause. Psychologically the second alternative represents completion of self by alliance with what is more complete. Sociology confirms psychology, but in a way that makes even more dubious the concept of the lost generation.

A docility among readers of literary journals is responsible for much bad thinking. They accept writers' own judgments of themselves and so interpret evidence of mere fashion, caprice, and even log-rolling as the spirit of the age. Let us be quite explicit here. To sociology, the *Cosmopolitan* is more significant than *Broom*, and the *Saturday Evening Post* more significant than either; the *New Masses* more significant than the old *Masses*, and the *National Ripsaw* more significant than either; O. O. McIntyre more significant than Michael Gold, Kathleen Norris more significant than either, and Edgar Rice Burroughs more significant than she. The social function of literature is to express the sentiments of groups and to heighten awareness of the aggregates that constitute the emotional vitality of groups. Socially, it is much better for any writer (or any realtor, farmer, or stevedore) to increase his sense of personal integrity by identifying himself with a group than it is for him to suffer impairment in that sentiment by remaining just an individual. The health of the state is the vitality of its groups, but it is an error of the first magnitude to suppose that only a single group can be vital. Socially a capitalist state is unhealthy unless its communists have vital aggregates; a communist state is just as unhealthy unless the aggregates of its counter-revolutionary groups are furiously active. Socially, it is the base and not the form that is important, and the true social function of

literature in America during the post-war years was performed on levels that the lost generation never touched.
Mr. Cowley is quite right in advising the remnants to identify
themselves with a group, for by doing so they will achieve
the identity which he finds they lack, but when he commands them to attach themselves to the workers, who alone
are the true church, he lapses from sociology to autobiography.

The last paragraph above is an analysis by abstract principles, those of Vilfredo Pareto, precisely as the principles
behind Mr. Cowley's analysis are, somewhat improved upon,
those of Karl Marx. Although the Paretian approach has here
the support of psychology and anthropology, no abstract
analysis is worth much. Let us get back to the repository of
social facts, history. As history, *Exile's Return* is extremely
dubious, the simple fact being that most of the generation was
never lost at all.

Mr. Cowley's narrative has defects of statement and assumption. It is of little importance that Mr. Cowley's controversy with Gorham Munson (abbreviated since its appearance in the *New Republic*) shows an altogether different
color when one turns to the *Sewanee Review*, or that there
may have been other reasons for the rise of *The American
Mercury* than the article by Ernest Boyd in the first issue
which intensely annoyed Mr. Cowley. But it is important
when we are told that, historically, "everyone felt lost and
directionless," that bourgeois society collapsed, and that the
capitalist system was "convulsively dying." The first two
of these assertions are simply untrue, and the third is a
prophecy which needs only a difference of opinion to attain the same falsity. All three are statements of sentiment,
not of fact, and Mr. Cowley's treatment of the whole era
is in the same terms. His account of the years is altogether

subjective and he continually mistakes the emotions of his friends for the structure of society. A part of this insufficiency is merely defective experience, as when he derives a principle of history from a belief that Greenwich Village invented the drinking party — Ogden, Utah, could have shown him otherwise in 1910. Mostly, however, it is a defect of his original assumption, that some literary people are a generation and that their biography must be a history of America. There finally we must leave him altogether.

For it is a fact, however painful to writers, that the literary have only a slight importance. Among the people who were of draft-age or below in 1917, there are a few to whom the writers of their time are tremendously important. To a larger number they are moderately important, but in ambiguous ways — at best as a form of diversion, at worst as an accessory aid to peristalsis. But to much the greatest part of the generation they have no importance at all, being either quite unknown or effectively disregarded. The heart of Mr. Cowley's fallacy is right here. What about the men and women who, since 1917, in a period of rapid social shifts and readjustment, have established the pattern of our time and given shape to our institutions? To number writers among these people or to regard them as lost or to assert that they so regarded themselves is either a literary affectation or a delusion. As a symbol, the doughboy, when he got out of uniform, went to work. He entered into the process of activity, he neither fled from it nor tried to coin it into art, he became it. In the mill or the A. & P., or on the farm or in the office, he went about earning a living, rearing a family, defending his present, and safeguarding his future as well as he could. The processes of shift and adjustment, of disintegration, occurred in him and not in the disembodied, theoretical discussions of literary people. To be sure, he was the material and not the mechanism of the adjustments and the patterns. The mechanism is to be observed at the foci of power — and will be seen more clearly there, now that the generation reaches the age at which it takes complete control. No writers are resident at those foci — to think otherwise is a form of fantasy, in the interest of consolation. Primarily the laboratory scientists and the politicians (the engineers of economic and social pressure) are the determinants of the actual generation. It is unwise to forget them, as Mr. Cowley does. The man who has perfected a serum for the treatment of encephalitis, who has measured a star's recession, or has discovered new ways for the utilization of energy, has worked straight toward an alteration of the social equilibrium, as no writer can. Similarly, the humblest member of the Brain Trust and any active spokesman of a business group or a labor group has applied the very power whose absence is, by Mr. Cowley's book, a diagnostic character of the literary.

Among these men the past seventeen years have revealed no vocational neurosis. The actual possessors of power show no sense of frustration. They, like the symbolic doughboy, have not considered themselves a lost generation. It is time for the adjective to receive a closer examination than anyone has given it. Mr. Cowley has defined it as meaning that certain writers of books and their admirers, in effect a coterie, a fraternity, a literary clique, experienced despair and either committed suicide or saved their souls by deciding to favor communism. To the class of 1916 in the high schools of the United States as a whole the definition obviously does not apply.

FROM *The Saturday Review*, APRIL 25, 1936

Genius Is Not Enough

~~~~~~

SOME months age *The Saturday Review* serialized Mr. Thomas Wolfe's account of the conception, gestation and as yet uncompleted delivery of his Novel, and Scribners' are now publishing the three articles as a book. It is one of the most appealing books of our time. No one who reads it can doubt Mr. Wolfe's complete dedication to his job or regard with anything but respect his attempt to describe the dark and nameless fury of the million-footed life swarming in his dark and unknown soul. So honest or so exhaustive an effort at self-analysis in the interest of esthetics has seldom been made in the history of American literature, and *The Story of a Novel* is likely to have a long life as a source-book for students of literature and for psychologists as well. But also it brings into the public domain material that has been hitherto outside the privilege of criticism. Our first essay must be to examine it in relation to Mr. Wolfe's novels, to see what continuities and determinants it may reveal, and to inquire into their bearing on the art of fiction.

Let us begin with one of many aspects of Mr. Wolfe's

novels that impress the reader, the frequent recurrence of material to which one must apply the adjective placental. (The birth metaphors are imposed by Mr. Wolfe himself. In *The Story of a Novel* he finds himself big with first a thunder-cloud and then a river. The symbolism of waters is obviously important to him, and the title of his latest novel is to be that of the series as a whole.) A great part of *Look Homeward, Angel* was just the routine first-novel of the period which many novelists had published and many others had suppressed, the story of a sensitive and rebellious adolescent who was headed toward the writing of novels. The rest of it was not so easily catalogued. Parts of it showed intuition, understanding and ecstasy, and an ability to realize all three in character and scene, whose equal it would have been hard to point out anywhere in the fiction of the time. These looked like great talent, and in such passages as the lunchroom scene in the dawn that Mr. Wolfe called nacreous some fifty times, they seemed to exist on both a higher and a deeper level of realization than any of Mr. Wolfe's contemporaries had attained. But also there were parts that looked very dubious indeed — long, whirling discharges of words, unabsorbed in the novel, unrelated to the proper business of fiction, badly if not altogether unacceptably written, raw gobs of emotion, aimless and quite meaningless jabber, claptrap, belches, grunts and Tarzan-like screams. Their rawness, their unshaped quality must be insisted upon: it was as if the birth of the novel had been accompanied by a lot of the material that had nourished its gestation. The material which nature and most novelists discard when its use has been served. It looked like one of two things, there was no telling which. It looked like the self-consciously literary posturing of a novelist too young and too naïve to have learned his trade. Or, from another point of view, it looked like a document in psychic disintegration. And one of the most important questions in contemporary literature was: would the proportion of fiction to placenta increase or decrease in Mr. Wolfe's next book?

It decreased. If fiction of the quality of that lunchroom scene made up about one-fifth of *Look Homeward, Angel*, it constituted, in *Of Time and the River*, hardly more than a tenth. The placental material had enormously grown and, what was even more ominous, it now had a rationalization. It was as unshaped as before, but it had now been retroactively associated with the dark and nameless heaving of the voiceless and unknown womb of Time, and with the unknown and voiceless fury of the dark and lovely and lost America. There were still passages where Mr. Wolfe was a novelist not only better than most of his contemporaries but altogether out of their class. But they were pushed farther apart and even diluted when they occurred by this dark substance which may have been nameless but was certainly far from voiceless.

Certain other aspects of the new book seemed revealing. For one thing, there was a shocking contempt of the medium. Some passages were not completely translated from the "I" in which they had apparently been written to the "he" of Eugene Gant. Other passages alluded to incidents which had probably appeared in an earlier draft but could not be found in the final one. Others contradictorily reported scenes which had already appeared, and at least once a passage that had seen service already was reënlisted for a second hitch in a quite different context, apparently with no recollection that it had been used before.

Again, a state of mind that had been appropriate to the puberty of Eugene seemed inappropriate as the boy grew older, and might therefore be significant. I mean the giantism of the characters. Eugene himself, in *Of Time and the River*, was clearly a borderline manic-depressive: he exhibited the classic cycle in his alternation between "fury" and "despair" and the classic accompaniment of obsessional neurosis in the compulsions he was under to read all the books in the world, see all the people in Boston, observe all the lives of the man-swarm and list all the names and places in America. That was simple enough, but practically every other character in the book also suffered from fury and compulsions, and, what was more suggestive, they were all twenty feet tall, spoke with the voice of trumpets and the thunder, ate like Pantagruel, wept like Niobe, laughed like Falstaff and bellowed like the bulls of Bashan. The significant thing was that we were seeing them all through Eugene's eyes. To a child all adults are giants: their voices are thunderous, their actions are portentous and grotesquely magnified, and all their exhibited emotions are seismic. It looked as if part of Eugene's condition was an infantile regression.

This appearance was reinforced by what seemed to be another stigma of infantilism: that all the experiences in *Of Time and the River* were on the same level and had the same value. When Mr. Gant died (of enough cancer to have exterminated an army corps), the reader accepted the accompanying frenzy as proper to the death of a man's father — which is one of the most important events in anyone's life. But when the same frenzy accompanied nearly everything else in the book — a ride on a railroad train, a literary tea-fight, a midnight lunch in the kitchen, a quarrel between friends, a walk at night, the rejection of a play, an automobile trip, a seduction that misfired, the discovery of Eugene's true love — one could only decide that something was dreadfully wrong. If the death of a father comes out even with a ham-on-rye, then the art of fiction is cockeyed.

Well, *The Story of a Novel* puts an end to speculation and supplies some unexpected but very welcome light. To think of these matters as contempt of the medium, regression and infantilism is to be too complex and subtle. The truth shows up in two much simpler facts: that Mr. Wolfe is still astonishingly immature, and that he has mastered neither the psychic material out of which a novel is made nor the technique of writing fiction. He does not seem aware of the first fact, but he acknowledges the second with a frankness and an understanding that are the finest promise to date for his future books. How far either defect is reparable it is idle to speculate. But at least Mr. Wolfe realizes that he is, as yet, by no means a complete novelist.

The most flagrant evidence of his incompleteness is the fact that, so far, one indispensable part of the artist has existed not in Mr. Wolfe but in Maxwell Perkins. Such organizing faculty and such critical intelligence as have been applied to the book have come not from inside the artist, not from the artist's feeling for form and esthetic integrity, but from the office of Charles Scribner's Sons. For five years the artist pours out words "like burning lava from a volcano" — with little or no idea what their purpose is, which book they belong in, what the relation of part to part is, what is organic and what irrelevant, or what emphasis or coloration in the completed work of art is being served by the job at hand. Then Mr. Perkins decides these questions — from without, and by a process to which rumor applies the word "assembly." But works of art cannot be assembled like a carburetor — they must be grown like a plant, or in Mr. Wolfe's favorite simile like an embryo. The artist writes a hundred thousand words about a train: Mr. Perkins decides that the train is worth only five thousand words. But such a decision as this is properly not within Mr. Perkins's power; it must be made by the highly conscious self-criticism of the artist in relation to the pulse of the book itself. Worse still, the artist goes on writing till Mr. Perkins tells him that the novel is finished. But the end of a novel is, properly, dictated by the internal pressure, osmosis, metabolism — what you will — of the novel itself, of which only the novelist can have a first-hand knowledge. There comes a point where the necessities of the book are satisfied, where its organic processes have reached completion. It is hard to see how awareness of that point can manifest itself at an editor's desk — and harder still to trust the integrity of a work of art in which not the artist but the publisher has determined where the true ends and the false begins.

All this is made more ominous by Mr. Wolfe's almost incredibly youthful attitude toward revision. No novel is written till it is revised — the process is organic, it is one of the processes of art. It is, furthermore, the process above all others that requires objectivity, a feeling for form, a knowledge of what the necessities of the book are, a determination that those necessities shall outweigh and dominate everything else. It is, if not the highest functioning of the artistic intelligence, at least a fundamental and culminating one. But the process appears to Mr. Wolfe not one which will free his book from falsity, irrelevance and its private encumbrances, not one which will justify and so exalt the artist — but one that makes his spirit quiver "at the bloody execution" and his soul recoil "from the carnage of so many lovely things." But superfluous and mistaken things are lovely to only a very young writer, and the excision of them is bloody carnage only if the artist has not learned to subdue his ego in favor of his book. And the same juvenility

makes him prowl "the streets of Paris like a maddened animal" because — for God's sake! — the reviewers may not
like the job.

The placental passages are now explained. They consist
of psychic material which the novelist has proved unable
to shape into fiction. The failure may be due either to immature understanding or to insufficient technical skill:
probably both causes operate here and cannot be separated. The principle is very simple. When Mr. Wolfe gives
us his doctors, undertakers and newspapermen talking in a
lunchroom at dawn, he does his job — magnificently. There
they are, and the reader revels in the dynamic presentation
of human beings, and in something else as well that should
have the greatest possible significance for Mr. Wolfe. For
while the doctors and undertakers are chaffing one another,
the reader gets that feeling of the glamour and mystery of
American life which Mr. Wolfe elsewhere unsuccessfully
labors to evoke in thousands of rhapsodic words. The novelist makes his point in the lives of his characters, not in tidal
surges of rhetoric.

Is America lost, lonely, nameless and unknown? Maybe,
and maybe not. But if it is, the conditions of the novelist's
medium require him to make it lost and lonely in the lives
of his characters, not in blank verse bombast and apocalyptic
delirium. You cannot represent America by hurling adjec-
tives at it. Do "the rats of death and age and dark oblivion
feed forever at the roots of sleep"? It sounds like a high
school valedictory, but if in fact they do, then the novelist
is constrained to show them feeding so by means of what his
characters do and say and feel in relation to one another,
and not by chasing the ghosts of Whitman and Ezekiel
through fifty pages of disembodied emotion. Such emotion
is certainly the material that fiction works with, but until

it is embodied in character and scene it is not fiction — it is only logorrhea. A poem should not mean but be, Mr. MacLeish tells us, and poetry is always proving that fundamental. In a homelier aphorism Mr. Cohan has expressed the same imperative of the drama: "Don't tell 'em, show 'em." In the art of fiction the *thing* is not only an imperative, it is a primary condition. A novel *is* — it cannot be asserted, ranted or even detonated. A novelist represents life. When he does anything else, no matter how beautiful or furious or ecstatic the way in which he does it, he is not writing fiction. Mr. Wolfe can write fiction — has written some of the finest fiction of our day. But a great part of what he writes is not fiction at all; it is only material with which the novelist has struggled but which has defeated him. The most important question in American fiction to-day, probably, is whether he can win that encounter in his next book. It may be that *The October Fair* and *The Hills Beyond Pentland* will show him winning it, but one remembers the dilution from *Look Homeward, Angel* to *Of Time and the River* and is apprehensive. If he does win it, he must do so inside himself; Mr. Perkins and the assembly-line at Scribners' can do nothing to help him.

That struggle also has another aspect. A novelist utilizes the mechanism of fantasy for the creation of a novel, and there are three kinds of fantasy with which he works. One of them is unconscious fantasy, about which Dr. Kubie was writing in these columns something over a year ago. A novelist is wholly subject to its emphases and can do nothing whatever about them — though when Mr. Wolfe says that the center of all living is reconciliation with one's father he comes close to revealing its pattern in him. There remain two kinds of fantasy which every novelist employs — but which everyone employs in a different ratio. Call them identification and projection, call them automatic and directed, call them proliferating and objectified – the names do not matter. The novelist surrenders himself to the first kind, but dominates and directs the second kind. In the first kind he says "I am Napoleon" and examines himself to see how he feels. In the second kind, he wonders how Napoleon feels, and instead of identifying himself with him, he tries to discover Napoleon's necessities. If he is excessively endowed with the first kind of fantasy, he is likely to be a genius. But if he learns to utilize the second kind in the manifold interrelationships of a novel he is certain to be an artist. Whatever Mr. Wolfe's future in the wider and looser interest of Literature, his future in the far more rigorous interest of fiction just about comes down to the question of whether he can increase his facility at the second kind of fantasy. People would stop idiotically calling him autobiographical, if he gave us less identification and more understanding. And we could do with a lot less genius, if we got a little more artist.

For the truth is that Mr. Wolfe is presented to us, and to himself, as a genius. There is no more dissent from that judgment in his thinking about himself than in Scribners' publicity. And, what is more, a genius of the good old-fashioned romantic kind – possessed by a demon, driven by the gales of his own fury, helpless before the lava-flood of his own passion, selected and set apart for greatness, his lips touched by a live coal, consequently unable to exercise any control over what he does and in fact likely to be damaged or diminished by any effort at control. Chaos is everything, if you have enough of it in you to make a world. Yes, but what if you don't make a world – what if you just make a noise? There was chaos in Stephen Dedalus's soul, but he thought of that soul not as sufficient in itself but merely as a smithy wherein he might forge his novel. And listen to Mr. Thomas Mann: "When I think of the masterpiece of the twentieth century, I have an idea of something that differs essentially and, in my opinion, with profit from the Wagnerian masterpiece — something exceptionally logical, clear, and well developed in form, something at once austere and serene, with no less intensity of will than his, but of cooler, nobler, even healthier spirituality, something that seeks its greatness not in the colossal, the baroque, and its beauty not in intoxication." Something, in other words, with inescapable form, something which exists as the imposition of order on chaos, something that *is*, not is merely asserted.

One can only respect Mr. Wolfe for his determination to realize himself on the highest level and to be satisfied with nothing short of greatness. But, however useful genius may be in the writing of novels, it is not enough in itself — it never has been enough, in any art, and it never will be. At the very least it must be supported by an ability to impart shape to material, simple competence in the use of tools. Until Mr. Wolfe develops more craftsmanship, he will not be the important novelist he is now widely accepted as being. In order to be a great novelist he must also mature his emotions till he can see more profoundly into character than he now does, and he must learn to put a corset on his prose. Once more: his own smithy is the only possible place for these developments — they cannot occur in the office of any editor whom he will ever know.

A REVIEW FROM *The Saturday Review*, OCTOBER 5, 1935

Proletarian Literature in the United States

BY JOSEPH FREEMAN

SOME of the inclusions in this collection, the first offering of the Book Union, are surprising to a middle-class reader: if they are proletarian literature then a good many American writers have been speaking prose without knowing it, and an excellent proletarian anthology could be assembled from people who would be alarmed if they found themselves classified as anything but boorjoy. Some of the omissions are even more surprising and make one suspect that some of Mr. Freeman's six editors have applied the principle he quotes from Edwin Seaver — have divided authors into Party writers and non-Party writers and let it go at that. If you are a Trotskyite, it appears, you may write about the exploited as much as you please but you will not produce proletarian literature. Which may be sound dogma but is confusing.

Some confusion is implicit in any attempt to make an anthology of class literature, but it is increased here by unsatisfactory definition. Mr. Freeman's otherwise excellent introduction fumbles pretty badly when he undertakes to tell us just what proletarian literature is. Messrs. Phillips and Rahv are more illuminating — their "Recent Problems of Revolutionary Literature" is one of the best things in the book — but they too ignore a fundamental principle.

Class literature, the literature of any class whatever, quite apart from its esthetic function which may in part at least affect all classes, must serve at least one of two functions. First and most important, there is the function of heightening and unifying the sentiments of the class which it represents. It may confirm or increase their group-consciousness, step up their solidarity, make stronger their sense of power and injury and communion, and create, propagate and enliven those vital myths, beliefs, ideals, aims, dogmas, slogans, personifications, purposes and sanctions which are at once the bonds that hold the class together and the energy that makes action possible. Second, there is the interclass function. Literature may be an agency of attack on other classes or of conversion among them. It may assist disintegration, weakening the other classes by making them pity or fear the class it represents, giving them a sense of shame or guilt or futility, hammering at their doubts with ridicule or horror or terror. Or it may proselytize among them, converting the essentially religious symbols of its own myths into symbols acceptable among the religions it invades, and carrying the position by outflanking it with visions of the greater glory to come — or the equivalent in the eschatology of the period.

These functions are usually quite distinct. Only rarely and only in great literature will they coalesce. A work of genius may well fuse them, achieving symbols that are both incandescent for its own class and immediately authoritative for other classes. But the usual disparity between them is especially marked in proletarian literature. For the proletariat is composed of the least educated, least sophisticated, least intellectually complex elements of society. The fact may be distasteful to champions of the proletariat, but it must be taken into account by writers and critics, whatever their class. Literature, to be "live" for most of the proletariat, must employ simple, crude, naïve symbols, must work primarily with caricature or sentimentality or invective or the pink spot or the offstage violin, must use the simplified technique of the pulp story and the sex movie and the cheap melodrama if it is to be understood and effective in its most important function. No sophisticated art of the proletariat is possible till the proletariat becomes sophisticated, yet the more faithfully and effectively literature serves this function, the less effective it must be in the other one. That is why literature that can really inspire the proletariat will, except by accident, continue to be written by actual proletarians for a long while yet. That is why intellectuals who join the movement from outside will continue to be effective writers principally as they are evangelists or propagandists among the heretics.

Such considerations must be kept in mind while reading the present collection. It contains, for instance, a number of exhibits which demonstrate that some proletarian authors can write as badly as any on earth — that they can be clumsy, derivative, imitative, sprawling, uncorseted, priggish and damned dull. But, considering the purposes of the anthology, that judgment is in part irrelevant, since the esthetic shortcomings of such writing may facilitate its class function. Thus Tillie Lerner's "The Iron Throat," which is crude and awkward, and Grace Lumpkin's "John Stevens," which is as mawkish as any temperance apologue in a Methodist weekly, may conceivably serve the primary purpose of class literature far better than, say, the subtleties of John Dos Passos which only sophisticates can appreciate.

By the more usual criteria, the fiction selections are the

worst in the volume, drama esthetically the best, and literary criticism the most interesting. The fiction is badly chosen. Any bourgeois critic could have made a better showing for proletarian literature from novels of the last five years, frequently from the same writers represented here. Much of it is either plain bad or pretentiously bad. A good deal of it vindicates bourgeois Hollywood by painting up its goblins of the exploiting class in shapes and colors accommodated to the mental age of eight. On top of this, a surprising amount of it is tricked out with the arty spellings and punctuation that Dos Passos took over from Joyce, and one wonders why such an accessory of decadent capitalist art is essential to the literature of the workers. Ben Field's "Cow" would be first-rate stuff if the author were a Trotskyite or a millionaire, and no pitch of Party orthodoxy could make Philip Stevenson's "Death of a Century" anything but lousy.

Poetry goes better but is uneven. Eliot — who is probably to be classified as Fascist — is imitated in it almost as often as Dos Passos is in the fiction; and, whatever their ardor, such people as H. H. Lewis, Norman MacLeod and Charles Henry Newman are bad poets. Kenneth Fearing and Horace Gregory, on the other hand, are very good ones. They are too mannered and elliptical to be much read by the proletariat and will be acclaimed chiefly in infidel parts. Isidor Schneider and James Neugass work far more directly with the emotions and symbols of the class for which they speak: they are within the myth-making function of proletarian literature. But probably the truest class poetry of· all is that which, rather ambiguously, is called Folksongs. More of it might well have been included, and surely there should have been selections from the Little Red Songbook.

Proletarian literature in America has so far had its finest artistic achievement in the drama. *Black Pit, Waiting for*

Lefty, Stevedore, and *They Shall Not Die,* are represented here. They are accompanied by Alfred Kreymborg's *America, America,* which does not live up to them. The section called "Reportage" (Mr. Freeman assures his audience that the term has Moscow's *nihil obstat*) contains some excellent writing but one wonders why it was included. It must be intended solely as an exhibit, for reportage fully as sympathetic to the workers appears regularly in the capitalist press. Meridel LeSueur's "I Was Marching" is easily the best of it.

The essays grouped under "Literary Criticism" can mean nothing to the general proletariat, but they are more interesting to an inquiring infidel than anything else in the book. Here is where the theology of proletarian literature is formulated, its canon determined and the tests to be applied to it for orthodoxy set forth — with holy water and exorcisms to reveal the presence of Fascism. It varies, of course, in intelligence and maturity, and includes one bit of collegiate smarty-pants that tends to discredit the serious work it appears with. But the sum is valuable and arresting: here, so far as literature is an offensive weapon, is the actual front of class aggression. Here is where the myths, dogmas and philosophies of history are being selected, validated and implemented. This dialectical department is, and is likely to remain for a long time, the most active field of proletarian literature and, in its secondary function at least, the most important.

The collection has the defects of a first attempt, and the solid virtue of putting into one book a number of representative selections. It has one serious blemish: the biographical identification of authors is much too brief. If, as we are told, writing is to be classified as Party and non-Party literature — Christian and pagan, Mormon and Gentile, Eddyite and

M.A.M. — then we boorjoys want to know whether a writer presented to us as proletarian has taken out his papers. Does he or doesn't he belong to the Party? So far as we are concerned the question of whole-hog honesty is a typical middle-class sentimentality. But conceivably the proletariat might feel the same curiosity in a more realistic frame of mind.

Green Hills of Africa

BY ERNEST HEMINGWAY

~~~~~~~~~~

"THE writer has attempted to write an absolutely true book to see whether the shape of a country and the pattern of a month's action can, if truly presented, compete with a work of imagination." So Mr. Hemingway describes his intention, in a preface which is shorter than the average sentence that follows it. Later, in one of the "bloody literary discussions," he praises prose that is "without tricks and without cheating" — a phrase which sums up an ambition that has been constant in all his work. Then he records his satisfaction "when you write well and truly of something and know impersonally you have written in that way and those who are paid to read it and report on it do not like the subject so they say it is all a fake." In another passage, "the lice who crawl on literature will not praise" a work of art. Either the reviewers have been getting under his skin or he is uneasy about this book.

Mr. Hemingway should have his answer: *Green Hills of Africa* cannot compete with his works of the imagination. It is not exactly a poor book, but it is certainly far from a good one. The trouble is that it has few fine and no extraordinary passages, and long parts of it are dull. And being bored by Ernest Hemingway is a new experience for readers and reviewers alike. The queer thing is that this novelty springs from the same intense literary self-consciousness that has been a large part of the effectiveness of his books up to now. He kills this one by being too assiduously an experimental artist in prose, out to register sensation and find the right words for the countryside and activity and emotion, and, by way of the bush and the campfires and the rhinoceros dung, carry his prose to the "fourth and fifth dimension that can be gotten." He has reverted to his café-table-talk days, he is being arty, and Africa isn't a good place for it.

Only about forty per cent. of the book is devoted to the shape of the country and the pattern of action. That part isn't any too good. He is magnificent when he is rendering the emotions of the hunt and the kill, but those passages are less frequent than long, confusing, over-written descriptions, and these are lush and very tiresome. They are, I seem to remember, the sort of thing you have to skip in Tolstoi. Besides, there are a lot of tricks and some cheating. Mr. Hemingway plunges into the rhetoric he has monotonously denounced, and he overlays a good many bits of plain brushwork with very eloquent and highly literary researches into past time.

The rest of it runs about twenty per cent. literary discussion, twenty per cent. exhibitionism, and twenty per cent. straight fiction technique gratefully brought into this unimaginative effort. The literary discussion, though it contains some precious plums, is mostly bad; the exhibitionism is unfailingly good. Mr. Hemingway is not qualified for analytical thought. His flat judgments and especially his papal rules and by-laws are superficial when they aren't plain cockeyed. He has written about writing, probably, more than any other novelist of his time: he is much better at writing and we should all be richer if he would stick to it. But he is a first-rate humorist, and the clowning is excellent. When he gives us Hemingway in the sulks, Hemingway with the braggies, Hemingway amused or angered by the gun-bearers, Hemingway getting tight, Hemingway at the latrine, Hemingway being hard-boiled or brutal or swaggering or ruthless, Hemingway kidding someone or getting sore at someone — the book comes to life. It comes to life, in fact, whenever he forgets about the shape of the country and the pattern of action, and brings some people on the stage. Working with real people, Pop, P.O.M., Karl, the casuals, he is quite as effective a novelist as he is with imaginary ones. He imparts the same life to the natives, some of whom do not even speak. Droopy, Garrick and The Wanderobo are splendid creations; one sees and feels them, accepts them, experiences them. They live. And that is creation of a high order, a *tour de force* all the more remarkable since it is done without the dialogue that is Mr. Hemingway's most formidable weapon. When he is being a novelist, he achieves his purpose. His book has the life and validity he tells us he set out to give it; he gets the experience itself into prose. It successfully competes with the imagination — because it uses the tools and technique of an imaginative artist.

The big news for literature, however, is that, stylistically, there is a new period of Hemingway. He seems to be fighting a one-man revolution to carry prose back to *The Anatomy of Melancholy* or beyond. There have been omens of it before now, of course, and Mr. Hemingway, in his café-table days, pondered Gertrude Stein to his own gain. The repetitious Stein of *Tender Buttons* doesn't show up here, but the Stein who is out to get four or five dimensions into prose is pretty obvious. But he also appears to have been reading a prose translation of *The Odyssey* too closely, and something that sounds like a German translation of Hemingway. With the result that whereas the typical Hemingway sentence used to run three to a line it now runs three to a page. And whereas he used to simplify vocabulary in order to be wholly clear, he now simplifies grammar till the result looks like a marriage between an E. E. Cummings simultaneity and one of those ground-mists of Sherwood Anderson's that Mr. Hemingway was burlesquing ten years ago.

The prize sentence in the book runs forty-six lines, the one I should like to quote as typical ("Now, heavy socks . . ." p. 95), though less than half that long is still too long, and a comparatively straightforward one must serve. "Going down-hill steeply made these Spanish shooting boots too short in the toe and there was an old argument, about this length of boot and whether the bootmaker, whose part I had taken, unwittingly first, only as interpreter, and finally embraced his theory patriotically as a whole and, I believed, by logic, had overcome it by adding onto the heel." This is simpler than most, is unencumbered by the clusters of participles that hang from the more typical ones, and has the verb where you can grab it as it goes by, but it shows the new phase. The effort is to make words do more than they say, to get the fourth and maybe the fifth dimension, to convey significance and immediate experience as well as meaning. Usually the material is not so factual as this and we are supposed to get, besides the sense, some muscular effort or some effect of color or movement that is latent in pace and rhythm rather than in words. But, however earnest the intention, the result is a kind of etymological gas that is just bad writing. The five-word sentences of *The Sun Also Rises* were better. You knew where you stood with them, and what Mr. Hemingway was saying. He ought to leave the fourth dimension to Ouspensky and give us prose.

An unimportant book. A pretty small book for a big man to write. One hopes that this is just a valley and that something the size of *Death in the Afternoon* is on the other side.

Green Light

BY LLOYD C. DOUGLAS

$\sim\sim\sim\sim\sim\sim\sim\sim\sim\sim\sim\sim\sim\sim\sim\sim$

A SUMMARY of the Reverend Dr. Douglas's new novel will indicate its classification. In a city never quite identified as Chicago a crippled clergyman named Dean Harcourt mends shattered lives by discovering to their possessors their own Personal Adequacy and bringing them into knowledge of the Irresistible Onward Drive of God's purpose. (Hence the symbolic title: the road is clear before you — Go Forward.) The dean is a mighty preacher and so sways multitudes, but also he is a mystical psychoanalyst, a priest in the consulting room, and thus exercises his inspiration on individuals. Persons who come in contact with him are never again quite the same. Once a patient of his has heard the message, he has thereafter a harmonious personality, makes a success in his career, and achieves a happy marriage — except Sonia Duquesne, who has committed adultery and has to be content with becoming the dean's secretary. Several minor couples are conducted to God-consciousness and the marriage bed, but both the dean and his message are focused on Newell Paige and Phyllis Dexter. Paige is the most brilliant young surgeon anywhere. He is about to succeed to the place of the most brilliant older surgeon, whom he loves and idolizes, Dr. Bruce Endicott. (Note the influence of Mrs. Southworth in the characters' names.) A patient whom Dr. Paige is treating has received Dean Harcourt's message and seems to the doctor the most inspiring woman he has ever known. But alas, on the day when Dr. Endicott is to operate on her, the bottom falls out of the stock market and so he botches the job. The patient dies, Dr. Paige accepts the responsibility for his chief's mistake, Dr. Endicott permits him to, and he begins to wander over the earth, disenchanted, very bitter, his life a ruin. Being a great soul, he can't help doing good here and there, but he is still Hamlet when he drops in on Dean Harcourt. In the dean's office he meets the daughter of the dead woman, and though they love greatly they misunderstand. Paige therefore wanders some more and the dean finally has to discover him in a laboratory where deckle-edge scientists are risking their lives with Rocky Mountain spotted fever before he can make his message clear. Even so a setter bitch is killed and she has carried some of the most touching scenes in the book. Dr. Endicott repents and everyone, including the adulteress, is saved.

It would be absurd to call this sort of thing bilge. It belongs to one of the oldest traditions of literature, the mystically therapeutic. Its equivalent is always with us and always serves an important end. Dr. Douglas is, briefly, a Harold Bell Wright — a streamlined Wright with knee-action wheels and chased silver dials on the cowl, to be sure, but with the identical engine under the hood. His milieu has changed from the desert to the metropolis, he deals with the maladjusted rather than the impure of heart, fear and frustration rather than lust and dishonesty are his monsters, but he tells us exactly what Mr. Wright used to tell us and he employs exactly the same technique. He tells us: one increasing purpose runs. He tells us: let not your hearts be troubled. He tells us no more — but do not be disdainful. He tells us what Mary Baker Eddy and Ralph Waldo Trine told us — or, if you like, what Emerson and Whitman told us. Or Woodrow Wilson. Or Karl Marx.

Millions want to be told just that. This audience combines wish-fulfillment with its spiritual sustenance, and it is Dr. Douglas's audience. He gives them what they need and desperately desire: assurance. In a time of economic chaos, it is comforting to be told that the Long Parade is moving onward in God's plan. In a time of disaster, it is comforting to be told that one is being Dragged Up. It is always comforting to frightened, weary, and discouraged men, to be told that they are the masters of their fate, that they have a spiritual power which will bring them through, that they have the Kingdom of Heaven within them, that the God-spirit of which they are a part has given them unused and even unguessed capacities for heroism and eventual success. It is comforting and, when told in terms of metrical and crepuscular vagueness, it is convincing. Thoughts so noble, so impalpable, so incapable of precise statement, must be true.

Comfort is what his readers ask of Dr. Douglas and comfort is what they get. His books would not sell by the carload — as at least *The Magnificent Obsession* did, which had the same message — unless his public found what they were looking for. It is a legitimate literary quest. He works with the humbler symbols of art, but they are eternal symbols. Their success on the lower levels of literature, in the sub-basements where yearning and exhortation and incantation dictate their form, requires no explanation. Does *Molly-Make-Believe* need to be explained? Or *St. Elmo?* Or *Tempest and Sunshine?* Or *If Winter Comes?*

Mark Twain: the Ink of History

~~~~~~~~~~~~~~~~~~~~~~~~~~~~~~~~~~~~~

THE instinct that leads us to honor the memory of our great dead is buried deeper in the racial mind than exploration can trace it down. Nevertheless, such commemoration is precarious. For if our great men replenish us, it is also true that we insist on their confirming us. As the years pass, the unstable race changes the ways in which it must be confirmed, and so the memory and significance of a great man are changed in obedience to no more dignified force than mere fashion.

Again, no man is ever single, simple and consistent — but when he is dead there is a powerful need for him to seem so to the rest of us. With not too much intelligence but with the greatest sincerity, we ask, "What did he mean? What has he to say to us? What is the significance of his career?" But he was a man, and so he meant many things. To-day he meant this, and a week later he meant its opposite. Both may have sprung from fundamental truths at the bedrock of his personality, and the whole force of his sincerity may have been concentrated in each of the incommensurable words. But the disparity troubles us, and we require him to resolve it in something single and eternally meaningful. Since he is dead and cannot make that reconciliation, we make it for him with good grace, in order to protect ourselves. He has many things to say to us, and most of them are confused and contradictory. The significances of his career are hazards of intersecting forces which war with one another so furiously that only in our minds and only years later can an illusion of simplicity develop. Precisely that is our opportunity. Out of the richness of the dead we may select what is most conformable to our needs, and the shadow that lengthens down the years comes more and more to be our own shadow.

The great Missourian in whose name we meet to-day had harder words for what I have said softly. In "Pudd'nhead Wilson's New Calendar," he remarks: "The ink with which all history is written is merely fluid prejudice." That saying should make us wary in this effort to declare what, a century after he was born, Mark Twain means to American literature.

Fifteen years ago Missouri was observing another centennial, the completion of a hundred years of statehood. It was a time to look back over the past and bring into judgment the culture of the commonwealth. A good many men divided that effort, and to one of them fell the duty of reviewing "A Century of Missouri Literature." [1] It was a task to be done with a searching mind and a heart not too affectionate, and the point of this episode is that the gentleman who did it met both requirements. He selected fifty-three Missouri writers for examination and judgment. There are fifty-three of them on that honor roll, and there is room to praise the

---

[1] *Missouri Historical Review*, October, 1920.

editors of county newspapers that died fifty years before
Salt Creek ran dry, for the authors of tracts destined to
Christianize the heathen, and for poets whose lyrics once
brightened the last page when the office was too tired to
find other filler. And here is what Mark Twain meant when,
fifteen years ago, his state looked back over its century:

"It has always seemed to me impossible that a writer who
violated nearly all the canons of literary art and whose
themes were so thoroughly commonplace, should become
so extensively known and so widely popular as Mark Twain
has become. . . . He deals of [*sic*] the everyday and ordinary; he is often coarse (as in *The Adventures of Huckleberry Finn*), irreverent if not blasphemous (as in *The Innocents Abroad*), and unnatural and straining after effect
(as in *The Adventures of Tom Sawyer*). He has not one
tithe of the refinement of Lowell, the delicacy of Irving, or
the spontaneous geniality of Holmes; and yet in public estimation, he is greater, or at least he is more popular, than all
these combined! As a humorist he paints no typical character — he describes individuals whose peculiarities, and the
unexpected conditions in which they are placed, awake our
risibilities for the time being, and leave no lasting impression. . . . Mark Twain lacks the education necessary to a
great writer; he lacks the refinement which would render it
impossible for him to create such coarse characters as
Huckleberry Finn; furthermore, he is absolutely unconscious of almost all canons of literary art."

That was only fifteen years ago. Yet the meaning of this
gathering to-day is that the author of that judgment was
wrong and that the "public estimation" of which he com-
plains was right. Our critic was one more in a long line of
those who objected to Mark Twain and the judgment is
typical of many that rejected him. Not the least amazing of

many paradoxes that Mark Twain presents to us is this: that, although only in the very last years of the century now ending have critics been willing to discuss him as a literary artist, from the very first the people who read books and incorporate them into their lives have recognized the artist whom the critics only now begin to acknowledge. In the minds of the public, American and international, there has never been any doubt about the greatness of Mark Twain. It is only among the literary that the recognition now fulfilled in centennial exercises has delayed.

Let us examine this paradox in the history of Mark Twain, the ink in which his history has been written. For it is the key to his meaning for American life at the end of his century.

The critic I have quoted voiced a tradition that had passed even its twilight, when he wrote. It was a tradition which students have agreed to call the genteel tradition. The virtues which it admired may be observed in our critic's epithets, and in the writers he chooses to attach them to. Observe that he speaks not of the Lowell who wrote in the vernacular, shared the dust and clamor of popular causes, and spoke savagely of public abuses and national dishonor. He speaks instead of the "refinement" of Lowell — the Lowell who wrote gentle verses about Sir Launfal and elegantly bloodless essays about the books on his study shelves. He speaks of the "delicacy" of Irving and the "geniality" of Holmes. Refinement, delicacy and geniality — there, in three words, you have the genteel tradition. It dominated American criticism during all the years in which Mark Twain's books were written. To such a tradition, *The Adventures of Huckleberry Finn* must necessarily seem coarse, and its creator must seem "absolutely unconscious of all canons of literary art."

The genteel tradition governed American critical opinion

during the last three decades of the nineteenth century and
the first decade of the twentieth. It was a tradition that narrowed literary values to those three, refinement, delicacy
and geniality. You will note that there is no mention of vigor,
of fidelity to life and human experience, of understanding
of human problems, of insight into and sympathy with the
dark heart of man, or of realization of man's tragic destiny.
It was a tradition that looked abroad for its models, especially
to England, and especially to those parts of English literature
which were refined, delicate and genial. When — and rarely
— it looked at American literature at all, it naturally saw only
such literature as had also looked eastward across the Atlantic
and not westward, whither the nation's most vigorous life
had moved. It saw the refined Lowell, the delicate Irving
and the genial Holmes. It did not see the exuberant Whitman
or the rebellious Melville.

Note as a further paradox that this tradition had curiously
usurped the place of one much nearer to Mark's own temperament. If there had been Whitman and Melville, there had
also been the flowering of the New England genius — there
had been Hawthorne, Emerson, Thoreau. Our critic does
not mention them, for the genteel tradition with its abhor-
rence of native roots and the native mind had forgotten them.
They bulk to-day far larger than Lowell, Irving and Holmes.
And their permanence is just this: that as New England first
of the sections developed an articulated culture, in the
shrewdness and earthiness and canny nativeness of those
Yankee minds, the nation for the first time saw types and
eidolons in which it could recognize itself. Here were not
transported or translated or impaired Englishmen but Americans. They were men of the First Republic, the nation of
Adams and Jefferson, the seaboard states, tidewater America.
The First Republic saw its own face and heard its own voice

in what they wrote. Let us remember this native tradition which the genteel tradition displaced, for its sequel will be important.

Yet at the very moment when our critic wrote, the genteel tradition in American literature was itself being displaced by a new orientation of ideas. It was in 1920 that the liberal critics who had come to maturity in the preceding decade, and were to dominate our literary thinking for another ten years, first consolidated their thesis. It is not surprising that the book which achieved the first synthesis of this new criticism was a study of Mark Twain. What is surprising is that the new criticism, which fiercely rejected the genteel tradition and fiercely demanded native standards of judgment and an untrammeled native literature to apply them to, also rejected Mark Twain. Rejected him, what is more, in almost the same terms as the genteel tradition had done. The new critics found him lacking in refinement and delicacy, and though they did not take him to task for being coarse (they sighed that he ought to have been much coarser), they did insist that he had missed the meaning of his times, that he had not risen to a decent level of understanding of American life, and that he was "absolutely unconscious of almost all the canons of literary art." He was to these achingly intellectual men just what he had been to the genteel critics — a jester, a buffoon, a mountebank. He was an improviser, and extemporizer, a popularizer. He was a time-server and a trimmer, who pandered to low tastes and the inferior preferences of the mob. Above all he was a child-like mind incapable of mature thought or mature emotion and, consequently, hardly an artist at all. He was born with a talent that might have matured in art, but subversive elements in American life arrested its development. The society in which he grew up was squalid, "a mere desert of human sand"; the puritanical and materialistic civilization of America suffocated the genius which his birthplace had stunted; and the paltry and regrettable books of Mark Twain were the result.

Accompanying all this, let us remember, was the repeated demand that America must find an artist who should be shaped by the national life and should in turn plumb and interpret that life in his books.

So that the two critical traditions that have dominated American literary thinking since Mark Twain began to write both rejected him. He was not to either of them a literary artist, not a mature writer of full stature or first importance. . . . And throughout all this time he was read more widely and with more pleasure, admiration and love — by more classes, kinds and conditions of men — than any other American writer. Through all this time his fame, as distinguished from his critical reputation, grew steadily till it became unshakable and remains so to-day. There has never been any doubt of Mark Twain's greatness in that court of appeal whose jurisdiction over literature is final, the reading public. The verdict of that court has been a universal and sustained acclaim never equaled by any other American, and equaled by only a few writers in the whole history of literature.

Why? What is the explanation of this curious anesthesia of criticism to one of the few writers unmistakably of the first rank that the national literature has produced? The answer is complex but not difficult.

To begin with, his personality, his mind, his genius and his books were original, contradictory and richly various. It has never been possible to say, this is the sole burden of his work, for his work is so many-sided that prejudice has been able to select anything it desired and exploit that, ignoring the rest. But with one part of him criticism has seen its way quite simple before it: he was a humorist. To both the genteel tradition and the tradition of liberal thought, humor was distasteful. A laugh was vulgar to the former, when it was not sanctified by the whimsicality of the gentler English humorists or such shadows of them as the genial Dr. Holmes. But if it was vulgar to them, it was positively indecent to the liberals, for was not mankind, especially the Americans, still to be saved? and with salvation unachieved, levity is sacrilegious. It is quite clear that his whole life long Mark Twain was a deliberate laugh-producer, a writer who would go any length to evoke laughter. It is equally clear that his earliest fame rested on that alone, and that a great part of it from that day to this has rested on it and will continue to do so.

It is a humor infinitely various, from mere word-play, frequently strained and dull, to comic intuitions that illuminate with the suddenness of lightning something fundamental and immortal in humanity. To-day we do not reprobate that humor. Much of it is, of course, as lifeless as any dead thing in the dustiest alcoves of literature. But also in much of it we can discern authentic America dealing with its conditions, finding its adaptations, larding the bones of its culture. It deals with the irrational pettiness and grandeur of the damned human race. It is a sword against injustice and oppression, a scourge for folly, an armor against hypocrisy and cruelty and greed. But its sources go deeper still. For laughter is a final refuge and a final solace of the human spirit: it is a shape that pity takes in great and sensitive minds, a lenitive and emollient of the soul that is a basic strength, a basic courage and a basic reconciliation, making life tolerable by making it defiant.

Yet there is a far deeper cause than his humor for criticism's half-century of bewilderment about Mark Twain. As hundreds of thousands read him, America found itself in his books. Criticism neglected to make that discovery for a reason which I have already suggested. Once before America had seen the lineaments of its character and heard its own accents in our first national literature. But the First Republic was a smaller, more localized, more simple nation, and its roots were on the seaboard. That simpler nation was passing when Mark Twain was born, and had gone altogether when he reached maturity. Yet criticism curiously went on expecting America to speak with that selfsame voice. It is the all but inconceivable absurdity of the genteel critics and the liberal thinkers who unhorsed them that both expected the transcontinental America, the melting pot, the industrial revolution, the American empire, when they should at last find an art — to sit on the shore of Walden Pond and speak with the tranquil twang of Henry Thoreau chatting in the cool of the day with Neighbor Emerson. No wonder that, when the voice of imperial America proved to be that of Davy Crockett, half-horse, half-alligator and all snapping-turtle, roaring from the canebrakes and the river bottom, the voice of Big Bear of Arkansaw, the Wild Humorist of the Pacific Slope — no wonder that criticism required fifty years to understand what had happened.

When William Dean Howells called Mark Twain "the Lincoln of our literature," he meant more than the pat alliteration may at first suggest. For, without pushing a happy intuition too far, it is fruitful to think of them together. Both were born of the great migration — born too, each in his respective place, after the migration had gone far enough and sunk its roots deep enough to produce an unmistakable issue of its own. The stamp of mid-America is on them both, and equally the stamp of the frontier. You could never mistake Lincoln for Daniel Webster or Calhoun, still less for Washington, for any of the founding fathers. The very lineaments of the American have changed. Instead of the massive face and features that make a century of our statues Roman, you have the lean face of the frontiersman. Compare the formal rhetoric of Jefferson's First Inaugural Address with the broken, far subtler music of Lincoln's Second Inaugural — "with malice toward none, with charity for all, with firmness in the right as God gives us to see the right" — and you will see that a fundamental change has found its way to the ganglions of thought. We cannot say that one is better than the other, we can only say that they are fundamentally different. Compare the images they take in our thinking, Jefferson the philosopher of the state, Lincoln the humanizer of the state. Again it is idle to say that one is better than the other or more fundamentally American But obviously they are different. And obviously Jefferson is of the First Republic and Lincoln of the Empire.

Now if you bring Mark Twain into comparison with, say, Emerson, the same observation strikes you with the same force. You would never mistake Lincoln's famous letter to General McClellan or to Mrs. Bixby for one of Jefferson's Ciceronian epistles. Similarly, to pose the mind or the writing of Emerson against the mind or the writing of Mark Twain is to see vividly what has happened to America as the effective center of its life moved from the Concord and Merrimack Rivers to the Mississippi. Emerson is the classic literary man of the First Republic. We may understand if we cannot pardon the failure of criticism to perceive that Mark Twain was the classic writer of the Empire that succeeded it.

But observe that our first nationalists never made that mistake. They knew what was happening, they understood the transmutation better than the genteel critics or their liberal inheritors have ever understood it. Thoreau was an inveterate walker. He found that whenever he started out without any definite objective his steps turned naturally, involuntarily, toward the west. He felt the current that, from the very beginning, had held the needle of the national life true to the western pole. The apocalyptic visions of Walt Whitman saw the Great Valley as an "incubator of a radical, true, far-scoped and thorough-going Democracy" which would be free from the "conventionalism and arti-ficialized influence of older-settled sections," whose litera-ture would be "spontaneous and unconventionalized," free of the "patent-leather, curled-hair japonicadom style."

"The millions that around us are rushing into life," Emer-son said, two years after Mark Twain was born, in the address which ever since has been called the declaration of independence of the American mind, "the millions that around us are rushing into life cannot always be fed on the sere remains of foreign harvests. Events, actions arise that must be sung, that will sing themselves." (In, be sure, the spontaneous and unconventionalized style that Whit-man prophesied.) And, Emerson said, "We will walk on our own feet; we will work with our own hands; we will speak with our own minds." This was a prophecy of the American artist. And what, according to the prophetic Yankee, would be the symbols which the American artist would vitalize till they inclosed the significance of the native American way of life? "The meal in the firkin, the milk in the pan, the ballad in the street, the news of the boat." Our own firkin, our own milk-pan, turned and coopered in our own shop — the America on which, in Hawthorne's words, "the damned shadow of Europe" had not fallen.

A new America and a new American were taking shape.

The nation's center of gravity had shifted. The nation's energy had entered a new phase. The generative and truly imperial culture had moved beyond the mountains to the great central valley. In art, nothing happens capriciously or by chance. Certainly it was not by accident that Mark Twain, who was the first to give the new America a shape in art in which the nation might see itself — it was not by accident that Mark Twain was born here in the young, unfinished and even unformed commonwealth where the three great rivers of the continent meet. Where all the streams that fed the western expansion met also and flowed together. The commonwealth plumb in the center of the shaping empire, where a hundred migrations and a hundred racial strains met, merged and became something altogether different from what any of them had been before. Where in the tremendous heat of the fires thus generated, the tremendous heterogeneity of the flux was moulded to the long, spare, native stature and features that for three-quarters of a century no one has ever been able to mistake for something else. The commonwealth that was savagely shaken and almost destroyed by that basic division which shook and almost destroyed the nation, and which had to be fought out and ended before a seal could be put on the empire. All America had, like Thoreau, walked westward. That wayfaring is our greatest saga, to whose majestic rhythm our very consciousness has been shaped. From the falls line of the eastern rivers to the Pacific beach the Americans marched for two and a half centuries till their very pulses carried the drumbeat of the westward passage.

Mark Twain is in nothing accidental. His mother's family crossed the mountains by our oldest gateway, to the limestone and savannas of Kentucky. His father carried this westering to frontier Missouri. And Mark was born in the center of the great valley at the exact moment when the westward nation, hurrying toward empire, leaped from the frontier into the continental void. Step by step, year by year, he accompanied the accelerating empire, a part of that gigantic shaping. Year by year its experience was his, registering in his nerves, piling up the accretions of knowledge in muscle and sinew and bone, while the empire whirled toward climax — and after climax could judge itself, read the registration of the nerves, and determine what, for good or ill but forever, had been changed, gained and lost.

Small wonder if critics have needed fifty years to understand what happened. As history goes, fifty years is a short time for criticism to lag behind revolutionary art. For, of course, Mark Twain was a revolutionary artist — not in the trivial and transitory meaning now much hymned by dissociated minds, but in the only meaning that literature knows. The bonds and constraints of a national life had been altogether rearranged, and literature had not adjusted itself to the difference. A wedge had been driven between American life and American literature. To drive that wedge out, to bring our literature once more into organic relationship with our national life, to give our life a new, cleared channel in letters — that was the recurrent task of the revolutionary artist.

Mark Twain, both critical traditions assure us, was "absolutely unconscious of all canons of literary art." But what does that mean? Only that the life of the new America was a new life, changed forever from what American life had been before, and the expression it found was necessarily new also — and very strange. Criticism must necessarily be absolutely unconscious of the canons of an art that expressed this new native life — and so must honestly, sincerely, and with the deepest regret tell us that it had no canons. For the canons of any art are bones grown from within itself, not a set of blue-prints and specifications imposed upon it from without by someone who has a textbook in his hand.

To keep our bearing true, to italicize what had happened, think again of Lincoln. He was hewn from the same rock as Mark Twain, their ancestors neighbored in the same trans-Allegheny frontier, living in log cabins, scalping Indians, sleeping on bear skins before an open fire. Lincoln's habitual speech was the same metaphorical, highly vernacular humor as Mark Twain's, shadowed with the same knowledge, singing the same tune. He was a famous raconteur; humor was so interstitially a part of him that it became his every-day expression. Crises of state were illuminated by the kind of vernacular epigram that Mark habitually wrote, or by the tall tale from the river-lore or the frontier newspaper. We know how he could compress a political issue or a military principle into an anecdote about his Springfield neighbors. We know how, having called the Cabinet together to announce the most momentous decision he had to make as President of a great nation divided by civil war, he first, before reading the Emancipation Proclamation, read to them Artemus Ward's "High-Handed Outrage at Utiky." That scene in the White House, with the nation's destiny hanging on the immortal state paper which he would not read till he had first read Ward, is surely one of the most amazing in all history. The very soul of Lincoln shows in it. Something unmistakably American shows in it too, something uniquely American. For you cannot imagine that scene in an English chancellery — or in the Government House of any other nation. And note well that you cannot imagine its taking place in the White House at any time until the mysterious chemistry that began when America surged over the mountains into the great valley had had time to work its change.

And surely the native humor of the frontier President, the new native way of life, in this scene achieves a great dignity, a great calm, and a tragic beauty.

It defines, I believe, the Mark Twain whom it is at last possible to see, when his work has been over for forty years and he has been dead for twenty-five. The great writer who was shaped by the experience of a westward-making people during the great years of their rise to empire, and who shaped their experience to the finest, fullest and greatest art the empire produced.

He was a complex, various and contradictory man. Being so intimately a part of the experience he recorded, he necessarily shared its insufficiencies and its faults. He was often wild and untamable, a very jingo of the stumps. He was often grotesquely exuberant, silly, trivial, oratorical, sentimental, lachrymose. He was often undisciplined, a rank improviser of hasty, ill-considered and now distressing fustian. He tumbled blindfold into a hundred delusions of his people during their incandescent years. But also another hundred delusions that victimized them he had the prophetic sense to see through and denounce. That realist was just as truly as the jingo one of the multitudes whom Mark Twain contained. One who survives and speaks to us to-day, when the trivial and preposterous in him is dead. The court of final appeal has already taken care of him. Much that he wrote is only dreariness now and will be altogether forgotten by the time another change in our organization of ideas makes another assay of him essential. But also, with that realist, others of the multitudes remain to us to-day, and will remain. Let us name some of them.

First the frontiersman, the native Missourian on the fringe of settlement, in whom the most deep-seated pattern of the American experience is embodied. The stage of vital interlinking with the wilderness, the commonwealth bringing itself to be on the cleared land, is a stage through which the whole nation has moved. It has conditioned many things about us. It gave native, characteristic shapes to our political and social institutions, it was the last authoritative mould of our democracy. It gave native, characteristic shapes to the Americans themselves. Necessarily, when America speaks in art something of that experience must also shape the artist, and Mark Twain is nowhere more truly of his people than in the indigenous perceptions of the frontiersman. Where else has the beauty of the untouched continent, as well as the terror of that beautiful wilderness, had the magnificence that it has in his books? Nothing is more native to us even now, generations after that loveliness has been destroyed. That countryside, the new and strange and satisfying wilderness, is not only the oldest theme in our literature — it is even to-day a constant, below the threshold of awareness, in the thought-stream that flows through our minds. Something of what we are, one of the differences that sets us off in our nationality, comes from that conditioning, and its very moment and rhythm are in Mark Twain.

And the habits of mind of the frontiersman are also his. Accuracy of observation and instant and exact application of it were once necessities for survival. These were the "hard old Injun" that Charles Godfrey Leland noticed in him. It is, of course, a customary characteristic of American fiction, as distinct from a certain elegant vagueness of the English, but nowhere else has the swift, discriminating eye of the trailer achieved such notable effects as in Mark Twain. Add to this something of the border shrewdness, the hard-headed realism of a race whose first condition was the realistic struggle with the wilderness. Add, too, the tropical luxuriance of his imagination, the hellish terrors and the almost cosmic jubilations it could achieve — is not this, at least in part, a product of the largeness, the vigor and the violence of frontier life? Is not, in fact, most of his humor the humor native to the frontier — the democratic leveling, the shrewd analysis of character, the pure fantasy of the tall talk and the tall tales? The frontier is the master-pattern in his work.

Not forgetting humor's tragic beauty, as I have pointed out in Lincoln. In both of them we see, for all their mirth, for all their inexhaustible enjoyment of the world and mankind, for all their recognition of vitality and the rich grain and the coarse texture of experience accepted and affirmed — for all this, we perceive in both of them a constant sense of the tragedy of human life. Something that I associate with the illimitable space and time of the great forests and the prairie wilderness.

Again, the vernacular. When we are summing up Mark Twain's permanent achievement, we must not forget that with him, for the first time, the American language became a medium of art. This too goes back to the humble joke-maker who had learned the use of his tools from a hundred long forgotten humorists and to the frontier's inexhaustible delight in sketching its own types. There had been, heaven knows, much talk about the American language before Mark Twain, from Noah Webster's day onward. But though the language steadily differentiated itself from the mother tongue, and though by mid-century no first-rate American writer wrote English, still vernacular American had only a timid and clumsy use before Mark Twain and, after him, lapsed again into timidity and clumsiness almost to our own generation. In his earliest work you will find it in the dialogue he records, already with a sureness and a delicacy never before brought to the rendition of American speech.

And then, suddenly, a miracle. That coarse character Huck Finn begins to recount his adventures — and at one step the American language has become a medium for the highest reaches of prose fiction, for as subtle and complex effects of architecture, music and psychology as our fiction has ever known. This astonishing achievement alone would rank Mark Twain among the great innovators, and it was, historically, a decisive turning-point in our literature.

There is also the satirist of America and of the human race, the damned human race. His was a dynamic nature, explosive, even volcanic, and like most sensitive and kindly men whose personal relationships are rich, he hated the cruelties, injustices, hypocrisies and stupidities of life. From his earliest to his latest work, his books are crammed full of satirical finalities. That, rather than any specific themes he treated or specific abuses he attacked, it is proper to recall to-day — that they were, sometimes, finalities, that they sometimes attained a level beyond which no satire in all literature has gone. Recall the scene in *A Connecticut Yankee* where, after the burning of the castle at Abblasoure, King Arthur and the Yankee find some children playing mob and hanging one of their number with a rope of bark. Or recall the passage in *The Adventures of Huckleberry Finn* where Jim has said he intends to work till he can buy his wife and children out of slavery, and if their master won't sell them he'll get an Abolitionist to go and steal them. And Huck Finn — it was by as heavy a stroke as literature knows anywhere that this whole journey through America is seen through the eyes of a shrewd boy — Huck Finn says:

"It most froze me to hear such talk. He wouldn't ever dared to talk such talk in his life before. Just see what a difference it made in him the minute he judged he was about free. It was according to the old saying, 'Give a nigger an inch and he'll take an ell.' Thinks I, this is what comes of not thinking. Here was this nigger, which I had as good as helped to run away, coming right out flat-footed and saying he would steal his children — children that belonged to a man I didn't even know, a man that hadn't ever done me no harm."

In such passages as these something final has been said — and something immortal. Be very sure they belong to world literature. The frontiersman has joined the company of Swift and Rabelais and Voltaire.

Frontiersman, idyll-maker, innovator, satirist. It is right to name these from the multitudes, for they are fundamental in the American artist. Yet two others of the multitude go far deeper into America and are lodged more securely in our hearts. Let us give them names that would please Emerson, whom I have already invoked, calling them the myth-maker and the prophet. It is here that Mark Twain comes finally into judgment.

The myth-maker is the novelist rising to universals by absolute fidelity to the life of his own nation, even his own section. We have many tests to appraise the value and degree of fiction, but the final one must always be this: with what illusion of human life does the novelist endow the characters in his books? It was fifty years before criticism thought to apply its basic criterion to Mark Twain. But when it is applied, disputation, bewilderment and irrelevance are cleared away. He was a maculate and episodic genius, but that he was the foremost genius of our fiction is at once too obvious to need any further argument. His was a careless fecundity but it was a fecundity so rich, instant and overwhelming that the creativeness of any other American novelist whom you may care to set beside him will seem pinched and poor. By the vitality of the casuals you may judge the vitality of the

novelist, so that if the first and second gentlemen who ac-
company Hamlet to the portals and have, it may be, only a
single line to speak, speak it in such a way that for the moment they live as truly as Hamlet does — then you will know
that their creator is himself a king. Look now at any person
in the books of Mark Twain who enters for half a page and
then disappears forever — a voice heard by night as the
raft drifts southward on the June flood, some loafer spitting
in the mud on the sunny side of a village store, the hapless
Muff Potter who though accused of murder has after all
shown generations of boys where the best fishing holes are,
old man Finn whose dozen pages of prose lift him to immortality. Into these and literally hundreds of others has
gone such a prodigality of creation that they instantly live
for us and, no matter how brief their actual appearance, have
identities as real and as vivid as the Hamlets of fiction. It is a
simple thing, if miracles are ever simple, this charged life
with which they are endowed. But it is a simplicity that
exists only on the highest level of fiction.

This, of course, is the population in which the new America which the nineteenth century had brought to be, recognized itself. The westward-making America moving from
the frontier through expanding industrialism to empire.
"What would we really know the meaning of? The meal in
the firkin, the milk in the pan, the ballad in the street." Seldom
has a population been measured with such Olympian detachment, seldom have the scales been held so steadily, never has
the unpitying good humor of the judge been so unmoved as
the uglier balance fell. Note also that the population are members one of another, that they form a social whole. The
American community has seldom existed in fiction, which
has mostly had to content itself with individuals, however
splendidly seen, insulated from the organism of which they

are a part. Well, here is the community. Strange to find this most mature, most adult, most profound merit that fiction can have, the sense of the community, native and immediate in the work of a man who "lacks the education necessary to a great writer." Strange to find it more fundamental in Mark Twain than in any other American novelist. . . . And therefore as a stranger give it welcome.

Thus by the prodigal fecundity of genius and the community which the living Americans create, by his own firkin and milk-pan, Mark Twain came to the universal. It is only by immersion in his own people and his own time that any writer has ever crossed a national boundary into the timeless citizenship of world literature. Render your own moment in your own living-room well enough and, without intending it, you will tell all nationalities something true about themselves. We must remember that, at his highest reach, Mark Twain has become not nineteenth-century, mid-continental America alone and not the possession only of ourselves. The best of him belongs in fee simple to the damned human race itself, and in that small bulk of pure gold, American fiction has made almost its only and by far its greatest contribution to world literature.

It is easy enough to say that Colonel Sellers belongs to a company which has endured, whose select fellowship is headed by Don Quixote. But for Mulberry Sellers and a half-dozen other immortals of the collected works literature has a comparable fellowship. For Tom Sawyer, Nigger Jim and Huck Finn it has not. For sixty years they have lived in the delight of people the whole world over, regardless of race or nationality or condition of intelligence. We can be sure that they will go on living in that delight until the nature of mankind shall have changed beyond all recognition of what mankind has been. They are the summation

of genius, and all other tributes that can be paid to him, as
well as the just reservations we must take into account, are
far less important than that fact. Tom Sawyer whitewashing
the fence, doing broadsword combat in the forest, agonized
by night in the graveyard with Huck Finn, terrified by the
sight of murder and tortured by remorse, lost in the cave
with Becky Thatcher, paralyzed when the hand of Injun
Joe lifts a candle through the darkness — these are in the
king's lineage of literature. How much more so, then, the
downstream voyage of Huck Finn. This passage of a lumber raft through a continent, a people, a century and a civilization is a pageantry of the strangeness, the wonder and
the horror of life. It has many levels of significance. From
the fascinating surface of adventure so rapt, so warm with
reality that all degrees of understanding fall captive to it —
from that bright, exterior fabric to the obscure symbols at
the basis of awareness, symbols of freedom and need, symbols of the deepest satisfactions and the deepest horrors of
experience — there has been wrought one of the abiding
miracles of literature. It is here, in the lives of these boys,
that Mark Twain is an elder poet. They belong to the living
myths of the world. Alone in American literature, they have
attained timelessness and eternity. They are, and be sure
they will remain, one of the myths that fructify and console
humanity and give it reassurance. They are part of the
spiritual inheritance of mankind.

And one thing more must be acknowledged. I doubt if
all the facts that I have described are sufficient to explain
the shift in opinion of the last few years. They are facts and
each of them has its part in the slow maturing of his critical
recognition, but the shift among our self-conscious critics is
so complete and has been so rapid in the last four or five
years, that something more immediate and topical must ex-

ist. It does, and this too has always been known to thought-
ful men who find literature a judgment passed on life,
though it has abundantly been hidden from the critics. It
is likely to be foremost in the estimate of Mark Twain that
will be made in this place a hundred years from to-day. It is
this: That, just as nineteenth-century America found itself
in his works, so his works embodied a perception of its end.
The Mark Twain who has conspicuously come into his
own in the last few years is — the Mark Twain we recognize
as our contemporary. In our day has perished the New
Jerusalem of the democratic hope. Democracy has perceived the difference between vision and reality. The confident era when Mark Twain was born, when there was no
limit to our aspiration but the stars, and the stars would soon
be within our reach, ended, if not in the Civil War, then
in the undreamed-of evocation of new energies in the thirty
years that followed it. The nation that gazed down a new
century in 1900 — down what vista of war, upheaval and
catastrophe we now know something of — was an older,
less hopeful, less visionary nation than the expanding certainty of 1835. It was learning to come to terms not only
with realities but with self-knowledge. Neither man nor
society, it was coming slowly to perceive, had in itself the
seeds of perfection. The human race was after all the human
race, and the pronouncement of that dead end is first made,
for American literature, in Mark Twain's books. Democracy
had been young, hopeful and seemingly irresistible; democracy was now tired, tested and disenchanted, aware that
it could rise no higher than its source and that its source is
the human race, for which old Mark was willing to find
the conclusive adjective. Are we settled in our beliefs to-
day? Do we read into ourselves the confident virtues and

heroisms our great-grandfathers had no difficulty in discovering in themselves? Are the stars so near as they seemed in 1835, or are we confident the road we travel leads toward them? Well, that is the intellectual history of democracy in the century now ending. Mark Twain's life covered the period of the greatest democratic hope, and his work means that he shared the hope and came to understand its eternal frustration.

He has been called a pessimist. Pessimism is only the name that men of weak nerves give to wisdom. Say rather that, when he looked at the human race, he saw no ranked battalions of the angels. Say that, beginning as a sharer of the democratic hope, he had eyes keen enough to see the collision of that hope with the reality of its eternal conditions — the world and mankind. Say that with a desire however warm and with the tenderness of a lover, he nevertheless understood that the heart of man is wayward, a dark forest. Say that it is not repudiation he comes to at last, but reconciliation — an assertion that democracy is not a pathway to the stars but only the articles of war under which the race fights an endless battle with itself. Say, in short, that the great humorist, the great novelist, was also a prophet, that he worked through the pieties and timidities of his time to the realities of ours. For that is what has happened to him in these years of our disaster — that we have finally, after much nonsense, learned that, dead these twenty-five years and silent almost for fifty, he is nevertheless one of us. For good or ill it may be, but in so far as our own time has courage, it is the courage not of hope but of realism, the knowledge that the conditions of life are infinitely difficult and the armies of evil infinitely strong. And that is the judgment passed in those sunny and leisurely pages where a shrewd boy is drifting down the great river on a raft, looking with undeluded eyes on the strange and various spectacle of the human race.

Well, this is the major prophet, the great novelist, the artist as American I declare unto you on his centennial. Recognition of the true greatness of this Missouri frontiersman has had, among the critical, a slow and amazingly obtuse progress. He looks to-day far otherwise, I judge, than he looked to the gentleman whom I quoted when I began to speak. He does not seem a commonplace, coarse, uneducated buffoon, absolutely ignorant of all the canons of literary art. He looks instead like the foremost artist in American literature.

Mark Twain and the Limits of Criticism

I

THE purpose of this essay is to examine some of the critical judgments that have been made about the books of Mark Twain, and to determine how far their results are acceptable. The undertaking will involve a consideration of various critical assumptions, and an application of such tests as those of relevance, logic and common sense to various methods of criticism. If successful, it will define certain limitations which criticism has not transcended in its study of Mark Twain. By implication it may suggest that some of the ends which literary criticism sets itself are either meaningless or impossible of achievement.

In all literary discussions we should state some of the assumptions and prejudices which are liable to influence our findings. I therefore make the following declarations about my point of view. I believe that criticism is necessarily an imprecise method of studying literature: it must never ignore two of the conditions under which it operates, that it cannot phrase its aims unequivocally and cannot apply its methods objectively. I believe that both its methods and its results are indissolubly bound up with the preconceptions and unconscious trends of those who practise it. I believe that critical generalizations are never completely applicable to literature. I believe that critical systems, however learned, logical and exhaustive, and however valuable as social or intellectual documents, are separated from the material with which they undertake to deal by intellectual and emotional barriers and by the conditions of the creative process, and so have only a secondary importance for literature. I accept the extension of these beliefs to the essay I am reading.

Mark Twain serves as a convenient example by means of which the processes of criticism may be studied because he is an "important" writer, because his work is copious, varied and contradictory, because he has been dead long enough for us to approach him with some detachment and historical perspective, and because a great deal of criticism has been written about him from various points of view and with various conclusions. If we examine his books, the books written about them, and the differences of judgment which critics have expressed, we may be able to say something of importance about criticism. We may be able to establish errors of fact, contradictions of principle and fallacies of reasoning. By so doing we may reveal more or less fundamental dilemmas or paradoxes in the critical process and, with luck, may define some of the limits of criticism.

II

I begin with the humblest level of academic criticism, the study of vocabulary. Its aims are so unpretentious that they need not be questioned. Its results are reasonably sure and sound, but they have no relation to literature, or have a relation so small and obvious that it may be disregarded. That it has a considerable value for philology is certain; that it has a real but smaller value for history is also certain. I know of two published studies of Mark Twain's vocabulary and some ten unpublished ones; doubtless a number exist of which I do not know. I am not a philologist and so cannot say how valuable they are to that science, but their potential value is obviously great. And because of them historians may hereafter speak with more certainty about the use of language in the United States and so may make somewhat more useful statements about the differentiation and growth of that language, together with limited statements about geographical and cultural conditions that bear on the use of language and the development of dialects. Such statements are precarious unless made under qualifications so rigorous as to impair their generalizing power. That being understood, however, they are valuable. Certainly they provide an acceptable answer to the ever-present problem of what to do with the candidate for the M.A. in American literature.

But what do they tell us about literature? Nothing, I am afraid, that any intelligent man might not have known before they were made. They show that Mark Twain was tirelessly interested in words, in idiom, and in the vernacular. But practically all writers have that same interest, and no one could read a hundred pages of Mark Twain without finding it in him. They tell us that his vocabulary was in part conditioned by the language of the section in which he grew up and the other sections in which he lived, by the trades he practised and the literature he read. But is that news? The man who began a study of Mark Twain without assuming it would be naïve; the man who read one of his books without realizing it would be a fool. They analyze and classify and interrelate his words, an excellent service to philology but quite useless to criticism beyond obvious platitudes which no one needs to support with evidence. They reach conclusions about innovation and obsolescence which may be useful to the historian of culture but have little bearing on *The Adventures of Huckleberry Finn* as a work of art.

The next level of criticism, the determination of texts, introduces a confusion that will become drastic on the next level but one. Happily, Mark Twain offers us few textual problems and not much labor has been spent on them. I trust that I am not unsympathetic with that labor, having certainly shouted louder than anyone else for the privilege which alone will make it successful, the privilege of examining the Mark Twain manuscripts. But even if that privilege were granted to us, very little of importance would result, and what did follow would be important to criticism not in relation to the texts themselves but in relation to the artist's mind as he revised, altered, suppressed, condensed or expanded what he wrote. Here we confront a fundamental which criticism, and especially academic criticism, tends to ignore: that we deal with works of art, that these particular works of art are books, and that any book ever written is far more important as an existing whole than in any doubtful or disputed passage it contains. Remove altogether from Shakespeare's *Hamlet* the first one hundred cruxes of textual inquiry, thus taking them quite out of consideration, and the problems which *Hamlet* presents to criticism would be quite unchanged. It does not matter what "miching mallecho" means or what Shakespeare may have written instead of the phrase that has come down to us. That is a problem in detective work or, it may be, in philology, but if the phrase were entirely cut out the criticism of *Hamlet* would not be in the least affected. Similarly, the fact that Stedman made Mark Twain change "sewage" to "waste," that Howells or Gilder made him change "stink" to "smell," that Livy made him change "Hell" to "Sheol" or "son of a bitch" to "beggar" may interest us as social historians concerned with shifts in the ephemeræ of judgment that we call taste, but *The Adventures of Huckleberry Finn* as a novel, as a work of art with which criticism must deal, is just exactly what it was before the fact was established, and any conceivable sum of such alterations tells us nothing. I confess a furious interest not in these minute censorships but in the successive stages by which Mark Twain moved to the ultimate version of *Huckleberry Finn*. I should like tremendously to observe him correcting himself, moving, it may be disastrously, by the trial and error of actual composition, toward the book which he finally published. But what could I tell you, if I had been able to study those manuscripts? I might describe the process of revision, but all writers revise and it is not critically important to know how they revise, and besides any deductions would be dubious to an extreme. And my dubious deductions would still be localized in psychology — in the psychology, furthermore, of rejection. Criticism must necessarily deal with the version of *Huckleberry Finn* that was given to us. Great interest may conceivably exist in the stages by which it was arrived at — but that is an accessory and even irrelevant interest.

These are the two sub-basements of criticism. Come now to the main basement, the level before criticism essays systematic analysis. The level to which, alas, so much academic criticism is confined, and on which a portentous activity suggests that Mark Twain is going to be subjected to a tireless, repugnant and quite meaningless exploitation. I refer to the study of influences.

Let me say at once that this activity may exist on two planes, and that on one of them criticism performs one of its most important services. So far as the study of influences is an effort to determine the total cultural possession of a literary artist, his liaisons with his time and the civilization of which he is a part, just that far it is the most valuable branch of literary studies. It is certain to be incomplete always, wrong more often than it is right, grotesquely wrong a good part of the time, and right chiefly in flashes of inspiration and by the grace of God. Nevertheless it gives us dependable information and ideas, and it establishes a skeleton and outline on which to base ethical, social and esthetic judgments by which we record and may even assay our own culture.

But the study of influences does not always or even often exist on that plane. More often it attempts to erect bit by bit a foundation on which, presumably, others may build the edifice. And this humble effort turns into a hunt for sources. The study of literary influences is mostly uncontrollable by fact, and almost always the search for specific sources of works of the imagination is usually evidence that the person who engages in it does not understand the creative process. He is disqualified by ignorance of esthetics and particularly the psychology of esthetics. He is disqualified by ignorance of general and individual psychology. And he is deficient both in practical experience and in the associative functions of intelligence that qualify one to understand literature.

We come at once to a paradox that is seldom absent from the study of literature: that general statements can be made most confidently of the worst writers, and that as we move from the worse to the better writers generalizations progressively fail us, till with men of genius we must make so many individual qualifications of everything we say in general that most of its meaning is taken away. Thus, ephemeral writers do in fact influence and imitate one another, do in fact borrow ideas and emotions from contemporary and earlier books, and do in fact fall into recognizable groupings within which influences may be determined. But even a negligible writer, if he can be called an imaginative or creative writer at all, is usually restrained by the conditions of individual psychology from such direct appropriation of the ideas, emotions and inventions of others as the source-hunter believes in. So that even on the rubble heaps of literature, what the source-hunter may say with authority is more a finding in cultural history than in literary criticism. His findings, that is, are likely to be in "sources" and mistaken, whereas his search may have been in cultural inheritance and, beyond his intention, quite legitimate. Every writer is a product of his time and must in greater or less degree be shaped by the intellectual and emotional currents and fashions of his time. The opportunity of social history is to study how he was shaped by them. Thus, the critic may point out conventions, trends and tendencies and may more or less harmonize the work of a writer with them and relate it to the forces of philosophy, science, economics, politics and social change — in a ratio always individual and always beyond exact determination. But if he may not achieve exactness in such general terms, he is altogether unable to say with certainty that any given idea, emotion, situation or even phrase has its source anywhere under the sun. And step by step as he gets away from negligible writers, he encounters complexities and prohibitions that make his study of sources increasingly absurd. Generalized in the sum of cultural forces, it may be legitimate; localized in specific instances it is always undependable and it is usually stupid as well.

Another conditioning force works to the same end, the historical fact that modern literature has developed not only an implicit ethics but, what is much more important, a specific organization of mental processes. The problem of borrowing a mediaeval convention for the purpose of embroidering it with individual variations of one's own, is obviously and fundamentally different from the problem of describing the world in one's own terms, which has been increasingly the effort of literature for three hundred years.

When we deal with, say, Chaucer's use of a literary legend used by many writers before him we are obviously on different ground than when we undertake to determine, say, where Henry James acquired the moods and ideas of *The Wings of a Dove.* The change thus illustrated is flagrant by the Eighteenth Century, and by the Nineteenth an inquiry that might be sound and promising for the Fourteenth is both meaningless and impossible.

Thus, though it may be possible to find that a writer has borrowed a literary convention, anything further than that is usually either obvious or meaningless. When we show that Holinshed's chronicles gave Shakespeare a framework for a play, or in general when we find that a "plot" has been borrowed, the conclusion has no meaning in esthetics. Beyond that, the search rapidly degenerates into psychological absurdity. Minute research may show a possibility or even a likelihood, though almost never a certainty, that some part of a writer's reading has closed a circuit of association or acted as a release of fantasy. Even here the announced results must be dubious to an extreme, for such research must necessarily be uncontrolled and can never hope to be complete — it must remain, that is, in great part speculative. But even if its results be acceptable, they have not carried criticism very far. They have only brought us through a preliminary study to a psychological problem which they have not even begun to solve. What gave this particular item of the. author's reading, rather than another item, its power to fuse or release the psychic material from which his books are composed? What made it generative or fruitful? The answer is still buried in the experience and personality of the author, and the source-hunter cannot follow his drifting item into that mystery nor analyze its power nor measure its effect. What he can say is at best accidental and subsidiary to the process of creation.

For instance, the obscene activity of American scholars on the works of Poe. I am not, thank God, familiar with all of it, but I have read enough to see the figure of the artist which scholarship has by now assembled. It is the figure of a man who had no faculty of fantasy, who received no direct impetus to his work from the circumstances of his own life, who felt and experienced nothing on his own behalf, whom life and death, joy and grief, thought and reverie did not shape at all. It is a man who read widely (more widely than seems possible to a man who thinks of himself as no slouch at reading), forgot nothing that he read but found long-dead *curiosa* supernaturally charged with immediate significance to him, and spun from them a close fabric of literary derivation. I do not know whether scholars believe in the Poe they have reconstructed. I hope for the sake of the American colleges that they do not. But, if they don't, why do they persist in their absurdity? Certainly I do not believe in him. I am not much interested in Poe, but I know that Poe the literary artist was an astronomical distance away from the Poe of scholarship.

Fashion, convention, trend and tendency influence an important writer only in general terms, and he will transcend them in exact proportion as he has talent or genius.

Specific appropriation of specific ideas, emotions, situations, scenes and expressions is all but impossible for him, and when possible can occur only in the parts of his work that are insignificant interludes between the waves of intense, creative fantasy that give his books all the worth they have as literature. Take, for example, a passage with whose gestation I am familiar, in Mr. Sinclair Lewis's *It Can't Happen Here*. The Holinshed's chronicle of this work of art is plainly the fact that Mr. Lewis's wife is Dorothy Thompson. But when you have said that you have announced the obvious and pursued it to the farthest limit: no search of Miss Thompson's own books or of the newspapers of the time will discover sources. The sources of that book are the events of the last ten years, Mr. Lewis's faculty of associative fantasy which happens to be the most active in contemporary fiction, and the conditioning necessities of his basic wishes, fears and ideas — all of which are beyond analysis. Now, it happens that I can isolate one of the catalytic agents, one of the circuit-closing fuses, that produced an unimportant and minute passage in the book. In the course of a meditation on dictatorship, Doremus Jessup, the hero of the novel, alludes (on page 135) to Vilfredo Pareto and (on page 138) to Brigham Young. I can assure you flatly, of my certain knowledge, that Mr. Lewis has never read Pareto and knows nothing about Brigham Young. A source-hunter who traced this passage to *The Mind and Society* and *The Journal of Discourses* would be tracing it where Mr. Lewis has never himself ventured. The allusions are a by-product of a long argument I had with Miss Thompson one afternoon when I exhibited Brigham Young as an illustration of certain phenomena which Pareto discusses, and when Mr. Lewis was principally occupied in denouncing a fool who had written to him asking for a contribution to a new little magazine. Observe that the allusions come not from Mr. Lewis's reading but from his social intercourse, that they are affixed to a fantasy that was already complete and articulated, and — much the most significant fact — that they occur in an unimportant and comparatively unimpassioned portion of his book. That is the significant thing. The vital portions of imaginative literature are so thoroughly a transmutation of the artist's private and complex experience that analysis is quite unable to isolate the parts.

Techniques the artist may and does borrow and adapt. That is the flagrant, basic fact which betrays the source-hunter. Literary people are forever trying to strain their experience, ideas and fantasies through the styles, devices and technical inventions that are fashionable, or anti-fashionable, at the moment when they write. The study of such borrowings and adaptations is, of course, thoroughly legitimate for criticism. But the source-hunter invariably projects a purely stylistic inquiry into an emotional and esthetic one, and invariably goes wrong. Consider, for instance, how altogether different in every genuine value of literature the work of John Dos Passos is from that of James Joyce, from which many of its stylistic devices are adapted. To consider *1919* and *Ulysses* side by side is to bring together two works which are fundamentally and irrevocably different. To discover in the former any literary material from the second would be to achieve a fourth dimension of critical imbecility, yet the technical influence is demonstrable on nearly every page. Now, the stylistic devices of Mr. Dos Passos, which we may assume originate in Joyce or beyond, freckle and sometimes blight many novels of what, at the moment, we are calling the proletarian movement. Practically every proletarian novelist shares Mr. Dos Passos's forthright revolt against the hyphen, and the fact that many inferior novelists have adopted his stylistic and even his typographical devices clearly shows the process of technical fashion. Yet if we study *1919* and any inferior proletarian novel — say *Marching! Marching!* — we perceive at once that the two have, as literature, as any of the values in which criticism is interested, nothing whatever in common. This perception is triply underlined when we substitute for the inferior novel such a mature and distinguished work of art as *Studs Lonigan*, which is in my opinion much the best novel that the proletarian movement has so far produced. Mr. Farrell's trilogy borrows freely from the styles and techniques of *1919*, yet it is altogether different. A source-hunter who made findings from one to the other would go as far astray as human folly can ever go. Why? Because *Studs Lonigan* has become what it is, like every work of art, by a process of interior, organic growth which is absolutely unique to Mr. Farrell.

Techniques the artist may borrow or adapt — the content to which technique is applied he cannot borrow. He can only grow it as a horticulturist grows fruit. He may imitate as a young man, though even then he cannot well incorporate in the way the source-hunter chooses to believe in (see Mr. Wolfe's reveries in *Look Homeward, Angel*), but when he matures, if he is a writer who any two critics can agree is important, he is bound to an effort whose entire process is the transmutation of his own experience into the symbolism of art. We come at once to the source-hunter's assertion that literature is experience, supported by the precept and practice of the T. S. Eliot coterie. Mr. Eliot conscientiously annotates his appropriations and the whole burden of his critical analyses is that there is, psychologically, no difference between what a man feels in his own right and what he feels as the result of his reading. Yet the "total-personality" theory is in flagrant conflict with the teachings of psychology, and in fact Mr. Eliot's poetic practice escapes into a dimension where a study of the act of appropriation becomes quite meaningless. No man has ever suffered the pangs of despised love at first hand out of Shakespeare's sonnets nor responded to the symbolism of the *Wasteland* by means of someone else's castration anxiety. Mr. MacLeish uses the style of Mr. Pound as an instrument in the development of his own style, but *Conquistador* and the *Cantos* are as incommensurable as weight and velocity.

Certainly what a writer reads may serve as a trigger to his associative faculty. But you cannot be sure he has read any specific passage, even if he tells you he has, and if you could be sure you would have learned exactly nothing. The trigger, release or focus is merely an item on the surface flux of the mind, one of the infinite impressions of the exterior world that constantly swarm there. Its entire force, even as a trigger, is exerted beneath the flux in the organic emotional life of the individual, which alone gives it meaning as a symbol or power as a trigger, and which is beyond the reach both of influence and of critical analysis.

An enormous amount of criticism thus exists in a world not only fallacious but meaningless as well. It pivots on those most durable of fallacies, *post hoc ergo propter hoc* and *non causa pro causa*. Here in *A's* book is a passage *b;* here in *C's* book, or in a newspaper or an almanac or a letter from *D*, earlier in time, is a passage *e* which has striking similarities to *b*. The two passages are similar in thought, emotion, situation or phraseology. The facts stated are unquestionable. Scholarship then moves by easy steps, each one of them fallacious, to an experimental absurdity. The passage *e* was earlier than *b*, therefore *A* may have read it; it is similar to *b*, therefore he must have read it; he must have read it, therefore he did read it; therefore *e* is the source of *b*. And, applying the same inexorable logic, somewhere in past time must exist a passage *x* which is the source of *e*, and behind it a series, x_1, x_2, x_3 . . . , which carries the source back to infinity and which it is the occupation of scholarship to discover. For, as George Foote Moore once told me, "originality, young man, is only ignorance of one's predecessors." No doubt. But observe that it is ignorance of them.

Let me give an example which I can guarantee. A couple of years ago a novel by Hans Fallada called *Little Man, What Now?* was published in this country. It contains a scene wherein a young wife, pregnant, and depressed by poverty and fear, sees a luscious sausage in a shop-window and impulsively commits the extravagance of buying and eating that sausage, using money, of which she had so little, that she should have kept for the inexorable necessities of family life. Some eight or ten months after *Little Man, What Now?*, an American novel was published. Written by *A*, it contains a passage *b*, in which a young wife, pregnant, and depressed by poverty and fear, sees a luscious French pastry in a shop-window and impulsively commits the extravagance of buying and eating that pastry, using money, of which she has so little, that should have been kept for the inexorable necessities of family life. A study of the dates of publication and the probable rate of composition suggests that scene *b*, in the American novel, was probably written a month or so after the American publication of *Little Man, What Now?*, at a time when the latter was a best seller, was being widely read and discussed, and was probably a common topic of conversation among literary people. The journal of *C*, a faithful diarist of the contemporary literary world, records a party at which *A*, the American novelist, was present and at which Fallada's novel was one of the books discussed. The records of a lending library in the town where *A* lives show that *Little Man, What Now?* was rented for several days to a member of *A's* family shortly after it was published. Finally, the files of *A's* publisher contain a carbon copy of a letter which the president of the firm wrote to *A*, dated some six weeks before the publication of *A's* novel, in which the publisher alludes to the striking similarity between the two scenes.

These facts have never before been noticed by a critic, but in the face of them what source-hunter would fail to decide that Fallada's scene was the source of *A's?* The evidence is conclusive. But there is this further fact: that *A* had not read Fallada's novel when his scene was written, has not read either the novel or the scene in question to this day, and heard nothing whatever about Fallada's scene until months after his own scene was written. He first heard of it, in fact, in the publisher's letter referred to, when the publisher, looking over the page proof, saw the similarity and inquired about it. He did not know, until that time, that such a scene existed. In the face of this further fact, the source-hunter is flatly wrong.

The author of the novel heard discussions of *Little Man, What Now?* and read several reviews of it when it was a best seller, but did not read it, has read no part of it to this day, and neither heard nor saw any mention of the scene in question till the publisher mentioned it long after his was written. His wife read Fallada's book shortly after its publication, but the similarity did not occur to her when his was written — for the best of reasons — and she never mentioned it to him. When the publisher spoke to him, he said, "The scene stays in. It is my scene and I'm going to keep it." And it is his scene. For it was a literal transcription of an incident which actually occurred and with which he was intimately and emotionally involved, being the husband of the woman to whom it occurred. The character in his book is pregnant for purposes not of this scene but of the book itself, and the incident of the French pastry was conferred on her to heighten the effect. So that the source was not a scene from a contemporary novel which he has not read. The source was human experience.

That is, of course, almost exclusively the source of all creative writing. Striking parallels and similarities appear in literature not because writers are influenced by one another but because there are striking parallels and similarities in human experience. Literature has similar patterns because the patterns of life repeat themselves. Human experience, infinitely various in detail, is eternally the same in the basic emotions with which literature deals. The exterior circumstances in which these emotions find expression repeat themselves in identical or nearly identical ways. Two writers whose experience and understanding of life is in part mutual, in part based on the same experience, must always write books that are in part alike, whether or not the later one has ever heard of the earlier one.

The womb of literary art is the daydream. Poets, dramatists and novelists are people in whom the faculty of fantasy is highly developed. People who, under the impact of experience, make up fantasies elaborating, developing and proliferating experience in accordance with the fundamental drives of their own emotional life. The process by which this faculty works the transmutation of experience that we call art occurs in three areas of cognition. It is in small part conscious, in greater part unconscious and so beyond the exploration of writer and critic alike, and in the greatest part half-conscious, the warm but unguided flux of the mind where emotion drifts freely but thought can exercise no control and only partial selection. Reading, books written by others, can become experience for the first and to a much smaller extent for the third but never *directly* for the second. And in any area such books are not the material on which the process works, but only a catalyst that may put the process into action. Even so, this catalytic power depends upon the sum of the writer, on the primary drives of his emotional make-up as chance and experience have shaped them — on, that is, the entire organization of the writer's individuality. And purely as a catalyst, literature is infinitely less powerful than the omnipresent stimulus of the writer's moment to moment existence. That stimulus is beyond recovery by the writer or by any critic. A given passage in a masterpiece may proceed from something as tremendous as the death of a father or an act of incest. But such is the nature of associative fantasy that the same passage may just as well proceed from a stimulus so apparently weak and irrelevant as the distant echo of an engine whistle or the casual fall of a red leaf. It may have proceeded from any of these stimuli, or from any of a myriad more. The critic can never know.

So when Professor Lorch tells me that a possible source of "The Dandy and the Squatter" was a sketch in an Iowa county newspaper, I do not believe him. Too much hangs on the word "possible." Thirteen seems an early age at which to acquire a literary influence for two inconsiderable pages of type. There is no evidence whatever that Mark read the Iowa newspaper. Nor is there any such thing as the source of a joke. Jokes are, individually, older than literature. "The Dandy and the Squatter" describes the discomfiture of an absurd foreigner to the great enjoyment of provincial natives. Surely this is a pattern of experience as old as the first venturer who went over the hill from his own tribe to the country of those uncouth and inferior folk who worshiped not a wolf but a turtle. The emotions it utilizes are immortal and recurrent. May we not more safely assume that a writer was describing experience as he knew it?

When Professor Wagenknecht, following other critics, tells me that *The Adventures of Tom Sawyer* was strongly influenced by *Don Quixote*, I can only say: nonsense. In the first place, Tom is not a visionary like the Don, he is not set off against Huck Finn, Huck does not correct his visions, Huck is not an earthy realist like Sancho Panza, and the book is not an attack on chivalry or on romance. In the second place Mark's known admiration for Cervantes is slight and unimportant, being mostly his satisfaction in the comparison made by Howells and not demonstrably an admiration of his ideas or his methods. And even if he had worshiped Cervantes and read him once a week, still the decisive appeal is not to literature but to the artist's fantasy as exhibited by the book itself. The situations, emotions and sentiments of *The Adventures of Tom Sawyer* are those of life itself, for which Cervantes held no title in fee simple. They are obviously, flagrantly, clamorously the fantasies of Mark Twain moving among the known circumstances of his boyhood in the landscape of his experience. That is precisely why *Tom Sawyer* is a great book: because, as we at once recognize from our own experience, it is shaped by life — not because it is influenced by Cervantes.

When Dr. Brashear describes to me a Hannibal so cultured, so acquainted with literary tradition that, it seems, the natives acted first from the library and only secondarily from the appetites and passions of life, when she presents

Mark Twain to me as a writer steeped in the thought and feeling of eighteenth-century literature — I can only say, this is the process that has made a literary dictaphone of Poe, and it is wrong. Let us appeal to experience and to Mark Twain's books. I do not doubt that the western town where I was ten years old in 1907 contained fifty copies of Xenophon's *Anabasis*, for there were at least fifty people who could have carried them there from school — as Miss Brashear has found a great many eighteenth-century classics in Missouri private libraries when Mark Twain was ten. Yet fifty Xenophons do not make my home town a cultured society deeply imbued with the Greek spirit. It was in fact a crude, coarse, ignorant and even illiterate society, for all its libraries. I did not read the *Anabasis* till I was thirty-five, and though my father's library contained a copy of the *Noctes Ambrosianae*, it remains to me and in my library a set of four books into which I have never looked, and would remain that though a hundred sets were found in Utah between 1905 and 1915. Are Mark Twain's books full of wit, "characters," discursive essays, and formally developed satirical sketches on human folly? So are many books of his own time and every other time. Those are not indexes of an eighteenth-century inheritance, they are the common and perennial modes of literature. And, *in fact*, is the Hannibal which exists in Mark's books a focus of eighteenth-century culture? Are, *in fact*, the emotions, sentiments and patterns in them eighteenth-century? The whole force of intelligence is that they are not — that they issue directly and concretely from their time and place, a frontier Missouri settlement before the Civil War where a new, native way of life was in process of formation, a way of life that had as little in common with the eighteenth century as with the eighth. In short, Mark Twain was a literary artist employing his fantasy on the immediate material of experience.

III

Let us turn from criticism *ad hoc* to theoretical, systematic criticism. Here generalization is always intended. A logically unified system of criteria is set up: esthetic, ethical, theological, political, economic, or several of these in combination. The works of a writer are then measured by these standards, and judgment is pronounced. This is the most ambitious form of criticism; here criticism becomes itself a department of literature and undertakes to express creatively a judgment on life, at second hand by way of literature. That very fact, that criticism here usurps a function of the literature with which it deals, opens a way to error: in pursuing one of its ends it is liable to betray another. In expressing judgments on life, time, the world and society, it is liable to distort the literature from which it starts. That those judgments may be more important than the distortion, that the critic's general ideas may be more valuable than the literature in relation to which he expresses them — that is as may be. It is another problem and I do not treat it here. I am concerned with the limits of the critical process as it deals directly and in the first instance with imaginative literature. So I confine myself to pointing out certain fallacies.

Imaginative literature is like science, in that it deals with concrete experience. Criticism is like metaphysics, in that it deals with general ideas which it abstracts from literature. A system of critical criteria is an assumption, latent or explicit, that there are right ways and wrong ways of writing books, that there are ways in which books must or ought to

be written. Here is the primary contention between the
artist and the critic, which may be more or less ameliorated
but never reconciled. We must take one side or the other
of this quarrel, and the artist's appears to me the more realistic. We know that there are many ways in which books have
been written, many ideas and sentiments and beliefs they
have contained. We may assume that there is an infinite
number of ways in which they may be written, an infinite
number of sentiments they may contain. Logic does not
constrain us to decide that there are any ways in which they
must be written, or any sentiments they must contain. The
systematic critic says in effect, your book is good because
it is written in this way, or bad because it expresses this
sentiment. Such a judgment commits the critic to a dogma,
and the artist can only reply: dogmas are subjective; there
is no external judge; you say I must write in a given way
because some imperative in the nature of literature, the
structure of society or the moral universe commands me
to. But there is no such imperative. There is only your assertion of one. The critic says: you must. He means: I think
you must. This difference between assertion and meaning
must never be disregarded in a discussion of the critical
process.

Again, the effort of systematic criticism is to discover a
unity in the literature it examines. It is forever trying to
reduce a writer to a total single meaning, on which it may
pass judgment. Yet experience is complex, and the components of any writer's work are multiple if not inchoate.
A constant danger is that criticism, in trying to enforce
unity on them, will select some and represent those as the
whole, ignoring the rest. This, in fact, is what the metaphysical critic, the systematic critic, usually does. It is why

systematic criticism is usually more descriptive of the critic than of the artist with whom he deals. It has been conspicuously true of critics of Mark Twain.

This fallacy is itself complex, containing several lesser ones. I will examine only one. A primary effort is to establish just what a writer means. Few critics have ever analyzed this effort, and none has ever kept such an analysis in mind while dealing with Mark Twain. It is at least a fourfold effort, and the critic usually shifts from one to another of four inquiries without being aware that he has shifted. When we ask what a writer means we are asking not one question but at least four: What does his work as a whole mean? What does he mean in a given passage? What was his thought, his psychic state, when he wrote a given passage and how did he come by that psychic state? What was his meaning considered to be by the people to whom it was addressed, or by any given group or groups of those people? The critic asks these questions one at a time at different stages of his inquiry but usually does not realize that they are different questions or that he is asking them alternatively. He believes himself, and represents himself to the reader, to be asking only a single question. Furthermore, only the second and fourth of them can be answered with any real objectivity — what a given passage means and what it was considered to mean by a given group. Only the last can be confidently established.

A writer has many ideas, many emotions, many sentiments. They are frequently at war with one another and usually achieve contradiction from period to period of his work. Often they may establish flat contradictions in a single volume, even on a single page. His experience changes; promptly the emotions it evokes and correlates change also. The shape in ideas that the emotions take must change with them. Indeed, the same emotion may produce flatly contradictory ideas, which the writer may hold simultaneously, with equal fervor, and without perceiving that they impair each other. So transitory a stimulus as, say, an interruption of a love affair or a quarrel with a friend may result in an emotionally charged passage which, by accident of circumstance, may be developed at great length. The stimulus passes, new considerations occupy the writer, and he reverts to an earlier, different attitude, which, by accident of circumstance, never finds expression except in a short, unemphasized passage tucked away somewhere in a parenthesis. I have, of course, simplified the process; but what are you going to do with the two incommensurables?

What the critic invariably does is to make a choice. He selects one idea and says that that is the "true" Mark Twain — rejecting the other as ephemeral or insignificant, or, more usually, ignoring it. He justifies his selection in various ways. He says that he knows which is true and which false, which the writer "really" meant, which is consistent with the writer's "true nature" or with the "main current" of his thinking. He says that, throughout the writer's career, as we progress from book to book, we can make out a "basic structure" of ideas, proliferating, organizing, articulating itself. The current is interrupted at times, it momentarily contradicts itself, sometimes it veers in false directions toward dead ends. But the "plain burden" and implication can be determined, and on that we shall concentrate for it is the "true" or "essential" Mark Twain.

Which is all very well. Only, a writer's work is so multiple that two critics, or ten critics, who have different sets of first principles, will find in it two or ten basic structures, main currents and plain burdens. The ten significances make merciless war on one another. And then come other ten critics and find — as they have signally found with Mark Twain — that the plain burden and main current of his thinking is not to be discovered at all in the books that he wrote, but instead is clearly indicated in the books he meant to write or should have written but, for ten different reasons, was prevented from writing.

What happens is that the critic establishes his system *a priori*. It is, in a way, his own experience projected in a theory. He then hides the main current and plain burden of Mark Twain's work behind the Household Edition and sets out in search of it, employing the most sensitive and delicately calibrated instruments. As, volume by volume, he takes the Household Edition down, increasingly he is able to make out the significance of Mark Twain, until he has read them all and there, revealed on the bare shelf, is what Mark Twain means, single, simple, organic and clear, and the critic is silent upon a peak of Darien.

Thus the prepossessions of Professor Parrington require him to bring all things into judgment by means of Thomas Jefferson's libertarian commonwealth with its individualism, its personal and political liberty, its small artisans and small landholders, its democratic opposition to concentrations of wealth and all the rest of a great tradition. Here, says Mr. Parrington, is the pure vision. Books which reflect it are good; books are bad insofar as they fail to reflect it or as they dissent from it. In other words: here is the way that books must be written. So poor Mark, who never in his life had any clear idea of politics and especially of the theory of politics, whose ideas about democracy changed quite as often as he changed his clothes, who was Jeffersonian and Hamiltonian, Andrew Carnegian and Henry Georgian, a black Republican and a red revolutionist — Mark Twain is held, for literary judgment, against Mr. Par-

rington's idea of the good life. Where he can find the good
life in Mark Twain, he praises Mark for writing books as
they ought to be written. Where he finds something else,
he condemns him. Mark, he says, attacked all the minnows
of the Gilded Age but never went after a single whale. All
right. But maybe icthyology has relative classifications, and
maybe Mr. Parrington's whales were minnows to Mark
Twain, and certainly to condemn Mark for not attacking
them is merely to exhibit Mr. Parrington's ideas about the
categorical imperative of harpooning. The expression of that
imperative may have the first importance in politics, sociology or the perfect state — but, wherever, its importance
is of Mr. Parrington, not of Mark Twain.

And clearly, in his effort to establish what Mark Twain
meant to write and ought to have written, he seriously, if
unconsciously, misrepresents what Mark Twain wrote. He
examines (to give only one instance) *A Connecticut Yankee*
and finds that Mark Twain was drifting steadily toward the
left — in his phrase, toward socialism. Alas, this means only
that Mr. Parrington wants him to drift toward socialism,
believing that he ought to, and so finds that he does. For
consider the catastrophe of *A Connecticut Yankee*, with the
damned human race gratefully, eagerly, unanimously rushing to assume voluntarily the oppression, tyranny and exploitation from which it had been delivered. Consider the
Yankee's repeated declarations that the race loves cruelty
and injustice, that it wills its own oppression and exploitation, that it gets the treatment it really desires and will never
be capable of anything better. This does not look like a
drift toward the left: it is an explicit repudiation of socialism. The *Yankee* is a contradictory book. I do not know
what its plain burden and significance are. I do know that
it contains these judgments and that Mr. Parrington ignores

them in order to harmonize it with his system. And that means that the process of criticism has moved away from Mark Twain to Mr. Parrington.

Seldom has a more confused and contradictory book than Mr. Lewisohn's *Expression in America* been published. I am in danger of committing the error I am undertaking to define when I try to decide what its critical criteria are. For Mr. Lewisohn is unlike most critics in that, instead of one system, he has several and they agree only in rejecting what he dislikes in American life. Wherever sexual timidity or repression can be denounced, wherever the Protestant sects can be held responsible for phases of our civilization distressing to Mr. Lewisohn, wherever German or Jewish culture can be exhibited as the productive leaven in what he approves — there the theories come together. But certainly the main current or plain burden he detects in Mark Twain is that of what he calls "our one folk artist." "His triumph is the triumph of the balladist, the writer of the folk-tale that corresponds to the epic on a higher level, that necessarily becomes, in certain times and under certain civilizations, the picaresque romance." This judgment has been widely applauded and imitated; one sees it increasingly in discussions of Mark Twain. But it merely represents the necessity of one of Mr. Lewisohn's theories to prove that the villainous American life has prevented American art from achieving adult emotions and mature forms, and the necessity of another of his theories to prove that the American folk (who are somehow to be distinguished from the American people, a scurvy lot) are rich and warm with humanity and far finer, purer, idealistic, free and sexually impulsive than the oppressive civilization that has been imposed on them. Yet the phrase "folk-artist," an absurdity in the civilization of the industrial nineteenth century, implies an almost complete unconsciousness of what the artist is doing, an acceptance of "folk" sentiments and myths and wishes so instinctive that it never reaches consciousness, and a lack of conscious intent so complete that the artist must serve merely as the vicar of the "folk." Well, if there exist more adult emotions than those which go into the portrayal of the society that *The Adventures of Huckleberry Finn* embodies, if there is a more self-conscious or more mature understanding of the damned human race than that book announces, or a more deliberate rejection of the "folk" — then either my reading of world literature has missed it, or Mr. Lewisohn is using a phrase which expresses not objective meaning but his personal sentiments. I find for the latter hypothesis. Folk-artist? Nonsense — nonsense double distilled. If Mark Twain is a folk-artist, then so are James Joyce and T. S. Eliot.

Mr. Lewisohn's confusion is a simpler repetition of what happened more complexly in the most brilliant theoretical criticism of Mark Twain that has ever been written. I have elsewhere devoted some fifty printed pages to the system of Mr. Van Wyck Brooks, which, in my opinion, was the most important critical idea of the last pre-war and first postwar decades. Let me say that I am in complete sympathy with Mr. Brooks's intent as he announced it, to study Mark Twain's books in relation to American life, and that of all theories, the one he announced as his basis seems to me most fruitful and most nearly tenable, that literature is in great part a social phenomenon and is most accessible to study as such. But Mr. Brooks neither carried out his intent as he announced it nor held to his critical base, and he was not equipped with the proper instruments for such an inquiry as he proposed. He did not study American life, he only denounced it. He did not, that is, study what existed, he asserted what, in the light of his own sentiments, ought to exist. He was well trained in European literature, he knew too little of American literature, and about all he knew of American life was that it had disastrously failed to produce European literature. He lamented that American life had failed to produce the novels of Dostoevski: he did not understand that only Russian life produces Dostoevski, whereas American life produces Mark Twain. He knew very little about American life but knew what he felt about it. Feeling strongly, he wrote an elaborate and very brilliant analysis of Mark Twain's books that exists in an ideal world completely insulated from the books with which it pretends to deal. It is an elaborate rationalization of Mark Twain's failure to write books as Mr. Brooks believes books ought to be written, but it does not at any point touch the reality of what Mark wrote. It may be a document in ideas of absolutely first importance — as a social historian, I believe that it is — and certainly it is a passionate revelation of Mr. Brooks, but it is not criticism of Mark Twain.

Mr. Calverton's criticism parallels Mr. Parrington's but is oriented in a different system. What Mr. Calverton calls "the petty bourgeois ideology of the frontier" serves as his touchstone to Mark Twain. He reaches conclusions quite different from any others by means of this phrase, but it is a meaningless phrase except as it reveals how Mr. Calverton believes that books ought to be written. It cannot be squared with the facts about Mark Twain's books, about the many bourgeoisies of American history, or about the frontier. But it serves to uncover the great general truths that Mr. Calverton hid behind the Household Edition and then went out to find. Criticism has revealed not the criticized but the critic.

Mr. Hicks has the same general ideas as Mr. Calverton and makes the same assumptions. But he comes to no such solid conclusions. Instead, Mr. Hicks is conspicuously tentative and inconclusive about Mark Twain. What he says is qualified, limited, and for purposes of systematic criticism, including his own system, very nearly useless. This is a suggestive fact and, I think, an important one. If I may hazard an explanation, I guess first that Mr. Hicks knew Mark Twain's work better than Mr. Calverton and had a greater respect for facts, and second that a book about Mark Twain which appeared a year or two before *The Great Tradition* and which pointed out the dangers of theorizing, made him cautious. If these guesses are right, then we come to an interesting conclusion (which I hid behind the Household Edition some time ago): that knowledge of an author's work and respect for fact are deterrents to systematic criticism. If that is so, then it leads directly to further conclusions.

But first let me take a brief plunge into that other uncontrolled activity of criticism, prophecy. On the basis of my knowledge of Mark Twain's work and my observation of the cycles of critical fashion, I prophesy another critical revaluation of Mark Twain, toward which Mr. Lewisohn took the first step and Mr. Calverton and Mr. Hicks the decisive steps. The process thus begun will eventually make out Mark Twain to have been a revolutionary writer (revolutionary, that is, in intention, content, sympathy and technique), a champion of the exploited class, and a forerunner if not a prophet of proletarian literature. This fashion will assemble impressive evidence from the Household Edition. It will be based, I promise you, on quite as logical and quite as organic a set of plain burdens and main currents as any system up to now has pointed out.

IV

Now consider this. Mr. Parrington, Mr. Brooks, Mr. Lewisohn and Mr. Calverton have all brought Mark Twain to the judgment bar of different critical systems. Add the genteel critics and the humanists, whom I have not had time to examine here. Add my own suggestively systematized attempt to avoid systematic criticism. Here we have seven different systems. They give us seven different sets of findings. Each one of them presents a different Mark Twain, and asks us to accept him, forsaking all others. The seven Mark Twains thus derived are mutually contradictory. The inhibited artist of Mr. Brooks contradicts the freely functioning folk-artist of Mr. Lewisohn. The petty bourgeois of Mr. Calverton is incompatible with Mr. Parrington's Jeffersonian and socialist. Any one of them obliterates all the others. Yet all seven systems are applied to the analysis of the same body of facts, the books which Mark Twain wrote, which are available in the Household Edition, and which remain unchanged.

I conclude that Mark Twain's books are something apart from and independent of the criticism that seven different systems have applied to them. I conclude that criticism has found no way of representing literature that is divorced from the critic's temperament, no way, that is, of compelling a skeptic's acceptance. I conclude that these seven systems are arbitrary and subjective.

My further conclusions are themselves arbitrary and subjective. I summarize them briefly because they are, after all, of no interest to you and because this paper has been intolerably long.

It seems to me that the most fruitful fields of criticism are esthetics and social history. Esthetic criticism is flagrantly and frankly subjective, and experiences a cyclical shift of fashions similar to the one I have pointed out in systematic criticism. The despair of such a critic as Mr. Krutch or Mr. Richards proceeds from an unwillingness to accept its comparatives and an attempt to ground them on an absolute in psychology or revelation. Mr. T. S. Eliot struggled with the same dilemma until esthetic revelation merged with theological revelation and made him a systematic critic. So long as esthetics frankly accepts the relativity of its results, however, it avoids the morass and remains indispensable to the study of literature. It is the immediate nexus between literature and the student. It is furthermore, a record of taste and so an index to and vehicle of the culture of any given period.

Social history treats esthetic criticism and systematic criticism as objective facts and uses them as points of orientation in its descriptive study. Its opportunity for analysis, however, is in the fourth field of inquiry that I described some pages back, the study of what a writer was understood to mean by a given class at a given time. To determine what a writer "meant" in his work as a whole is clearly a subjective undertaking. But what a writer meant at any given time to any clearly defined group of people is an objective fact and can be determined with some objectivity. Such an inquiry seems to me not only the most meaningful but also the most important occupation of literary criticism. By pursuing it criticism can reveal significant facts and linkages of facts in culture and civilization, and can escape the subjective whirlpools that make certain of its other inquiries so nearly impotent.